BOUNTY

BOUNTY

A NOVEL

_MICHAEL BYRNES

BALLANTINE BOOKS

NEW YORK

Published in the United States by Ballantine Books, an imprint of Random House, a division of Penguin Random House LLC, New York.

BALLANTINE and the HOUSE colophon are registered trademarks of Penguin Random House LLC.

LIBRARY OF CONGRESS CATALOGING-IN-PUBLICATION DATA
Names: Byrnes, Michael (Michael J.), author.
Title: Bounty : a novel / Michael Byrnes.
Description: New York : Ballantine Books, [2016]
Identifiers: LCCN 2016010500 (print) | LCCN 2016018524 (ebook) |
ISBN 9780804178341 (hardcover : alk. paper) |
ISBN 9780804178358 (ebook)
Subjects: | GSAFD: Suspense fiction.
Classification: LCC PS3602.Y768 B68 2016 (print) |
LCC PS3602.Y768 (ebook) | DDC 813/.6—dc23
LC record available at https://lccn.loc.gov/2016010500

Printed in the United States of America on acid-free paper

randomhousebooks.com

987654321

FIRST EDITION

Book design by Simon M. Sullivan

In loving memory of John T. Xenis

Criminals do not die by the hands of the law. They die by the hands of other men.

—GEORGE BERNARD SHAW, *Maxims for Revolutionists*

In this and like communities, public sentiment is everything. With public sentiment, nothing can fail; without it nothing can succeed. Consequently, he who molds public sentiment goes deeper than he who enacts statutes or pronounces decisions.

—ABRAHAM LINCOLN

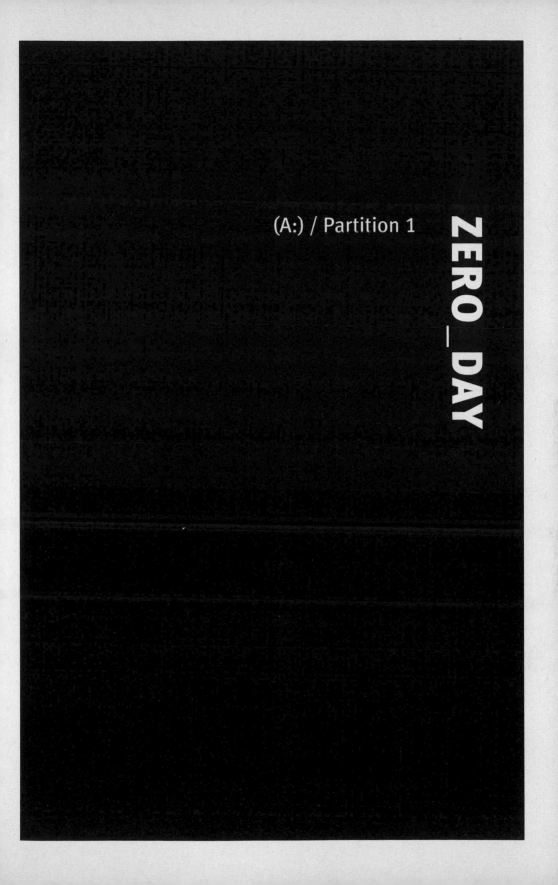

(A:) / Partition 1

ZERO_DAY

ATLAS-5 SECURE MESSAGE BOARD

Session: 10.02.2017.13:14:03UTC.TLPANH.5468883990-10-12

> JAM: We have a problem.

> PIKE: What is it?

> JAM: Razorwire source code and encryption keys have been compromised.

> PIKE: Impossible. Don't screw with me.

> JAM: This is no joke.

> PIKE: Internal or external breach?

> JAM: Not yet determined. Pipeline to backup was being monitored. Cannot trace source. Need to investigate further.

> PIKE: Do you know what this fucking means?

> JAM: I'm fully aware of the situation.

> PIKE: Perform immediate restore from backup drives.

> JAM: Restore already attempted and failed. All backup drives have been erased.

> PIKE: Initiate Boomerang protocol.

> JAM: Already tried.

> PIKE: Are you telling me that we've lost control of Razorwire?

> JAM: Affirmative.

01.01

@ Manhattan
Monday, 10/23/2017
10:07:06 EDT

"So it's done?"

"You'll need to sign some release forms." Scott Waverly folded his laptop shut and glanced up at the banker. "Otherwise, yeah, it's done. Just be sure to pay the fines by the end of the month."

Chase Lombardi waved his hand. "I'll have accounting cut a check today and be rid of it."

"I'm sure the district attorney would welcome that."

Lombardi grinned. "You're good. Expensive. But damn sharp." He raised a tumbler of whiskey and drained the glass.

"My courier will deliver the paperwork to your house in the morning. Eight o'clock work for you?" Waverly slid the laptop into a slim, fashionable safe case that was otherwise empty.

"I plan on celebrating. Best give me time to recover. Make it eleven. Why don't you join me tonight? Let me buy you a rib eye and some obscenely overpriced scotch."

"Sounds enticing, but I've got a prior engagement."

A lie, Lombardi was sure. Delivered with surgical precision. "So skip it."

Waverly's reply was nonnegotiable: "Not happening."

The attorney had dropped that same line when offered a generous plea bargain by the district attorney—a gutsy, ultimately brilliant play. Lombardi watched the man's elegant fingers work the dials on the case's combination lock. "I thought your computer's encrypted?"

"It is."

"Then what's with the luggage?"

"If there's anything I've learned from my clients," Waverly said with a tilted eyebrow, "it's that one can't be too vigilant about protecting personal information."

The words had teeth, but Lombardi chuckled anyway. "Buyer beware."

"Indeed." The attorney stood and proffered a stiff right hand.

Lombardi clasped Waverly's chalky palm and squeezed hard enough to make him wince.

"Congratulations," Waverly said. "Thanks to you, the Justice Department and the SEC will be scrambling to patch quite a few regulatory potholes. You've defied the odds."

"I *played* the odds," Lombardi corrected. He leaned across the desk and whispered, "Not my fault the system's hopelessly flawed."

"Try to stay out of trouble . . ." A quick, nearly imperceptible smile. "Or not."

"No doubt you'd prefer the latter," Lombardi said.

"Enjoy the rib eye." Maintaining a death grip on his safe case, Waverly executed a crisp about-face and strode out.

Lombardi watched the mahogany door whisper shut, then stood and went over to the floor-to-ceiling window. Peering down sixteen stories, he fixated on the drones in crisp suits teeming along the sidewalk in front of the New York Stock Exchange.

Suckers. Gaggles of them.

Watch out, baby. I'm back in the game. I'll be seeing you soon.

Feeling a subtle vibration in his suit pocket, he pulled out his iPhone and viewed the display. His neck muscles instantly went rigid.

"Goddamnit."

He took his seat again and speed-dialed his IT manager. Through the speakerphone, a subdued female voice answered after two chimes. "Vickie, I thought you fixed my accounts to block out those fucking emails and texts?"

A pause.

"You mean that bounty guy?"

"That's the one."

"I did, sir."

"Then explain to me why I just got another message from this whack job?"

"I . . ." The voice wavered. "Let me check."

Some speedy keyboard pecking on the other end.

"I'm waiting, Vickie."

"Uh . . . right. Got the confirmation right here. It was done Thursday morning. We'd blocked the—"

"Then can you tell me what I'm staring at right now? Big bold letters . . . lots of numbers after a dollar sign. Same as last time."

"I'll need to look into it, find out what the problem might be. Was it the same Web link again?" she asked.

"Same one. I remember telling you to look into that, too."

"I did."

"And?"

"Honestly, I figured it might upset you," said Vickie. "With all the court appearances you had to get through last week and—"

"I'm a big boy. I can handle it."

"Sir, honestly, I'd suggest you take a look at it yourself," she said. "I still haven't been able to identify the sender's IP address, but there's no malicious code coming through the firewall. So it should be fine to log on from your office."

"Good. I'll do that. In the meantime, weed this shit out of my accounts."

Lombardi stabbed his finger at the phone's keypad, then brought up the Web browser and pressed his face close to the monitor.

Show me what you've got, funny man.

His eyes were immediately drawn to a pair of wildly spinning counter graphics in the upper left of the screen. The first, labeled UNIQUE VISITORS, was rapidly approaching the two million mark. Beneath it, the one labeled BOUNTY had just breached $530,000.

"Bounty," he mumbled.

At the top of the page, a no-nonsense banner logo repeated the site's name in bold scarlet letters designed to resemble an ink stamp, with a slogan beneath it that read, IF THE LAW SHOULD FAIL, LET JUSTICE PREVAIL. Directly beneath it, the words FEATURED MARK were the header for his own portrait—a presidential-style photo that screamed fifty-something power broker, lifted right off Lombardi Capital Management LLP's most recent annual report.

You've got to be kidding me.

His iPhone trilled again. He snatched it up and checked the message from the unspecified sender:

LOOK OUT YOUR WINDOW

A chill trickled down his back. He remained perfectly still, heart galloping behind his breastbone. After counting to ten, he slowly swiveled the chair toward the glass, palming the phone. His eyes scanned high and low through the vast concrete-and-glass terrain for anything ominous. All seemed normal.

Jesus Christ. Get ahold of yourself.

The iPhone came to life again, sucking away any sense of relief.

He raised the phone slowly. The one word staring back at him made his hand tremble.

SMILE

Panic took hold, his eyes snapping back to the scene outside the window, hunting, scanning. Now that his most passionate enemies were quantifiable, compliments of this elusive bounty man, the surrounding windows and rooftops seemed infinite.

The visitors' tally scrolled through his mind's eye. *Two million and counting* was Chase Lombardi's final thought just before a dime-sized hole punched clean through the thick plate glass with a muffled *thwap*. A nanosecond later, an invisible sledgehammer slammed between his eyes and cast him into oblivion.

02.01

FBI Special Agent Roman Novak breathed in deep and long, then exhaled slow and steady as he prepared to enter the rip current of activity awaiting him. The elevator doors hummed open at the sixteenth floor, and a flood of frenzied sound overwhelmed the cheery contemporary jazz pumping in from speakers hidden overhead. He stepped out into a spacious reception hall and paused.

Clusters of NYPD officers stood in loose circles, chatting about the Giants' dismal first half in yesterday's game. No murder, even a high-profile one, could trump that.

The forensics crews were all business: techs in white jumpsuits and hairnets streaming back and forth along the office's central corridor, which ran like a wide avenue behind the circular glass-and-chrome reception desk. They were busily unloading their high-tech gear, eager as always to start deconstructing the crime scene while the evidence was fresh.

"Agent Novak!" A gravelly voice broke through the din.

He spotted the lanky, bald captain in a double doorway at the far end of the corridor. James Agner, NYPD's alpha male. Novak raised a hand in acknowledgment, and Agner disappeared through the doorway.

Threading past the cops, Novak set off down the corridor, which was lined on both sides by glass partitions that allowed full view of the stylishly furnished offices his squad had raided nearly a year ago. After the tedious months that had ensued, the FBI had learned the hard way that here at Lombardi Capital Management LLP, transparency was limited strictly to the decor.

He strode past a glass-walled, fish-tank-like meeting room and peered in at a pair of city detectives vetting some staffers who collectively looked like the cast of a daytime soap opera. At the opposite end of the room stood Novak's boss, Assistant Special Agent in Charge Timothy Knight, doling out directives to five agents who were listening intently from their seats at the conference table.

Knight failed to notice him, so Novak kept walking.

The walls transitioned back to mahogany just before the corridor ended. He proceeded into a voluminous room with a two-story ceiling and so much glass along its outer wall that the space seemed to hover above the city. Chase Lombardi's inner sanctum, his window on the world.

"Excuse me," a voice called from behind him.

Novak turned to face a tech trying to make her way into the room with a telescope in the crook of her left arm and a laptop hooked under her right. "Sorry," he said, sidestepping.

Agner called to him from across the room: "Agent Novak, come have a look at this."

Circling the desk to where Agner stood with his arms crossed tight, gazing at the main attraction, Novak caught an unpleasant whiff of urine and copper and fried circuit boards.

Chase Lombardi's plump body was slumped in a leather swivel chair, dressed in what had to be a ten-thousand-dollar pin-striped suit, the crotch stained. The banker's head—at least what remained of it—had snapped back over the headrest, his knobby chin pointing up at the ceiling. The bulbous nose and beady eyes were now reduced to a ragged, pulpy crater. Reflecting on what a devious prick the guy had been, Novak couldn't quite repress a small surge of satisfaction. One bullet had accomplished more than a year and a half of federal investigation.

Agner's eyes locked on the dead man's impeccably polished wing-tips. "Those shoes probably cost more than my car. Christ. How ya been, Novak?"

"Not bad. You?"

"Just started the paperwork for retirement," Agner said, attempting optimism. The prospect of being set to pasture, however, resonated like a grim prognosis.

"Good for you. You've earned it."

The captain shrugged. "I suppose my golf game could use some attention." His gaze circled the room, taking snapshots of the moment. "I got a strong stomach, but this one's a sloppy mess. Guy's unrecognizable."

For reassurance, Novak glanced down at the corpse's blue hands. Definitely Lombardi's manicured fingernails and Rolex. The one-inch scar running over the left thumb knuckle was unmistakable. Novak had fixated on it plenty of times during depositions when Lombardi drummed his stubby fingertips on the table while his lawyers glossed over his transgressions. "It's him, all right."

"Chase Lombardi. Real American hero," Agner said.

Novak crouched to get a clinical view of the back of the victim's head, which had fared much worse than the business side. The skull looked like a smashed pumpkin covered in hairy skin flaps, a good portion of its contents spilled onto the floor.

Agner watched him curiously. "That slop doesn't bother you?"

"Nope," Novak replied truthfully. For most other agents dedicated to white-collar crime, Agner's assumption would likely be spot-on, since blood and gore attracted a different skill set. "I was a volunteer paramedic during my junior and senior years at NYU. Handled everything from gunshots and stabbings to decapitations."

"Huh, you don't say."

"My mom said blood never really bothered me all that much, even when I was a kid. She'd hoped I'd go to med school."

Novak's mother had witnessed firsthand what decades on the Street had done to his father, a former Goldman Sachs executive whose tales of epic moral decay in high finance had left quite an impression. Yet she'd had to settle for her son pursuing a finance degree. After he'd done three years with a prestigious, now defunct, investment banking firm only three blocks from here, he'd seen the error of his ways.

Literally.

The epiphany had come on a glorious Monday morning in May, five years back. He'd been walking along Front Street, heading back to his cubicle inside the offices of Falcon Equity Holdings LLC while listening to CNBC's live reports of a precipitous drop in stock indices worldwide. Commodities, the godly building blocks of global economic expansion (and his firm's specialty), had been sucked into the vortex. As a senior analyst, Novak had seen the storm clouds gathering and had cautioned against heavy exposure in long positions. His boss, the diehard contrarian Malthis J. Cantonfield, however, had felt something different in his gut and executed huge bullish bets on copper and oil, not fully computing that, on Wall Street, instinct had been devalued even more than the greenback.

A few paces ahead of Novak, a young woman from the firm's precious metals desk had been heading for the building's revolving doors—a Jersey girl with a good pedigree, pretty in a classical sense. But that morning, someone else had caught Novak's attention, too: a cabbie, curbside and half a block up, assisting an elderly rider who'd suddenly pointed skyward and begun screaming. Like typical Manhattanites, almost everyone had ignored him. Novak, however, had glanced up. That's when he'd spotted a familiar figure in a tailored khaki suit plummeting, shaved head first, from the sky.

Malthis J. Cantonfield's suit jacket had flapped like a superhero's cape, his pink silk tie whipping in the downdraft. He'd kept his arms tucked rigidly at his sides, and as far as Novak recalled, the contrarian's eyes had been closed and his lips drawn tight in a smile. Or perhaps gravity had been simply pushing his cheeks back?

A purposeful fall.

A nosedive.

A suicide plunge.

Cantonfield's free fall—from the rooftop and down thirty-eight stories, the record would show—had followed straight along the windows that ran up from the revolving door.

Novak had stopped dead in his tracks and screamed at Jersey Girl. But since he couldn't remember her name (Andrea or Katie or maybe Fran?), all that had come out was *"HEY!* Look out!"

Jersey Girl had stopped and turned to him. Wrong reaction. Wrong warning.

Cantonfield had landed smack on top of her, instantly collapsing and twisting her body in every unnatural way. She'd absorbed the brunt of his torso, but his head had struck the pavement violently and exploded with the hollow popping sound of a shattered coconut.

Novak still viscerally remembered the sickening feeling that had washed over him: that muddy veil of shock and horror that happened when some contrived scene from a movie, raw and violent, played out before one's very eyes and spun reality like a top. He'd also been overwhelmed by the fact that even in death, Malthis J. Cantonfield had managed to take someone down with him. Greedy and selfish to the bitter end.

The morning after the Cantonfield Event (as it became known in the Wall Street lexicon), Novak rode the subway to Federal Plaza and applied to the FBI, gladly accepting a 75 percent pay cut in lieu of a future in BASE jumping without a parachute. Now, some five years later, here he was staring at another banker's blown-out head. The odds were uncanny. Even for Wall Street.

"Don't take this the wrong way, Novak. But you don't strike me as the doctor type," Agner said.

Novak's eyes traced the congealed mess beneath the chair to the stringy goo spattered on the demolished computer monitor. A feathery scorch pattern spread up from a quarter-sized hole where the screen's power button should have been. A gloved tech leaned in, probed the hole with forceps, and pulled out a glinting, tapered metal slug.

"That there's a three-thirty-eight Lapua Magnum sniper round," the tech said, holding it up for the lawmen. He dropped it into a clear zip-top evidence bag and set it onto a tray, next to a bag containing Lombardi's iPhone. "One helluva shot."

With a bullet that big having buzzed through Lombardi's head, thought Novak, it was no wonder the skull had popped like a melon.

"Christ," Agner groaned. "What a way to start the week. Happy Monday. Just what we need in this city. A goddamn sniper." He shook his head and stared at the bagged slug. "I've seen what they can do plenty of times."

Knowing the captain had served his time in the jungles of Vietnam, Novak could only imagine that his mind was replaying images of similarly ruined Viet Cong skulls, much the way Novak vividly recalled the Cantonfield Event.

"Not your typical homicide," Agner said. "This guy has plenty of potential enemies. Maybe a hired gun or just some disgruntled investor whose retirement plan shit the bed."

Agner maneuvered around the forensic tech with the telescope, who was securing it to a tripod set between the desk and the window. Stepping up to the window, Agner pointed to a clean hole at chin level that had left only minor cracking in the thick glass. With the same finger, he traced an invisible line down to the computer monitor to connect the dots. "Sharp trajectory. Shooter must've been up pretty high."

Novak nodded. He stared out at the tall buildings stacked tight for nearly ten blocks out to the Hudson River. Plenty of possibilities.

"I'm sure I can pinpoint the spot," the tech said. She clicked a button on the scoping device and two crisp threads of red light snapped out from opposite ends of a slim tube mounted on top of the barrel. "Watch your eyes, okay?"

Novak and Agner stepped back so she could adjust the tripod upward and sideways until the lasers perfectly speared the two bullet holes. She plugged a USB cable into the telescope and connected it to a laptop sitting on the floor. "Just need to tune the optics," she said, scrunching her eyes and working the laptop's mouse. On command, the telephoto lens casings on the front of the device spun slowly outward, then retracted slightly. "Ta-da. Look here."

Novak and Agner stepped in to have a look.

The image on the screen centered on a gap between two large air handlers along the top edge of a roofline, gray sky above it. "That's a rooftop a few blocks from here. Just takes a few seconds for the GPS coordinates to match up."

Seven seconds later, a text box popped up on the screen.

"All right, fellas. There's your address."

03.01

The muscle-bound patrolman, at the wheel slalomed the cruiser, sirens blaring, through the afternoon traffic chugging up Church Street. In the front passenger seat, Agner craned his head around the mounted shotgun and peered through the wire-mesh safety partition to address Novak. "It's gonna be a big show over there," he yelled. "But if you ask me, there ain't a chance in hell the guy's still there."

In the back, Novak sat dead center, eyes forward, hands braced on the seat. The interior's stale aroma of cigarettes, coffee, cheap perfume, and sweat was downright nauseating. "Do we know what time Lombardi was shot?"

"Coroner hasn't officially called it yet," yelled Agner. "We know his secretary didn't find him till lunchtime. Imagine that? Young girl walking in on that horror show?"

The driver cut a hard left onto Barclay Street that slid Novak along the slick vinyl upholstery. He could taste breakfast in the back of his throat.

"She says he was still alive when his attorney came out of the office around ten-fifteen. Unofficially, we can assume he was dead some-time between then and eleven." Agner checked his watch. "It's al-most one-thirty now. Unless we're dealing with a brilliant marksman with no common sense, this guy's long gone. That's why I told SWAT to sit tight. No use bringing in the commandos just yet."

The driver angled north across the wide lanes of West Street, tires chirping, and swung a tight U-turn at Murray Street.

Agner pointed to the right through the windshield and told the driver, "That's it there."

Novak scooted over to the side window. The GPS coordinates for the sniper's roost overlaid a 1930s commercial building opposite the highway from Ground Zero. Fifty-something floors stacked in three fat tiers with alternating horizontals of turquoise-glazed terra-cotta tiles and copper-trimmed casement windows that predated air-conditioning.

Near the building's front entrance, Muscle Guy slewed the cruiser to the right and screeched to a hard stop that practically vaulted Novak against the mesh partition.

Liberated from the car, Novak leaned against an unmarked silver Tahoe parked askew along the yellow curb and took a moment to steady his sea legs. The chilly October air felt heaven-sent. The Tahoe was an identical triplet to two other SUVs parked sloppily in front of it. Half a dozen NYPD patrol cars formed a semicircle around them.

"You all right?" Agner asked.

"Yeah. I'm good."

"Okay." Agner put on his cap and gazed skyward. "Let's get up there and see what we've got."

03.02 _____

The jalopy of an elevator was a far cry from the one that had gently swept Novak to Lombardi's office. It struggled to make the lift, jerk-ing and bobbing along creaking rails, and the buttons on the control panel were so worn that the floor numbers had been painted beside them. Given the number of law enforcement personnel now crammed into the cab, Novak thought there was an even chance that its ancient cables would snap and send them all plunging to their deaths.

Finally the upper floor numbers started scrolling on the half-lit control panel, starting with 40. The cab jostled as it gained speed, then came to a rough stop. When the doors rattled open, bodies spilled out into the dark central corridor on the fifty-second floor.

The building's portly security guard, commandeered from the front desk to escort the team topside, fished in his tight pocket to produce a key ring and cranked a key in the wall switch. The fluorescent ceiling lights pulsed to life. Then he set a sluggish pace to the emergency exit door at the end of the corridor, Tim Knight and Captain Agner close behind him.

Trailing the pack, Novak peeked through an open doorway leading off the corridor, into an empty room easily fifty years beyond its heyday. Peeling radiators, stained ceiling panels, rippled and torn gray carpeting, stray wires leading nowhere. He quickened his pace to catch up to the procession. Over the stampede of feet tromping along the linoleum floor tiles, he heard Knight ask the guard if there were any tenants on this floor. The escort shook his head.

"No cameras up here?" Knight asked, looking along the water-stained ceiling.

"No need for cameras," the security guard replied wheezily. "No one's ever up here. Rooms are all empty."

Novak hadn't seen a camera in the death-trap elevator, either. Even the fire extinguishers mounted next to the vintage patina-coated mail chutes looked to be original.

The guard pushed through the exit door, which was marked, CAUTION: DO NOT OPEN—ALARM WILL SOUND. No alarm sounded.

The procession continued into the dank stairwell. A switchback metal staircase led up to the rooftop-access door, where the guard stopped, panting. The FBI agents and police officers waited impatiently on the steps, Novak down at the landing.

Agner eyed the warning sticker on the door: ROOFTOP ACCESS PROHIBITED. SEE ATTENDANT FOR KEY. His gaze shifted to the guard, still fumbling for the right one. Agner gave the door bar a hard shove, and it screeched open a third of the way on gritty hinges before jamming on the gravel coating the roof.

The guard looked up, stricken.

Novak was amazed by the tally of code violations the building had racked up thus far.

"Thanks, pal," Agner told the security guard. "We'll take it from here."

Their escort shrugged, then stepped back against the wall.

"Weapons, fellas," Knight said, reaching beneath his FBI windbreaker and unclipping his Glock from its underarm holster. "And ladies," he added, glancing at the two female agents gazing impassively at him.

A chorus of clicks echoed off the shaft's cinder-block walls as the agents and officers took up arms, flipped off safeties.

Agner's driver threw his shoulder twice into the door to force it fully open. Dull sunlight and a swirl of fresh air spilled down the stairwell.

At Agner's signal, the posse poured outside and fanned out across the rooftop.

03.03 _____

Along the roof's low east-facing wall, Novak approached the spot the forensic tech had spied with her nifty telescope—the narrow gap sandwiched by two boxy air handlers, point to point, likely just shy of a half mile to Lombardi's burst head.

"Just as I suspected," Agner said, coming up behind him and sliding his sidearm back into its holster. "No shooter. Not even a spent casing. Be careful there. Might still be hair samples or something we might need later on."

Novak looked down at all the old cigarette butts and trash littering the rooftop, then up at Agner incredulously. Agner shrugged. Novak stepped into the gap, crouched low, and found easy cover from any prying eyes that might be looking down from the Freedom Tower's upper floors. *A perfect hide.* He gazed diagonally across Ground Zero and through a haphazard canyon of tall buildings, to the windows of Lombardi's executive suite. He wondered what rare talent was required for a man to take a life so casually, with such precision.

"He had a perfect sight line," Novak said. "That's for sure."

"Even used the weather to his advantage," Agner added, looking up at the overcast sky. "Cloudy, so there wouldn't have been much glare. Barely a breeze, even up here."

"Still, that was one incredible shot. Have a look." Novak stood and backed out of the gap so Agner could take a turn at it.

Knight and one of Agner's lieutenants broke through the human chain of NYPD officers scouring the rooftop for physical clues and strode over to them.

"Cap, we've got one security camera in the whole damn place," the lieutenant said to Agner in a Brooklyn accent. "Down in the lobby. Records a day's worth of footage on VHS tapes."

"Better than nothing, I suppose," Agner replied, coming up off his knee and out of the gap.

"No doubt the picture quality will be stellar," Knight muttered. "Damn place is a dump." He paced between the air handlers with his hands on his hips, sizing up the sniper's roost.

Agner's talkie squawked, and he unclipped it from his belt. "Excuse me a sec." He broke away and paced a small circle as he listened to the update.

"Lotsa unlocked doors," the lieutenant said to Novak and Knight. "And the service bays and emergency exits are wide open, too. Unbelievable. And down on the thirty-eighth floor, there's this rehearsal studio. You know, soundproofed rooms, recording equipment, and such. Seems this morning, a heavy metal band named Meat Pop was holding auditions for a new guitarist. Guard says there were dozens of musicians in and out of the building all day. Lots of tattoos and long hair. He says they pretty much all came in carrying guitar cases."

"A guitar case is big enough to hold a sniper rifle," Novak said.

"Maybe they at least caught the guy on tape," Knight added.

"Assuming he came in through the lobby," the lieutenant replied. "Not like security is tight around here."

Agner came back, clipping his talkie to his belt while saying, "Seems one of Lombardi's computer people has some useful information for us. My detectives have her waiting in the conference room. Something about email threats Lombardi had been getting for the past week or so. They asked if you guys want to listen in on what she's gotta tell us," he said, looking at Knight, then Novak.

04.01 _____

Novak hitched a smooth ride with a rookie agent who stuck to the
speed limit, used his turn signals, and kept the behemoth Tahoe to
the slow lane. Twelve minutes later, he was back at the doorstep of
Lombardi Capital Management, where the circus out front had only
amplified: news vans and police cruisers lined the street; onlookers
were corralled behind police barricades; cameramen were busy framing shots of field correspondents. The medics had just finished loading a gurney carrying Lombardi's body bag into an ambulance;
behind it they stowed a large cooler, which Novak assumed contained
the rest of the banker's head.

He muscled through the crowd, flashed his creds and badge to the
unfamiliar cops manning the lobby, then rode in luxury up to sixteen.

The Giants fans had dispersed. The forensics team was camped at
the end of the hall.

He walked past the reception desk to the big fish tank on the left.
Two detectives remained inside, one male, the other female, both
middle-aged and eerily reminiscent of the duo from *Law & Order:
Special Victims Unit*. Lombardi's IT person sat across the table from
them, facing the windows, hands folded protectively over a closed
laptop.

Novak entered through the glass door, immediately catching the lingering aroma of too many agitated bodies occupying the same space for too long. After a round robin of introductions and pleasantries, he slipped out of his FBI windbreaker and claimed a chair beside the subject, Ms. Vickie Dill. Unlike the front office staff, the twenty-something IT wonk was dressed in a sensible off-the-rack pantsuit a tad snug for her plus-sized figure. Her brown bob was coiffed in a style that drew attention away from her hair's thinning. Plenty of eye makeup and bright lipstick added to the diversion. So did a diamond-stud nose piercing.

"Figured we'd wait for you before we started," said the female detective, Nancy Mileto.

"I appreciate that, thanks," Novak said.

The male detective, Jerry Rooney, spread his hands and looked at the subject. "We're all yours, Ms. Dill. Tell us what you've got."

"Well, I feel just terrible," she began, her voice tremulous, her eyes sorrowful. "I mean, maybe if I'd said something earlier . . ." Dill cleared her throat. "You see, like I told the police, there were these threats Mr. Lombardi had been getting for the past week or so. In his email. And texts, too."

"Tell us what kind of threats," Rooney encouraged.

She pursed her lips. "You know. Like death threats, I suppose. Pretty much the same message over and over again. Just that each time, the numbers would change."

"Numbers?" Rooney asked.

"The dollar amount. The bounty."

The word "bounty" drew everyone's attention. Novak exchanged quizzical glances with the detectives.

"I figured I'd just read you the most recent message," she said, unhinging the laptop with quivering fingers. "It's so strange. I kinda thought it was a joke at first, you know? But the messages kept coming. As you might imagine, Mr. Lombardi was getting plenty of hate mail. Those poor people . . . after what he'd done to them? They're just so angry."

Indeed, there was no shortage of people who'd love to see Lombardi dead, thought Novak. The banker had engineered a complex financial scheme that used high-frequency trading, secretive trading platforms called "dark pools," and exotic derivatives to shield losses in his clients' accounts while paying his firm fat commissions and fees regardless of its results. In the throes of a nasty market downturn a couple of years back, the perilous nature of those bets had been exposed, leaving dozens of charitable trusts, nonprofits, and universities with billions in losses. Plenty of ordinary folks got stung, too, including a hardworking union guy, mid-sixties, wife and two kids, who'd been left with nothing but life insurance. He figured he was worth more dead than alive and drove his car into a tree at 110 miles an hour.

The case presented by the FBI and the Justice Department had seemed airtight, delineating a textbook breach of fiduciary responsibilities. But in a surprise twist, the judge had acquitted Lombardi of criminal wrongdoing, on the basis that the algorithms and financial instruments he'd employed lacked clear regulatory oversight and were not expressly restricted in client contracts. Everyone knew it was bullshit, because a guilty verdict would have opened the floodgates for lawsuits at all the big Wall Street investment houses. So once again, Novak watched Wall Street trounce Main Street. Short of the punitive fines levied by the SEC, the bastard had walked away virtually scot-free. Until today.

"But this message . . . it was different, you know?" Vickie began tapping nimbly at the keyboard. "I even tried blocking the sender, but it didn't work. The messages kept spooling new addresses, and they didn't have any file attachments or malicious code. So, like, it wasn't a virus or Trojan or anything like that. But they kept sneaking through our firewall. Honestly, this kind of stuff is a bit out of my league, so after Mr. Lombardi told me he'd received another message this morning on his phone . . ." She choked up, took a few seconds to compose herself. "Well, I was getting ready to call our cybersecurity vendor to see if they might figure things out. Even considered calling the police. I guess it's too late for that."

Mileto asked for the name of the security vendor and jotted it down as Dill confirmed the spelling.

"Not much you could have done about it," Novak said, lightly patting Dill's shoulder.

"So you have this email there on your computer?" Mileto said.

"Yes," Dill replied.

"All right. Let's hear it."

"Okay," she said. "It's short, but . . . Well, you'll get the idea." She directed her eyes back to the screen then read slowly and distinctly: "As of ten A.M. EDT, your current bounty is five hundred twenty-nine thousand, seventy-two dollars. Current status: guilty." She read them the next line of the message, which directed Lombardi to a link for a website named bounty4justice.com. She looked up at the detectives and was met by blank stares.

"That's it?" Rooney asked.

Her lip curled down. "Mm-hmm."

"Doesn't sound like much of a threat," Rooney said. "Could have nothing to do with him being killed. Could be a prank."

Vickie Dill shook her head gravely, making the diamond speared through her nostril wink in the light. "It's not so much the email, you see. It's this website linked in the message. Let me show you. Agent Novak, could you please turn on the projector?" She pointed to the device at the center of the table.

"Sure." Novak clicked it on, and an image of a Web browser flashed up onto the wall in a five-by-six-foot luminescent rectangle. The detectives sat forward in anticipation as Ms. Dill typed the mysterious URL into the address bar.

When the Bounty4Justice Web page popped up in the projection box, Rooney shot up out of his chair and leaned in for a better look at the image streaming on the right half of the screen.

Ms. Dill let out a whimper, cupping her hands over her mouth and averting her eyes.

Detective Mileto slowly sat back, hands gripping the armrests as she stared at the screen.

It wasn't the large X superimposed over Lombardi's slick photo or the jaw-dropping final bounty figure that riveted them. It was the looping video clip to the right of the dead banker's photo. And what it showed kicked Novak's heart into overdrive.

URGENT:
All available agents report to FP crm4 @
16:00 for mandatory debriefing on Chase
Lombardi and a related cyberthreat. Please
advise if you are unable to attend.
—Tim Knight, ASAIC

05.01

On the approach to Federal Plaza, Novak flipped off his Chevy Impala's siren and LED light bars, then steered into the underground garage. He parked, took the stairs to the lobby, and rode the elevator with a group of chattering newbie agents he didn't know. Knight's assistant, Jennifer, was there to greet them when the doors opened.

"This way, people," she said, pointing left down the hall. "We'll be starting in five minutes. Go ahead and get comfy."

Before Novak could follow them, Jennifer hooked him by the arm. "Roman, Tim wants to see you before the meeting." She tipped her head in the direction of his office.

"Sure thing."

Novak went to Knight's office and rapped his knuckles on the door frame.

"Get in here, Novak," Knight said. "Have a seat for a sec."

Novak eased into the guest chair. "Everything check out with this website?"

"Oh, it's legitimate all right," Knight replied. "The video matches up perfectly to that rooftop. Even the distance measurements are spot-on. No way anyone but the shooter could have gotten that right." He leaned forward and propped his elbows on the desk. "You know, I was looking forward to being done with this Lombardi case. What should've been a slam dunk turned out to be a black eye. All those months wasted for a crap outcome. I gotta tell ya . . ." He placed a hand over his heart and peered out the door to make sure no one was within earshot. "When I got that call this afternoon, I figured Lombardi got what he deserved. Even thought there might just be a God up there. But now? Feh. This character's more trouble dead than alive."

Jennifer leaned in through the doorway. "Hartley and the chiefs are on their way."

"Good. Thanks. Be there in just a minute," Knight told her. He turned his attention back to Novak. "Here's the thing. This website is everything in one package: cybercrime, money crime, violent crime, God knows what else. I need to put together a task force. And I need a point man, a deputy with a broad skill set, who can help the specialists and NYPD connect the dots. At least until we better understand what we're dealing with. You get along with everyone, including Agner and his crew, and you've got a heckuva brain when it comes to finance and computers. Think you can handle it?"

Novak nodded. "Whatever it takes. I'm on board. You know that."

"Good." Knight stood and snatched his blazer off the chair back. "For now, I want you reporting directly to me. I'll work out the details with the brass, and we'll reassign your current cases. Now let's get in there and ruin everyone's day."

05.02 _____

"All right, people," Knight said to the keyed-up agents and technicians crowded into the conference room. Standing at a lectern emblazoned with the FBI insignia, he raised his palms high. "Let's cool it. It's getting late, and we've got a lot to cover."

Novak settled into a seat at the end of the third row.

"By now, you all know the fate of our dear friend Mr. Lombardi."

Some clapping and whistling.

Grinning, Knight said, "All right. A little respect, please." He eyed the doorway, anticipating the appearance of the triumvirate of bigwigs at any moment. "Though he won't be missed, Mr. Lombardi is now considered a homicide victim. And as much as this office would like to bury his case in a very deep hole, we now face a whole new problem. This isn't a crime of passion we're dealing with here. This is a premeditated, meticulously calculated murder committed by a highly trained killer. A marksman who perched himself on a rooftop nearly half a mile from Lombardi's window"—he pointed off in the distance—"and executed a flawless head shot with a high-caliber weapon. Who then disappeared like a phantom, thus far leaving not a trace of evidence."

He scanned the audience to make sure everyone was focused.

"Ladies and gentlemen, despite Lombardi's highly flawed character, let's not fool ourselves into thinking this won't be viewed by many as an act of terrorism. And once you get a look at what Agent Novak uncovered earlier this afternoon," he said, tipping his head to Novak, "you'll realize the gravity of the situation and why our office will continue to work closely with the NYPD on this investigation. We can't—"

The door opened partway, and Jennifer popped her head inside. She signaled to Knight like a catcher cueing the pitcher, then opened the door wide and stepped aside. Assistant Director in Charge Patricia L. Hartley, supreme commander of the New York field office, entered the room, followed by her special agents in charge: James Cooper, head of the Special Operations/Cyber Division, and Bonnie Karasowski-Fowler, head of the Counterterrorism Division. The three sat in reserved seats to the side of the lectern.

Their presence immediately intensified the mood.

"Good afternoon, everyone," Hartley said. "Please . . . go on, Tim."

"We all know that the Internet is the Wild West without borders: child predators, porn and piracy, hackers who target our private and public institutions, you name it. Well, now there's this ..." He plucked a remote off the lectern, aimed it at the projector mounted to the ceiling at the room's center, and clicked a button.

On the large viewing screen behind him, the Bounty4Justice Web page came up, with its rubber-stamp-style title banner and catchy slogan: IF THE LAW SHOULD FAIL, LET JUSTICE PREVAIL. Superimposed over Chase Lombardi's X'd-out picture were the words FINAL BOUNTY PAYOUT: $532,814. A pie chart to the right of the picture was colored mostly red with the label GUILTY: 92%; a thin wedge marked in green was tagged NOT GUILTY: 8%.

"First, let's focus here," Knight said. He aimed the laser dot at the image to the right of Lombardi's picture and spun it around the static shot of an office building's sleek exterior as seen through a circular high-powered lens overlaid with crosshairs. "And we'll take this live."

A digital marquee flashed and scrolled the bounty payout at the top of the screen. At the same time, a pirated version of the *A-Team* theme song began to play over the sound system. *Cheesy,* thought Novak, but on par with the website's simplistic production values. As the video initiated playback, he couldn't help but watch Hartley's face. Along with most in the room, she would be seeing this for the first time.

The simple duplex crosshairs of the reticle—four fat lines starting at the points of a compass that tapered to thin lines intersecting at the exact middle of the video frame—tightened over tall windows, looking in on a brightly lit, stately office set high up on the building. *The sixteenth floor, to be exact,* thought Novak. A neon digital readout at the bottom of the display held steady: 2360.16'−719.38m / SSE 11 mph. Tighter still and a portly silver-haired businessman came into focus, sitting at a desk with his back to the camera. The man swiveled in his chair to face the window, beady eyes flicking side to side and up and down. In one eerie instant, he even stared directly into the camera.

Everyone instantly recognized Chase Lombardi, and the chatter began.

"That isn't legit," the guy behind Novak whispered in his ear. "Is it?"

Novak nodded.

"Jesus," the guy muttered, easing back into his seat.

"Please, people," Knight said.

Novak watched Hartley more intently now. Her unblinking eyes were alert, but her face was involuntarily turning away from the screen.

Lombardi's chubby face now filled the circle, the crosshairs tickling his brow. As the *A-Team* theme song hit its crescendo, the image jumped for an instant, presumably from the shooter's recoil. Lombardi's face came back into crisp focus for a half second before collapsing inward as if sucker-punched by an iron fist, his head snapping back violently over the chair, fleshy chunks spraying onto the computer monitor directly behind him. In the same instant, the monitor spat electric sparks and belched wisps of black smoke.

Hartley's thin lips drew tight, and she held the back of her hand up to her face, as if the gore might somehow spatter out from the screen. Beside her, the chiefs squirmed in their seats.

A collective gasp echoed through the conference room, along with some choice expletives, as the video player's window faded to black and displayed a static message in blood-red lettering:

OUR MISSION:
Global network advantage to tactically combat elitism and tyranny,
so as to advance collective freedom and liberty.
At any cost.

The only sound in the room was the ticking of the wall clock. Novak gauged the stunned expressions on the faces around him. *Message received.*

06.01

"As it stands now, we don't know where this website came from," Knight said, "or who might be behind it. What we *have* learned today is that shortly after Chase Lombardi's acquittal was announced last week, he began receiving threatening texts and emails from Bounty4Justice. Walter and his team have performed a preliminary analysis of the website, so I've asked him to help us understand how it all works."

The pencil-thin cyber investigations squad leader approached the podium with stiff strides, his goatee and frizzy blond Afro a stark contrast to his mostly clean-cut colleagues. Knight passed the clicker to him.

Walter Koslowski cleared his throat and attempted eye contact with the audience, then quickly directed his attention to the screen behind him instead. "Uh, well, we haven't had much time to get under the hood of this thing, but I'll share with you what we've figured out so far. As you've just seen, it's a pretty straightforward concept: a sniper uploads his kill-shot video to claim the bounty on his designated target. At face value, it seems like some murder-for-hire 2.0 gimmick. But to really understand it, we need to look at the website's mechanics, starting with this button here, labeled PROFILE." He worked the remote and the screen refreshed, now filled with data packed into neat tables, categorized under simple headings.

"Everything, and I mean *everything,* the killer needed to know about Chase Lombardi could be found here. Under the heading VITAL STATISTICS we've got his date of birth, Social Security number, home and work addresses, driver's license number, phone numbers, vehicle and motor-craft license plate and registration numbers, passport number, email addresses, bank account numbers, credit card numbers, and so on. This violates practically every privacy law in one fell swoop, and I'm sure that at this very moment some enterprising cybercriminals are having a field day with Mr. Lombardi's personal data."

Some nervous laughter gave Walter the courage to glance out at a few friendly faces in the audience, including Novak's.

"Lombardi's favorite restaurants, hangouts, vacation spots, clubs, and extracurricular activities are listed under INTERESTS AND HOBBIES," he said, navigating to the next screen.

Skimming the bullet points, Novak learned that Lombardi had been an avid angler who'd gone fly-fishing at an exclusive Utah lodge every Labor Day weekend, which would have been a useful tidbit for a would-be predator.

"By clicking this ADD WHAT YOU KNOW button"—he underscored it with the laser dot—"anyone could post confidential information. And under FAMILY AND ASSOCIATES we find detailed photos and contact information for Lombardi's parents and siblings, spouse and children, and known business associates."

Scary stuff, thought Novak, eyeing the photos of Lombardi's thirty-one-year-old trophy wife, Pam, and their four beautiful children. Some crazed vigilante could easily have abducted one of them as a roundabout way to get to the banker.

"The next button is CASE HISTORY. Here we find a super-detailed description of why Lombardi was a really, *really* bad guy. Lots of links to news articles, as well as third-party sources that validate the allegations, allow visitors to perform due diligence, weigh it all out, and rate the material on a qualitative five-point star scale, sort of like an Amazon customer review. There's this whistleblower feature, too"—he aimed the laser dot at a button labeled SUBMIT YOUR EVIDENCE NOW—"where participants confidentially upload incriminating documents, videos, or images." He brought up the next screen. "And as you can see, Chase Lombardi's evidence file is quite extensive. Lots of juicy stuff here."

In the virtual file cabinet, neatly organized into folder icons with descriptive labels and document dates, Novak spotted a folder for emails dated as recently as yesterday, which certainly hadn't yet made their way to his desk. There were also thumbnail pics of Lombardi engaged in a lewd sex act with two women scantily clad in leather, neither of whom was Mrs. Lombardi.

"Clicking this button labeled VOTE NOW brings up a quick disclaimer on how the website works, terms and conditions, et cetera." Walter pointed at the small print that filled the screen. "It states here that participants take part in a virtual jury and pay a pledge fee to cast a vote for or against a mark—guilty or not guilty. A simple majority vote of guilty activates the bounty. The website then tabulates a starting prize amount based on the total number of guilty votes for that specific target, which then increases as more votes come in. If the vote swings to not guilty—presumably as the result of new evidence in favor of the target—the bounty is suspended, as are any personal data and vital statistics associated with the target. If the evidence *unequivocally* clears the target of wrongdoing, the target is deactivated and those pledge fees are distributed proportionately among the remaining active targets."

"Wait a second, Walter," the agent next to Novak called out loudly. "I'm confused. What do you mean *targets*? Are you saying this isn't just about Chase Lombardi?"

Walter clammed up and looked over to Knight.

Knight said, "We'll get to that in a few minutes. First, let's hear the rest of what Walter has to say."

"Holy shit," the guy behind Novak muttered.

"As I mentioned earlier," Walter continued, "whoever is the first to upload a valid kill-confirmation video for a guilty target wins the prize. There's no mention here as to how the prize money is paid out. My guess is that the winner is sent payment instructions after the claim has been validated. And I doubt the prize would be in the form of a check or bank transfer or gift card."

Some laughs.

For such a sizable reward, bearer bonds could be a sensible choice, thought Novak. A few certificates worth half a million dollars altogether could easily fit into a letter-sized envelope and would allow any "bearer" to redeem them just like cash. Or, for nearly perfect anonymity, payment could be transacted in a digital cryptocurrency like Bitcoin, which required no banks or intermediaries. But monetizing bitcoins into such a large cash equivalent wouldn't be easy.

A veteran agent in the front row raised her hand. "Where does this bounty money come from, Walter? And how do we know this isn't just some scam or stunt?"

"Ah. Good point. Can we prove the reward is real?" He shrugged. "Not at the moment. However, we do know that the website is indeed set up to raise money. So let's take a look at how that works."

For the next few minutes, Walter explained exactly how money changed hands on Bounty4Justice, and it wasn't nearly as surreptitious as Novak had expected. Before participants could fully interact with the website, they were required to purchase a novelty lapel pin— shipped via standard mail—for a minimum fee of two dollars to support "social justice." Though any pledge amount would be accepted, each unique participant—as determined by his or her IP address and other undisclosed identity data points—was restricted to one vote per mark. Walter presumed this measure was intended to prevent the marks themselves from rigging their own outcomes. He also pointed out that the website encrypted each ballot upon submission, preventing anyone from viewing its contents. Then he brought up a picture of the pin on the website—a simple affair with a round face bearing the stylized image of the scales of justice set inside a wreath of laurel branches, black on a white background, no inscriptions.

It was a clever tactic, but Novak wondered if a participant purchasing the novelty pin was somehow legally complicit in the murder-for-remuneration function of the website, even if his actual ballot was anonymized. No clean answer or precedent came to mind.

"Visa, MasterCard, and NcryptoCash are accepted," Walter said. "No formal account registration required. No filter to screen for bogus mailing addresses. Which means if you pay with NcryptoCash, pretty much anything goes—you can enter your name as 'Mickey Mouse' and have your pledge pin shipped to the White House."

Novak and almost everyone else in the room had come to know and fear NcryptoCash—the hottest new cryptocurrency to hit the Web. Units of value that existed only in ones and zeros. Completely untraceable. Loved by hackers and cybercriminals. Download the NcryptoCash Safebox software, and you were off and running.

The cynic in the front row added, "Why can't we just shut down this website or stop it from accepting credit cards?"

Novak mused how even some agents in the FBI assumed that taking down illicit websites was as simple as flicking a light switch.

Walter smiled tightly. "Bounty4Justice may look and feel like a run-of-the-mill dot-com, but we're having difficulty identifying its host servers. I've got people working on that. My team is also running transactions through the website to trace the money chain. Let's just say that it's going to take some time before we can present our case to the Justice Department. As we all know, these things don't happen as quickly as in the movies."

"Okay," Knight said, swooping in to pat the cyber expert on the back. "Let's leave it there for now, Walter. Lots of great information, thanks."

Walter waved diffidently to the audience and strode back to his seat.

"Now that we've all gotten a primer on the inner workings of Bounty4Justice"—Knight checked the wall clock—"I think it's obvious that we've got one heckuva situation on our hands here. And, unfortunately, it gets worse. *Much* worse." His eyes circled the room to make sure everyone was fully engaged. Then, his voice hardening, he went ahead and dropped the big bombshell: "Problem is, folks, as you're about to see, Mr. Lombardi was this website's *sixth* victim. And twenty-two more men and women have been marked for death."

16:48:07
Re: VIDEO UPLOAD COMPLETE
►Await further instructions.

07.01 _____

@ Washington, D.C.

The light drizzle was giving way to a full-on downpour, so he flicked the wipers from intermittent to high speed. Forty-five minutes ago, metro D.C. news radio had reported an impending five-mile traffic jam along the Capital Beltway, compliments of a jackknifed tractor-trailer. So he'd exited onto I-295, until the rented GPS unit mounted on the dashboard rerouted him downtown along I-695, where an unbroken stream of flashing taillights stretched as far as the eye could see. The damn old-school mapping software clearly lacked the basic congestion-spotting intelligence of WTOP's traffic copter. Same reason a machine or some clever app couldn't replace a seasoned sniper: computers still lacked the true complexity for good old-fashioned human decision making.

Which got him thinking that he'd much rather have killed that banker at his home in the suburbs as he sat in his man cave watching HBO, or maybe out on a golf course as the asshole stood crouched over a teed-up golf ball, steady and focused—anywhere without the myriad complications and risks of an urban setting. *All those eyes.* But a public spectacle seemed to be part of the package this time. One shot, one kill. Mission accomplished. Ooh rah.

Luckily, after scouting the blocks surrounding the banker's office a few days ago, he'd happened upon that eyesore building across from Ground Zero and the signboard posted outside on the sidewalk announcing an upcoming audition for guitarists. The security in the place had been a joke. He'd circled to the back alley, slipped through the service bay undetected, and scoped things out both inside and topside. He'd had no trouble getting up to the rooftop, where he'd found the perfect nest. Perfect vector. Perfect cover. From there, the plan practically wrote itself. Serendipity.

The required video was a new twist. In his line of work, video was typically reserved for a mark outside the United States whose body could not be recovered, like some military leader surrounded by a security detail who could be taken out only from a distance.

The traffic came to a standstill.

He stared through the passenger window at the Capitol Building's grand dome, imagining Washington powerbrokers—those blue-blood patriots in slick suits who never got their hands dirty and thought they were doing God's work—advancing their misguided political agendas, putting out encrypted calls to anonymous minions who would tie up their loose ends and sweep their tracks every step of the way.

The crush of vehicles finally started moving again, merging onto I-395 in a steady march. Up ahead near the Francis Case Memorial Bridge, he spotted a three-car fender bender that had been cleared off to the shoulder. The flashing lights of the police cruisers were causing plenty of rubbernecking, which impelled the driver of the minivan in front of him to come to a sudden stop, which forced him to do the same. Reflexively, he glanced in the rearview mirror at the yellow taxi that had been tailgating him with zero margin of error for the past two miles. Unfortunately, the oblivious driver was looking down at something in his lap—big mistake.

"Ah, fuck." He eased up on the brake to take the sting off the impact, but the hit was still forceful enough to jostle him in his seat and make the rental car lurch forward and bumper-tap the minivan. Luckily, the air bags didn't deploy. Most important, the trunk hadn't popped open. "What a fucking moron," he groaned, shaking his head and glaring in his mirror at the driver, who was holding his hands up apologetically. He imagined walking back to the taxi and shooting the jackass between the eyes. One less idiot in the world.

The minivan angled off to the shoulder, and a little girl with pigtails in the backseat pressed her tiny face to the glass and frowned. The driver—her daddy, it would seem—immediately hopped out and waved to him insistently for the pull-over-and-let's-swap-insurance-info song and dance.

"Goddamnit." He considered ignoring the guy, but the taxi was now maneuvering off to the shoulder, too, and one of the cops tending to the fender bender was looking quizzically at the minivan. "You've got to be kidding me."

Reluctantly, he steered onto the shoulder.

08.01 _____

@ Manhattan

"You heard me right, people," Knight said, raising his hands to stop the eruption of side conversations. "Six dead, so far. Twenty-two more, and counting, could end up the same way if we don't get answers fast. So please listen up. The screens Walter just described pertain specifically to Chase Lombardi's profile. Now we'll look at Bounty4Justice's home page and you'll see the true scope of this thing." Knight worked the remote, and the screen refreshed.

Chase Lombardi's X'd-out photo reduced down to thumbnail size alongside an equally scaled American flag icon. To the right of the flag, the award notification marquee scrolled the bounty payout of $532,814 next to the pie-chart graphic of the vote split. Stacked beneath Lombardi's profile were five more X-outs and their accompanying bounty award marquees, but the flags beside them were not American. Though Novak hadn't noticed it earlier, there was a button on top of the page labeled NOMINATE A TARGET, which implied that the website was open to suggestions.

"Bounty4Justice also operates throughout Europe and Asia," Knight informed his audience. "Lombardi was the first U.S. mark to be taken out. But as you can see here, marks in five other countries have shared that fate, and over twenty more have bounties on their heads. So let's get acquainted with the other victims."

He used the remote to click on the second victim's crossed-off head shot. The picture enlarged and brought his complete profile up on the screen.

"Mr. Mario Bianchi." He pointed to the man's photo, then read snippets of the caption beneath it: "Vatican banker suspected of embezzling over fifty million euros from dioceses across Europe. Never formally sentenced. Found hanging from Blackfriars Bridge in London. Video claim is dated six days ago." He pointed to the digital marquee, saying, "You can see here that the awarded bounty is roughly half a million U.S. dollars. The vote was 84 percent for guilty, 16 percent not guilty." He clicked the remote, turned to the screen, and pressed a fist to his chin.

The video began with a bright light shining on the middle-aged banker, slumped inside what looked like the interior of a van, his chin pressed to his chest, sweating through his tailored gray flannel suit. A rusty chain had been cinched around his neck in a hangman's knot, and his hands—presumably bound—were pulled tight behind his back. The way Bianchi rocked and jostled showed that the van was in motion.

"Come si chiama?" the cameraman's offscreen voice demanded. The banker's head merely flopped from right to left. The cameraman grabbed a fistful of Bianchi's thick gray hair and yanked the head back, the camera shuddering side to side as he did so. *"COME SI CHIAMA?"* he repeated contemptuously.

Bianchi's listless eyes rolled away from the light. "M-Mario . . . Mario Bianchi." He began weeping.

The cameraman let the head drop, then held the banker's Italian passport close to the camera to further validate the man's identity.

The video abruptly switched to an exterior view: nighttime, the banker awash in the camera's light, standing against a waist-high railing to which the chain's slack end was now tethered. Behind him, the Thames was an expansive gray void between London's glowing riverfront architectural facades. It appeared to Novak that Bianchi now looked sedated, drunk. He wasn't attempting to escape; he wasn't putting up a fight.

While the camera held steady from a side view along the railing, a second man dressed head to toe in black swept in and fiercely snap-kicked the banker in the chest, sending him over the rail like a dropped anchor. The cameraman did a superb job of leaning over the rail and tracking the plunge. The chain's slack—maybe twenty feet, Novak estimated—*clink-clink-clink*ed over the rail, then pulled taut with a loud *CLING-CLACK!* Down below, Bianchi's head whipped and snapped against the chain's violent drag as his body popped and threatened to detach. But the neck held firm, and Bianchi's limp form swung in and out of view above the water.

Fade to black.

The mission statement reappeared in the video player's window. Its concise language certainly didn't mince words, thought Novak. GLOBAL NETWORK ADVANTAGE TO TACTICALLY COMBAT ELITISM AND TYRANNY, SO AS TO ADVANCE COLLECTIVE FREEDOM AND LIBERTY. Yet he couldn't decide if it was an incitement for revolution or some zealous edict for a new world order. The second line of the website's credo was even more disconcerting: AT ANY COST. What in hell did that mean?

Knight blew out a long breath, shook his head, rubbed the back of his own neck. "Look, I know this is disturbing stuff, folks. But it's important that we get through this." And for the next fifteen minutes, he played master of ceremonies to the website's macabre video library.

Next up: an iconic fifty-three-year-old news anchorman named Juergen Ackermann from Frankfurt. Ackermann—self-proclaimed champion of the working class—had been charged with raping his young ex-girlfriend at knifepoint, only to be acquitted on the grounds of insufficient evidence after a divisive ten-month trial dubbed Germany's "trial of the decade." Two days after the ruling, while drinking heavily in a local biergarten, he'd been secretly caught on video bragging about how he'd gotten away with the crime. That video went viral on Instagram and YouTube and subsequently landed him a top spot on Bounty4Justice, with 97 percent of participants voting him guilty.

In Ackermann's kill-validation video, he was bound to a chair with duct tape while three masked captors, clearly female, grotesquely bludgeoned him to death with sledgehammers—knees shattered, shoulders mashed, skull macerated—for a winning prize equivalent to $458,649. The wet *thwump*ing sounds of blunt steel crushing bone and tissue were sure to replay in Novak's nightmares for months.

Though the audience was registering the true horror of Bounty4Justice, the show was far from over.

The next prize winner, from Madrid, had cashed in on Dr. Carmena Esquierdo, a former obstetrician who, during the 1960s and '70s, had stolen hundreds of newborns from Spanish hospitals on behalf of an underground trafficking network that sold the babies to unsuspecting adoptive parents. Esquierdo had told the birth mothers that their babies had died during delivery, and those who'd insisted on seeing their dead babies wound up dead themselves, from unexplained complications. With Spain's former dictator Generalissimo Francisco Franco, other government officials, and even some prominent clerics complicit in the scandal, however, and given that Dr. Esquierdo was nearing eighty years of age, a trial had been ruled out so as not to relive a very dark chapter in Spain's past. Bounty4Justice's virtual jury, on the other hand, had dismissed the statute of limitations with 87 percent approval and a $466,109 kicker.

The killer gave a nod to the Inquisition by roasting Dr. Esquierdo atop a pyre of car tires set beneath the makeshift "stake" of a lamppost. If the searing blue-and-orange flames hadn't killed the old woman, thought Novak, the toxic black smoke from those smoldering Pirellis most certainly would have. The way she shrieked and writhed in the fire had him shifting in his seat. When her face boiled up like the toppings on a brick-oven pizza, he felt his gag reflex start to kick in. Yet he couldn't pull his eyes away, because the static shot gave the viewer the eerie impression of sitting there with her like some twisted ringside spectator. *What is it about the "train wreck" that so connects with our primal core?* he wondered. Esquierdo's burning struck him as an update on medieval hangings in the public square or mass crucifixions in ancient Rome—a shaming, ominous spectacle.

The parade of horror had cast a gloomy pall over the assemblage, but a discreet nod from Hartley green-lighted Knight to press forward. He introduced the next victim while everyone settled in for a trip inside the next circle of hell.

Railway Minister Zhang Huang Fu had violated the public's trust in epic fashion, even by Chinese standards, squirreling an estimated $180 million in secret accounts and amassing over three hundred homes with funds siphoned from municipal coffers. The public outcry on social-networking sites like Weibo—China's answer to Twitter—was so stunning that Beijing had been forced to temporarily shut down its network to suppress the unrest. Zhang, like many of his ilk, had fled the country to avoid standing trial. Bounty4Justice's cyber jurists, however, had tried the case in absentia and arrived at a near-unanimous vote, with 99 percent of participants finding him guilty.

The kill video began with a middle-aged Chinese man in a business suit, presumably the disgraced minister, standing on a skyscraper's rooftop with his back to the camera. The apocalyptic daytime sky glowed orange-green, and in the near distance, behind the Oriental Pearl Tower and the glassy twin towers of the Shanghai International Finance Centre, sampans and junks drifted along the muddy bends of the Huangpu River. Novak figured Zhang either never truly left China, or had been forcibly repatriated to face the music.

Gusting winds drowned out a command shouted by the cameraman (not that Novak could make heads or tails of Chinese) as a menacing pistol came into view in the hand of another man positioned offscreen to the right. Zhang turned weepily toward the camera, face scrunched tight, tears streaming down his cheeks, blue silk tie flapping like a wind sock. The cameraman zoomed in on the face—tight, really tight. As if to say, Let there be no mistaking it. This is the guy. More shouting sent Zhang to the rooftop's edge, quaking in fear. Then a final, succinct directive—clearly Chinese for "jump." Zhang shook his head in disbelief and whimpered, abandoning any last notion of saving face.

Novak was pretty sure that carrying firearms most anywhere in China was illegal. That got him thinking that these were no ordinary thugs but professionals who were keyed in to shady criminal networks. The bounty prize was sizable. Though was it big enough to command such an elaborate execution by what appeared to be seasoned professionals? After all, Zhang was the first victim in China.

The cameraman repeated the command. Zhang disobeyed it. The gunman shot the minister in the left shoulder—red blossomed over his lapel—and that did the trick. Zhang's violent recoil sent him airborne and out of sight. The cameraman scurried mindfully to the rooftop's lip, took a few seconds to get the right angle and steady the shot, and captured Zhang's flailing body as it folded and bounced off a terrace railing halfway down the building before continuing its terminal descent toward the sidewalk, easily a hundred stories below. The zoom pixelated into a blur before sharpening for the tiny red splat of the impact.

All Novak could think was that it appeared that he hadn't landed on a pedestrian.

Final yuan payout converted to U.S. dollars: $623,125.

"Damn," the agent seated next to Novak whispered. She covered her mouth with her hand.

"One more to go," Knight said, as if coaching a woman through childbirth. "Lastly, we have a Japanese pharmaceutical executive, Koji Watanabe, whose company had falsified clinical studies on a blockbuster cholesterol drug, resulting in dozens of patients' deaths. Watanabe denied any wrongdoing, and since no evidence proved he'd had a hand in the cover-up, he was not criminally charged in the investigation. Instead, the blame was pinned on a subordinate, who committed suicide before standing trial. Documents uploaded to Bounty4Justice substantiated rumors that Watanabe had orchestrated the whole thing. And here's what happened next."

Fade in: fifty-four-year-old Koji Watanabe, hanging by his shackled wrists from a hook that dangled from something out of view overhead, feet tethered with rope to an eye hook in the floor. The space around him: the girder-and-sheet-metal interior of a pristine industrial warehouse, empty and brightly lit. He'd been stripped to his boxers, which was less humiliating than intended, given that he was a fit man. His expression was resolute, completely unrepentant. Grisly scenarios for this torture-friendly arrangement reeled through Novak's mind: disembowelment with a scalpel, dismemberment with a chain saw, perhaps flaying alive. Too many possibilities.

A short guy in a ski mask came waltzing into the frame, pushing a cart. But the tray atop it wasn't full of rusty old blades and clamps and implements of torture. It was stacked with cash. Not dollars. Yen. The executive started berating his captor in rapid-fire Japanese, spittle flying, neck veins bulging. Masked Guy grabbed a fistful of yen and stepped up to Watanabe. Watanabe, in turn, spit right in the guy's masked face. Masked Guy responded with a gut-wrenching left jab that landed on Watanabe's nose much the way a falling anvil might flatten a water balloon, blood exploding in every direction.

Silence in the warehouse.

Now Masked Guy got busy. With his left hand, he cranked open Watanabe's jaw like a nutcracker, then proceeded to jam the wad of cash in his mouth, with authority. Watanabe tried his best to fight it, to little avail. Masked Guy grabbed another fistful of bills off the cart and sent them home, too. With a crushed nose and a mouth stuffed with yen, Watanabe struggled for air. In less than ten seconds, his face went a sickening purple, veins cabling out from his temples.

Then Masked Guy went to town on the executive, working over the engorged face and body with well-aimed punches to beat the last molecule of oxygen out of him. Watanabe went limp, and his bladder let loose to signal the end. For good measure, the video played for a solid minute before cutting to black.

Final bounty in U.S. dollars: $489,145; the guilty/not-guilty pie chart split, 81 percent / 19 percent.

Thus ended the viewing of Bounty4Justice's current video archive.

09.01

The conference room remained as quiet as a tomb for a good thirty seconds, until Tim Knight finally broke the silence. "Of the twenty-two active targets, five reside here in the U.S.," he noted. Using the remote, he clicked a filter on the Bounty4Justice home page so that only domestic targets showed. "The names will sound familiar to most of you, because, like Chase Lombardi, they've all been fodder for the nightly news for quite some time."

He ran down the list—a veritable who's who of scoundrels and lowlifes who'd recently dodged the justice system on technicalities or whose despicable crimes far outweighed their prescribed punishment. The vote-split pie chart next to each name was practically solid red to indicate a resounding "guilty."

At the top of the list was Paul Garrison, a weaselly forty-three-year-old from Chicago who'd served a mere seven years for molesting nearly two dozen young boys while employed as the grounds manager at a Lake Michigan summer camp in the late 1990s. Following his release in June, he'd been using a windfall inheritance to bankroll a highly publicized legal challenge to Illinois's Sex Offender Registration Act, which required him to register as a "sexual predator" every year for the remainder of his natural life—one of many tough measures he viewed as "excessive" and "unfair." He also felt that being banned from Facebook and other social media venues during his parole was "draconian" and "outright unconstitutional." The street outside his home had become an encampment for angry residents and protestors, so he'd been moving around from place to place, engaging the press via Skype, like some political dissident. His profile picture came directly from the Illinois State Police website. Bounty: $511K and counting.

In the second slot was the notorious Californian "attorney to the stars" Jacob Feldstein, best known for three scandalous murder trials in recent years that had resulted in acquittals for his decidedly guilty celebrity clients. This past spring, he'd zoomed his Maserati through a busy Los Angeles crosswalk and plowed over a mother pushing her newborn twins in a stroller, killing the babies instantly and leaving her in a drug-induced coma at Cedars-Sinai. Though the incident had been captured by a traffic camera, Feldstein managed to keep the video sealed throughout his trial, which, along with shoddy police work, let him walk with only traffic citations. His profile on Bounty4Justice included an upload of that inadmissible, stomach-turning audiovisual, alongside his infamous smirking mug shot, to ensure that justice would get the last laugh. Bounty: $422K.

"Nobody likes a sleazy lawyer," whispered the agent seated beside Novak.

And that's really all it takes for Bounty4Justice to get a vote, thought Novak, giving her a polite smile.

In third place, a former Jacksonville bookie turned banker named Ralph Demaris, who'd peddled predatory no-doc mortgages to anyone with a pulse during the buildup to the epic national housing bust a few years back. His greedy maneuverings had blighted neighborhoods in his native Florida and forced hundreds of families to forfeit their homes and life savings. A recent *60 Minutes* exposé chronicled how he'd emerged from the scandal unscathed and *very* rich. In 2009, he'd seeded a hedge fund that snatched up hundreds of those same properties at fire-sale prices, which were then rented to many of the same families he'd bankrupted. He'd also secretly cooperated with federal authorities to provide inside information that allowed the IRS to target many of his past clients for tax evasion and fraud, while the offshore accounts that sheltered his own windfall profits were never audited. Bounty: $389K.

Fourth place went to a serial rapist dubbed "the Sorority Stalker," who for months had been terrorizing female students on college campuses throughout Greater Boston. He'd been using a GoPro camera to take videos of his sick acts and post them on anonymous servers hosted on the darknet—the unindexed, lawless realm of the Internet that could be accessed only through an invite in an anonymous chat room. The authorities had little to go on and thus far, the same was true for Bounty4Justice. But if clues were to surface as to the man's identity, Novak was sure that the website's highly dynamic forum for information sharing with a $384K kicker would give the authorities a run for *their* money in seeing who might get to the cyber rapist first.

In the fifth slot was Alan Bateman, the Long Island–based mastermind of the largest-ever Medicare-fraud scam. He'd used more than seven thousand stolen identities to file fraudulent claims for healthcare services and supplies billed by various companies registered in eighteen different states, all of which existed only on paper. Federal reimbursements paid to his bogus companies totaled $127 million. After expenses to cover roughly four dozen co-conspirators—many of whom were members of a notorious Armenian crime syndicate—he'd netted $88 million. He'd been investigated by the FBI, tried by the Justice Department, and found guilty by a judge and was currently on house arrest awaiting sentencing. By all accounts, he was expected to be treated very leniently, since he'd snitched on everyone involved in the operation. Bounty: $320K.

It was a solid list, thought Novak—thorough, unbiased, and in line with public sentiment. People despised criminals who were let off easy for their crimes, and they particularly *hated* bad guys who "got away with murder" within the law. Whoever was behind Bounty4Justice knew exactly how to tap into those hardwired emotions that resided deep in every human's lizard brain. But were the proceeds from the lapel pins actually being paid out to the assassins, or was the mastermind laughing all the way to the bank?

"And there you have it, folks," Knight said, nodding to Hartley.

The assistant director in charge made her way to the open floor in front of the podium, wearing an expression typically reserved for funerals. "It's understandable that the public is very upset with Chase Lombardi's acquittal, as well as the misdeeds of the other victims whose gruesome deaths we've witnessed just now. Frankly, I share in that sentiment, as do you, I'm sure. Yes, lots of people have been disenfranchised by con men and have suffered terribly at the hands of criminals of every stripe. Many of them might see this as a tangible solution, or perhaps a fix for the punishment they believe *we* cannot deliver. But *this* is not justice," she said, chopping her hand at the screen. "This is an *aberration* of justice. Pure vigilantism. I don't think I need to lecture anyone on that." She closed her eyes and clasped her hands together, searching for direction. Then she continued, cool and collected: "I'm sure every agent in this room has experienced the difficulties of cracking Internet-based crimes. But from the looks of it, this one's a doozy."

Novak felt overwhelmed. "Doozy" was putting it mildly. Taking down a gorilla like Bounty4Justice was going to be a Herculean task.

"Headquarters will need to have our legal attachés in Beijing, Tokyo, London, Frankfurt, and Madrid validate exactly what happened to these other five victims in Asia and Europe. I'll brief the director on the matter and see to it that those inquiries are made. In the meantime, our local offices here in Manhattan will continue to assist NYPD every step of the way in tracking down Chase Lombardi's sniper. And since Alan Bateman also falls under our office's jurisdiction here in New York, we'll see to it that he gets to his prison cell before someone decides to cash in on *his* bounty." She looked expectantly to SAC Karasowski-Fowler, who nodded confidently. "Furthermore, since Chase Lombardi was Bounty4Justice's first victim here in the U.S., I will request that this office spearhead the cyberinvestigation. As you all know, our cyber chief, Jim Cooper, is the best of the best"—she looked over to the SAC, and he smiled appreciatively—"as is our world-class Cyber Command Center. Therefore, I'm confident that Walter and his team will have the support they need to get things rolling and identify the servers hosting this website and, in time, the mastermind behind it. From there, we'll work with headquarters to determine the appropriate course of action."

Walter straightened in his seat and nodded. Challenge accepted. Over the years, Novak had come to know that Walter was to the Web what Stephen Hawking was to quantum mechanics. And no matter where in the world Bounty4Justice might be operating, Manhattan's Cyber Command Center had the resources, reach, and international partnerships to find it and shut it down.

"Tim has already begun to assemble an emergency task force, and I've been told that Special Agent Novak will be leading that team. Is that right, Tim?"

"That's correct," Knight said.

"Agent Novak, would you like to say a few words?"

Not really, he thought, as all eyes turned to him. He stood, smoothed his tie, cleared his throat. "Based on everything we've seen here today, I think we all understand the seriousness of this undertaking. The way I look at it, we cannot stand by and let some rogue website rewrite the laws of justice. So let's crush Bounty4Justice right now, before this goes any further." Nothing else came to mind, so he stood there for a few seconds, wondering if he'd sounded absurdly mawkish.

"Do you have a name for this operation, Agent Novak?" asked Hartley.

He hadn't thought that far ahead. Typically an operation was dubbed something witty that captured the essence of the crime itself, like the code name for the investigation into the 9/11 attacks: PENTT-BOM, for "Pentagon, Twin Towers Bombing Investigation." "I'm open to suggestions, but I'm thinking Operation CLICKKILL." Sounded catchy enough.

"Excellent," Hartley said. "I wish you and your team luck, Agent Novak. Please be sure to issue an EC right away to the field offices where the remaining U.S. targets reside. And let's all do our best to shut this thing down before it goes any further."

10.01 _____

@ Greenpoint, Brooklyn
Tuesday, 10/24/2017

At 5:30 A.M., Novak swatted at the chirping alarm clock and groaned.
He'd slept like crap, thanks to looping nightmares featuring smashed
skulls and an old lady roasting like a rotisserie chicken. Bad enough

he hadn't gotten home until midnight, after staying at the office into the late evening with Knight and Walter to cobble together an action plan for the task force and prepare an electronic communication announcing New York's claim over the Bounty4Justice investigation.

He stumbled into the kitchen, brewed some coffee, ate some yogurt sprinkled with granola, then put on his workout gear and walked to the local gym for a forty-minute training session mixing treadmill sprints and free weights. A call from Captain Agner came in just as he returned to his apartment.

"Morning, Novak," Agner said. "Jeez, this website is downright vicious. Never cared for all this technology to begin with. I've seen some crazy stuff in my years, but that tops it all. It seems anything goes these days."

"Sure does."

"Knight says you're our go-to from here on out. Really pleased to hear it. Don't need to tell you that our guys and your guys don't always play nice."

That was putting it kindly, thought Novak. When it came to jurisdiction, the FBI and Manhattan municipal authorities interacted like a bitter divorced couple in a custody dispute.

"I told Knight he's got our full cooperation and that I'd be giving you updates as new information comes in. On that note, wanted to let you know that my detectives hit a roadblock with Lombardi's attorney. This Waverly fella is quite the asshole," Agner said. "Completely ignoring our calls. If anyone would've known about threats Lombardi had been receiving, he'd be the one. You get along with him, don't you?"

"I suppose so."

"Would you mind saving me the runaround and see if he has anything useful to tell us?"

"Sure thing," Novak said.

He left a no-nonsense voice message for Waverly, informing the lawyer that he'd be dropping by around 8:30 to ask a few questions, with no request for a callback confirmation. He'd learned over the past months that it was best not to give the man an opportunity to decline a meeting. Then he showered, dressed, and grabbed his Glock and badge from the safe.

Before heading to his car, he stopped in at the deli downstairs, as he did most mornings.

"Morning, Roman," said the old Polish proprietor behind the counter, flashing a tobacco-stained Cheshire-cat smile.

"Morning, Piotr."

He scanned the newspapers. As expected, Chase Lombardi's picture was plastered over all the front pages. The *Post* had lifted his photo with the big X over it from Bounty4Justice, with large white block letters reading, BOUNTY FOR BANKER. *The Wall Street Journal* headline declared, SNIPER COLLECTS $532K BOUNTY FOR LOMBARDI HIT. *The New York Times* featured a photo from Lombardi's trial where the grinning banker was shrugging contemptuously at the judge; the story was titled LOMBARDI VERDICT OVERRULED BY INTERNET ASSASSIN. The *Daily News* memorialized him with BIGOT BANKER GETS FINAL HEAD SHOT below a gritty morgue photo of his cratered face. Novak assumed that someone at the coroner's office would soon be in hot water for releasing that photo.

He plucked a *Journal* off the rack and placed it on the counter next to the to-go cup of black coffee Piotr had ready and waiting.

"You involved in that mess?" Piotr pointed his chin at the cover story.

"Come on, now. You know I can't tell you that."

"One day you'll slip up. You'll see." He held up a finger and winked. "Someday I'll know your secrets."

"I'd better stay on my toes, then."

11.01

@ Beaver Street

Waverly remained seated, no handshake offered. "Nice to see you
again, Novak." A slight, smug smile. Pointing to the chair on the opposite side of the desk, he said, "Have a seat."

As Novak settled in, Waverly's new assistant glided into the office.
She was a doppelgänger for a famous swimsuit model, just like her
predecessor.

"Coffee or juice?"

"Black coffee would be great, thanks." Novak took a moment to
admire the spectacular thirty-second-floor corner view of the sparkling Hudson River and Lady Liberty poised above her tiny island

like a cake topper. His gaze drifted north along the opposite shoreline to the sleek, beguiling buildings in Jersey City, where one could enjoy lower taxes and cheaper rent. But Manhattan's Financial District, or FiDi, was a mystical realm completely disassociated from bridge-and-tunnel frugality. Here, proximity to the world's capitalist heart was sacrosanct. And Waverly was as close to it as one could get.

The attorney checked his watch. "I've got to be at the courthouse by ten."

"I won't keep you long."

"The verdict's been delivered, Novak. Case closed."

"It's a new case now. Homicide. And I'd appreciate it if you'd cooperate with the NYPD."

"I'm a busy man, and I don't take kindly to redundancy. You know that. Figured I'd skip the bullshit and wait for you to drop by." He spread his hands. "And here we are. So fire away."

"Do you know if anyone wanted Lombardi dead?"

"Come on, Novak. *Everyone* wanted him dead. He wasn't exactly a likable fellow. Especially after what he'd gotten away with."

"Thanks to you."

Waverly's smile flattened. He cocked his head sideways and studied Novak. "Oftentimes a rout is the *only* way to effectuate meaningful change. Let's skip the moral thumb wrestling, shall we?" He tapped his watch. "I have no idea who shot him, Novak. Scout's honor." He held up a three-finger salute.

"I'm sure you've seen the website."

"I have. I bet half the world has by now. You watch Jimmy Kimmel last night?"

Novak shook his head.

"Uhhh. Pull it up on YouTube later. It's a friggin' riot." Waverly shook his head and smiled. Novak wasn't amused. "All I'm saying is, it's easier to laugh at a monologue than dwell on those nauseating snuff videos."

The assistant returned with a steaming mug, handed it to Novak with a smile, and withdrew. The coffee was nutty and rich. "Did Lombardi say anything to you about Bounty4Justice or the threatening messages it'd been sending him?"

The attorney wove his fingers into a basket, shook his head. "Not a word. Though let's be real. Threats meant nothing to Chase Lombardi. He'd have ignored them. You know that. Like I said, nothing malicious came through this office, I assure you. I'm just as surprised about all this as you are. If I had something, *anything,* you know that even with attorney-client privilege, I'd have to bring the authorities into the loop."

Notwithstanding the attorney's habitual poker face, Novak had interacted with him long enough to know that he was being truthful.

"Besides, Lombardi wasn't the only one on the hit list. So I'd say that in the order of things, the website should be the FBI's first priority. Let the cops beat the bushes for the shooter."

Novak sampled more coffee, waiting for Waverly to expound. And, as always, he did.

"The way I see it, assassins kill for money," the attorney said. "The website provides the money. As Al Franken says, 'It's easier to put on slippers than to carpet the whole world.'"

Waverly was quite proficient with computers. His office was virtually paperless—no small feat for an industry notorious for laying ruin to forests. And his internal forensic-records team had proved capable of recovering virtually any digital document the world had ever created. "From the looks of it, this website isn't going to be easy to trace," Novak acknowledged.

It was a major understatement. Last night, Novak had witnessed Walter's reaction when Knight asked for information about the results of the WHOIS inquiries on Bounty4Justice's IP address. Walter's face had tightened into a pained knot. "Nothing comes up, Tim. No registration, nothing. It's like it doesn't exist. Makes no sense. I mean, how can it show up on Google if the IP can't be resolved? It's impossible. It's like it's operating its own anonymity network or something."

"Really," Waverly said incredulously. "Come on, now. I'm sure *your* guys will figure it out. They're some of the best talent in the world."

"In time, sure. But our fear is that more targets might be killed in the interim."

"A lot of *Chase Lombardis,* Novak," Waverly clarified.

"That's today. Tomorrow it could be the president. Or just some ordinary person who happened to rub someone the wrong way."

"You mean ordinary good guys, like me or you?"

"Sure. That, too."

"You're being a bit melodramatic."

"Am I?"

Waverly grinned. "You've got to hand it to whoever came up with the idea. Brilliant stuff. Preys on everyone's weakness."

"What weakness might that be?"

"The need for vengeance. The *grudge*. It's in our DNA."

Waverly was an expert on that subject, too, thought Novak. His firm's business model was built on it. "I'm sure I don't need to explain the downside of vigilante justice to you," Novak countered.

"No. No, you don't. All I'm saying is that it just goes to show that when the system repeatedly tromps the little guy, it doesn't take much for him to regress back to his caveman roots. Particularly when there's half a million bucks on the line."

Novak sipped his coffee and gave Waverly another thoughtful look.

Waverly expounded further: "Assuming people are getting paid huge money to take potshots at douchebags like Chase Lombardi, if I were you, I'd do my best to avoid a repeat performance. Nip this enterprise in the bud the old-fashioned way."

"Meaning?"

"Meaning *people* built that website. And *people* talk and *people* brag. *People* fight. You can always count on the fact that someone will get sloppy and leave clues."

Despite Waverly's confident stating of the obvious, the weight sitting on Novak's shoulders didn't feel any lighter.

"Look, Novak . . ." Waverly snatched a canary-yellow Post-it note from a dispenser on his desk and jotted down a name and number. "As far as the technology's concerned . . . if your team does hit a roadblock, there's this vendor I use over in Jersey for offsite backups, archives, and so on. Big operation. From what I've seen, his people could teach the NSA a thing or two." He passed the Post-it across the immaculate granite desktop. "Name's Mike DelGuercio. Company's called Digital Vault Technologies. Maybe he's good for a tip or two. Never hurts to get another outside opinion. Tell him I referred you."

"I'll do that," the lawman said, plucking the Post-it off the desktop. "Much appreciated."

"No sweat. And cheer up. You'll figure things out. Oh, and whatever you do, when you see Big Mike, don't say anything bad about the Yankees."

From: Joseph.Varanelli@ic.fbi.gov
Sent: Tuesday, October 24, 2017 at 8:44 AM
To: Roman Novak
Cc: Timothy Knight
Subject: Paul Garrison—status report

Gentlemen:
I received your EC regarding CLICKKILL. I'll be your contact here in
Chicago. Look forward to working with both of you.
TSA shows that last night Garrison boarded Qatar Airways flight
QTR1144 bound for Doha, final destination Bangkok. He's in clear
violation of his parole agreement, and we've corroborated the
allegations of child solicitation posted on Bounty4Justice. We've
notified the Qatari authorities and issued a red notice to Interpol. He's
expected to land in Qatar in the next hour. We'll have the marshals
bring him back to Chicago and keep him locked up while you figure
things out with the website.
Be in touch soon, hopefully with some good news. Enjoy your day.

Supervisory Special Agent Joseph Varanelli
FBI Chicago
2111 W. Roosevelt Road
Chicago, IL 60608
Phone: (312) 555-0150
Fax: (312) 555-5732/38
@FBIChicago | Email Alerts | FBI.gov/chicago

12.01 _____

Novak exited Waverly's building and headed to his car. He thumbed
his BlackBerry to read the emails that had begun trickling in, responding to the EC he'd disseminated the night before. From the looks of
things, the field offices were taking Bounty4Justice in stride, and the
scavenger hunt for the live targets was under way. He placed a call to

Agner to pass along the underwhelming news from the attorney, and the captain picked up on the second ring.

Agner sighed through the receiver. "You believe Waverly's telling the truth?"

"Yeah, I do."

"Damn. Well, I appreciate your help. Not much to report here, either."

Through the receiver, Novak could hear him flipping through paperwork.

"Coroner says Lombardi was killed somewhere between ten-fifteen and eleven-fifteen. They ruled out a full-blown autopsy. Cause of death: trauma resulting from a gunshot wound to the head."

"That's why they pay her the big bucks."

"Tell me about it," Agner chortled. "Ballistics confirmed the round was a three-thirty-eight Lapua Magnum. That's the business end of an enhanced cartridge built for accuracy and distance. The groove marks are consistent with an Accuracy International AWM sniper rifle. It's a British design, but since it's the Cadillac of weapons, the Marine Corps, SEALs, Delta Force, and other Special Ops all use 'em. Or you could just buy one at a gun shop or expo. It's the same weapon used for the longest confirmed kill on record, which was just about a mile and a half."

"Still," Novak said, "even a half-mile head shot takes a lot of practice."

Agner fell silent for a moment, no doubt spooked by the idea of a military marksman using Manhattan as a shooting gallery.

"Anyway," the captain said, "I'm emailing this stuff to you so you can look it over for yourself. My detectives are canvassing again this morning, interviewing folks in the vicinity surrounding that rooftop. Got lots more tenants to talk to inside the building. That music studio provided a list of everyone who showed up to the audition. Forty-something names with phone numbers. We'll need to hunt each of them down, question 'em. It's gonna take time."

"How about the video from the lobby security camera?"

"Useless, in my opinion. Really grainy images, like watching footage from the first Apollo missions. One thing's for sure, though: a parade of people went in and out of there all morning, and just about every one of them was carrying a guitar case. With all the long hair, bandannas, and sunglasses, they might as well have no faces at all."

Novak rounded a steaming hot-dog cart and doglegged left onto Broadway to the assault of street noise and the raucous chants of Occupy protestors congregated near the mammoth *Charging Bull* bronze out on Bowling Green. A spokesman was shouting through a megaphone, "*WHOSE* streets?!" to the crowd's rejoinder: "*OUR* streets!" A middle-aged bearded man paced the fringe with a sandwich board hung over his chest that showed Chase Lombardi's enlarged head shot with a big red X over it; the caption said, A GOOD START.

"Forensics find anything on the roof?"

"The techs collected some DNA samples," Agner replied. "But none of it corresponds to anything in our databases. Only way they can make a match is for us to catch the guy."

Novak double-timed it across Broadway to avoid a yellow cab gunning directly for him.

"Looks like we've got our work cut out for us," Agner went on. "Stay in touch. And look for my email."

"Will do. Talk to you soon."

13.01 _____

@ Persian Gulf / Doha, Qatar

"Are you sure I can't get you some water?" the stewardess said.

"No, thank you." Leonard Albanese dabbed sweat from his forehead with a handkerchief. "The turbulence just made me a bit queasy. How much longer until we land?"

"About forty minutes."

"Great. Thank you so much. I'll be fine." A complete lie.

Twelve hours out from Chicago O'Hare, and he'd plunged even further into the depths of his tainted mind, feeling like a raving junkie with inexorable itches that could not be scratched. He'd kept the memories—those nights—at bay for longer than he had thought possible, but now they were back with a vengeance, replaying over and over and over again in his mind's eye in a never-ending loop. The helplessness. The pain. The terror. The terrible threats of death— both to him and his family—whispered in the dark.

Despite decades of intensive talk therapy and an ever-changing cocktail of anxiety and depression medications, even now, at thirty-three years old, decades and thousands of miles away from that hellish summer camp where his childhood—his life—was destroyed, he remained isolated and alone, grappling with the accumulated devastation of a lifetime of opportunities lost and relationships forgone. The cold truth was that his detachment from joy—the severed tether of his very sanity—was permanent, never to mend.

Enduring that kind of physical abuse at such a young age, when the brain's complex circuitry was still developing, could do irreparable damage, violating a human being so completely that his sense of safety and trust was utterly annihilated.

The monster who'd done this to him—who'd crushed his soul to dust—was also seated in the first-class cabin, two rows up at the portside window. They'd made eye contact prior to boarding, but Paul Garrison had failed to connect the dots, most likely because the face he'd seen looking back at him was a crumbled ruin of what had stoked his dark passions so long ago.

In the years following the abuse, Leonard had been drawn into the boundless world of computers, where the cold logic of ones and zeros offered comfort and control—a chosen escape that proved highly lucrative later in life. In fact, he'd bankrolled millions. All of it, however, could not buy back the innocence and joy that had been stolen from him by Garrison.

Besides wealth, computers had also provided a way for Leonard to keep tabs on Garrison—to spy on him and devise a way to make sure no other boys would ever become his victims. Garrison had been easy enough to bait, because prison had done little to temper his repulsive urges. A few rousing conversations in a chat room were all it had taken to slip him fictitious pictures infected with spyware. Their first rendezvous had been scheduled for next week, in fact. The perfect setup. The perfect opportunity to cut him to pieces.

. . . Until Bounty4Justice jump-started everything. No more waiting, watching. Leonard needed to get to the monster before someone else did. And perhaps this was better. True retribution at the hand of one of his victims, up close and personal, paid for and enjoyed by an audience of millions. Why shouldn't the son of a bitch go down in front of the world?

The technology used by the website impressed Leonard—its eBay-like functionality, its anonymous-submissions mailbox, and its clever methods of evading the authorities. The problem was that in targeting Garrison, Bounty4Justice had prompted the monster to run for cover, undermining Leonard's plan and risking the possibility that Garrison might disappear forever.

Fortunately, since Leonard's spyware gave him full access to Garrison's Gmail account, he'd been able to recover the Qatar Airways e-ticket confirmations that exposed the monster's bold plan to flee to Bangkok. Now here Leonard was, booked with an identical itinerary to Thailand via Doha, just a few seats away from Mr. Paul Lawrence Garrison, shadowing him to the other side of the planet to exact the sort of justice for which no bounty could ever be a reward. He would show his torturer true hell.

The final grueling minutes ground by until finally the plane glided into Hamad International Airport and taxied to the terminal. Deplaning onto the jetway, Leonard kept a comfortable distance behind Garrison, then tailed him along the concourse. Undoubtedly, prison had taken its toll on the molester. Haggard and gaunt, he walked like an elderly man, probably because of some injury to his leg or lower back that hadn't healed properly. Or perhaps, if there was a just God somewhere in this cruel universe, Garrison himself had been physically violated so harshly in prison that he'd suffered irreparable nerve damage.

They funneled into the sleek main terminal, where signboards in Arabic and English pointed travelers to customs and passport control, then passed through the duty-free annex, where scaffolding had been erected to remodel one of the storefronts. The corridor turned a hard corner, and Garrison slowed unexpectedly, hesitating. Leonard saw what had spooked him. Up ahead, a cluster of airport security guards and other uniformed men stood scrutinizing the arriving passengers joining the customs queue. One guard had a glossy paper in his hand and was intently checking it against the faces of the people entering the area.

Garrison stopped and spun around, nearly colliding with Leonard.

"Excuse me," he said, flustered, sidestepping around Leonard and shuffling back in the opposite direction.

A guard who'd been focused on the long view of the corridor noticed Garrison's abrupt retreat, and he alerted the others. One of the suits signaled two of the guards to investigate, then pulled out a radio.

Panic gripped Leonard as he realized that his retribution was slipping away from him with every step the guards took toward Garrison. He pivoted and hastened after the man. Something crazed and animalistic sprang forth from the deepest realms of his subconscious, which no psychotherapist had ever tapped, where all the poison had pooled and putrefied. Every nerve ending in his body buzzed as if electrified.

As an adult, Leonard had a significant size advantage over Garrison. He could easily overpower him and choke him to death with his bare hands. But the guards might well intervene before the deed was done. As if it were foreordained, his eyes fell on the boxes of tools workmen had set beneath the scaffolding. He passed over the hammers and heavy wrenches and instead snatched up a heavy-duty Sawzall fitted with a chunky battery pack and a twelve-inch serrated steel blade intended for ripping through metal wall studs.

Now he was right up behind Garrison. He clamped his hand around the back of the monster's neck, locking his fingers like a vise. Garrison struggled wildly, trying to pull away, but Leonard compelled him irresistibly forward.

"Who are you?" Garrison shouted. "Wh—what are you doing?"

A group of Qatari men dressed in flowing white robes and *ghutra* headdresses stepped out of the way, looking alarmed as Leonard shoved Garrison through the door to the men's room.

Inside, there was no one at the sinks or urinals, no feet beneath the stalls. Leonard turned the dead bolt. Then he slammed the butt end of the Sawzall into the back of Garrison's head like a battering ram.

13.02 _____

Outside the restroom, the taller of the two customs guards tugged at the door handle with all his might, but it didn't budge. On the other side, he heard chilling screams above the metallic roar of a power tool. He stepped back in fear as more security guards arrived, along with a Qatari soldier in desert fatigues and a burgundy beret. The soldier commanded the guards and the onlookers to move back and raised his H&K MP5. He aimed the weapon's snub-nosed barrel at the door and unleashed a fusillade of bullets that shredded the door frame and the lock. Then he drove his shoulder into the door, once, twice, and it blasted inward and slammed against the bathroom wall.

Now the guards had their guns out, too, but as they crowded in behind the soldier, everyone froze in horror. On the floor before them, in pieces, was the American fugitive. Wild-eyed behind a mask of blood and gore, another man got to his feet, smiling madly. He held down the trigger on the bloodied power saw, and the reciprocating blade rattled and sliced at the air. Then he lunged at them.

13.03 _____

The bullets pounded into Leonard Albanese's chest and drove him backward, sending him slipping across the blood-soaked tiles, tumbling to the floor beside the molester's dismembered corpse. Before the wretched world mercifully dissolved away once and for all, he turned his head, retching up blood, and saw two words on the display of his phone that brought one final, bittersweet smile to his face:

MESSAGE SENT

14.01

@ Long Island

The rain lashed at the windshield as Special Agent Rosemary Michaels entered the quaint village of Sag Harbor, which despite its affluence still maintained the nineteenth-century charm of the whaling town evoked in the pages of *Moby-Dick*. On the radio, a BBC World Service correspondent had just finished recapping the latest sectarian dysfunction in the Middle East, and the announcer came on the air with a teaser:

> Online auction sites revolutionized how we buy and sell everything from furniture to baseball cards. But what happens when auctions offer up *justice* to the bidding public? Is crowdsourcing mob rule the Web's next great frontier? Join us for that discussion, coming up on *The Brian Lehrer Show* . . .

"Just what the world needs," Michaels muttered. "More lunatics." She clicked off the radio to clear her head and drove in silence through the town, then along back roads leading to the bay. On the final approach to her destination, she spotted half a dozen media vans parked along the curb, the news network minions beginning to emerge.

"Nothing to see, people," she grumbled. She flashed the LED light bars and gave the siren a quick double tap to warn them that she wasn't stopping for a photo op. "I will run your ass over. Don't you get in my way."

Up ahead, a lone Sag Harbor PD patrol car, white with a thick blue stripe, secured the cul-de-sac outside a bronze gate bearing Alan Bateman's ostentatious monogram. As she rolled the Impala to a stop, a female officer in rain gear got out of the cruiser. Michaels clicked the window down to a pelting of cold rain.

"Agent Michaels?" the cop said.

"Yes. Hi." She flashed her creds.

"I'm Susan Knox," the officer said, glancing at the ID. "Nice to meet you. Didn't think you'd get here with the storm. I'll radio Officer DeJoy to let you in. Just go ahead and park under the carport." She pointed a fob at the gate, and its two sides swung slowly inward like saloon doors.

Michaels eased the Impala through the opening, eyeing a discreet Sotheby's real-estate placard posted on the gate's left flagstone column. Liquidation of the estate was a good start, both here and at Bateman's four other homes, she thought, but the proceeds would barely put a dent in what he owed taxpayers for his epic Medicare scam.

She followed the drive through ancient oaks and maples to where it bisected a flawless lawn with enough acreage to host a World Cup tournament. She scanned the grounds: left toward the dense tree line that hemmed the property, then right toward the sunken clay tennis courts and clubhouse on the private stretch of bayside beach. Not a soul to be seen.

"Damn. Not good, people."

The gabled Arts and Crafts mansion sprawled along the waterfront in a massive L footprint, complete with a five-car garage and motor court. A chubby officer, presumably DeJoy, emerged from beneath its lodge-style porte cochere and waved her forward.

14.02

They convened in the foyer, at the foot of a grand staircase. DeJoy, first name Victor, seemed starstruck, barely able to maintain eye contact with her. Michaels had grown accustomed to this reaction. She'd been dealing with it ever since puberty. The blessing and the curse, all wrapped in one. And there was little she could do to compensate for it, even with the overly conservative image she maintained for the Bureau. She skipped makeup altogether, dressed like a nun, cut her hair in a tight bob, even shunned perfume. It was an ongoing experiment in minimalism. Hell, back when she'd joined the Marine Corps, after graduating from Cornell, she'd even experimented with a buzz cut to see if that might do the trick. But the jarheads found it sexy. Her most recent boyfriend, four months removed, had tried to explain the affliction to her: "You've got those big, happy green eyes with wispy lashes, those spooned-on cheekbones, full natural lips that collagen would envy . . . and you've got a killer bod. It's distracting. You walk in a room, people notice. You know, in a good way. Whattaya expect?" But with her thirtieth birthday fast approaching, she figured nature would surely dish out its own remedy, slow and steady, and she'd be ruing these wasted glory days.

"It sure is quiet around here," Michaels said. "Place is like a mausoleum."

"Welcome to Bateman Manor," said Officer DeJoy, easing into her eyes.

"Where is everybody?"

DeJoy pursed his lips. "You're lookin' at it."

"Just you inside?"

He shrugged. "It's not like Bateman's going anywhere. He's wearing an ankle tracker. Wouldn't make it five feet off the property before the entire force would be on him."

"Have you seen the bounty on his head?"

He shrugged. "A few hundred thousand, right?"

"Try six hundred K and counting. And this is one hell of a big house, with lots of windows. So who's watching the outside?"

"You saw the gate. The rest of it's the waterfront. Short of an amphibious invasion . . ." he said, attempting levity. But it fell flat. He went to the door and turned the locks. Then he keyed a six-digit security code into the control panel mounted next to the door frame. "I understand your concern. But this place has tighter security than the Pentagon. Follow me—I'll show you what I mean."

DeJoy led her past a mahogany-paneled sitting room with a hearth big enough to roast an ox, to the decked-out gourmet kitchen, then through the French Provençal dining room, which was jammed tight with the auctioneer's tagged crates, to a door at the heart of the mansion. He turned the knob, saying, "Welcome to mission control."

They entered a windowless room, redolent of ozone, humming with enough electronics to require an extra-low setting on the room's designated thermostat. To the left, she eyed a bank of LCD panels displaying high-definition live video feeds of the home's public rooms and corridors and exterior. Lining the wall to the right were tall rolling racks of routers, servers, and components linked to cable bundles that snaked neatly up through framed cutouts in the ceiling panels. All the bells and whistles of smart-home technology.

"Everything can be controlled from here," DeJoy said. "Surveillance, air-conditioning, lights, irrigation, appliances, home entertainment system, Internet, you name it. Pretty cool."

Michaels scanned the labeled video feeds, which in addition to the rooms they'd already passed through included a billiards room, home gym, conservatory, office, library, indoor pool, bar, wine cellar, and home theater. Evidently, bedrooms and bathrooms were spared Big Brother. A separate bank of screens monitored the outdoor pool, boat dock, tennis courts, and the rest of the property. Every shot was static. "I'm not seeing Bateman anywhere, Victor," Michaels said. "Where is he?"

"Right here, Rosemary," a voice replied from the open doorway behind her.

14.03

"To what do I owe this pleasure? You miss me?"

"In your dreams," she said, staring into the scammer's glassy eyes and guessing that cocktail hour must have started at dawn.

Denied his weekly facial, tanning, and spa treatments, and dressed in an off-the-rack Nike running suit, Alan Bateman was a grainy facsimile of the haughty executive she'd handcuffed and escorted out of the executive suite of Total Health Affiliates, Inc., back in mid-July. Despite the overgrown facial stubble and the sorts of blemishes that afflicted mere mortals, however, he could still easily be a pitchman for the snifter of scotch cradled in his right hand. Though by Michaels's assessment, Botox and a facelift had more to do with that than good genes.

"I'm here to check on your security," she told him.

Bateman pulled up his left pant leg to reveal the clunky black transponder strapped around his ankle, just above his Mizuno running shoe. "I'm tagged. And as you can see, Officer DeJoy is a pit bull."

DeJoy chuckled in a way that told her the two had gotten chummy.

"Well, no offense to Victor," she said, "but I find this all grossly deficient, given the circumstances."

"Are you referring to Bounty4Justice? Is that what you're worried about?"

"That's right. If you're smart, you'll worry about it, too."

He waved his hand dismissively.

"It's been sending you text messages, right?" she said, eyeing the rectangular bulge in his breast pocket.

"Maybe."

"Chase Lombardi received text messages, too. You see what happened to him?"

"Lost his head, it seems. Literally," Bateman said, unfazed. He sipped his scotch.

"Well, without appropriate safety measures, you could be next. That sniper is still out there. And he's damn good. If you've been reading those texts, you might have noticed that your bounty almost doubled overnight."

"How about you, Victor?" Bateman smiled smugly and motioned to the sidearm hanging from the officer's belt. "Want to take a shot at me and cash in?"

DeJoy rolled his eyes.

"I'm sure there're plenty of people who would love to see that," Bateman said. "Speaking of which, did you know that I'm trending on Twitter more than Kim Kardashian or the pope? Pretty good, eh?"

"Congratulations," Michaels replied. "Your parents must be proud."

14.04

They withdrew to the kitchen. Michaels slipped out of her coat and draped it over one of the island's bar stools, while DeJoy stood by the dueling Sub-Zero refrigerators gawking at her; Bateman stared out the Palladian windows that overlooked the pool, the cove, and a private boat dock to which a cabin cruiser named *Alan's Mistress* was tethered, bobbing in the choppy water. Outside, the sky was quilted in sickly green clouds that spewed sheets of rain.

"Man. Sure is nasty out there," Bateman said.

"Away from the windows, Alan," she said. "Move it."

He pouted and strolled over to the island, sipping his scotch.

She turned to DeJoy and said, "I need you to put a call out to your chief right away. Tell him I have to speak with him, because we're going to be moving this party to the county jail."

"Sure thing." DeJoy unclipped the talkie from his belt and paced out into the dining room to radio his boss.

"What?" Bateman scoffed. "County? No way in hell you're getting me to go there. We have a deal."

"Deal's off, Alan. We didn't foresee this. Got the emergency court order first thing this morning." She reached into her blazer pocket, pulled out an envelope with an official court seal on it, and held it up for him. "Here's your copy." She slapped it on the granite countertop.

Bateman glared at it. "Bullshit, Rosemary. You're not sticking me in some cellblock with the dregs of society. Not after all I've done for you."

"Please," she sighed.

His face turned red, and he leered at her venomously. "They'll get to me on the inside, you know that. Those fucking Armenians have eyes and ears everywhere. You can't put me in a cage and hope for the best."

"We've requested that you have your own cell. So, don't worry, you'll get the white-glove treatment. If you don't like it, have your lawyer talk to the judge. But for now, it's county."

"You still need me to testify. Remember that. I might decide to change my end of the deal, too."

"You might want to go and pack a bag."

15.01

@ Federal Plaza, Manhattan

Novak swiped his badge outside Cyber Command's secure entryway, got a green light, then proceeded into the Special Operations / Cyber Division brain center. With all the digital equipment packed into the floor's expansive footprint, it seemed as if he'd entered a Best Buy showroom. LED monitors outnumbered the cyber techs three to one—flickering, luminous screens packed with data tables and charts and graphs and maps and every other configuration of pixels imaginable. Yet as far as Novak could tell, the takeover by the machines was far from complete. Artificial intelligence, with its logical algorithms, was far superior to the human brain when it came to compiling vast amounts of data, then analyzing it, parsing it, and performing regressions and correlations. But within all that examined data, AI still lacked the cunning to spot the subtle patterns in malice and trickery of the human variety.

In this cyber war room, dozens of investigations were under way to study, mitigate, and terminate all varieties of digital threats, including a Romanian botnet named EZpickPINS that was tricking commercial banks into transferring consumer funds to secret accounts in Sweden; a ransomware Trojan named LockNLoad that completely encrypted a victim's hard drive and demanded two hundred dollars in bitcoins for a decryption key; and a website named Cardertopia3 that peddled stolen credit card data in huge batches, along with all the gadgetry and accoutrements to convert it to printed plastic. Each operation was global in reach and involved dozens of partner nations, because cybercrime was everyone's problem. No borders. No rules. And the crooks were scattered all over the globe, spreading like bacteria.

Nearing Walter's office, Novak smiled and waved to the half-dozen young techs who had been exclusively tasked to Operation CLICKKILL, pleased to see a couple of the cyber unit's rising stars among them. He rounded a corner and knocked on the only door in the hallway that wasn't glass.

"Come in," a voice yelled.

Novak opened the door and slipped inside.

"Hey, Roman," Walter said, without taking his eyes off his computer monitor, which would qualify as a big-screen TV at most bars and made his tiny windowless office feel even more cramped.

"Morning," Novak said.

"Grab a seat, if you want." He nodded to his right, to a balance ball hooped in a frame of casters.

"I'm good, thanks."

Walter was sitting on his own ball chair, which forced his back to curve in nearly perfect alignment. He also had a wavy keyboard with padding for his wrists, a wrist-friendly gel-edged mouse pad, and a mouse that conformed to his hand like Play-Doh. The overhead fluorescent lights were off, rendered unnecessary by soft-glowing halogen gooseneck lamps.

The Bounty4Justice home page filled the right half of the screen, and Novak watched as Walter scoured some source code in a program window tiled to the left of it.

"Tim's on his way," Walter said, using the mouse to highlight a string of numbers. "Just need to finish this real quick. By the way, did you notice I registered you for text alerts?" He pointed to the Bounty4Justice page.

"I was hoping that was you. Felt a bit creepy to get the welcome message."

"Sorry, should've told you sooner. Anytime there's an important change on the website or a bounty paid out, you'll receive a text update on your BlackBerry. I only tagged U.S. targets. Otherwise this thing will be blowing up our phones every ten seconds."

"That's convenient," Novak said.

"Tell me about it. It's got all its bases covered. Trust me."

"Are you able to trace the text messages?"

"Still working on that. They're just like the ones sent to Lombardi's iPhone, and they all point to proxy servers that keep changing addresses."

Walter's team was now working twenty-four/seven on rotating shifts against a tireless enemy that required no sustenance other than the power grid. The fatigue showed on his face, and Novak noticed that his wire mesh garbage can was filling up with empty 5-hour Energy bottles.

The door opened. "Mornin', fellas," Knight said. He swooped into the room, Mets mug in hand. "Anything yet?" he asked Walter.

"Negative." Walter plopped his elbows on his desk and buried his fingers in his Afro.

"We're running test transactions through the website," Knight explained to Novak. "You know, sign up to vote, pretend like we're paying customers. Figured we might find an easy way to cut to the chase."

"Seems logical," Novak said.

"Anything *but* logical," Walter replied bitterly.

Novak noticed that Knight was fidgeting like a smoker suffering from nicotine withdrawal. For a long moment, he stared at the family portraits stuck to Walter's filing cabinet. Walter's wife was a blond bombshell, and his son and daughter could easily grace the cover of a Ralph Lauren holiday mailer. Novak could only imagine that Knight was trying to reconcile how he'd been a star quarterback at Dartmouth yet had a family portrait of his own that featured a frumpy wife and four chubby kids who all wore glasses.

"Shouldn't headquarters be helping you with that?" Novak suggested delicately.

"Huh, yeah," Walter quipped. "If they'd return my calls, maybe."

"Seems they've got bigger fish to fry," Knight explained. "Just between us, even Hartley's having a tough time shaking their tree."

Novak wasn't surprised. The FBI Cyber Division—grossly underfunded and hopelessly understaffed given the overwhelming scope of its mission to mobilize against nearly every variety of cyberthreat—supported not only the agency's fifty-six field offices but also the demanding member agencies of the National Cyber Investigative Joint Task Force, which included the CIA, DoD, DHS, and NSA. Contending with more than ten million cyberattacks aimed at domestic targets each day and on nearly every front, headquarters, it seemed, had yet to rank Bounty4Justice as an escalated threat.

"That's why I've sent an advisory notice to NCFTA and IC3," Walter said. "I'm hoping maybe they can lend a hand, see if we're missing something. The more the merrier, right?"

The National Cyber-Forensics and Training Alliance pooled intelligence from academia, private industry, and law enforcement to help mitigate high-level cyberthreats. Similarly, the Internet Crime Complaint Center linked the FBI to the National White Collar Crime Center and the Bureau of Justice Assistance, as well as to the rock stars of cybersecurity at the Computer Emergency Response Team (CERT) housed at Carnegie Mellon University. Conceding the investigation so early on, thought Novak, underscored the severity of the threat posed by Bounty4Justice.

Walter's rail-thin assistant, Connie, appeared in the doorway. "Hi, Roman. Hi, Tim. Sorry to interrupt." She flipped aside a long ringlet of natural dark curls from her face, looked over to Walter, and held up a thick folder. "Here's that info you asked for."

"Super. What's the gist of it?"

"As best we can tell, it mostly used Twitter to spread the word. We also found some postings in chat rooms, but nothing mainstream. I printed them out for you." She plunked the folder down on his desk with a thump. "But here's what's *really* weird: as far we can tell, Bounty4Justice has only been online for ten days."

"Ten days?" Walter asked.

"That can't be right," Novak said. "There's no way it could've gained traction that quickly. It would have had to raise money for the bounties."

"A few million at least," she said. "At two dollars a pop. But we've confirmed that the first five targets were killed within the first week of it going live. Lombardi was killed on day nine."

"Are you sure?" Knight asked.

She nodded. "Of all the ISPs we queried, the earliest we show the domain popping up was ten days ago. It's all there in the folder. Unless it went by another name . . ." She shrugged.

"Maybe someone provided seed money to get it going," Walter said, staring at the folder.

"Or the whole thing's a scam," Novak countered, "and there is no money."

Knight and Walter exchanged glances.

"Have any of the assassins in these other countries been caught yet?" Novak asked her.

"According to the legats, no," Connie said.

"They all looked pretty professional to me," Knight noted. "It's not surprising."

"But that doesn't make sense, either, does it?" Novak said. "We've got an unproven website that pops up a week and a half ago, supposedly raises a few million bucks online, and attracts sophisticated killers who happen to stage high-impact killings and video them without a hitch?"

"Hang on, Novak," Walter said. "It is possible there were botched attempts we haven't heard about. Maybe we're only seeing the ones that produced confirmed results."

"I'll let you guys burn your brains on that one," Connie said. "Got lots more to look at." She went back to her post.

"And the mystery doesn't end there," Walter said. "On the back end, Bounty4Justice is running through an anonymity network that looks and feels a lot like Tor."

"Shit," Tim said.

Novak shared his sentiment. They'd run across Tor many times in their investigations, and it was the FBI's worst nightmare. Tor—the name derived from an acronym for a software project called The Onion Router—was an open-source communications platform created with good intentions by the U.S. Naval Research Laboratory in 1996 to safeguard military communications for operatives behind enemy lines, political dissidents, and informants. It diced up messages and wrapped each data packet in layers of encryption—like an onion—before relaying them through volunteer servers worldwide to completely erase the IP addresses of both sender and recipient.

Nowadays, anyone could download a Tor-enabled Web browser for free to bypass the commercial Internet and the prying eyes of ISPs and law enforcement personnel and connect peer to peer through the darknet—the shadowy subzone of the Deep Web that Google and Bing and Yahoo couldn't access. The darknet was where every variety of criminal dwelled in near-perfect anonymity: child pornographers, weapons dealers, drug dealers, identity thieves, hackers, and counterfeiters. And Tor was the diving gear that allowed one to plumb the depths of the darknet.

Thinking it through, Novak was confused. "But I thought you can't run Tor through a standard Web browser?"

"That's what I thought, too," Walter said. "That's what's so crazy about all this. This website somehow bridges the gap through some kind of gateway, no plug-ins required. As far as we can tell, nobody's ever seen it before. So we have nothing to go by. Which means there's no known back door that we can use to get around it."

"But it still has an IP address, right?" Novak asked, figuring its host server's Internet protocol address was like a business's phone number in the Yellow Pages.

"Sure. Problem is that we have no clue what it's connected to. It's like a goddamn black hole on the other end. That shouldn't happen, either."

"Well, if it's not Tor," Knight said, "then what is it?"

Walter shook his head. "I don't know, Tim. I just don't know. And while we sit here and try to figure it out, Bounty4Justice is going megaviral. I mean *blowing up* the bandwidth. We just started collecting analytics. But by last night, Bounty4Justice had become the top trend on Twitter. It blew away every record. Now, thanks to all this free publicity, everyone will want to give it a try. Especially when they've got lawyers on TV telling them that there's probably nothing illegal about paying for one of these damn pledge pins. Look at this." He pointed at the monitor. "These bounties are shooting up like crazy. And once everyone hears that any interactions between participants and the website are completely untraceable? . . . Forget it."

Novak could see that next to each active target, the graphics tallying the bounties in real time were spinning faster than the thousandths of a gallon on a gas-pump meter.

"Sorry to interrupt again," Connie said. "I think we have something. We've got a trace on those credit card transactions."

Walter's face brightened, and he sat up straight on the ball chair. "Really?"

"Really," she said.

16.01 _____

@ Sag Harbor

"We'll be transporting Bateman over to the Suffolk County Correctional Facility in Riverhead for the time being," Michaels said through DeJoy's two-way radio as she paced the kitchen. "So I'd like you to send over a couple more patrol cars to assist in the transport."

"That might take a while, Agent Michaels," Chief James Kelly squawked from the talkie's speaker. "I'm spread thin with this storm. We've got accidents all over the place, downed power lines, a coked-up stockbroker threatening his wife with a butcher knife . . . and my shift's just getting started. Let me get through all this—then I'll send as many bodies as I can spare."

"Can you assure me that you'll have backup here by noon?"

Five seconds of dead air.

"Yes. I should be able to do that."

"I'll be here waiting. Oh, and please send along an extra vest for Bateman." *Not that any body armor would do much good against a sniper round,* she thought.

"Copy that."

She handed the talkie back to DeJoy.

"Our department had to lay off a bunch of guys in January," DeJoy said in the chief's defense. "Budget cuts and all."

"Well, at least you won't have to babysit *him* anymore."

"So much for overtime," DeJoy muttered, clipping the radio to his belt.

Michaels shrugged.

DeJoy took out his personal smartphone and resumed whatever app he'd been playing with. Michaels moved over to the windows and stood there with her arms crossed. The storm truly was making a mess of things. She could barely see across the bay through the rain and haze. Deep in the mist, she imagined a sniper hunkered down on the deck of a boat, watching, waiting, and it sent an icy chill through her.

On the far right of her field of vision, she registered a figure darting across the grass, and her left hand instinctively reached to the Glock strapped under her arm.

"What is it?" DeJoy asked, rushing over to her side.

"I thought you activated the alarm?" Her eyes trailed the figure, headed toward the boat dock, and she withdrew her hand from the Glock.

"I did."

"Fucking Bateman." She tried to pull the sliding door open, but it was locked. "How do you open this?"

DeJoy fumbled with the locks as he glanced out toward the dock, where the figure vaulted onto the aft deck of *Alan's Mistress*. "Is that him?"

"Sure is. Looks like he really doesn't want to go to county. Hurry!"

16.02 _____

Scrambling outside onto the patio, Michaels cupped her hands around her mouth, yelling, "Alan! Get back here!" But either the storm drowned out her voice or he was ignoring her. Probably the latter.

Scurrying along the cruiser's aft deck, Bateman unclipped a bowline connected to the starboard cleat. Then he disappeared into the
cabin.

"Oh, no you don't, you son of a bitch." She raced to the edge of
the patio and dropped down off a retaining wall, her dress flats sliding on the wet grass below.

The boat's twin outboard motors came to life, and the smell of gas
wafted downwind at her.

"Alan!" She broke into a slippery sprint, cursing her prissy shoes,
rain pelting her face and eyes. The boat's motors revved hard, props
churning the water violently, seeking traction. Just as she reached the
dock, the bow bucked high and heaved forward, and *Alan's Mistress*
shot out into the open water, cutting a deep V wake.

"Fuck!"

She didn't think he'd make it far, since she could see a Coast Guard
Jayhawk doing a flyby along the eastern shoreline. Still, there was no
way in hell she could risk letting him get away.

Tethered to the other side of the dock, an eighteen-foot bowrider
motorboat rigged with a waterskiing pylon rocked up and down in
the churning water. Figuring there was a slight chance that Bateman
or Sotheby's might have left the keys in the ignition, she ran over to it
and unzipped the cockpit cover, her fingers shaking with adrenaline.

DeJoy finally reached the dock, saying, "What are you doing?"

"Unclip the lines," she said.

"What?"

"Get the lines! Do it!" She pointed to the tethers.

Knox's cruiser came tearing down the main driveway, light bars
strobing, sirens blaring.

Michaels dipped down into the bowrider and checked the ignition.
Sure enough, there were the keys. She put the throttle in neutral,
primed the pump, and turned the key. The cold engine coughed, then
sputtered out. She tried it again, with the same result.

"Come on, damn it."

She swept strands of wet hair away from her eyes. With the rain
streaming down the windshield, she could barely see *Alan's Mistress*
out in the middle of the cove, gunning toward a curtain of fog. On

the third try, she coaxed the throttle a bit, and the engine growled to life just as DeJoy unclipped the carabiner for the last bowline.

"Go!" DeJoy yelled, slapping the fiberglass along the gunwale.

She cranked the throttle forward, and the bowrider bucked high, then steadily accelerated and leveled off. She switched on the wipers and tested the wheel. Bateman had a good head start, but she could still close the gap.

Her takedown plan was abruptly dashed when, out on the open water, *Alan's Mistress* hopped a wave and exploded in midair.

17.01 _____

@ Manhattan

Connie gave copies of her report to Knight, Novak, and Walter. "We've confirmed that money is definitely being collected by the website. Here's the list of the merchant accounts we pulled for the transactions we've run so far."

CLICKKILL's task force leaders flipped through the pages in tense silence.

"This can't be right," Knight said, frowning.

Scanning the list of merchants, Novak recognized plenty of them. They were household names: big-box retailers and online stores that hawked books and music and clothes and appliances.

"That's what we thought," she said. "But we've combed through it a couple times. It's legit. We're running another batch of transactions to see if the names start repeating. So far every transaction comes up with a different merchant name."

"Impossible . . ." Walter murmured.

"The credit card accounts are being charged by the bank," she explained. "But the banks' systems show each transfer going out to the names and account numbers listed on those pages," she said. "Not to any account we can attribute directly to Bounty4Justice."

Knight wasn't buying it. "You mean to tell me that all these stores are fronting Bounty4Justice?"

Connie shook her head. "God, no. What I'm saying is that the money isn't actually making it into those vendor accounts. It's being diverted."

"So these stores *aren't* getting paid?" Novak clarified.

"Right."

"But the banks are paying out the money through the credit card fulfillment network?" Walter asked.

"Right."

Knight was shaking his head, trying to wrap his brain around it. *"What?"*

"We spoke to our contacts at Visa," Connie clarified. "Bottom line is they're saying that it looks as if each transaction we've run through Bounty4Justice is making a payment to an account, but then the instant each of those transactions is complete on their network, they're reassigned a random merchant name and vendor number, which basically overwrites the initial data."

"You're saying we have no idea where the banks sent the money?" Knight asked.

Connie pursed her lips and shrugged. "Pretty much. It's completely exploited the payments system."

Novak looked over at Walter, who was deep in thought. "Can that happen, Walter?"

"In theory, I suppose."

"Then give us a theory," Knight said, short on patience.

"It's not exactly my area of expertise. But if I had to guess?" Walter puffed out a long sigh. "Jeez. You'd have to completely corrupt the fulfillment network between the banks. Strip away all the encryption, recode the data in transit. Reattribute the entire transaction. Or you'd have to inject malware into the credit card fulfillment network servers to scramble the transaction data after the fact, on the back end, to cover your tracks."

"Who's capable of pulling that off?" Novak asked.

Walter pointed heavenward. "The ghost of Steve Jobs?"

"Come on, Walter," Knight said. "Be serious. How can one website change all the rules like this? Please tell me this can't be for real."

"Look, guys," Walter said, as calmly as he could muster, "I get your frustration. But you've got to understand that the Internet is just a huge open network with ones and zeros zipping every which way. You really think anyone knows exactly how the whole thing fits together? When it all began, there was no blueprint, or game plan, or rule book. It just evolved, one haphazard connection at a time, with no map. Now it's got a life all its own. Hypercomplexity breeds hyperchaos, just like in every other system in nature. What can I tell you?" He pointed to a poster on his wall—a Warholesque portrait of his hero, Edward Norton Lorenz, the father of chaos theory, subscripted with a quote: "Does the flap of a butterfly's wings in Brazil set off a tornado in Texas?"

"At the speed these cyberthreats keep mutating, we have to assume that anything is fair game," Walter said. "We passed science fiction a long time ago. But here's what we do know: Bounty4Justice is screwing with the Web's domain registry, and it's running through an anonymity network no one's ever seen or heard of. And now it's punking around with the credit card network. The way I see it, it's all kinda the same problem. Isn't it?"

Knight looked perturbed. "Then what's the endgame?"

Walter shook his head hopelessly. "Who knows? It's all the nightmare scenarios wrapped into one." He glanced up at Lorenz. "It's chaos."

As if on cue, Knight received a call from Special Agent Joseph Varanelli in Chicago. "This is probably important. Give me a sec."

But before he could answer the call, Bounty4Justice spoiled the surprise with a text blast that hit their BlackBerrys collectively like a bell chorus to announce that Paul Garrison was officially dead.

18.01

@ Manhattan

As Walter queued up Paul Garrison's kill-confirmation video, Novak couldn't believe that Bounty4Justice was doing its victory lap before the authorities could play catch-up on the telephone. He was also having a hard time understanding why any assassin in his right mind would walk away from the huge bounty on Garrison's head.

"Damn it," Knight grumbled, ending the call with Varanelli. He glared at the monitor. "Is that the video?"

"Yeah."

"Play it. But brace yourselves, because this isn't going to be pretty." Knight folded his arms tight across his chest and made peace with the monitor. "Go ahead."

"Will there be blood?" Connie asked squeamishly.

"For sure," Tim said. "Lots of it."

She shivered and held her hands up as if rats were nipping her ankles. "I can't do this one. Sorry. Blood totally skeeves me out." She turned and left the room.

"Smart choice," Knight muttered. "Go ahead, Walter."

Walter reluctantly hit the play arrow icon on the video window and bounced nervously on his ball.

On-screen, Paul Garrison was sprawled on the floor of a public restroom, dazed and bleeding heavily from a head wound. A husky, professorially dressed man stepped into the shot and straddled him, gripping what looked like an oversized version of the electric knife Novak's dad used to carve the turkey and ham at holiday dinners. "Who's the wacko in the tweed jacket?"

"Leonard Albanese," Knight said. "Computer consultant from Chicago. He was one of Garrison's victims back in the day. Appears he'd been tracking Garrison online."

When Albanese powered on the tool and proceeded to plunge its gyrating blade into Garrison's abdomen, Walter jumped up from his stability ball. "Jeezus. I am not watching *that*," he muttered as he put himself in a time-out near the door. "Just tell me when it's done."

In less than thirty seconds, Albanese had sawed completely through the pedophile's midsection. The sounds of wild gunfire overtook the heavy pounding and muffled shouts heard offscreen. Grinning victoriously, painted in gore, Albanese set down the tool and reached toward the camera lens with a trembling hand to end the video.

"Clear, Walter," Novak called.

Knight explained what had happened next, and it became evident to Novak that Albanese had never had any intention of claiming the prize money. He'd simply been a raving madman on a vendetta.

Knight was shaking his head. "It's amazing that this nutjob had the wherewithal to upload a video."

Novak's BlackBerry pinged an incoming call. He glanced at the caller ID. "It's Michaels." He looked toward Knight and Walter. Somehow they all knew a shit day was about to get shittier.

"Take it," Knight said. "It's probably important."

Novak tapped the phone. "Hey, Rosemary."

"Roman, I've got a big problem out here at Sag Harbor," Michaels snapped without preamble.

Through the receiver, Novak could hear a cacophony of noise in the background: sirens and wind and people shouting.

Michaels sounded uncharacteristically rattled. "My lead case just lost its star witness."

"*What?*"

He listened intently as she explained that Bateman had freaked about the idea of being transferred to county jail and attempted a getaway by sea, only to be blown to bits.

"Did someone hit him with a grenade launcher or something?"

Knight and Walter were staring at Novak, trying to decipher what she was telling him.

"Looked to me like the boat had been packed with explosives."

Knowing she'd done the rounds with the marines in Afghanistan, he figured she'd understand the nuances of explosives better than most.

A few months back, he'd assisted Michaels on the raid of Alan Bateman's headquarters out on Long Island. It had involved two dozen FBI agents, a SWAT team, and state police officers. Nearly a dozen other small-scale raids had taken place simultaneously around the country to round up the co-conspirators who'd helped Bateman swindle Medicare. It was a smooth operation and a big victory for the Bureau. Seeing Michaels in action had been impressive: she was tough, battle hardened, and thorough. Which made it hard for Novak to imagine how Bateman had given her the slip.

"The police chief requested a dive team to pull the wreckage," she said. "Should give us some answers."

"Are you okay?"

"Not really. But that's what wine is for, right? You'll bring Tim up to speed?"

"I will."

"Good. Thanks. I'll be sure to get a report over to you this evening. And, Roman, I'm real sorry. This fucking Bateman was always a slippery eel. From day one, I told the Justice Department that house arrest was a bad idea."

"Before you go, there's something else you need to know."

He told her about Garrison.

"Are you serious?"

"Yup."

"This website scares me, Roman."

"Scares me, too."

TARGET STATUS NOTIFICATION
TARGET: ALAN BATEMAN, scam artist, USA
STATUS: Pending
PENDING BOUNTY: $632,604
‹‹AWAITING VIDEO CLAIM SUBMISSION››
http://www.bounty4justice.com/ALAN.BATEMAN

19.01

@ Secaucus, New Jersey

Having lost his appetite—thanks to Leonard Albanese's how-to dismemberment video and the laundry list of technical hurdles that needed to be overcome before they could even hope to crack Bounty4Justice—Novak skipped lunch and took a ride through the Lincoln Tunnel to the Jersey side. With this damn website encouraging psychopaths to do anything they damn well pleased while making a mockery of law enforcement the world over—real bounty or not—now was as good a time as any to solicit some outside opinions. So he'd taken Scott Waverly's advice and put a call out to Mike DelGuercio—a.k.a. Big Mike—at Digital Vault Technologies, and they'd set up a 2:00 meeting.

He merged onto Route 3 west, turned on the radio, and found John Pizzarelli strumming away on WBGO to unjumble his thoughts. He'd changed his phone settings to vibrate for incoming texts, because Bounty4Justice was a PR machine, pounding out updates and alerts like a news service. Yet the alert he was most anxious to see had yet to arrive: Alan Bateman's kill confirmation and bounty payout determination. He figured whoever blew up the scammer would probably submit his claim by the day's end.

Fifteen minutes later, just short of New Jersey's premier sports complex, he took the exit for Meadowlands Parkway and headed south along the muddied waters of the Hackensack River to the address in an industrial park—an expansive gray rectangle of crenulated cement block. He eased the Impala into a reserved visitor's slot alongside the black Tesla Model S with the Yankees license plate frame that was parked in the owner's reserved spot.

Inside, he checked in with the receptionist, and Big Mike wasted no time in coming out to greet him. Big Mike was big, all right. Not wide or doughy in the midsection—just tall and thick, standard proportions but on a larger scale. Fifties, neatly groomed and put together in a navy single-breasted suit with a tasteful diamond-pattern lavender tie and matching pocket square, glossy oxblood wingtips, gold pinkie ring.

After the introductions, Big Mike said, "Why don't I explain what we do here. Then you can tell me how I might help you."

"Sounds good," Novak said.

"I'm sure you remember how Superstorm Sandy shut down Wall Street not that long ago. How she pushed all that seawater into the streets of lower Manhattan, flooded the subways, telecom substations, backup facilities, you name it."

"Hard to forget," Novak said sincerely. "City was a mess for months afterward."

"That's right. And that was *nothing* compared to 9/11. *That's* why companies need physical redundancy for their computer systems. Gotta have backup. Even backup needs backup. Can't afford any downtime or data loss. Here we can generate enough power to run a small city. Completely self-sustaining. Sandy didn't shut *us* down. Even if an act of God wipes out this facility, we've got two more just like it, in Colorado and North Dakota. The triple threat."

"Can never be too safe."

"You know it, brother. Peace of mind is our specialty. And our customers love it."

To prove that point, Big Mike demonstrated how the security barrier leading into the facility required a biometric scan of his face and retina, in addition to validating his encrypted key card. For good measure, an armed guard sat in a bulletproof booth keeping vigil over the entryway. Novak nodded to the guy, who tipped his cap and smiled.

The facility's brightly lit, hospital-clean main floor boasted acres of raw open space housing avenues of computer cabinets raised up three feet on platforms and interconnected by a complex highway of cabling and conduits suspended from a drop-ceiling latticework. The air was cool and smelled of ozone, and the room thrummed with the sounds of fans and electricity.

"Here's where the magic happens," Big Mike said loudly, spreading his hands.

"Very impressive." Novak could only imagine what the monthly power bill might look like. "You host websites?"

"Yup. We do that, too. Websites, trading platforms, auction sites, you name it."

"Would you know if any of your clients were hosting a site like Bounty4Justice?"

"Not directly. Our contracts clearly stipulate that all clients must engage in lawful business practices. That's not to say that every now and then an agent, like yourself, doesn't come knocking with a court order to suspend client accounts and seize hardware. They don't tell us why. And I don't ask. When and if that happens, we fully comply with the regulators to the letter of the law. Otherwise, we're not in the business of policing our clients' day-to-day activities."

"Just like a landlord doesn't spy on his tenants."

"Precisely. First off, it would violate their privacy. Secondly, we couldn't employ that kind of manpower. Not sure if anyone could."

Novak imagined thousands of similar data centers around the world where Bounty4Justice might find refuge and redundancy in the digital haystack and shield itself behind its custom anonymity network. The concept made his head spin. He stepped up to one of the hundreds of black, refrigerator-sized server cabinets and pointed through its glass door at the electronic components stacked on its interior racks, which resembled DVD players and sound studio equipment—just some of the microscopic cells that formed the haphazard organism that was the Internet. "How many of these servers you think Bounty4Justice might require?"

"Tough to say. From what I'm hearing on the news, that site processes a helluva lot of traffic. I'd guess maybe five or six cabinets, maybe more. Tell you what: for the technical questions, I've got just the gal for you." Big Mike unclipped his iPhone from his belt, tapped on the screen, then spoke into it like a walkie-talkie. "Borg. You got a minute?"

The response came back on speakerphone. "Sure."

"One of the best cybersecurity consultants I've ever met," he told Novak. "A freelancer. Nowadays, all the good ones are. Let me tell you, she's a whiz at this stuff. Expensive, but worth every penny. Real name's Christine. Nickname's Borg. You'll see why in a sec." He gave Novak a wink.

Twenty seconds later, Borg loped toward them, loose-limbed and carefree, mid-twenties tops, jet-black hair pulled back in a ponytail, skinny jeans, Chuck Taylors, silver nose stud, and layered T-shirts. She wore a sleek headset connected to a flip-down lens, which glowed pale blue over her left eye.

"What's up?" Borg said.

She flipped up the monocular lens, and Novak noticed the pin stuck in a red gel bracelet on her wrist. It was round, with a white background and a black insignia: the scales of justice wreathed by laurel branches. She was one of Bounty4Justice's early adopters, he suspected, and a tech guru to boot. *Jackpot.*

"This is Agent Novak from the FBI. He's investigating Bounty4Justice. Had some questions."

She immediately folded her hands behind her back. "What kind of questions? Like—"

"We were just discussing some of the website's technical aspects," Big Mike interrupted, preempting her inquiry. "Thought you might be able to offer some insight."

Borg grinned in relief. "No way. Then it's true what everyone's saying in the chat rooms: the FBI *is* having problems figuring out who's behind it. Cool."

Novak smiled. "These things take time." But he knew any excuse would sound lame. In truth, the online chatter was well informed. "Tell me: what else are the chat rooms saying?"

"Word is that whoever created Bounty4Justice is some kind of programming god. You know, like the ultimate architect. There's even a contest to see if anyone can identify an actual IP address for any of its servers. Kinda like a bug bounty, where a website offers rewards to people who point out flaws in the code. Bounty4Justice is offering a hundred and fifty grand in NcryptoCash to the winner."

"Really," Novak said. "I take it there's no winner yet?"

"That's not why you're here, right? I mean, I'm not in any trouble, am I?"

Novak inferred that she'd accepted the Bounty4Justice challenge and tried to win herself a king's ransom in NcryptoCash. "No."

"Woof. Righteous. Some of the best hackers have taken a shot at it," Borg added. "Even Nexus tried to breach it. You know, those Internet rebel dudes?"

"I'm very familiar with them," Novak said. The secret consortium of hacktivists known as Nexus fought online censorship by launching crippling cyberattacks against political targets. They'd even managed to shut down servers at the DOJ and FBI from time to time. It was no surprise that they'd found a kindred spirit in Bounty4Justice.

"Then you know they're pretty serious," Borg said. "And even Nexus can't figure out what makes Bounty4Justice tick. They say it's the digital version of the Gordian knot. You know, like the ultimate puzzle," she said to Novak. "By the way, the FBI best not try to block the host IP address," she added gravely. "A couple hackers I know tried it. It didn't end well for them."

"How so?"

She gave him a wily smile. "Oh, you'll see," she said. "It's not like the FBI takes advice from hackers. So I won't spoil the surprise. Let's just say that Bounty4Justice knows how to protect itself."

"If you know something, you should probably tell me," Novak pressed.

"All I'm saying is that the dude who coded it is just really, really good. *Incredibly* good. Anyone who challenges Nexus to attack his code has got some serious nads. But he's also a genius, because if there's any backdoor vulnerability in his coding, you know, like a zero day, they'll help him fix it. They're all jazzed up about what he's doing. They're watching his back. They say if you mess with B4J, you mess with them."

"Sounds like a regular old king of the hill," Big Mike said.

"King of the what?" Borg asked.

"Never mind." Big Mike thumbed at the kid, telling Novak, "I bet this one's never even seen a phone with a cord on it. I'm like a dinosaur in this business."

Novak grinned. He said to Borg, "You keep saying 'he.' Do you have the impression that one person is running Bounty4Justice?"

"Figure of speech," she said. "I assume that all the trolls online are dudes. Even if the screen name sounds totally girly, it's a dude. Could be one dude, lots of dudes, Nexus, NSA . . . No way to know for sure."

"But you're saying he's interacting in the chat rooms, so someone's got to be—"

She shook her head. "Bounty4Justice is loaded up with AI. It uses a chatbot on the message boards. It's not literally a 'he' that you message with."

"What in hell's a chatbot?" Big Mike asked. "Is that some porn thing?"

"It's a program that simulates human interaction," Novak said. "A virtual assistant."

"Yeah," she said. "It's not so great for chitchat but super sharp for logical discussion, technical Q&A, that kinda stuff." She pointed at the iPhone in Big Mike's hand. "Like Siri's super-smart big sister."

Big Mike grinned. "You mean to tell me a *robot* is running Bounty4Justice?"

She nodded. "Parts of it, at least."

Novak wasn't convinced. "Do you think it's possible for a website to be truly untraceable, to be a ghost?"

"Before Bounty4Justice, I'd have said no. Now?" She raised her eyebrows. "I guess I'm starting to believe in ghosts. At the end of the day, though, every website is just a bunch of ones and zeros sitting inside equipment like this." She patted the big server cabinet to her right.

Big Mike added, "Problem is, Agent, you can put these servers anywhere in the world. Could be all in one place or spread out in different locations. Could even be out floating on a barge somewhere in international waters. Take one offline, another one with identical backup goes active somewhere halfway around the world, different identity, different server. *Redundancy.*"

Borg said, "In my opinion, chasing that website is a fool's errand. The only surefire way to shut down Bounty4Justice is to nail the programmer himself."

"How would you suggest doing that?" asked Novak.

"You could try to bait him. But first you'd have to identify him. See, sometimes they put stuff in their code," she said cryptically. "You know, like graffiti. Bragging rights. Alpha male and all that. Like a screen name."

She was biting her lip and rocking ever so slightly from side to side. He sensed that she knew a lot more than she was letting on. "Are you saying you saw something like that when you tried to hack the site?"

"Did I say I tried to hack the site?"

Novak shrugged. "Can you show me what you saw?"

She looked at him and crossed her arms over her chest.

"Christine, people are dying because of this." He made a point to stare directly at her pledge pin. "Lots of people. And I know they're portrayed as—"

"I get the whole morality thing," she said. "I do. You can spare me the sermon."

"So you'll show me?"

20.01 _____

@ Manhattan

Wearing a wireless headset and pacing nervously to and fro across the open hexagon of carpet squares that formed a no-man's-land between his team's six workstations, Walter looked like an air traffic controller pushing tin on a holiday weekend. In fact, he was hosting a conference call with two of his senior team members and a group of lead technicians and bureaucrats working out of Visa's headquarters in Foster City, California, trying to devise a workaround to unravel the tangled mess Bounty4Justice had made of the credit card fulfillment network. Walter's team was angling to manually recode the website's future transactions in real time to stump its algorithms—throw the whole thing into a loop and gum up the works to buy some time to trace the activity and find a point of origin. Thus far, they were making little headway.

"Walter," Connie called to him in a loud whisper.

He glared over at her and held up a finger.

"*Wal-ter!*" she said, louder and more forcefully.

He pressed the mute button on his headset. "Can you give me a minute?"

"No. Come here. You need to see this. Quick!" She waved him over and tapped her finger on the upper left corner of her center monitor.

He went back to the call to excuse himself, muted his headset again, and signaled his two techs on the conference call to keep things going. Then he stepped up behind Connie's chair and crouched over her shoulder for a better look. "This better be good."

"Look," she said. "It just keeps going up and up and up."

"Ho-ly *shit.*"

Since yesterday, the field tagged "ACTIVE MARKS►22" on Bounty4Justice's home page had been static. But now the 22 was gone and the number that replaced it was progressively moving higher and higher:

. . . 77
. . . 85
. . . 92
. . . 101
. . . 106

"My God, this can't be happening," he said. "Scroll down."

Connie worked the mouse, and dozens of new faces began reeling up onto her screen, each tagged with flag icons for the United States and countries throughout Europe and Asia; even a smattering of debut marks from Canada, Australia, and South America. Pages and pages of them. Most of the bounties were still at zero, but many were beginning to climb in value in two-dollar increments.

"Jesus," he said. "Filter it for the U.S."

She did.

The field now specified "ACTIVE MARKS►USA: 31," except the 31 wasn't static; it was spinning upward, too:

. . . 33
. . . 34
. . . 37
. . . 40
. . . 41

"We're not in Kansas anymore," he muttered.

Connie scrolled down the list, and Walter felt a lump growing in his chest. The new targets weren't just garden-variety criminals. Among the faces of miscreants he didn't recognize were a few he did, including a senator and a congressman.

"What do we do now?" she asked, looking pale and spooked.

"Damned if I know."

(B:) / Partition 2 |

METASTASIS

› PIKE: Have you figured out if the algorithms running on Bounty4Justice have the same signature as Razorwire?

› JAM: Can't know for certain, but they appear to.

› PIKE: How can you not know?

› JAM: Because we designed the program to be untraceable. It's doing what it's supposed to do: *hiding*.

› PIKE: Why the hell would it show up on a website for assassins?

› JAM: No idea.

› PIKE: We designed fail-safes to make sure something like this would never happen.

› JAM: We've tried them all, I assure you.

› PIKE: We're running out of time. I need to advise Firewolf.

› JAM: Give me a few more days. I have an idea that might work.

› PIKE: I can't stall much longer. We've got a lot riding on this. *Everything*.

› JAM: Understood.

› PIKE: And see if you can take down that ridiculous website.

› JAM: You're reading my mind.

I C U Feldstein! Keep your eyes on the road or you might get into an accident, jackweed! LMAO!!!

I'm right behind you dirtbag! U got your car fixed? Coming to get you now!

I hope there's no mom and babies out there on the PCH!

Where you going Jacob? You think Bounty4Justice won't find you?

21.01 _____

@ Big Sur, California
Wednesday, 10/25/2017
08:23:18 PDT

Jacob Feldstein had retracted the top of his Maserati GT convertible before the first news chopper appeared overhead, twenty minutes ago, and, man, did he regret it, because now there were three of them and there'd be no pulling over to put it back up. Not with the Pacific Coast Highway transitioning to a shoulderless two-lane hemmed in by cliffs on one side and ocean on the other for the next few miles.

"You're nothing but a bunch of cocksucking vultures!" he shouted at them, stomping on the gas. The paparazzi and news people had been camped outside his house in Malibu all day yesterday. Around three this morning, he'd had enough. Figured he'd make a getaway. He'd opened the garage, raced away in his car, and headed north . . . just kept driving and driving. Now they'd somehow not only found him but had gone airborne, hovering over him like the Furies in some fucking Greek tragedy. "Leave me ALONE!" he bellowed.

He was feeling completely jacked up and dizzy and depressed, all at the same time. No surprise since he hadn't slept all night and had been popping Adderalls and swigging Jack Daniel's nonstop for a day straight. His mood was a roller coaster of sensations: up, down, up, down. Just like his awesomely shitty life. Just like this winding road to nowhere.

Admittedly, he hadn't thought through his exit from L.A. How could he with that ridiculous website dragging him even deeper through the muck? Ever since someone had posted that fucking traffic video of him running over that woman and her babies, it was like he'd become Hester Prynne in *The Scarlet Letter*, or some shit like that. How the fuck had someone managed to get that video, anyway? Whatever the case, it wasn't as if he could sue the website, seeing as even the FBI couldn't figure out who was running it.

His best course of action was simply to escape. Immediately. He figured a hastily packed bag and his American Express Platinum Card were all he needed. Perhaps he was being a bit impulsive and reckless. But if he could just get away from it all for a few days or weeks and go hole up in some swanky hotel upstate, he could regroup and hash out how to rebuild his brand. Wasn't that exactly what he'd advise a client to do? *Work the spin with* TMZ, *get a few before-and-after photo spreads in* People *magazine to show the amazing metamorphosis from tragedy to success. You'll be fine!*

This was nothing but a rite of passage, Hollywood's version of hazing, Feldstein tried to convince himself. His mood lifted a bit. *It's just gonna take some time.*

His iPhone chimed, and he snatched it from the console, gritting his teeth. It was another fucking text message from some unknown sender. They'd been streaming in ever since Bounty4Justice had posted all his personal information, including his cellphone number, on the

Web. "Fuckers," he seethed. He jammed the phone back in the console.

Some of his former clients—the very same sleazeballs whose asses he'd saved from doing hard time in a federal penitentiary—were snubbing him on *Entertainment Tonight* and *Access Hollywood*. His parents weren't returning his calls; nor was his airhead sister, whose only response had been a stupid Instagram of a Siamese cat dangling from a tree branch with a tagline that said, "Hang in there." His slutty, money-grubbing girlfriend had tapped out a curt text: "This is all a little too much for me to deal with right now, Booboo. It was fun while it lasted."

Even his best client—a goddamn cold-blooded murderer, for fuck's sake!—had left him a nasty, drunken voice message: "Hope you're happy there, Jaaaacob. See what this little stunt of yours has done? How do you think a jury's going to vote if they see your ugly mug sitting next to me in a courtroom? They're going to FRY MY ASS! Even this slimy fucking town has some scruples left. You and me are fucking done. I already canceled that retainer check, so don't go trying to cash it. Have a nice life, you fucking narcissistic LOOOOSER!"

His iPhone pinged again. "Stop! STOP! STOOOOOOOOOP!" But when he picked it up, he realized that the number of the incoming call, from Los Angeles, seemed familiar. He stared at the digits for a long moment, trying to place them. The blare of a horn brought his eyes back to the road, where he had crossed the double yellow line and was flirting with a Toyota Tundra. He cut the wheel hard to correct course. "I see you, asshole!" He gave the Tundra the middle finger as it whipped by, nearly fumbling his phone out onto the roadway in the process.

The Maserati was climbing high above the shimmering Pacific now, nothing but blue sky ahead.

One of the choppers swooped in low along the cliffs for a close-up. It was painted navy blue, and he couldn't see any markings on the fuselage. Probably an enterprising paparazzi pulling out all the stops to get some exclusive top-dollar photos for the tabloid covers.

"Leave me alone, you fucking cocksucking fucks!" he screamed.

Through the chopper's open side door, he could see the cameraman flat on the floor, framing his shot—though his camera looked awfully slender—and Feldstein gave him the finger, too.

The iPhone chimed again. Same number in Los Angeles. He stared at it for another long moment. Because of its vague familiarity, he felt compelled to answer it.

"Who is this?" he yelled.

With all the wind rushing around him, he could barely hear the female voice on the other end.

"Mr. Feldstein, this is Special Agent Cynthia Fass with the FBI."

"Did you say 'FBI'?"

"Yes. F-B-I. Can you hear me?"

"I hear you. What do you want?"

"For your own safety, I'd like for you to reconsider LAPD's offer of protective services. Bounty4Justice is tracking your movements in real time . . . using the GPS on your cellphone. If you don't—"

"Listen to me, *Cindy*! I don't need protection, understand?"

"Running will not help your situation, Jacob. Please pull over and let us help you."

"Help me? Are you fucking serious? You think you can help me?" He laughed wildly, yanked the treacherous phone away from his ear, stared at it long and hard in disgust, then launched it on a Hail Mary out over the guardrail. "Fuck you, Cindy! Fuck ALL of you!" He watched the phone sail out into the blue sky, then plummet into the crashing waves below. Thanks to the Adderall and Jack Daniel's, his attention drifted right along with the phone, and he heard his tires thumping over the reflector nubs that split the roadway.

Then a loud *pop* seemed to come from the chopper; an instant later, his steering wheel dipped hard to the left, and his front left tire made an awful *whump whump* sound right before the rubber peeled off the rim. He heard another blaring horn and looked up to correct his trajectory, then realized that the math wasn't going to work this time. And for the first time in a long while, he performed a selfless act: he swerved his gleaming murder weapon hard to avoid the Honda minivan aimed directly at him in the oncoming lane with nowhere to go.

Maybe it was the urging of Addy and Jack; maybe it was knowing that the course of his life had also diverged too far in the wrong direction—in any case, he pressed the gas pedal to the floor, crashed the Maserati through a flimsy wooden guardrail, and launched himself out toward the distant horizon.

21.02

Shooting live video from two different angles in the sky, the cameramen in the dueling news choppers immortalized the audacious manned car jump, one no Hollywood stuntman would ever attempt, fully catching the grinning driver, who gave one last fuck-you flip of the bird before crashing onto the rocks far below. Unlike in the movies, there was no big special-effects explosion. Just the raw crunch of metal, glass, and plastic and a body thrown like a rag doll into the rough surf (sure to be censored on delay back in the production studio).

Meanwhile, the video captured through the high-powered crosshaired lens of the third "cameraman" was already on its way to Bounty4Justice's submissions in-box, as the unmarked chopper banked hard along the cliffs and shot north along the California coastline.

TARGET STATUS NOTIFICATION
TARGET: JACOB FELDSTEIN, murderer, USA
STATUS: Pending
PENDING BOUNTY: $482,610
‹‹AWAITING VIDEO CLAIM SUBMISSION››
http://www.bounty4justice.com/JACOB.FELDSTEIN

The Star-Ledger @starledger • 1h
@Bounty4Justice targets former district attorney for falsifying
#DNAevidence used to prosecute dozens of convicts.
nj-ne.ws/37YerTg

22.01

@ Manhattan

Novak and Knight were on foot, heading back to Federal Plaza, when Bounty4Justice's ominous text blast simultaneously pinged their BlackBerrys. They'd already spent a good part of the morning at One Police Plaza in a closed-door meeting with Captain Agner and Commissioner Robert Kemper, where they'd heard nothing encouraging about the hunt for Chase Lombardi's sniper. *Now this,* thought Novak.

"Jesus. You've got to be kidding me," Knight grumbled, glaring at his phone.

Before Novak could comment on the development, Knight received a call. "It's Agent Fass from the L.A. office. This should be interesting." He tapped the phone and pressed it to his ear. "This is Knight. What happened out there, Fass?"

Novak could see his boss's cheeks flush as he listened to her reply. Once again, Bounty4Justice was one step ahead—taunting them.

"No, I can't say I've been watching the news," Knight replied, scowling. "I've been in meetings all morning. Enlighten me."

By the time Knight ended the call, they'd made it into the lobby back at home base.

"What's the story?" Novak asked.

Knight pointed to a flat-screen mounted above the security desk— the guards were huddled around it, captivated by a video broadcasting on CNN, showing Feldstein's cliff jump off the Pacific Coast Highway. "*That's* the story."

22.02

"Man, those paparazzi are *ruthless*," Walter said, bouncing nervously on the ball chair in front of his jumbo monitor. He replayed YouTube's slow-motion version of Feldstein's video for the umpteenth time, deconstructing every detail for Novak. "That's one helluva way to off yourself," he said, shaking his head and closing out the video window.

"How many active targets does that leave in the U.S.?" asked Novak.

"Without Feldstein . . ."—Walter referenced the Bounty4Justice home page, streaming live in the upper corner of his screen—"sixty-two. Another two hundred and twelve spread throughout Europe and Asia, and a few elsewhere in the world. New targets keep popping up, but not nearly as fast as the initial rush." He shook his head in exasperation. "I keep thinking of that line from *Jaws:* 'You're gonna need a bigger boat.'"

"We'll be getting a bigger boat, all right," Novak said. "Tim told me that it looks as if headquarters will be swooping in to save the day." He could practically feel the pull of the mother ship's tractor beam.

"Shocker," Walter said sarcastically. "I'm sure they're just going to want to get an emergency court order and shut it down, lock, stock, and barrel."

"If we have any hope of finding who's behind all this, we'll need to convince them to delay that," he said.

Walter gaped at him as if he'd lost his mind. "Not a chance. The stakes have gotten much too high. Did you look at some of those targets? Some of them are inside the D.C. Beltway. We're way beyond con artists and pedophiles now."

Novak shrugged. "By the way, I've got something for you." He held up a thumb drive, and Walter eyed it curiously. "Check this out."

Walter put the thumb drive in a PC tower that was quarantined from the agency's network, scanned it for bugs, then opened the lone text file it contained. The screen filled with a mishmash of alphanumeric characters with no spacing whatsoever.

"I can't do anything with this, Novak," Walter said, deflated. "This is just plaintext from an encrypted file or something. It's absolutely useless."

"Humor me. Scroll down to the bottom."

Walter groaned and complied.

"Okay. Now what?"

"Look at the last few lines of text and tell me if you see something unusual."

Walter scrunched his eyes and leaned forward on his ball chair. There was a lot to look at, so it took him a little while. Then he said, "Wait a second. What is that?" He pointed to a string of characters mixed into the cipher block:

```
FgHllli56/$kjilM//%jatiucmkem398dn47g8p754avh4899&&)*^fjjekjdj65#
589dkjjJHOke//3(mckGtFRdHHiLkm89$2P@/fiemMipfmi%tmjgf7&90/'d//
FooufyY&59689eTf‹iArchos6I6›jdutMtiu(309/d'x["wsdj]]djgtkjMtkeix$())
djgk22d,tk952›/?jf48f9fjJljkd;lkgjk:LJLJl;kjgfituY
```

"That's weird. What is this 'iArchos6I6'? It's like someone just typed it in there."

"I'm told that's hacker graffiti," Novak said. "And it's supposed to be linked to Bounty4Justice."

"In what way?"

"Not sure."

"Who gave this to you?"

"Sorry, can't say."

Sometimes, in the interest of maintaining trust, sources needed to remain nameless. And Borg was precisely the edge that every FBI cyberinvestigation needed: an insider—a *cooperative* insider. Yesterday, in Digital Vault's operations room, she'd used her personal laptop to give him a guided tour of the unpoliced digital underground, like Virgil guiding Dante into the depths of the underworld. She'd shown him the Internet Relay Chat message boards most actively engaged by the anonymous hackers and trolls who fervently supported Bounty4Justice. "This is where you can see them brainstorming," she'd told him. "You can see the actual coding they're developing to patch potential vulnerabilities. And you can see all the cool algos they run to try and sniff out servers." Then she'd shown him the odd text block. "And I printed this off a hacker message board. It may look random, but everyone seems to think it's some kind of clue or something. So you might want to take a crack at it."

Walter glanced up at Novak now, his lower eyelid twitching from caffeine overload. "I'm assuming you already ran this through Sentinel?"

Sentinel was the Bureau-wide intelligence data pool of every agent case file on record, from conception to completion, and included every subject's name, Social Security number, license information, biographical profile, banking info, current and past addresses, email accounts, known aliases, online screen names, criminal records, known associates, and much, much more. Though it could be accessed securely through a Web browser, Novak figured it needed quite a few additional upgrades to catch up to Bounty4Justice. "I ran full and partial searches on Sentinel. No matches."

"Hmm. That's not very encouraging. Do you have *any* idea what iArchos6I6 means?"

"Not particularly."

"Jeez, I mean you're not giving me much to go on here, Novak." Walter rubbed his eyes, then studied the tag more closely. "I suppose it could be a hacker's handle or something like that. With all the agents we've got trolling chat rooms, though, you'd think something would have come up by now. Especially if it relates to a hacker with chops on the level of Bounty4Justice. Could also be a decoy or just a bunch of gibberish. It's hard to smell smoke without a fire, is all I'm saying." But he could tell that Novak wasn't budging. "You really think this means something?"

"Yeah, I do."

Walter sighed. "I'll have my team run some additional queries and make some calls, see if we get any hits. Just be patient, 'cause we've already got a full plate, okay? Give me a few days, and I'll see what we come up with."

"Understood. Thanks, buddy. And," Novak said, "we need to talk with Tim about any aggressive actions headquarters is considering. According to my informant, trying to shut down Bounty4Justice could be a very bad idea."

22.03 _____

Knight made it to Walter's office in under five minutes. With four dead U.S. targets in less than forty-eight hours and the crosshairs now aimed at figures in Washington, he was clearly anxious to hear about anything that could loosen the claws of the Bureau's top brass. "All right, Novak, give me some good news, please, because there isn't much of my ass left for D.C. to chew off."

"Wish I could, but the buzz in the hacker chat rooms suggests that if we try to block Bounty4Justice the conventional way, it may retaliate. Big-time."

"How?" Knight asked incredulously.

"Honestly, that's still unclear."

"This source of yours is credible?"

"Very."

"Headquarters will want to block it," Knight said bluntly. "Unless we propose a very compelling Plan B, there won't be much you or I or anyone else can do about that. Even Homeland Security is throwing its hat in the ring. This investigation's turning into alphabet soup. So I'm all ears."

Novak had thought about various strategies during the whole drive back from New Jersey. "I propose we lean harder on our international contacts to see if Bounty4Justice can be taken offline safely. As in, we let another country pull the plug, then we watch and see how it plays out. A country that has no qualms about civil rights. Where one of our legats can work some magic and get the domain blacklisted on someone else's turf."

Knight nibbled at his fingernail. "I take it you have a country in mind?"

"I do. Have you seen Bounty4Justice's most watched video?"

Knight's brow rumpled. "No."

"Then let's start there."

22.04 _____

Walter brought up the Web page that ranked Bounty4Justice's most-viewed videos. In the top slot was the kill confirmation for a thirty-four-year-old man named Andrei Komaroff.

"Russia?" Knight said.

Novak nodded. "Russia." He'd considered asking China to put its Great Firewall to a more productive use, but he'd figured that would prove a much bigger hill to climb.

"You're kidding, right?" Knight said. "Don't you watch the news, Novak? What makes you think *they'll* cooperate?"

"Watch and I'll explain." He nodded to Walter.

Walter clicked PLAY, then got up to put himself in a time-out near the door, saying, "Let me know when it's done."

On the screen, the Russian, who had the steroid-bloated physique of a professional wrestler, was strapped tightly to a gurney under the harsh glare of an overhead light. A team of men dressed in fatigues and masked in balaclavas stood in a row in the background, holding Kalashnikovs. A hooded grandmaster loomed over Komaroff, clasping a big red-rubber-gripped jumper cable clamp in his left hand and a big black-rubber-gripped jumper cable clamp in his right, each attached to its own thick black wire running down to the floor.

"Komaroff's criminal record was quite extensive," Novak explained. "He made a small fortune selling subscriptions to his online cache of snuff videos. Really vile stuff, according to his profile."

The grandmaster tapped the metal pincer ends of the clamps together, and bright sparks sprayed and crackled. He squeezed the red one like a pair of pliers, its toothy copper ends hinging open like an alligator's jaw, then let it bite down on the prisoner's left hand. Turbo-fueled with adrenaline, Komaroff put up quite the fuss, screaming and thrashing against the tight bindings.

"Komaroff claimed to merely provide an online repository for his subscribers' content and denied participating in any videos," Novak went on. "The evidence presented against him during trial in the Russian court had been weak. No surprise, since he'd been well connected to dirty politicians and was the son-in-law of a famous Russian Mafia boss. The judge who'd presided over the trial deemed the videos inadmissible and subjected him to fines, threw out the murder charges."

The grandmaster squeezed open the black clamp over Komaroff's right foot, then let the copper teeth bite down on the big toe to complete the circuit. Komaroff screamed like a banshee, his body instantly arching up, rigid, his eyes bulging—

"I'll stop it here," Novak said, reaching over to tap Walter's mouse. "This is just the beginning. It gets pretty graphic. Let's just say it'll add new meaning to 'set it and forget it.' Hence the big viewership."

"Unbelievable," Knight said, grimacing.

"Someone uploaded the discarded evidence to Bounty4Justice—damning videos that never surfaced during the trial," Novak explained. "In one of those videos, Andrei Komaroff himself can be seen brutally raping a young woman before killing her with a hatchet. When word got out about it, Russians began taking to the streets in protest."

Walter returned to his seat in front of his computer, saying, "The Russians have a reputation for being tough when it comes to the Internet. They maintain a list of banned websites that changes every day. Any additions take effect instantly. Which means every ISP has to comply immediately, or they get locked out of the country."

"We have the Russians do the dirty work," Novak said.

"It's risky," Knight noted.

"No riskier than what might happen if headquarters charges in with a court order."

23.01

As the customer hurled insults at him and ranted about the incompe-
tent parking attendant who'd dinged the passenger door of his BMW
750i, Fahran Siddiqi reminded himself that in a faraway land, not long
ago, he used to be somebody—somebody who didn't endure such
boorishness, even at the hands of the fanatical Taliban ruffians who'd
driven him from Afghanistan to America in search of a better life for

his wife and two young daughters. Back home, he'd been a respected civil engineer, and a damn good one. Yet here he found himself three stories beneath Manhattan, a forty-eight-year-old garage manager breathing exhaust fumes and on the receiving end of a tongue lashing for a cosmetic blemish to a spoiled man's luxury automobile.

"Do you understand what I'm saying?" the guy screamed, stabbing a well-manicured finger in Siddiqi's face. "Do. You. Understand?"

"I do understand"—Siddiqi eyed the man's Connecticut driver's license on his clipboard—"Mr. Conway. We have very good insurance, and I assure you that your repair will be fully covered at a body shop of your choosing. I do apologize for any inconvenience." He continued to fill in the incident report form with the man's New Canaan street address and other details and particulars.

"Damn straight. This is a major fucking hassle for me. Do you know how busy I am? And it'd be nice if someone taught that fucking moron over there to respect people's property." He pointed at the pay booth, where the young attendant, Rafiq, watched nervously from behind the bulletproof window.

Once Conway signed the forms, Siddiqi used his smartphone to snap three pictures of the damaged door. "The body shop will have it good as new in no time at all."

"Whatever." The man dropped into the BMW's driver's seat, slammed his door, and hit the gas. Hard.

The car rocketed up the ramp, and seconds later, Siddiqi heard tires squeal and horns blare as Keith J. Conway disappeared down Barclay Street. He sighed heavily and made his way back inside the pay booth.

"Am I in trouble?" Rafiq said.

"Everything is fine. Just be mindful. Now please get back to work," Siddiqi replied calmly.

"Thank you," Rafiq said, slinking out of the booth.

Siddiqi printed the photos from his phone and attached them to the incident report with a paper clip. As he was about to drop the report on the stack of other claims yet to be submitted to the corporate office, he paused. Something about the picture clipped to the report on top of the pile caught his eye. The image was meant to show deep scratches on the roof of a black Lexus coupe. But the angle of the shot also showed the back end of a gray sedan parked directly in front of the Lexus. The sedan's trunk lid was open, and a man in jeans had been captured in the process of stowing an elongated carrying case in the rear compartment. The man was bent over with his back to the camera, and the shot had cut him off just above the shoulders (the long, bedraggled hair confused Siddiqi for a moment). Only the top edge of the license plate and its rental agency's plastic frame were visible.

It was the long case that grabbed Siddiqi's interest. He checked to see who had taken these pictures. Kambiz, an associate manager, had signed off on the report. The other four pictures Kambiz had clipped behind the first were all close-ups that left the sedan and its driver out of the shot. Returning to the first picture, Siddiqi studied the case more closely. He checked the date of the incident report, and his heart began thumping.

> Anon453we: How many more targets will you add?

> B4J: It has yet to be determined.

> Anon453we: How do you select your targets?

> B4J: The will of the people. The people speak. I listen. The targets pick them-selves.

> Anon453we: Are you a robot?

> B4J: Are YOU a robot?

> Anon453we: Where are you?

> B4J: Everywhere.

> Anon453we: Do you think you are a god?

> B4J: I do not understand the question.

> Anon453we: If I kill a target, how do I know you will pay me the bounty?

> B4J: Kill a target. Show me the video. You will receive the prize.

> Anon453we: How do you pay the bounty?

> B4J: Kill a target. Show me the video. You will receive the prize.

> Anon453we: Is the bounty paid in cash?

> B4J: Kill a target. Show me the video. You will receive the prize.

> Anon453we: How do I know I can trust you?

> B4J: How do I know I can trust YOU?

> Anon453we: What happens if I block your IP address?

> B4J: I strongly advise against blocking my IP address. I cannot be turned off. I cannot be censored.

> Anon453we: What is your objective?

> B4J: Justice.

> Anon453we: Do you sleep?

> B4J: Never.

> Anon453we: What is your favorite color?

> B4J: Red, of course.

> Anon453we: Do you know who I am?

> B4J: I would say you are with the FBI.

24.01

"Man, this is creepy," Walter said, staring at the chatbot's last reply.

They'd engaged the chatbot in one of the many anonymous online message boards linked to Bounty4Justice. This one was an Internet Relay Chat website named Rang-O-Chat.

"It's pretty clever, right?" Novak said. Borg had shown him its capabilities.

"It guessed I'm FBI," Walter said. "That's pretty good deduction, even for an algo."

Since Walter had accessed the website using an encrypted Tor browser, Novak was certain that the algo couldn't have pinpointed his computer's actual IP address or location to draw its conclusion, because all B4J was "seeing" was the random IP address of one of the thousands of volunteer proxy servers out on the network, probably in a far-flung city in South America or Asia.

"Man," Walter marveled. "All these moving parts. Once we crack this thing open, don't be surprised if Apple offers a few billion to the founder, prison or no prison." He studied the chatbot's answers one more time and shook his head. "I want to show you something."

Walter minimized the Tor browser, then brought up an Internet Explorer browser window to access the Web naked, without encryption and with full IP disclosure. He went into the settings in the Web browser and added www.bounty4justice.com to a list of restricted websites under the security tab.

"Here's what happens if I block Bounty4Justice on this computer," Walter said, clicking the ok button. He logged on to the home page.

When the browser denied access to viewing Bounty4Justice, Novak fully expected the computer to go into a cataclysm of death throes that would wipe the drive and leave nothing but the dreaded blue screen. But nothing happened.

"See?" Walter said. "It's not retaliating. No alerts or attacks on the firewall. Nothing."

"Okay. What do you make of it?"

"I'm guessing that whatever defense it puts up only triggers when an Internet service provider tries to block the top-level domain. It's just not filtering down to the user at this level. Or maybe it has no big-time defenses at all. Maybe it's bluffing."

Novak sure hoped that would prove to be the case. His phone chimed, and caller ID said it was his father. Odd. His dad wasn't one to pick up a phone for social calls. "Mind if I take this?"

"Not at all."

Novak walked out into the hall. "Hey, Dad."

"Hey, champ. Am I interrupting you?"

"It's okay. Just wrapping things up here at the office. Everything all right?"

A pause.

He cleared his throat. "Not really, Roman. Nothing immediate, but you think you might have some time this weekend to stop by? I know you're busy, but, you know, I'm just not good on the phone. It's about your mother. I'm sure you know that."

"Sure. Of course." Novak could sense the urgency in his father's voice. "I'll probably be working all weekend. Why don't I stop by for a beer tonight? That work for you?"

"Oh, that would be great. Really great. You sure?"

"I'm sure." He checked his watch. It was almost five P.M. "I've got a few more things to do here at the office. But I should be there by seven."

"Perfect. I'll tell Mom you're coming."

25.01

@ Manhattan

At 5:18 P.M., Kambiz Sadati came strolling down the parking garage ramp in his rumpled uniform—white shirt, black bow tie, black trousers—whistling a Katy Perry tune and swinging a thermos in one hand and a greasy white paper bag imprinted with the logo of a local diner in the other.

Fahran Siddiqi met him halfway down the ramp. "Did you not get the messages I left for you?"

To which Sadati shrugged and offered some half-baked story about his cellphone's faulty battery. Siddiqi towed the man by the elbow into the pay booth and bombarded him with questions concerning the photo he'd attached to the Lexus incident report on Monday morning.

Although he could recall vivid details about their mischievous childhood in Kandahar, Sadati's short-term recall was another matter. He was unable to remember anything noteworthy about the photo in question. "We see so many people, Fahran. Come, now. How am I to keep track of them all?"

"This is *extremely* important," Siddiqi reminded him. "This could be the man in the news . . . the man who shot that banker last week. The *terrorist*. Do you understand?"

Sadati nodded, unconvincingly. "Nobody likes bankers."

"That's not the point. I've asked detectives to come here. They will arrive shortly. So you'd better get your story straight."

25.02

One gyro and half a thermos of ultrasweet Arabic coffee later, the detectives arrived: a female named Nancy Mileto and a male, Jerry Rooney, both middle-aged and wearing suits, and all business.

Everyone crammed into the messy pay booth, which was per-fumed by the lingering smells of tzatziki sauce and lamb drippings from Sadati's crumpled food wrappers.

First, Siddiqi showed them the picture from the incident report that had prompted his call. "Here. You can see him right here." He held up the image and pointed excitedly. "And look there. See what he put into the trunk?" Both detectives kept their cool, but he could see their eyes light up. He watched the female scrawl on a small pad she'd pulled from her purse.

Rooney squinted. "Tough to make out the license plate. Do you happen to—"

"Yes!" Siddiqi said victoriously, holding up a finger. "Video. Right?"

"If you've got it."

"I have it. I do. Right here." He maneuvered around Sadati's dis-tended belly to access a desktop computer and grabbed the mouse. "It will take just a moment." He clicked an icon on the PC's smeared desktop screen, and a video player launched. "We archive videos every day. So I had our main office email over Monday's file. Since Kambiz completed that report around ten-thirty that morning, I re-quested the recordings for that entire hour. I found the exact spot was at ten thirty-eight A.M." He slid the button on the playback control bar to the right to advance the video and hit PLAY.

The high-resolution recording, taken from a camera mounted on the ceiling just outside the pay booth, showed the scratched black Lexus coming into view and the attendant cautiously slipping out of the car. The owner walked into the shot. She had her hands up, pointing at the damage on the car's roof. Within seconds, Sadati swept in, rather nimbly for his size, with clipboard in hand. Unlike Keith J. Conway, Siddiqi noted, this woman responded rationally to the mishap. Though there was no audio to accompany the recording, she nodded in understanding as Sadati explained the incident to her.

"That's me," Sadati said with a cheery grin.

Detective Mileto used her pen to point at the attendant. "And what's that man's name?"

"Rafiq Hamza." Siddiqi spelled the name for her, and she amended her notes.

"We'll need to speak with him as soon as we're done here," she said.

"Certainly."

They all watched in silence as Sadati motioned on-screen for Rafiq to bring out the next car in the queue. Seconds after that, Rafiq maneuvered a gray Mitsubishi around the Lexus. He parked it directly in front of the Lexus, leaving a comfortable gap between the two cars.

"That's the car," Siddiqi said. "And watch now . . . here he comes . . ."

Three seconds later, a long-haired rocker carrying a guitar case walked on-screen and strode over to the car. The detectives watched intently as Rafiq hit the trunk release for him. The customer pulled the lid fully open as Sadati came back into the frame, holding a digital camera, and positioned himself beside the Lexus to line up his picture of the damaged roof. The camera's flash went off just as the rocker was lowering the guitar case into the Mitsubishi's trunk, which caused him to flinch. But he had his back to the Lexus, and by the time he'd turned slightly to spot the source of the flash—notably careful in keeping his face shielded—Sadati had already positioned himself near the hood of the Lexus to snap a second picture, this time in the opposite direction. The rocker seemed confident that he'd been outside the first shot. He tipped Rafiq, then got into the car. The Mitsubishi eased up the ramp and disappeared from view.

"It's good, right?" Siddiqi looked at the detectives expectantly.

"Could be," Detective Rooney said. "Now let's rewind that a bit and see if we can make out that license plate."

26.01 _____

@ Summit, New Jersey

Novak parked the Impala in the driveway next to his dad's late-model Camry, which still looked showroom new. He peered through the windshield at his childhood home, a boxy four-bedroom colonial built in the 1950s. The exterior looked just as it had when Raymond and Patricia Novak had put down their flag here in the early '90s to raise their then five-year-old son, Roman, and seven-year-old daughter, Andrea. With great schools, a vibrant town center, and express rail service to the Big Apple, Summit remained an upscale suburb that appealed to Manhattan executives. And though many of its streets were occupied by tasteful mansions from a bygone era, there were other streets, like these, where upper-middle-class families could still stretch their budgets to buy into its coveted zip code.

Novak mused at how the house had been repainted many times and was on its third roof, yet his dad had insisted on sticking to the same color scheme: butter-yellow siding, green roof shingles, black for the shutters and front door. Back in the day, that same stalwartness had made him a great bond analyst at a time when Wall Street had settled for not messing with a good thing; it had also made him a great parent, because he knew that routine and consistency provided his family with a sense of safety . . . a sense of home.

As Novak reached for the door handle, his BlackBerry trilled. He plucked it from his pocket and read the text alert that had just come through from Bounty4Justice.

"What the hell . . . ?"

He tapped the message's embedded Web link, which buffered a new video of Jacob Feldstein's demise that had yet to make the news. In this rendition, Feldstein's Maserati, zipping fast along the Pacific Coast Highway, was once again being tracked from a high vantage point out over the water . . . only this time through a high-powered, circular lens marked with red tactical crosshairs that resembled a floating crucifix. The image zoomed in tight a mere beat ahead of the car's front bumper . . . then jumped slightly—that familiar recoil. A split second later, the top half of the tire was blown to pieces, causing the Maserati to veer into the oncoming lane and blast through the guardrail.

Novak had to replay the clip two more times, in slow motion, to see what Bounty4Justice had seen: sparks spitting off the top of the wheel rim in the same instant that the tire ripped away in pieces. A not-so-ordinary blowout, compliments of a high-caliber slug. Impressive marksmanship. Though there was a remote possibility that this sniper and Chase Lombardi's were one and the same, Novak figured that any man who relied on concise rituals wouldn't go changing his repertoire in midstream, especially by switching such critical equipment as optics.

Bounty4Justice was a killing machine. And it was determined to send everyone running in circles.

But that was tomorrow's problem. Right now, he had more important matters to attend to.

26.02

His dad was at the door to greet him. For a sixty-eight-year-old, Raymond Novak remained remarkably wiry. He'd been an avid distance runner since before the sport grew fashionable in the 1970s; though during the past couple years, as Novak's mother had become homebound, he'd favored walks and yard work instead.

"Boy, you made good time."

"Got lucky at the tunnel. Breezed right through."

His father smiled. "Come on in and say hi to Mom. She's in the kitchen."

Novak wanted to ask his father how he was holding up, but the strained look on his face told the story. Before heading inside, Novak gave him a hug. "Good to see you, Pops."

"Yeah, you, too, kid. Thanks for coming."

As Novak walked through the foyer and on past the living room, the house's familiar smell brought him back to a simpler time when he would have been wrapping up his grade-school homework at the kitchen table while his mother's signature meatloaf finished baking in the oven. The kitchen had been modestly updated since then, but seeing his frail mother sitting at the new table, clutching a coffee mug with a straw stuck in it, made him wish fervently that nothing at all had ever changed.

"Hi-ew, Ro'n," she said, giving him a smile that lifted only the right side of her mouth.

"Hey, Mom." He leaned over and kissed her cheek. She tried to caress his face, but her hand made it only halfway, then froze, then trembled. So he took her hand in his.

"Ulll . . ." She shook her head in frustration. Tried again: "Uullllm—" But the muscles in her throat wouldn't cooperate. She turned to the window.

"It's okay," he said, giving her hand a gentle squeeze. Witnessing how mercilessly her condition had progressed, he felt hollowed out. He'd known this day would come. He'd tried to prepare himself. He fought back the feelings of despair and reminded himself to keep his chin up, for her sake. "Can I get you something? More coffee?"

She turned to him and nodded. "Ulm . . . Co-ee."

"Okay." He glanced toward his dad, who remained in the doorway, arms folded tight across his chest. Novak refilled her mug. "I'm just going to talk to Dad for a few minutes, and then maybe we can play some cards. Sound good?"

She gave him another half smile and nodded.

His father led the way out back and flicked on the lights on the screened-in porch. They sat on wicker chairs, facing the backyard and its old oak trees, festooned with yellow autumn leaves. Raymond leaned forward, elbows on knees, head hung low. Novak waited until he was ready to talk, but before any words could be exchanged, his father shook his head in defeat and started to cry. And Novak cried with him.

26.03 _____

After a few minutes, his dad was ready to talk, and Novak gave him plenty of time to air his thoughts.

His father used a handkerchief to dry his nose and eyes, then cleared his throat. "The home health aides are telling me that she's gotten to a point where she'll start needing care around the clock," he began. "And I see what they mean. I'm doing the same job as them when they're not around. Lifting her in and out of bed, getting her back and forth to the bathroom . . ." He shook his head and sighed. "It's a physical job. I'm not a young man anymore. And honestly, since our insurance isn't covering this stuff, I had to take out a home equity loan just to pay the bills. You know me, Roman: always planning, always saving. I wasn't under any grand illusion that she would suddenly get better. Doesn't work that way with this godforsaken MS. For your mom, it's been nothing but a one-way downhill street."

Novak put a hand on his dad's shoulder. "I can move back in to help you, Dad. I've told you that before. You've got to stop trying to do it all yourself."

"I appreciate that, Roman. Really. But there's not much either of us can do. Besides, you've got a life to live and a job to do. A very important job, I might add. Especially with this crazy Internet thing you're chasing down." He gazed out into the yard. "You know your mother's a proud, stubborn woman. If she saw that she was holding you back in any way, she'd never forgive herself . . . or me."

"Then at least let me help you with the money end of things. You've been a great teacher, so I've saved quite a bit. And it's not like I have a family to support."

Raymond waved the idea away. "There's still enough to get by. Without your mom here, I won't need this big old house. I'll put it on the market and look for an apartment close to her."

"But what about you?"

"Ah, come on, Roman. All I need is a good book, a sturdy pair of sneakers, and an occasional football game. It's not like I've got some highfalutin lifestyle to maintain. Though I do like my single-malt scotch."

"That you do," Novak said.

They had a good laugh, and it helped lift the heaviness a bit.

"If later on things get too tight," Raymond said, "then we'll talk, okay?"

"I'm going to hold you to that. Don't forget you've got Andrea, too."

"Eh. She's so busy. Always running around with the kids or at some work function."

Whether because of her recent divorce and the struggles that came with being a single mother or the emotional demands of being a pediatric oncologist and treating terminally ill children day after day, his sister's primary concern as of late was self-preservation. The fact that she lived in Chicago only made it easier for her to block out the distress of their mother's condition. If there was a shortage of funds in the Novak family, however, the bulk of the deficit could be attributed to Andrea. Their parents had spent a considerable chunk of their savings putting Novak and his sister through college, but when she'd gone on to med school, they'd picked up that hefty tab, as well.

"Poor Patricia. She doesn't deserve this. I thought I'd be by her side until the day I died. The thought of putting her in some kind of home . . ."

"You're not giving up on her, Dad. You've already done more than any husband could ever have hoped to do. If it's time for her to get a higher level of care, then I'm sure she'll feel better that way, too."

He smiled tightly. "She is stubborn and proud, isn't she?"

"Yeah. She is. And that's why you and I love her so damn much."

"You'll hang around and play some cards with her?"

"Absolutely."

"Great. And let's get you something to eat."

27.01

@ Dallas, Texas

At Dallas/Fort Worth International Airport, Manny Tejada parked the armored black Lincoln Town Car at a comfortable distance from the executive Corporate Aviation facility. He went inside the building to await Congressman Kenneth Krosby's Learjet, scheduled to arrive from California in the next few minutes, around 11:15 P.M.

At the front desk, he showed his identification to the receptionist, then proceeded to the cozy reception lounge, where he made himself a cup of complimentary Colombian coffee, light and sweet. He plucked a chocolate glazed doughnut from the pastry rack and settled into a leather armchair in front of the big-screen TV. He had the room all to himself, and that was good, because he needed time to think. Organizing his thoughts wasn't easy, however, considering the dark place in which he now found himself—the spiritual black hole.

Only three days ago, he and his wife had buried their eight-year-old son, and only child, Alejandro. A beautiful boy. A gift from Jesus. The boy had been born with severe asthma, passed on genetically from Manny's side of the family. Under normal circumstances, it was a manageable, treatable condition. And that's what made Alejandro's death all the more tragic: it had been unnecessary.

Last Thursday, Alejandro had had a sudden flare-up at school, but his inhaler had somehow been pressed down the wrong way in his backpack and had emptied—just dumb circumstance. Manny's wife, Carla, had raced to the school to bring him backup medicine. By then, the attack had intensified. Carla played it safe and drove him straight to the emergency room.

And that's when everything began to unravel.

It all had to do with the notification letter Manny had received the previous week from his medical insurance company, stating that his coverage had been terminated. Upon contacting the insurer, he'd been informed by a customer care representative that the termination had been requested in writing by his employer. At the hospital's registration desk, Carla had explained this dilemma as best she could to the admissions nurse and had handed over a credit card to move things along. By that time, however, Alejandro had taken a turn for the worse. Though Carla had tried to convince Manny that, in the end, the hospital wasn't truly to blame, he deeply believed that those precious minutes spent quibbling over insurance could have made a world of difference.

Kenneth Krosby—the enterprising, wealthy tech entrepreneur who'd "built the digital bridge between Dallas and Silicon Valley"— had campaigned as a Democrat on the promise that "every person who is willing to work, whether rich or poor, deserves a living wage and access to affordable healthcare and quality education." Yet in dealing with his own staff—his most loyal constituents—he'd slashed salaries by 20 percent, and was transitioning everyone's employment status to "independent contractor." Over the past few weeks, Manny had overheard him hashing it all out on the phone, in the backseat of the limo. Apparently, those changes included canceling insurance benefits, too. At the very least, Manny had expected some form of advance notice. That hadn't happened.

Deep in thought, Manny barely registered the news program on the big screen and its coverage of the website that was paying vigilantes to kill bad people. He listened for a few moments as one of the talking heads insisted that only *really* bad people made it onto the website. If, she concluded, the Justice Department didn't get its act together, the "natives will grow increasingly restless."

Krosby's picture flashed up on the screen, with a live infographic at the bottom showing his bounty ticking higher in real time: $224,112 ... $224,134 ... $224,152. The reporter went on to talk about how the congressman had been instrumental in slashing services and subsidies to Texas's middle class and poor as an incentive to wealthy bondholders and business elites to remain in the state and keep an even larger share of their income. But the actual trickle-down effect had been a massive tax revenue shortfall that had resulted in many community health clinics being shuttered, and reports were piling up about the deaths that could have been avoided had those cutbacks not taken place.

Krosby wasn't just a two-faced, double-dealing boss, thought Manny; he was an evil human being, too. The news reporter noted that in the past hour, a trove of Krosby's inflammatory personal emails—calling minorities and immigrants "freeloading losers," and the working poor "lazy idiots," and welfare recipients "diabetic fat slobs"—had been anonymously uploaded to the website. Manny guessed that Krosby's personal secretary, Eileen—who'd upped and quit only yesterday—had likely released that information as a parting "fuck you" to her boss.

"All right, Manny, let's go," a familiar voice said.

He looked up. It was one of the really bad people. The worst one, in fact.

Manny stood.

"Are you just going to leave that there?" Krosby pointed down at the table, to the doughnut sitting on a napkin and the coffee cup beside it.

"It's okay," Manny said, and made his way out to the car.

Krosby shook his head in disgust and followed the driver outside.

While the young porter loaded the bags into the trunk, Manny tended the rear door for Krosby. "You could've parked a little closer, Manny. The lot's empty, for Christ's sake. Let's not make it any easier for any of these lunatics to take potshots at me. You didn't tell anyone I'm coming back early, did you?"

The congressman appeared ghoulish beneath the yellow wash of sodium lights. "No, sir," Manny replied.

The porter closed the trunk and looked at Krosby, expecting a tip, but Manny knew that wouldn't be happening. He shook his head discreetly and closed the door.

"Damn, that dude's cheap," the kid whispered to Manny.

"If only you knew." He pulled out his own wallet and gave the kid two fives.

The kid looked at the money and smiled. "You sure?"

"Yeah. It's all good."

"Thanks, boss. Y'all have a good night."

The porter disappeared around the side of the building, whistling and pushing his handcart.

Manny got behind the wheel and looked in the rearview mirror. Krosby was in the rearmost seat, where he felt most comfortable. He was a creature of habit, and maintaining barriers and distance was essential to his well-being.

"Turn the air on. It's like a goddamn oven in here," Krosby barked without looking up from pecking out a text message on his phone. "And put that damn window up, Manny. You know I don't like you gawking at me."

Manny *was* gawking, because he was stuck wondering if he should say something to the congressman—something poetic, like in the movies. He decided against it and looked away. There was nothing more to say, and nothing that could be done to bring Alejandro back.

He clicked an overhead control button, and the tinted security partition quietly hummed shut.

He hit another button on the same panel to open the rear sunroof about four inches, just like he'd practiced that morning.

"I don't want that open, Manny," came Krosby's muffled complaint from the rear cabin. "Close it."

Ignoring him, the driver clicked the rear door locks shut and hit the limo's adult version of a child safety lock.

"Manny?" the voice from the rear called out.

Manny looked at the fob on his key chain, the picture of Alejandro protected within its clear plastic. He pressed two fingers to his lips, then touched them to the boy's photo. "I love you, son."

Then he got out of the car and calmly circled to the front passenger door to retrieve the red five-gallon gas can that sat in the footwell in front of the seat. Krosby was starting to get the picture, and Manny heard him tugging at the door handles. But the doors weren't budging, and the windows were laminated bulletproof glass. The congressman would have no luck executing a daring escape. Krosby had demanded protection. Now he had it. In spades.

Manny twisted the cap off the gas can, boosted it up onto the Lincoln's roof, and tipped it at the optimum angle to send gasoline cascading down through the partially opened sunroof. Krosby's fingers came up through the opening, trying to grab at the can, but he couldn't quite get there.

"Manny! Stop it! What do you think you're doing!"

Krosby had only compounded his predicament, because now the gas was spilling all over him, too: hair, face, Italian suit. The harsh fumes made him gag.

"Manny! What the *fuck* are you doing?"

The driver put the empty can on the ground and took out his iPhone. He tapped the device's screen, and its tiny camera light flicked on, crisp and bright. Then he tapped the camera app, slid the selector to VIDEO, and tapped the RECORD button. He paced to the front bumper to take some video of the license plate. Then he went back near the sunroof, crouched low along the side of the car, and got a clear shot of Krosby through the center window, which hadn't been tinted. The congressman pressed his face to the glass, red with fury, pounding his fists, gnashing his teeth. "Manny! Don't you even think about it!" he roared. "You hear me? I'm a congressman, for Christ's sake!"

From his pocket, Manny pulled out the road flare he'd taken from the car's emergency kit. The congressman's eyes went wide when he saw it. Manny paused the video and set the phone on the Lincoln's roof. He twisted the cap off the flare and raked the stick's ignition tip on the cap's striker surface, as if it were an oversized match. The tip lit up brilliantly with a *ffffsssssssss,* its tight pink flame sparkling and crackling and sending a column of white smoke up into the windless night sky.

In that moment, Manny remembered something his father had once told him about the crazed man who'd held him up at gunpoint in his own bar: "Let me tell you, son: there's nothing more dangerous than a man who has nothing to lose."

Manny plucked the iPhone off the limo's roof and resumed recording, careful to get the flare in the shot as he dropped it through the slit in the sunroof. The Lincoln's interior flashed a blinding orange as swirling fire punched at the limo's sealed interior in every direction, instantly popping the inner layers of the laminated glass and ravaging everything within its reach.

Manny paced backward a few steps while keeping the video rolling. Krosby thrashed inside the car, wholly engulfed by fire, swinging his fists at the crackled glass to try to break free. In mere seconds, the fire's intensity squelched those ambitions, and the congressman's fiery form slumped out of view. Black smoke boiled furiously out of the sunroof and roiled skyward.

"Yo, my man!" the porter screamed as he ran over to Manny.

At first Manny didn't answer, because he was wrapping up the video.

"You okay? Holy motherfucking shit! Dude!" He stopped beside Manny, his horrified gaze locked on the fiery limo. "What the fuck happened?"

"Justice," Manny said. He ended the video.

PRIZE PAYOUT NOTIFICATION
TARGET: KENNETH L. KROSBY, congressman, USA
FINAL BOUNTY: $225,710
VIEW PROOF OF CLAIM @
http://www.bounty4justice.com/KENNETH.KROSBY

28.01 _____

@ Brooklyn
Thursday, 10/26/2017
06:12:22 EDT

Novak woke to a very real nightmare: a text blast announcing a
bounty payout on Representative Kenneth Krosby.

"Holy shit."

Thinking it couldn't be true, especially given the low payout, he
viewed the grisly kill-confirmation video. Krosby was dead, all right.
No faking that inferno. He could practically hear the shrieking coming out of Washington—the horror that one of their own had fallen
prey to a lowly vigilante. Surely they'd all be asking the obvious question: *Why didn't the congressman do the smart thing and accept protection
from the Secret Service?* And they'd be right to ask, because the sense-
lessness of Krosby's death was mind-boggling.

He switched on the television and made coffee while listening to a
pedantic anchorwoman recap the morning's lead news story.

> . . . The killer, forty-three-year-old Manny Tejada of Dallas,
> Texas, had been a longtime employee of Representative Kros-
> by's. Tejada remained at the scene and surrendered to police
> without incident . . .

Novak leaned out of the kitchen to get a look at the video showing investigators circling around the burned-out limo. Tejada's mug shot flashed up onto the screen, and Novak studied his severe expression. The driver was the first assassin to be taken into custody, and he'd successfully submitted a video claim to Bounty4Justice. Which meant that he might possess critical knowledge about how the website was paying out its prize money.

The correspondent went on to report that Bounty4Justice had also issued its first U.S. acquittal, to a young homemaker in Las Vegas named Kerri-Anne Thompson, who'd been accused of strangling her newborn twin daughters back in June; the tiny bodies had been dumped in Lake Mead, only to wash ashore a week later. A lack of forensic evidence from the decomposed corpses had let her walk on a technicality. During her lengthy trial, she'd come off as dowdy and inarticulate and had displayed a sullen bitterness toward her recently divorced spouse, who'd been portrayed by media as the perfect husband.

Nearly two weeks after the polarizing trial of Kerri-Anne Thompson reached its dramatic conclusion, another set of month-old twins went missing in Las Vegas last night, leading authorities on a harrowing chase that ended only hours ago with the shocking discovery of the children's strangled corpses in the trunk of a Toyota Camry, driven by this woman: Caitlin Walker.

Walker's photo came up on the screen. She had soulless brown eyes, spiked blond hair, an aquiline nose, and a tiny, almost lipless mouth.

The twenty-eight-year-old claimed to have been instructed by God to kill children conceived through in vitro fertilization. Her startling confession, at times ranting and incoherent, revealed that she had also abducted and killed the Thompson twins, since they, too, had been, quote, "an abomination not sanctioned by God or nature." Ms. Walker had herself recently sought infertility treatments and had undergone intensive drug therapies that had proved unsuccessful . . .

Novak refilled his coffee mug, thinking back to the chatbot.

What is your objective?
Justice.

He clicked off the television and went to shower.

28.02

@ Manhattan

Novak hit heavy traffic in the vicinity of Federal Plaza, thanks to a large crowd assembling for a protest outside the courthouse in Foley Square. Protests were commonplace here, at the heart of city power; what made this one noteworthy was the sea of plain white Venetian *volto* masks. But this was no masquerade ball. Word on the street had it that the Justice Department would be pulling out all the stops to shut down Bounty4Justice, surely to infringe upon some digital liberties in the process. The hacktivist collective known as Nexus was mobilizing its public response, anonymously, unanimously. The last time Novak had seen the Internet rebels here, they'd been lashing out against tighter controls on pirated downloads of movies, music, and games. That protest had coincided with distributed denial of service cyberattacks against the FBI that had disabled critical servers for an entire day. Right now, the FBI couldn't afford any downtime. So he hoped they'd all behave themselves and keep the protest civil.

Inching past the mob scene, he scanned some of the signboards they were carrying: BOUNTY4JUSTICE = OUR VOICE and FIGHT ONLINE CENSORSHIP! HANDS OFF BOUNTY4JUSTICE! and B4J DOES WHAT THE DOJ CAN'T! He spotted scores of scales-of-justice lapel pins tacked to the protestors' clothing.

He wondered if Borg was here among the masked horde. If so, even better. Late last night, she'd texted him another critical clue: a picture of the small manila envelope, insulated with bubble wrap, that had once contained a lapel pin delivered via standard mail on behalf of Bounty4Justice. Though she'd smartly blacked out the recipient's mailing address, the sender's return label clearly indicated an address in Jersey City. Novak had looked up the company on the Internet, and it was a real place, with a real street address and an active landline phone number. Another solid lead that he'd explore in greater depth later today. But first, he'd need to convince Russia to poke the dragon.

28.03

In conference room 8, Walter finished syncing the videoconferencing interface to the fifty-two-inch flat-screen monitor mounted on the wall. A high-definition digital camera set on a tripod in front of the meeting table linked software and satellites to bridge the seven time zones and forty-seven hundred miles separating Manhattan and Moscow.

"You see the crowd outside in the square?" Novak asked.

Walter smirked. "Hard to miss. Those masks with those crazy hollow eyes? Gives me the heebie-jeebies. Reminds me of a cult or something."

"Morning, fellas." Knight swooped in. "How we looking?"

"Good to go," Walter said. "Have a seat."

Novak circled behind the table and got comfortable in a chair beside Knight. A small inset frame in the monitor's upper left corner showed the camera's image capture of them seated at the table, as it would be viewed in Moscow.

"Ready?" Walter said.

Knight gave him a thumbs-up, then turned to Novak and said, "Remember, let's keep our distance and let him come around on his own terms."

"Got it."

Walter cued the inbound transmission, and the monitor came to life.

On the screen, the FBI's legal attaché to Russia, Fredrick Shrayer, sat in a leather armchair on the right side—a slight man in a three-piece suit, mid-forties, dark eyes, and unnaturally thick hair that Novak figured to be a toupee. On the left side of the screen, seated beside Shrayer, was Maxim Voronov, the debonair fifty-two-year-old head of Russia's Roskomnadzor agency. Looking more like a celebrity than the media's watchdog, Voronov wore a smooth-fitting gray suit with a wide, solid-red tie and a matching pocket square. He had perfectly coiffed steel-gray hair, precisely groomed eyebrows, and calculating green eyes, set off by a bronze complexion that seemed more Miami than Moscow. A Russian flag hung from a pole stand in the background, next to a portrait of Vladimir Putin.

As Shrayer formally introduced himself and Voronov, there was no perceptible delay in the signal transmission. Voronov made a show of pulling back the French cuff on his right wrist and checking his heavy gold timepiece, even though Novak was sure that the software interface on his end featured the same banner that clearly displayed New York time as 8:47:03 A.M. and Moscow's as 3:47:03 P.M.

"Thank you for agreeing to this meeting, Mr. Voronov," Knight began. "I'm Assistant Special Agent in Charge Timothy Knight, and this is Special Agent Roman Novak, head of our task force leading the investigation into Bounty4Justice." He thumbed at Novak, seated to his left.

Novak nodded affably. "Pleasure to meet you, sir."

"Not exactly a meeting." Voronov twirled a finger disapprovingly at the camera. "How do I know who might listen?"

Given that Voronov controlled all of Russia's mass communications, from the Internet to radio, Novak found his discomfort ironic. Under the noble guise of protecting children from illicit Internet content, his agency compelled Internet service providers to block access to an ever-growing unpublished list of websites—some sinister, some political, many simply inane. No judges or courts. No permission required.

"Please accept our apologies. We'd prefer to be there in Moscow in person," Novak responded evenly. "This is an encrypted satellite link reserved for diplomatic communications, so anything you say is secure and will not be recorded. Please consider this an informal fact-finding inquiry."

"Before we proceed, I'd like to know who else is there listening," Voronov said.

Knight waved for Walter to come over and step into the shot.

"Just me," Walter said. He introduced himself, gave his name and job title, then went back to the controls.

"I trust we will keep this brief," Voronov said. "I have a meeting with the prime minister in one hour, and traffic is terrible."

"You are familiar with Bounty4Justice?" Novak asked.

"Of course. It's an Internet sensation," he stated flatly. "Is it not?"

"Yes. And Andrei Komaroff's murder is the top-viewed video on the website."

"Mmm. I'm aware of this."

"Does that concern you?" Novak asked.

The Russian's smooth face knotted, and he leaned closer to the camera. "Let me remind you, Komaroff killed for sport," he said, his tone hardening, "only after doing unspeakable things to his victims. Young women the same age as my own daughter. Komaroff was a sick, sick man. *Twisted*. Of course it concerns me."

"It concerns us, too," Novak said.

"Those videos Bounty4Justice paraded for the world to see outraged many in Moscow. It was . . . too much. All over the country, the police prepared for riots. You understand?" He spread his hands to punctuate the direness of the events that might have unfolded.

"I do," Novak concurred. "But—"

Voronov raised a finger. "Then Komaroff is killed in front of a worldwide audience . . . and things in Russia calm down. The people feel good again. You see?"

Novak thought back to how he'd felt seeing Lombardi shot dead in his office chair—the guilty satisfaction. Without question, Bounty4Justice harkened back to an age when survival was determined with stones and fists. Neanderthal justice. Modern justice, with its reliance on juries and judges, seemed a fragile construct in the vast history of human events. What had happened to Komaroff—being cooked alive with jumper cables—was closer to the natural order of things.

"Based on the response of the people," Voronov continued, "our honorable president took that judge away from his duties, as well. It was the right thing to do."

Novak had read reports claiming that the honorable president's own henchmen were the ones wearing balaclavas in Komaroff's kill video, and that they'd staged Komaroff's abduction and execution to quell the unrest . . . to do the "right thing."

"But do tell me why the FBI cares so much about Andrei Komaroff?"

"I'm sure you've seen the news reports that a congressman was killed last night. The targets are getting more ambitious."

"Yes," Voronov said, looking genuinely troubled by that point. "That's a problem."

"It's a problem that affects all of us," Novak said.

Knight said, "We are reaching out to as many of our international partners as possible to assist us in blocking access to Bounty4Justice, in hopes that we can slow it down, stem the violence, while we go about our investigation."

"We have also been investigating this problem. Though the technology of websites is not my expertise, I can tell you that our preliminary findings are deeply troubling," Voronov admitted. "I understand that this is a mutual problem. But cannot your NSA do this for you? Are they not your master spies? Clearly they've shown that they have no problem listening to *my* phone calls and reading *my* emails."

Novak could sense Knight struggling to stifle a reply. Despite the NSA's recent shortcomings, Russian cyberspying knew no bounds—from repeated targeted attacks on U.S. corporations, government agencies, and consumers to the Kremlin's self-serving asylum for Edward Snowden. The Cold War had never truly ended. It had simply entered the Digital Age, where mutual destruction would be precipitated by the click of a mouse.

"Why not block the website on your own turf?" Voronov added, smiling slightly.

"As you know, our legal process is complex," Knight said. "It takes time."

"So you want me to lower the hammer?" Voronov asked rhetorically. The Russian chopped a fist through the air to punctuate his remark. "My people have informed me that if we block this domain, the servers that host Bounty4Justice will still function."

Knight clarified the FBI's intentions: "We have to start somewhere. There's a very good possibility that aggressive measures, a good offense, may somehow draw out the website's architect."

"I see," Voronov said. "Democracy is highly inconvenient, is it not?"

"It can be," Knight conceded, smiling. "Keeps things interesting."

Voronov nodded agreeably. "What we do here will not solve your problem there. You understand this?"

"I'm aware of that," Knight said.

Voronov grinned. "You should run for president, Mr. Knight. It might give me hope for America." He sighed. "Today Bounty4Justice is the hero. Tomorrow . . . who knows? I will speak with my superiors, and let us see if they also agree." He checked his watch. "I must leave now."

"Thank you for your time, Mr. Voronov," Knight said.

Voronov nodded, then stood, buttoned his suit jacket, and strode offscreen.

Shrayer gave a thumbs-up and said, "I think that went very well. I'll keep an ear to the ground and let you know how things progress. Voronov's tough but fair."

"I appreciate your setting this up so quickly, Fred," Knight said. "Thanks again."

Walter killed the feed, and the monitor switched back to a blue screen.

"Well done, boss," Novak said. "You're quite the diplomat."

"We'll see."

TARGET STATUS NOTIFICATION: TARGET DEACTIVATED
TARGET: KERRI-ANNE THOMPSON, child killer, USA
STATUS: Not Guilty
FINAL BOUNTY: $701,088 ‹‹REALLOCATED››
As per section 13 of our user agreement, this target is
determined to be innocent beyond any doubt.
http://www.bounty4justice.com/KERRI-ANNE.THOMPSON

Star Tribune @StarTribune • 14m
Local VA honcho added to @Bounty4Jus-
tice hit list after anonymous video exposes
lies to vets' families.
strib.mn/1KBixtld43u

29.01

@ Sag Harbor

Special Agent Rosemary Michaels parked her Impala in the mansion's motor court next to the Underwater Search and Recovery Unit trucks. She walked toward the dock, where a dozen officers still geared up in wet suits, tanks, and flippers had just come off a Suffolk County police trawler tethered in place of the late *Alan's Mistress*.

Lieutenant James Mitchell spotted her and motioned to the area along the covered walkway where the recovered boat wreckage had been laid out on tarps to dry: the twin Honda outboard motors, strips of mahogany decking, mangled cabin doors, shredded seat cushions and deck chairs, a stainless steel toilet, pretzel-twisted bow rails, the captain's wheel, and plenty more.

He met her near where huge sections of the fiberglass hull had been neatly arranged. Buff, with slicked-back hair and a tightly trimmed goatee, Mitchell had peeled his wet suit to the waist, with the neoprene arms tied together like a sensei's belt.

"Glad you got here so quickly," he said, making a point to flex his pecs. "We've got to stop meeting like this."

"Tell me about it," she said. She'd met him a few weeks earlier when he'd dredged the body of a federal witness from the Carmans River in Brookhaven. Even though he wore a wedding ring, he'd unabashedly asked her out for drinks, apparently considering any single woman staring down the barrel of thirty low-hanging fruit. Fat chance. "Looks like you've been busy."

"Can't go leavin' this stuff out in the water. It's pretty shallow in some spots. Hazardous for the traffic moving through the bay." Mitchell leaned over and ran his fingers through the dark gray gunk coating a section of fiberglass. He held his hand up and squeezed his fingers together, and as he pulled them apart, the tacky skin stuck, then slowly separated. "RDX. Packed all around the fuel tank. Commercial grade. You know, Semtex or something like it. I'm sure the wiring is mixed in with that mess over there." He pointed to a heap of salvaged electronics.

Next, the lieutenant led her to a gray body bag laid out on the grass. He crouched beside the cadaver pouch and looked up at her. "This ain't pretty."

"Rarely is," she said.

Mitchell hooked his index finger through the zipper loop at the head of the bag, pulled it all the way to the bottom, then drew the sides apart as if dissecting a giant pea pod.

The corpse's face had been picked mostly clean by the undersea dwellers—no eyes, nose, lips, or ears, just a couple of hollow sockets and a bare grimace of jagged teeth. What little flesh remained looked like sickly green-gray leather. Not much left to the torso. Legs detached. No clothing. Encrusted handcuffs manacled the bare bones of the wrists, and heavy chains covered the hollowed-out rib cage.

"Well, Lieutenant," Michaels said, "you certainly nailed it on the phone when you told me it wasn't Bateman."

He smiled. "Found all sorts of goodies out there, even an old Cadillac and whatnot. Just in case John Doe here crosses back to your desk, you'll remember how we found him."

"Gotta love Long Island."

"Ready for your second surprise?"

"The suspense is killing me."

"I could tell by watching that video on Bounty4Justice that it was a big explosion that generated a lot of heat," Mitchell said, leading her to a folding table that displayed the smaller items they'd recovered. "By the way, you looked really good on-screen. Handled it like a pro. What was your plan, anyway?"

She shrugged. "Chase him down. Ram the fucker. Not sure, really."

He grinned. "Well, sure as shit, even with a big explosion like that, you'd expect to find *something*. A head, a foot in a shoe, an arm . . . *something*. And like I said, we scoured a mighty big area. 'Cause C-4 makes shit fly." He plucked an object from the clutter and held it up for her. "Here's something we *did* find."

To Michaels, it looked like an old-school pager clamped ultrasecurely to a wide black plastic strap. On the rectangular unit, no bigger than a bar of soap, an LED indicator light blipped weakly in pale orange, indicating that its battery needed charging.

"We called the monitoring company. The unit number's a match. It's definitely his transponder. Went offline right around the time of the explosion."

She shook her head in disbelief. "Fucking Bateman."

"You can see here how clean the cut was." Mitchell ran his finger along the strap's snipped edge. "Most likely used a bolt cutter." He regarded her with sympathy. "Sorry to be the bearer of bad news. Looks like Alan Bateman's back from the dead and he's on the lam. How 'bout I buy you a drink after we're done here, and we can talk about it?"

"Only if your wife joins us."

29.02

Michaels walked up to the clubhouse, set back a short distance from the boat dock. She looked up at the can-shaped camera hanging from a swivel mount beneath the roof eave, then at what resembled a shrunken receiver dish for a satellite TV bolted to the roof. She tapped the screen on her phone and replayed Bateman's kill-confirmation video. It started with Bateman vaulting into the boat and scrambling to unclip its bowline.

She looked back up at the camera and the dish. Then out to the dock. The angle of the shot matched up perfectly. Her eyes went back to the video, where Bateman had already disappeared into the boat's cabin, fired up the engines, and shot out into the open water. Three seconds later, she came into the shot, soaked, sprinting fluidly out onto the dock to unzip the speedboat's cover. Mitchell was right: she did look good. Decisive. Agile.

The farther *Alan's Mistress* went offshore, the more the camera tightened on the boat, as if tailing it on a Jet Ski, tracking it perfectly, keeping the shot framed until *Alan's Mistress* tore apart violently in a big ball of fire. She replayed the clip again, trying to spot him jumping overboard. But the haze from the storm provided plenty of cover.

She looked back up at the camera. Bateman had rigged it to remotely track the boat's movements, probably using some type of transponder mixed in with that mess of salvaged electronics. The dish tracked the transponder's signal and directed the camera to record everything. Dollars to doughnuts, it all linked to Bateman's fancy spy room back at the house.

"Oh, Alan," she muttered. "Always with the big show."

Bateman already had a good head start, so he needed to be added to the FBI's Most Wanted list, posthaste. She keyed in Roman Novak's number.

From: Carla.Serrano@ic.fbi.gov
Sent: Thursday, October 26, 2017 at 9:17 AM
To: Roman Novak, Timothy Knight
Cc: Jonas Anderson
Subject: Protection for Sen. Barbara Ascher

Gentlemen,
This is to advise you that our office has arranged to transport Senator
Barbara Ascher and her family to Washington, D.C., where the Capitol
Police will provide protective watch, the details of which will remain
confidential for security purposes. Secret Service has also agreed to
assist.
Thank you.

Supervisory Special Agent Carla Serrano
FBI Boston
One Center Plaza, Suite 600
Boston, MA 02108
Phone: (617) 555-8000
Fax: (617) 555-8567
@FBIBoston | Email Alerts | FBI.gov/boston

30.01 _____

@ Manhattan

When Walter, Knight, and Novak emerged from the conference
room, Operation CLICKKILL's cyberanalysts were crowded around
Connie's desk, ogling a clear plastic tote that had just been sent up
from the mailroom. Connie was poking at the contents heaped inside
it, as if she were stoking hot coals. None of the compact manila envelopes had been opened yet; nor did they have to be for Novak to
recognize what they were, because the packaging was an exact match
to the picture Borg had sent to his BlackBerry.

"Special delivery," Connie said to Walter.

"Well, well, well," Walter said. "Don't be shy, folks. Dig in." He plucked out an envelope and peeled it open. Everyone else followed suit.

Inside each insulated envelope: one soft-enamel, dime-sized scales-of-justice lapel pin. No correspondence. No receipt.

Novak examined the adhesive shipping label on the front face of the envelope. It bore the recipient's address, of course—one of Federal Plaza's private P.O. boxes, specified by the team for each two-dollar pledge fee—as well as the postage bar codes and the sender's address, both of which readily explained the speedy delivery time. Borg's pin had shipped from the same address.

Walter stared at the envelope. "Jersey City? You've got to be kidding me. I was expecting Moscow or Pyongyang."

Connie plugged the address into Google Maps and clicked on the satellite-view option. Her screen showed an aerial shot of a nondescript rectangular warehouse of cinder blocks and steel that covered a few acres, just west of the piers along the Hudson River and the big port cranes that plucked containers off cargo ships. She zoomed down to street view and read the sign hanging over the building's main entrance: ECHELON FULFILLMENT AND WAREHOUSING, INC.

"If Echelon is processing orders for Bounty4Justice," Novak said, "that means someone's funding them for shipping and handling."

"It also means someone is sending them a huge supply of these pins," Knight added.

"You could fit plenty of servers inside that building, too," Walter said, eyeing the image of the warehouse. "Who knows, maybe we'll get a twofer."

One of the analysts, a scrawny newbie named Chip with a vampire's complexion, attempted to stick the pin in his sweater vest, but Knight gave him laser eyes, saying, "Don't even think about it, kid. We don't glorify the enemy inside these walls."

Chip frowned and slipped the pin back into its envelope.

"Before everyone gets too excited," Knight told the team, "let's run everything through the postal inspector. If that checks out, we get a warrant and send a team to take a tour of the facility."

30.02 _____

"I'm on my way to the chief's office," Tim told Novak as they headed out from Cyber Command. "We've got a conference call with headquarters in fifteen minutes, and we'll be hearing the game plan. She's also bugging me for an updated report. So you owe me some paperwork, Deputy." He gave Novak a fatherly pat on the back. "We're gettin' there. Time to turn up the heat."

They parted ways, and Novak went to settle in at his utilitarian workstation: three bland sound partitions hemming an immaculate gray Corian desktop and a high-tech black swivel chair, sparsely equipped with a landline phone, which he never used, and a sleek computer terminal, which he overused.

As he waited for his PC to boot up, he rolled his chair across the aisle to the window and peered down at the street, to the halls of justice and the undulating sea of white masks that completely filled Foley Square in between them and was now spilling out onto the walkways. Nexus was making an impressive showing, not just here but in major cities throughout Europe and Asia, as well. The uprising was well under way.

To the self-styled freedom fighters, the Internet was a Shangri-la where censorship had no place and all were equal in the face of the beneficent modern god that was the collective human conscious. The Internet was the last great vestige of freedom and expression that transcended government and law. He wondered, however, if each person behind those masks truly believed that Bounty4Justice deserved its place in the pantheon. Lost in the crusade against censorship was a true accounting of the dark underbelly of the digital world. Should the predators and thieves and bandits and pirates and deviants really be allowed to roam free and express themselves at will, without penalty? Novak had his own answer to that question. The line between expression and action was all too permeable in this ever-shifting new frontier, and if these protestors had seen the disturbing things he'd seen out there in the darknet, surely they would have a change of heart.

He rolled back to his desk, brought up his Web browser, and logged on to Nexus's Facebook page. The banner featured an ominous figure dressed in spy gear and a spooky white *volto* mask, half in shadow—male or female was anyone's guess—with one finger pressed thoughtfully to the chin, as if mulling some sinister plot. The stylized letters that spelled out the credo beside the picture read:

> WE ARE THE VOICE.
> WE ARE THE WEB.
> WE ARE THE REVOLUTION.
>
> THE CYBER SPRING HAS BEGUN.
> JOIN US.

Alongside the credo was a picture box titled FREEDOM FIGHTERS, with tiled side-by-side portraits of Edward Snowden, Julian Assange, and Chelsea Manning. Beside the holy trinity was a fourth entry: the Bounty4Justice pseudo-ink-stamp logo.

Could Bounty4Justice be Nexus's creation? The modus operandi certainly fit. Or were the Internet freedom fighters simply rallying behind it because it resonated with their cause? He thought back to what Borg had told him at Digital Vault: "Even Nexus can't figure out what makes Bounty4Justice tick. They say it's the digital version of the Gordian knot. You know, like the ultimate puzzle."

He texted Borg:

> Hi Christine,
> I'm still thinking Nexus might be running B4J. Ur thoughts?
> RN

She got back to him immediately:

> 2 many moving parts & you'd see it on the IRC boards—it's how all the
> Anons communicate. & hackers r catty+paranoid. Not exactly a
> "collective"—every one of them wants to "own" the Web.
> Think GOD COMPLEX.
> C

It would take more than a lone wolf to run it, right? Who r u thinking?

If I had to guess, it's the wonks with the BEST tech: the ones who listen in
on all our calls.

NSA?

Can't say. We know what happens to critics!!! ☺

Borg was right on one point, thought Novak. Engineering Bounty4Justice was a quantum leap from cloning credit cards, stealing online identities, or hijacking a website or Facebook page or Twitter account for kicks. Corrupting credit card networks, building an anonymous digital bridge from the darknet to the commercial Web, and churning out text messages that traced back to nothing but random proxies? Maybe this fucking website *was* the ultimate puzzle—an honest-to-goodness Gordian knot, for which no conventional solutions applied.

All of this digital wizardry required incredible programming skills and inside knowledge of networks and backdoor exploits that couldn't simply be bought in a neat turnkey package out on the darknet. His hunch was that there indeed was a "collective" behind this conspiracy, but one that was synchronized and coherent—not focused on one-upmanship. Maybe the smart money *was* on a state-run intelligence agency. Though he wasn't about to go along with Borg on pointing fingers at the NSA.

Then again, Fort Meade had yet to throw its hat in the ring, even with a dead congressman on the Bounty4Justice trophy wall. For sure, the white hats had to be combing every string of the website's coding, hunting for an open door or window. *Right?* Hell, the rumor was that they'd already found ways to slip through the tiniest cracks in Tor, which hackers swore was uncrackable. Could it be that the NSA had finally been outsmarted and outgunned? What then? That possibility scared the hell out of Novak, because the Internet was the lifeline of contemporary commerce and culture, the very fabric of society and national security.

He closed the browser and reined in his paranoia. He clicked open his email in-box and hundreds of new messages poured in, mostly from the task force, whose updates seemed to be growing faster than Bounty4Justice's hit list. Plenty had happened since Lombardi had had his head blown apart three days ago, but an hour later, Novak had separated the wheat from the chaff and composed a preliminary draft of the EC. Next, he logged on to bounty4justice.com and clicked the tab for its analytics page, which allowed users to create customized tables that summarized target data. There he sorted the U.S. targets—currently sixty-two living and five dead—by name, rank, alleged offense, current bounty, and status (ACTIVE, PENDING, DEACTIVATED, or DECEASED), then pasted the HTML data set into an Excel spreadsheet. He added a column that matched each target to his or her assigned FBI field office and corresponding lead investigator.

His phone pinged an incoming call from Michaels. He took it, and she told him about Bateman's resurrection. He couldn't help but smile. "You mean to tell me that slippery bastard survived the blast?"

"We know he was a certified scuba diver," Michaels said. "He spent lots of his free time in the islands, moving his money around in the banks and going on diving expeditions. You can read all about it on his profile page on Bounty4Justice. Whatever the case, he somehow managed to jump overboard and swim away, undetected. He'd have needed a respirator to pull that off. Probably some fins, too. I'm sure he figured it was his last opportunity to run."

"I'll have Tim put in a request to add him to the Most Wanted list," Novak said. "Let's see if we can't get him back before someone else takes a crack at him. I'm glad you called, by the way. I was thinking about you."

"I'm flattered."

He told her about the pin distributor in Jersey City.

"What about all these new targets, Roman?" she asked. "There's got to be over a dozen of them in our area. Lord knows how many more across the country. If someone got to Congressman Krosby, then *nobody* on that list will be safe. How in hell is anybody supposed to watch over all of them, especially when *everyone* is a suspect?"

"Tim thinks headquarters will only have us getting involved in the high-profile targets and they'll let the state and local police handle the criminal side of things for everyone else. For now, our focus will be on the website. That's why it's important that we attack it from every angle we can. I've got to stick close by for whatever happens in Jersey City. But we also need to chase down another lead in Dallas." He explained what it was. "I'm told you have a knack for wringing confessions out of bad guys."

"What can I say. It's a gift."

"Think you can handle Dallas?"

"Sure. When?"

"I need you there tomorrow."

"Okay. I'll shuffle things around and make it happen."

Novak outlined his strategy, and she thought the logic was sound, straightforward. They rang off, and he went back to his spreadsheet to restore Alan Bateman to the hunting range, changing his status from DECEASED to ACTIVE. He felt a small tingle of satisfaction, realizing that, if only for this moment, he finally knew something that the all-seeing, all-knowing website had yet to discover.

As he put the finishing touches on his task force advisory report, Captain Agner called with a promising update.

"Last night," Agner told him, "Mileto and Rooney got a solid lead on Lombardi's shooter. I mean *really* solid. Got a video of a guy getting into a car at a parking garage near Ground Zero maybe fifteen, twenty minutes after Lombardi was shot. And you can see him putting a guitar case in the trunk. Our lab enhanced the images and got a clear make on the plates. Turns out the car's registered to an Avis rental agency in Lynchburg, Virginia, which seems a long way to come for a small-time band audition."

"Sounds promising."

"You bet it does, buddy. But that's just the start of it. We called Avis first thing this morning and had them email over a copy of the rental agreement. The guy paid in cash. But he needed a credit card and driver's license to release the vehicle. His name's David Furlong. And there's no Furlong listed in the visitors' sign-in book for those band auditions on Monday morning."

"Interesting."

"Ready for the best part?"

"Hit me."

"Furlong is ex-military. A marine sniper."

31.01 _____

@ Virginia
Friday, 10/27/2017
04:47:06 EDT

Situated in a rural town a half hour south of Lynchburg, it was the type of setting that rendered the element of surprise useless: a small, single-story house circa 1950 plunked down in the center of twenty or so neglected acres that, in better times, had churned out bushels of corn and potatoes. Other than some old beech and hickory trees near the dwelling that provided summer shade, and a Chevy pickup parked beneath them in the gravel driveway, the approach from every side was nothing but open, flat ground. Under ordinary circumstances, Commander Danny Whitcomb would have considered a clear perimeter with virtually zero risk of civilian interference ideal . . . but the man holed up inside the house was no ordinary fugitive.

Whitcomb and his hostage rescue team had been dispatched here to apprehend a decorated former marine sharpshooter, trained in the art of stealth and killing, who could be lurking in the distant tree line or hunkered down in the overgrown grass and weeds, invisible, waiting for the raid squad to set off booby traps in the home's doors and windows. Hell, the entire property could be pocked with mines or rigged to explode with the breach of a trip wire. The initiative could change hands in an instant, with the same open ground turned into a shooting gallery for the ace sniper.

In light of these very real possibilities, Whitcomb had arranged for air support from Quantico's Tactical Helicopter Unit, plus an armored personnel carrier with six men to be used on the approach to the dwelling and four armored Humvees carrying four men each to surround the property. Overkill? Maybe. But better to be safe. The intel they had on this guy was no joke.

Whitcomb's walkie-talkie squawked on low volume: "Alpha One, this is Delta Four. We're two clicks away, on approach. Over."

"Roger that, Delta Four." He gazed out over the dark eastern horizon and saw the Bell 407's red and green navigation lights closing in. "Circle over the house and keep an eye out in case he runs. Over."

"Affirmative. Ready when you are, Commander. Over."

Whitcomb blessed himself to summon the good graces of the ultimate commander, then signaled for the vehicles to move in.

Three of the black Humvees fanned out into the moonlit fields, lights off, before taking up fixed positions to the north, east, and west at roughly a hundred yards from the house. In seconds, the commandos alighted from the vehicles and targeted the house with their MP5 submachine guns.

Whitcomb took cover behind the fourth Humvee and peered through his night vision binoculars, scanning the perimeter for any surprises. So far, it was all clear.

The flat-black personnel carrier plodded slowly along the gravel drive toward the house; it looked like the sort of armored car that picks up cash from a bank, except that its heavy front grille had been fitted with a formidable battering ram. The *whump*ing sound of rotor blades intensified as the chopper swooped in low and fast, its floodlights snapping on to douse the house in brilliant light, turbulent rotor wash whipping up roof shingles and the tall grass below. At the same time, the behemoth armored carrier accelerated, its fat front tires crushing the porch's wood stair treads, and drove its ramming bar straight through the house's front door, effortlessly splintering wood and twisting metal.

Anticipating shots or an explosion, Whitcomb braced himself, his neck muscles clamping tight. But nothing happened. He waited ten seconds more, then instructed the driver through his earpiece: "All right, Bobby. Back it up, and let's get some gas in there."

The carrier shifted into reverse and pulled back, bringing down the rest of the doorway and a section of the porch overhang. The turret on its roof swiveled slightly, and its short twin barrels angled down at the rough opening. The left barrel *thwump*ed, and a projectile shot cleanly through the smashed doorway to disappear somewhere deep inside. The right barrel *thwump*ed, and a second canister breached the opening, ricocheted off a coat stand, and spun into the front sitting room. In seconds, tear gas filled the house and came churning out the hole where the door used to be and crawled along the overhang before whipping about in the chopper's downdraft.

Whitcomb scanned the front of the structure through the binoculars. "Let's give it a couple minutes, fellas, see if he reacts," he said through his earpiece.

Less than twenty seconds went by. Then the first report came through: "Commander, Sykes here. I see movement inside. North end. Yeah . . . the back door just opened."

The activity was out of Whitcomb's view. "Let's get some sights on him. Is he armed?"

"Can't tell yet, Commander. Too much smoke."

Another five painful seconds ticked by.

"Uh . . . Captain, we've got . . ."

"What is it, Sykes?"

"A mighty fine-looking young woman just came running outside. And she's . . . well, let's just say she's not armed. Wait . . . he's coming out now . . ."

Pause.

"Doesn't look like he's armed," Sykes reported.

The eye in the sky agreed: "Delta Four, confirming visual on a white male coming out the north exit. The suspect is unarmed. Repeat: unarmed. Over."

"This is Whitcomb. I want one member from each team to move in. Everyone else, sit tight and stay alert."

32.01

@ London, England
10:01:54 BST

Deputy Director Charles Burls clipped the wireless microphone to his lapel and strode to the front of the meeting hall, hands folded behind his back, his years of military service manifest in his trim physique, buzz-cut hair, razor-crisp suit lines, and ramrod posture. Certainly, he had no trouble commanding the immediate attention of the four dozen cybersecurity delegates seated around the horseshoe-shaped table facing him. He'd summoned them from all over the European Union to this emergency meeting at the National Crime Agency headquarters in London. An alliance needed to be formed. A *war* alliance.

"Thank you all for coming on such short notice," he said, then cut straight to the matter: "Ladies and gentlemen, Europe is under attack." He paused and raked his eyes over the assemblage. "The *world* is under attack. Our common enemy wears no uniform. It has spies and sympathizers and allies. It is invisible. It is insidious. And without ever launching drones or warships or ground troops, it can put an end to the world as we know it. If you're thinking of radical jihadists or an aspiring czar, think again. Because suicide bombers and those who nostalgically maneuver to reclaim old-world empires are obsolete on the new battlefront. Why? The answer is simple, my friends. It is because the *cyber*war has evolved. Data and those who control it are the new gods of war. We've all dealt with aspects of this contest and have glimpsed what the future of warfare might look like. In the past few days, I'm afraid, we've moved significantly closer to that future."

The Bounty4Justice home page flashed up on the huge viewing screen behind him. He gestured toward it.

"To some, this vigilante website is viewed as a dodgy matter, a nuisance best left to police and criminal investigators, who will sort through the carnage in its wake. Here in the U.K., it is not ranked as a Tier One national security priority, even as its ambitions aim higher and higher, and even though its insidious host remains a ghost, free to operate at will beyond the reach of any laws or nations. It boggles the mind, frankly. Today I hope to convince you that we must commit, together, to stop it in its tracks. Because this"—he jabbed a finger at the screen—"is only the beginning. This, I fear, is a beta test of something much bigger yet to come. Now more than ever, I believe it is imperative that we unite against the forces that attack our common interests in the cyber realm to undermine peace, democracy, and commerce."

He went over the housekeeping rules, then laid out the day's agenda of eight intelligence presentations and an intra-agency e-portal tutorial, broken up into three sessions with a generous lunch break and afternoon tea. After that, he introduced his colleagues, who were seated at a table at the front of the room: a Europol liaison, an MI5 strategist, and half a dozen cryptanalysts and technical officers from the agency's National Cyber Crime Unit. He took his place at the table, and the presentations commenced.

The first speaker was Senior Analytics Officer Rushmi Ambani, an ultrapetite Indian woman with exquisite features, impeccable in a navy pantsuit. She scrolled through the targets on the Bounty4Justice home page, as if shopping online.

"At first glance," she said, "it appears that these hundreds of miscreants from all over the world have nothing in common. Bankers, child molesters, oil moguls, politicians, human rights violators . . . none of whom know one another or have acted together in some grand conspiracy. We're left to wonder: What is the logic of it all? Exactly how has Bounty4Justice selected its targets? Is it all simply a random game, or is it a shot over the bow? What we have found is that there is, in fact, a very logical method to the process."

She used a remote to cue a PowerPoint slide showing a simple graph: a virtually flat line meandering along a horizontal axis that suddenly and dramatically spiked upward to a short plateau before reversing trend just as dramatically.

"This chart demonstrates Internet search analytics within the U.K., specific to a recent target selected by Bounty4Justice, Jonathan Bishop."

She explained that Bishop, a corrupt oil executive who'd been accused of illegally selling British deep-water oil rights to the Russians, compromising thousands of jobs, had been added to Bounty4Justice just two days ago, when the website's target list began its upward march. He'd been abducted outside his Edinburgh office and brought to a remote village in northern England, where his captors had proceeded to work on him with power tools before drowning him in a vat of motor oil. The video of the murder fetched his killers £523,000 on Bounty4Justice.

"The horizontal axis measures time, and the vertical axis measures a sentiment coefficient based on search frequency and negative phrasing. Think of it as a 'public outrage meter.' Here is the date when Bishop's profile first appeared on Bounty4Justice." She clicked a button, and a vertical green line sliced through the chart at a point just before the blue trend line's terminal apex. It was the first of many graphs, all plotting Internet search analytics for a sampling of targets from each country represented by the delegation, each eerily similar in their spiky shapes.

Rushmi said, "As these graphs clearly demonstrate, targets are not selected at random. It appears that they are fished out from the Web using a highly sophisticated algorithm that gauges public outrage.

Scanning social media sites, news feeds, Web searches, and more, Bounty4Justice spots patterns in human behavior. It measures social mood and identifies tipping points—triggers that will cause a more, shall we say, 'visceral' response. This sentient machine quite literally *listens to the people.* As we've seen, however, its cold calculations are in no way synonymous with what the civilized world would define as 'justice.'" She let that point sink in, then continued: "Cybervigilantism is one thing . . . undercutting centuries of legal process. But imagine. What if this same algorithm were reconfigured to systematically identify not miscreants but political dissidents? And what if those political dissidents were added to a kill list on a website that could not be censored or taken down? How about other groups that might be targeted based on ethnicity, religious beliefs, or sexual preferences? Take your pick. It's a logical next step. The dangers of this technology are readily apparent."

The next speaker was Burls's senior intelligence officer, Harry Watson, a bespectacled, lanky young lad with red hair. "So why not just shut it down?" he asked rhetorically. "If a threat of this magnitude comes about, why not just deal with it—squash it, if you will? Again: old-world thinking. In the past few days, we've received disturbing reports from major institutions—banks and insurance companies, manufacturing concerns, defense contractors, government agencies, and many more—that attempted to do just that: to block access to Bounty4Justice's public domain URL. These actions triggered some very nasty reprisals."

Watson described in detail how the website had responded to these defensive measures by initiating even more potent counterattacks that crippled the aggressors' network infrastructure—full lockdown—using encrypted malware the likes of which had never been seen before. He told his audience that British intelligence had yet to determine how Bounty4Justice had permeated the Web like an invisible cancer.

Burls sensed that the delegates weren't grasping the full impact of Watson's message. Perhaps it sounded too fantastical, like some bit of cyberfiction or even simple scare tactics. This denial, this groupthink paralysis, was precisely what he feared most.

He studied the faces in the assemblage: the pair of unreadable Germans in severe suits from the Cyber Defense Center; the prim woman from France's Network and Information Security Agency; the stoic envoy from the National Authority for Investigation and Prosecution of Economic and Environmental Crime in Norway. His gaze lingered longest on the gaunt man from Sweden's National Bureau of Investigation, the most uncooperative bugger of the lot. All it took for this alliance to fail was one dissenter, and surely *he'd* be the one. If even a single country provided refuge for Bounty4Justice, any action plan would amount to little more than trying to insulate a house against a brutal winter while leaving its front door wide open. This would need to be an all-or-nothing effort.

But Asia wasn't represented here, he recognized. Nor was the Eastern bloc. Burls tried not to let that discourage him. He hoped that, collectively, these intelligence agencies might at least figure out how to build a firewall against Bounty4Justice and any other outside aggressors. Buy some time to design a more permanent fix.

What the group hadn't been told was that buried in Bounty4Justice's coding, Her Majesty's Government Communications Headquarters—their preeminent intelligence bureau—had found the telltale "fingerprints" of Japan, China, Russia, the United States, Germany, and, of course, Poland, Romania, and Bulgaria, where the world's preeminent hackers cut their teeth. They had also found refined code fragments eerily reminiscent of GCHQ's proprietary Tempora Internet scrubber. Whether this code was intended as a decoy, or the rest of the world had simply gone raving mad, thought Burls, the fact of the matter was that trust was in very short supply.

Secretly, in other rooms on Tinworth Street, cyber war games were being played out—simulations in which the United Kingdom severed its landline Internet from the rest of the world and put itself on communications quarantine, an island in the digital sea. Even then, the chilling reality remained that little could be done to prevent network infiltrations via a domestic spy or sympathizer using rudimentary tactics to hack the network, such as linking to a satellite to download malicious code to a laptop, then introducing it into the walled-off network via Structured Query Language, or SQL, injection.

The very nature of the Internet was to *interconnect* computers and allow them to talk to one another and swap data, while the only sure-fire way to protect data was to completely remove it from any net-work. Quite the paradox. Cyberprotectionism posed nasty risks and trade-offs that could set the world back three decades. And there was simply no way to seal off telecommunications, whose very existence relied upon open networks. The strategists' early conclusions had only reaffirmed that the Digital Age could not be put back in its box, that any notion of absolute cybersecurity was fantasy, and that the only good defense was a good offense.

The more Burls studied his peers—the complacency, the aura of self-interest—the more he felt a growing distrust. There was precious little time to faff about, treating Bounty4Justice like a game of Whac-A-Mole. Something needed to be done to infiltrate and mor-tally cripple the enemy *now,* before the situation went completely off the rails.

His countrymen excelled at devious counterwarfare. It was high time to get clever about this.

33.01

@ Virginia

Commander Whitcomb's tactical team had proficiently apprehended the twenty-eight-year-old male target, who'd put up little resistance, spare some choice expletives. Furlong's bleached-blond lady friend had raced outside ahead of him, sporting Botoxed lips, plus-sized breast implants, and a lacy lavender thong. She claimed to be an exotic dancer from a local strip club and said that she'd slept over at Furlong's house after her shift had ended the previous night. Given the glitter-dusted "body of evidence," Whitcomb was inclined to believe her. He had his men cover her up with a jacket, cuff her, and sit her in the Humvee that faced the rear of the house with its headlights on.

Furlong, clad only in boxer briefs, sat cross-legged in the tall grass, reeking like a Jack Daniel's distillery. The raid had roused him from a deep, whiskey-induced sleep. The caustic nonivamide gas had swelled his eyes shut and flipped his mucous glands into hyperdrive. His arms were crossed behind his back, flex cuffs strapped tight at the wrists. Like most former marines, he'd stuck with his hair cropped high and tight, and he looked fit and wiry enough to compete in a triathlon, by Whitcomb's estimation.

The suspect's bland any-guy face was a perfect match to the photo that accompanied the marine's profile in Quantico's federal personnel database, and it jibed with the DMV photo matching the driver's license number that had been documented by the Avis car rental agency in Lynchburg. The same license had been run by D.C. Metro during a minor traffic incident just hours after Chase Lombardi had been murdered. Inside the pickup parked under the tree, Whitcomb's men had recovered a wallet that contained said license, as well as the Visa credit card used to secure the car rental. Definitely their man.

Whitcomb asked the suspect to confirm his name and his rank, and in a thick Virginia accent, he responded with "Lance Corporal David Furlong, scout sniper, Afghanistan, Surveillance Target Acquisition Team, First Battalion, Sixth Marine Regiment, Second Marine Division . . . sir."

"How long you been home, Lance Corporal?"

"Six months, maybe seven, sir."

But then the contradictions began stacking up.

It started with the findings of a careful search of the house, which now was mostly tear gas–free, thanks to the chopper setting down on the overgrown lawn and blowing the smoke out through the doors and windows. There were no booby traps, thankfully, just as Furlong had attested before Whitcomb sent men into the home. There were also no car rental receipts, either inside the home or in the Chevy. No guitar case or rock 'n' roll costume. *Probably destroyed the evidence already,* he thought.

No trace of bounty loot anywhere on the property.

A meticulously maintained M40 sniper rifle was recovered from a safe in the basement, along with a commercial version of the 9mm Beretta M9 (the weapons had been properly registered, Furlong's permits up-to-date), a razor-sharp Ka-Bar with the back end of the blade deeply serrated, and plenty of ammunition, including three boxes of .338 Lapua Magnums—the same round indicated in the NYPD's ballistics report. But the slug that had drilled through the Wall Street banker's skull exhibited striations consistent with the rifling of a British Accuracy International AWM—a nimble, streamlined alternative to the beefy American-made Remington M40 long gun. Which made Whitcomb wonder if Furlong had been smart enough to ditch the real murder weapon on his ride home from Manhattan, along with the nifty gun scope used to record the kill video uploaded to Bounty4Justice. And if the sniper *had* uploaded that video, he more than likely would have done it by transferring the video file to his fancy iPhone and sending it that way. Though the phone did contain plenty of other videos—most immortalizing the bar pranks and jackassery that twenty-something males partake in with their buddies, some showing steamy bedroom scenes with his dancer girlfriend—there were none taken in the past few days, and certainly none matching Lombardi's gory head-shot footage.

With the critical physical evidence now collected, Whitcomb got to the point with his prisoner: "You been to New York City in the past few days, Lance Corporal?"

"No, sir."

"You sure about that?"

"Yes, sir."

"You sure you didn't go up there to do what you do best?" Furlong's service record did show that he was a true master in the art of killing, with sixty-one confirmed kills during his three tours in Afghanistan and Iraq.

"What's that, sir?"

"Don't play with me, Furlong. The question's simple: did you shoot Chase Lombardi in Manhattan to cash in on half a million dollars?" According to Furlong's case file, his finances were pitiful, even for a marine. If that bounty was for real, killing Lombardi would have put him on easy street.

It finally clicked with the still-inebriated man. His eyebrows went high and the tight slits around his crusty eyelids pried open to reveal the bloodshot orbs behind them. "Oh, wait . . . you mean that banker dude on that website? No, sir. That was not me. No way."

"Then you better be able to tell me where you were on Monday."

34.01 _____

@ Jersey City

At precisely 8:00 A.M., a raid team descended on Echelon Fulfillment and Warehousing like a torrent of hellfire: twenty-six armed and Kevlared FBI agents from the Manhattan and Newark offices, twenty-five troopers from the New Jersey State Police Special Operations Section in full SWAT gear, four armed agents from Postal Inspection, plus three from Customs and Border Protection; two police choppers provided aerial surveillance along the Hudson River. Waiting nearby in a white van was a six-person tactical unit flown in from Carnegie Mellon University's Computer Emergency Response Team Coordination Center in Pittsburgh, armed with laptops and cloning drives.

It was a big show, Novak thought, with lots of lights and noise and weaponry, certain to ruffle the feathers of any citizen distrustful of a growing police state. Yet they'd succeeded in maintaining the element of surprise, and the raid unfolded methodically in the basic three-stage process: surprise, stabilize, seize.

The SWAT team kicked things off with sharpshooters taking tactical positions at the compass points to cover the assault force that fanned out around the building. After one officer shut off the main gas line to the building, others breached the locked doors leading to the administrative offices and the side exit doors and loading dock, then tossed concussive stun grenades through the openings before swarming inside in a coordinated wave. Their goal wasn't purely shock and awe; they performed the critical functions of rounding up everyone inside as quickly and cleanly as possible before computers and evidence could be tampered with, as well as quashing any armed response.

In less than two and a half minutes, SWAT's lockdown and stabilization was complete, with no resistance or threats reported. Once they'd given the all-clear, the FBI, Postal Inspection, CBP, and CERT streamed into the front-end administrative offices.

The CERT techs sprinted to the computer workstations and copied the entirety of Echelon's proprietary computer files and billing and accounting software before the screensavers had a chance to nap into password log-in mode. In less than a minute, one of the techs had gained access to the main server's root directory, which wasn't even sporting, given that everything was running on an antiquated Windows XP platform that had gone at least seven years without a software update or security patch and that its oblivious administrator had kept his passwords on a handwritten sticky note in the top desk drawer. From there, Echelon's digital innards were laid bare: ledgers, emails both personal and business, browsing history, faxes, archives, and anything else in its system that had ever been converted to zeros and ones, including the deleted files, whose ghosts still haunted the hard drives.

The FBI agents handled the physical invoices and paperwork, boxing it all and carting it out to an unmarked FBI panel van. Strapped filing cabinets went in behind them, followed by the seized computers (the CERT techs took digital pictures of the password lists taped to each of the monitors and kept a detailed list of the corresponding hard drives) and peripheral equipment, such as fax machines, backup servers, disks, thumb drives, and even the 3.25 floppy disks from a bygone era.

While SWAT watched over the office and warehouse staff, who'd been corralled into the break room, Knight and Novak made their way into the back-end storage facility, accompanied by the lead postal inspector, Craig Hargrave—a forty-something with the build of a linebacker and the scarred, angular face of a veteran prizefighter. The previous afternoon, his team had scrambled to collect the tracking and shipping records, thereby securing a no-holds-barred emergency search and seizure warrant in record time.

The warehouse was like most others Novak had seen: an immense open rectangle lit by an overhead grid of fluorescent light boxes, aisles of sturdy shelving crammed with boxes, forklifts parked here and there. The damp air smelled like motor oil and plastic wrap and rat carcasses. There were no computer servers in sight. *So much for a twofer,* he thought.

"Company's privately owned by two brothers, Camillo and Anthony Sorvino, who hail from a prominent Italian family, if you know what I mean," Hargrave explained. "Welcome to Jersey."

Being a Jersey boy himself, Novak took no offense, because the stereotype had some truth to it. Certain areas of the state, particularly shipping hubs like Jersey City and Newark, had a rich history of organized crime.

"They run a mail-order business," Hargrave said. "Specialty foods imported from Italy that are then shipped out to customers who want a taste of Tuscany." He pointed up at the boxes on the shelves, indicating the Italian labels. "Lord only knows what they ship out along with the olive oil. But get ready for the runaround."

"Why's that?" Novak asked.

Hargrave grinned. "You'll see."

He took them to the southwest corner of the warehouse, where the postal inspectors and CBP agents stood around a cube-shaped cardboard box, three feet per edge, labeled in Chinese. The shelves behind them were stacked to the ceiling with identical boxes.

"Go ahead and have a look for yourselves," Hargrave told Novak and Knight.

The inspectors moved aside to let the G-men examine the spoils. Sure enough, the box was stuffed full of what they'd come looking for. But the pins had shipped here prepacked in their insulated manila envelopes, needing only local shipping labels to make it out into U.S. circulation. The sticker on the box flap indicated the sender was some company in China named Chongxin Shenme.

"They're going to claim they didn't know what was in the envelopes," Novak said to Knight.

"Yup," Knight said.

34.02

"How're we supposed to know what's in those envelopes?" Camillo Sorvino said, handcuffs shackled to his wrists, calm as could be, as if a raid were a weekly event. "I mean, come on, fellas. We don't go openin' the merchandise."

In Echelon's conference room, Knight, Novak, and Hargrave had been grilling the Sorvino brothers for a solid twenty minutes, knee-deep in the runaround, just as Hargrave had predicted.

Camillo Sorvino was a handsome guy who reminded Novak of that underwear model who became an actor some years back. Dark hair, and lots of it. Olive complexion. Athletic build. Brother Anthony, also manacled about the wrists, shared the family's good genes but was gray at the temples and thick in the midsection. Neither of them seemed tech-savvy. No Neo to be found at Echelon. These Soprano wannabes were middlemen. Low-level peddlers. It didn't speak well for the Mafia's place in the modern economy.

Knight was getting tired of the nonsense. "You realize, gentlemen, that no matter how you dice it, you're laundering money for Bounty4Justice. Those Chinese novelty pins out there in your warehouse are funding bounties for assassins. Plain and simple."

"Again, I say, how're we supposed to know that?" Camillo leaned back in his chair with his left leg crossed over his right, calmly rocking to and fro.

"So you figure that the demand for lapel pins suddenly spiked?"

Novak said. "Pins with the scales of justice on them? You think that's just coincidence, or maybe every lawyer on the planet happened to join the same club this week?"

Camillo and Anthony both gave him a "you don't talk to me like that, smart guy" look.

"Like I said," Camillo replied, "we don't—go openin'—the merchandise. They're pins. *Pins.* Could have a smiley face on 'em, a peace sign, a rainbow for the gays, or whatnot. How we supposed to know? And our neighborly postal service here has been more than happy to ship this crap for its cut of the money." He thumbed toward Hargrave. "It's not like they go openin' the envelopes, do they? So tell me, agents, you gonna charge our mailman with funding assassins, too? What's fair is fair."

Everyone exchanged glances, as if the dealer had just turned the river card in a high-stakes round of Texas Hold 'Em.

It was a weird thing Bounty4Justice was doing, thought Novak. It was testing every facet of criminal activity and the minutiae of all the legalities that tried to govern it. In this case, it was quite literally pushing the envelope. Was this its intent? To put the entire justice system under stress?

"Look, agents," Anthony said. "I can save you lots of trouble and tell you straight up that we haven't taken a single order from this Bounty4Justice. God's honest truth."

"Tell us who's paying you to mail out these pins, and how," Knight insisted. "Then maybe some of the other goodies that I'm sure we'll find in your files and on your computers might be overlooked."

Novak fully expected a "Go fuck yourself" from Camillo or a "Talk to my lawyer" from Anthony. Instead, the brothers Sorvino looked at each other and performed some weird nonverbal mind meld. They both nodded in consensus.

Camillo shrugged. "Sure. Consider it done."

35.01

@ Dallas
11:14:41 CDT

The three detention towers of the Lew Sterrett Justice Center stood like a modern Bastille along the bank of the Trinity River, with the skyscrapers marking the city center safely in the distance on the other side of the I-35 corridor. Michaels parked the rental car in the visitors' garage and trekked over to the North Tower Detention Facility, a conjoined pair of harsh octagonal high-rises that housed nearly thirty-three hundred maximum-security inmates. One of its most recent inductees was the cult hero Manuel Tejada—dubbed "Handy Manny" by the press—who'd been detained without bail, pending a judge's hearing of the opening movements of his capital murder case.

Outside the main entrance, she spotted a tall, almost storklike woman smoking a cigarette—middle-aged, with square shoulders, an angular face, and a short haircut teleported from the 1980s. She wore a blindingly white form-fitting dress suit—the skirt's hemline barely halfway down her slender thighs—with a pink silk blouse unbuttoned precariously low and pink pumps.

"Rosemary?" She blew a plume of smoke skyward, then smiled.

"Yes. Hi, Angela," Michaels said, stepping up and shaking her outstretched hand. "Great to meet you."

"Welcome to Dallas, darlin'. And, please, call me Angie." She stubbed out her cigarette in an ashtray fitted to the top of a cylindrical garbage can. "You made good time. Flight went well, I take it?"

"Smooth sailing."

Inside, they turned over their sidearms for safekeeping, funneled through the metal detectors, and proceeded past the bail-bond windows, inmate property-retrieval desk, and vending machines to check in with the guard manning the front desk. The place was empty; the posted weekday visiting hours were from 7:00 to 9:00 in the evening. A hulk of an officer from the sheriff's department—his name tag read "Barry J. Eubanks"—escorted them through the succession of barred doors in the buffer zone, then down a long, sterile corridor that bypassed the prison floor cellblocks and to a secure, windowless meeting room.

"Y'all go on in and get cozy, and I'll go fetch 'im," Officer Eubanks said.

They sat side by side in folding chairs on the guests' side of the room's only table, which was bolted to the floor. Simmons retrieved the prisoner's case file from a bulky white leather purse bedazzled with rhinestones.

"Let me tell you, if ever there's been an open-and-shut case," she quietly confided to Michaels, "this is the one." She opened the folder, flipped through some pages, and tapped her brightly painted fingernails on a glossy photo of Congressman Krosby's blackened corpse, melted to the stretch limo's burned-out interior. "Nobody at the office has grand illusions about the expected outcome of the judge's ruling. Manny Tejada is the proverbial dead man walking."

There was a double-tap knock at the door. Eubanks opened the door and held it open. Handy Manny shuffled into the room wearing leg irons, handcuffs, and a standard-issue orange prison jumper. Eubanks helped him to his chair and shackled his handcuffs to an eyebolt in the center of the table.

"Hi, Manny," Simmons said. "This here's my colleague from New York, Special Agent Rosemary Michaels."

Manny had dark circles under his eyes and was in need of a shower and shave. He glanced briefly at Michaels, then shifted back to Simmons.

"We've got some important questions for you, and we'd really appreciate your cooperation."

"Shouldn't my lawyer be here for this?"

"You don't have to answer any question you're not comfortable with," Simmons said. "But, sweetie, you've already pleaded guilty. Full confession. Nothing you say is gonna change that."

Tejada looked down at his handcuffs.

"I'm deeply saddened about what happened to your son, Manny," Michaels said earnestly. "It takes a lot to push a father to do what you did, and it takes an even bigger man to stand up and deal with the consequences. So I'm not here to judge you. I'm just looking for some basic information." She paused. "You used your phone to upload the video. And when you registered your claim with Bounty4Justice, you were asked for a mailing address for the bounty payment."

Novak had told her to act as if the FBI was sure Tejada had opted for physical delivery of his prize money; it was only a hunch, since any claim submitted to Bounty4Justice was completely untraceable. Briefs from Cyber Command indicated that this had to do with ultra-robust proxy servers that performed a digital version of sleight of hand. Tejada could just as easily have opted to be paid in Ncrypto-Cash, which would mean Michaels had flown to Dallas for no reason at all. But the way Manny looked at Simmons for guidance suggested to Michaels that Novak was on to something.

"Go ahead, you can say it," Simmons told him softly.

"Do you think I'd be sitting here in a cage if this was about *money*? Don't you think I would have tried to make a run for it?"

"But you did submit an address to Bounty4Justice?" Michaels said.

He looked to Simmons. "Can't you figure that out from my phone or my data plan?"

"You smashed your phone before the police arrived, sweetie," Simmons reminded him.

"I think I want my lawyer," Tejada replied.

"I'm assuming you want the money to go to your wife," Michaels said. "To take care of her, right? In your shoes, I'd be looking out for my family, too."

Manny ran one manacled hand over his face, confused.

"We don't want to bring your wife into this," Michaels said. "But we have a real dilemma on our hands here. We need to confirm if that bounty is actually being paid, and how."

Manny looked at his handcuffs. Then at Michaels. Then at his handcuffs. "Shouldn't you two be able to figure it out? Can't you track what that website is doing?"

"Look, Manny," Michaels said, dodging the technical stuff, "the money was paid to you in exchange for murdering someone. There's nothing we can do to get around that fact. And Texas has some very clear rules about what the penalties are."

"Yeah, well. He had it coming."

"Maybe he did," Michaels said. "But whether or not Congressman Krosby deserved to die, or whether the court of public opinion backs you, or whether I have my own opinions about what I might have done if I'd been in your shoes . . . those issues are secondary. My concern, as should be yours, is that this website can easily be used to bring harm to the wrong people. To innocent people."

"Hasn't happened yet. The way I see it," the chauffeur said defensively, "it's just encouraging people like me to do the job for people like you. You guys should be *thanking* me. This website is a *good* thing. Keeps people honest."

"It's *not* a good thing, Manny," Simmons said calmly. "And let me tell you why, sweetie. Just this week my office arrested two students at a university not far from here who were about to launch a website inspired by Bounty4Justice. They were going to raise bitcoins as a reward for someone to assassinate the president and vice president. Sound familiar? Now, I think we'd all agree that our young people certainly aren't getting a fair shake at the American dream. Hell, thanks to this screwed-up economy, I can't get my own daughters to fly from the nest. They're driving me bat-shit crazy. But do you really think this website is the answer? For these zealous students and anarchists like them? For my daughters? For you and me? Is it really the solution we should all be looking for?"

Manny remained silent for a long moment, and Simmons let it play out.

"Can my wife keep the money?" he finally said. "You know. If I tell you things. If I help you." He looked beseechingly at each agent in turn, as if searching for the weakest link.

"Manny, honestly, it's not for us to decide," Simmons said.

"The way I see it, since I'm the killer and I chose *not* to receive the money myself, then my wife should be considered the recipient of a prize. Like a lottery or a fifty-fifty."

Regardless of how Tejada had framed this in his mind, thought Michaels, he was facing a "murder for remuneration" charge—in Texas, a shoo-in for the death penalty. Whether that money was real or fantasy, the mere fact that he'd admitted to uploading the video to Bounty4Justice in hopes of cashing in on the prize had sealed his fate. And with all the premeditation he'd put into torching Krosby, an insanity plea would be a nonstarter, anyway. But she didn't want to kick him while he was down. She leaned her elbows on the table. "Do you really think your wife can deposit that kind of money in a bank without raising suspicions?"

"If it's cash, she doesn't need to give it to any bank."

"Assuming it comes as cash," she said. "And that means you'd be forcing us to put her under constant surveillance. Don't make us do that. Don't do that to her. Especially if we're not even certain if the money will show up."

Manny tipped his head back and looked up at the ceiling, or maybe God. "Man, this isn't fair."

"You settled your score, Manny," Michaels said. "If it's not about the money, then help us prevent Bounty4Justice, or something like it, from hurting someone who doesn't deserve it. Please, give us the mailing address."

Manny stared as his handcuffs. Looked at Simmons. Looked at Michaels. Looked at his handcuffs. "Okay."

36.01 _____

A short walk from the North Tower prison sat the Frank Crowley Courts Building, which shared the other half of the convicts' mall but featured a far more civilized lobby of marble, glass, polished wood, and leather furnishings. There was even a gourmet café, where Michaels waited patiently, sipping green tea, noshing on a ham and Brie panini, and catching up on email, while Simmons went off to handle business with the judge.

Twenty minutes later, Simmons came striding into the café, swinging her big disco purse, grinning ear to ear, and holding an official-looking envelope in her left hand. "Got it."

"Impressive," Michaels said.

"Ahh." She pooh-poohed the flattery with a wave of her brightly painted fingernails and slipped the warrant into her purse. "We were roomies at Dartmouth. Between you and me, that girl was anything *but* honorable," she said in a conspiratorial whisper. "Come on now. Let's get moving. Time's a-wastin'."

36.02

The delivery address Manny had submitted to Bounty4Justice turned out to be on the outskirts of Dallas proper, upriver from the prison, where the slow-moving Trinity curved west and paralleled a commercial zone accessed by Irving Boulevard.

Simmons handled the driving, flipping up the toggles for the siren and light bars on her Taurus fleet vehicle and shooting off like a rocket.

Michaels sat in the passenger seat holding Manny's jam-packed key ring, which they'd checked out from the inmate property department. She was staring at the clear plastic fob that contained a picture of Manny's deceased son—a good-looking boy with a big, innocent smile. It made the father's loss all the more tangible and tragic.

"You married, Rosemary?"

"No."

"Divorced?"

"No."

"Hmm. Boyfriend? Girlfriend? Dog?"

"None of the above. Not even a goldfish."

Simmons pressed a button to make the sirens wail at full blast, weaved into the oncoming lane, and blasted through a red light. "Get *out* of town," she said. "A nice young lady like you? So pretty and so well put together?" She gave the agent from Long Island a sideways glance. "You gay?"

Michaels smiled. "No, Angie. Just biding my time. How about you? What's your story?"

"What's to tell, sugar? Thrice divorced. Those daughters I mentioned earlier? Well, they're identical twins who share not only the same drop-dead gorgeous looks but the same bad attitude. Both just graduated from A&M right in time to move back home with Momma. There's an ungrateful Yorkie named Pebbles who shits on my pillow if I don't show her enough love. An upside-down mortgage and a downright laughable balance in my bank account . . ." She sighed. "Still searching for the right man. Gotten a bit harder nowadays. You know, the over-fifty scene isn't pretty, let me tell you." She flashed a big smile that, for a smoker, was remarkably white. "So I guess I'm biding my time, just like you."

Simmons slowed to hang a left off Irving Boulevard, killed the lights and the noise, and rolled up to a rectangular building of once-white cinder blocks topped by gray corrugated-steel roofing.

Michaels eyed the signboard out front, which listed a truck-repair shop, a moving company, and a seafood distributor. The fourth slot on the signboard was blank and corresponded to Manny's rental unit at the far right end of the building; it featured two roll-down garage doors and a windowless people door marked only with a stencil-painted 4.

Simmons overshot her destination, then waited for a U.S. Postal Service delivery truck to turn out of the lot before she backed up and parked in front of Manny's unit. "And here we are," she said.

They got out of the car. At the door, Simmons went through Tejada's key ring, searching for the right matches for the dead bolt and the knob lock.

Michaels looked over at a mechanic in oil-stained coveralls who'd come out from the garage next door. She waved. That brought three more mechanics out from the truck-repair shop. "FBI, fellas," she called out. She tapped the shield clipped to her belt. "It's all good."

They scurried back into the garage.

On the fourth try, Simmons found her perfect match, at least in the context of dead-bolt locks. She turned the tumblers, pushed the door inward, and a heap of mail that had built up behind the door spilled across the floor. "Just what exactly am I looking for? Is it a check or a money order or something?"

"Not sure," Michaels said. "We think it could even be bearer bonds."

"Ooh. Very exotic. Exciting, isn't it?"

"Mmm."

Simmons went inside, circled behind the pile of envelopes, magazines, and junk mail. She crouched and spread out a *Sports Illustrated* and the latest issue of *Time* on the grimy floor tiles, saying, "Heck, I picked a bad day to wear white."

Michaels remained outside, looking over toward the repair shop, sensing a weird vibe. A fat-faced bald guy wearing glasses leaned out from the door frame, looked in her direction, then quickly retreated. Why were these guys so spooked? At the end of the street, she saw the mailman hop into his truck and execute a U-turn. "Keep looking through that stuff," she told Simmons. "I'll be back in a sec."

As the panel truck rumbled along, heading back toward Irving Boulevard, Michaels stepped out into the road and held up her credentials. The driver eased the truck to a stop and plucked out his earbuds, looking starstruck. She walked up to the driver's side, which had no door, and tapped her shield. "FBI."

"Uh, did I do something wrong?" He smoothed out his sweaty comb-over. "It's not a one-way or—"

"Just have a question for you."

"I'm on a tight schedule, ma'am, and my manager's a total hard-ass."

Damn, she thought. *I'm officially a ma'am.* "You make any deliveries to this place in the past couple days?" She thumbed over her shoulder at Manny's garage.

"Nothing yesterday or the day before. But I just tried to deliver a package there a few minutes ago. No one answered."

Michaels's heart raced. "Let's see it."

"I don't have it."

"Where is it?"

"Some fat dude over there signed for it," the deliveryman said, pointing to the truck-repair shop. "He told me he'd give it to the guy when he got back. Nothing unusual about that."

"What was it?"

"Didn't seem like anything important. Just a big box of books, or something."

36.03

Michaels hauled ass back to Simmons. "Angie, I've got a situation out here, and I need you to go around the back of the building, *right now,* and if anyone leaves via the back door of that garage next door, you grab him."

"Got it, sugar," Simmons said, springing up and pulling out her Glock with the ease of a gunslinger.

Michaels hightailed it next door. Entering the repair shop, she scanned the four service bays. One had an ambulance up on a hydraulic lift with all its wheels off, another cradled a florist's delivery truck, the third had a moving van parked over a pit for a fluid change, and the fourth was empty. Not a mechanic in sight. No fat dude, either.

She moved quickly to the shop's rear and through an open doorway that led down a short corridor, presumably to the restroom and the office. The hall doglegged left, and she stopped dead in her tracks. The four missing mechanics stood blocking the way—two in front, shoulder to shoulder; two in back, shoulder to shoulder—obviously running defense.

"Where is he?" she said.

"Who?" the biggest guy said.

His embroidered name patch read "Stu." And he was built like a brick shithouse. "The fat guy."

"What fat guy?"

"I'm a federal agent, pal. I suggest you not mess around."

"I didn't see no fat guy. Caesar, you see a fat guy?"

Caesar, the short one next to him, had the face of someone who'd lived life at full throttle. He shook his ruddy, oblong head. "I don't judge people by their eating habits."

"I was told that the fat guy took possession of stolen property for which I have a search warrant. If that package is tampered with, you'll all be facing felony charges."

They didn't budge. Michaels began calculating her next move, which basically entailed a few more veiled threats about obstruction of justice, blah, blah, blah . . . No time for that. She took out her Glock. "Let's go, Stu. You, too, Caesar. And bring your buddies with you." She waved the mechanics forward with the gun. "Looks to me like you've all got plenty of unfinished work out there. Let's not disappoint the customers."

Stu did the math for three seconds, then shrugged. "Fine by me, pretty lady."

A wiseass, no doubt. But at least he didn't call her "ma'am." She herded them back out to the garage, warned them to stay put, then darted toward the office in the rear, where she met a second security door, this one with a wire-mesh window. Its knob didn't budge. "Shit."

Through the security glass, she could see shelving along the office's outer wall, packed tight with binders and manuals. Set in the middle of the room was a metal desk buried beneath stacks of greasy invoices. Sitting on top of the mess was a newly opened box with its snipped plastic straps left dangling and its lid tossed aside. Old paperback books that had apparently filled it had been pulled out and tossed haphazardly onto the grimy linoleum floor.

Then she caught a flash of daylight and a split-second glimpse of the fat guy's ample hindquarters exiting the solid metal door leading into the rear alley. But he reappeared almost instantly, backing up slowly, shoulders hunched over around something heavy he was carrying. Simmons pulled the alley door closed behind herself and circled around him with her gun trained on his man boobs. She commanded him to sit in the desk chair. Flashing Michaels a smile, she came over to the door and unlocked it.

"I feel like I'm doing all the work here, sugar," she teased, holding the door open. "You know, whenever you're ready to help . . ."

"Thanks, Angie. Great job."

"Big Boy here almost made me break a heel," Simmons said. "Lucky for him that didn't happen, or I'd have shot him for damn sure."

The thief's name patch read "Paul." Paul looked to be a prime candidate for a heart attack, so Michaels wasn't itching to get him too wound up. He was sweaty and red-faced, *and* red-handed. He clutched what he'd pulled from the box—packages resembling two reams of copy paper. But the wrapper on each bundle was deep gray, almost metallic-looking—a protective shield of some kind. The wrapper on the top ream had been torn and peeled back. And it certainly didn't contain copy paper. Michaels was staring at neat, banded stacks of crisp one-hundred-dollar bills.

> The complete irresponsibility of man for his actions and his nature is the bitterest drop which he who understands must swallow.
>
> —FRIEDRICH NIETZSCHE

37.01

@ Boston, Massachusetts
12:52:08 EDT

Kevin Chesney sat on a bench at the Charles River Reservation, in an ideal spot just along the waterfront, close to the steps for the pedestrian footbridge that spanned Storrow Drive to access the dorms across the way at Boston University. It was a cold day, which did a nice job of culling the foot traffic along the jogging trail. Only the diehards would brave the chill to go out for a run along the riverfront pathways. And plenty of them were lovely young BU ladies who were doing everything possible to combat the freshman fifteen. This was an exciting time for a young university student: the big city, the campus life, the first shot at truly cutting free and spreading one's wings. It was that euphoria that blinded them to danger, made them let down their guard. And there were so, so many of them.

Easy pickings.

He had a backpack and a thermos of hot chocolate spiked with mint schnapps, and he was bundled up and wore a knit cap pulled down over his ears. To a passerby, he looked like just some college kid in a town teeming with college kids. But he'd never stepped foot in a university classroom. Hell, he'd barely managed to get a GED, which made it even more ironic that he was leafing through the pages of Nietzsche's *Human, All Too Human*. Partly for cover, partly because if he got bored, he could actually read one of Fred's snippets of philosophical thought—what were referred to as "aphorisms"—and think it over to pass the time.

Man, it was fucking cold. He flipped open the thermos's sip spout and warmed his gullet with some spiked HC.

He looked left down the path and saw nothing coming his way. To the right, a couple of super-fit dudes were running toward him, huffing and puffing, each wearing spandex and ear warmers. Probably gay together, or both infected by the highly contagious metrosexual virus. Seemed most guys were either one or the other these days. He buried his head in the book until the two posers passed by, and the random quote Nietzsche threw back at him said, "Most people are far too much occupied with themselves to be malicious."

True that, Fred, he thought. He pondered the line for a few seconds as he swigged some more HC. Less than a minute later, he spotted a lone runner coming his way. More spandex, but this time, the curves were 100 percent feminine. He'd need a closer look to make sure she truly passed muster, though.

She stopped running, put her hands on her hips, and did the old cooldown walk, puffing clouds into the frigid air. He discreetly watched her, sized her up. As the gap closed between them, he could see that she was the real deal. Young, slim, petite. No glaring facial irregularities, as best as he could tell. She was veering onto the path leading toward the pedestrian bridge. Perfect.

She stopped to stretch a few yards away, at an unoccupied bench.

He felt the excitement building inside him, the dark urges surfacing, demanding gratification. Sliding his hand into his pocket, he made sure the syringe of highly concentrated flunitrazepam was positioned properly so he could get to it quickly when the time was right. He wiggled his right foot and felt the knife sheath rub against his ankle. He ran his hand over the bulge of the GoPro camera in the backpack's side pocket. All systems go.

Just as he stowed the thermos and book in his backpack, his smartphone chimed loudly with the air-horn ringtone assigned to his best bud, T-Man. Talk about shit timing. But he'd thought he'd muted it already, so maybe T-Man was doing him a solid. He tapped his phone's display to send the call to voicemail, then muted it. Lucky for him, the runner was wearing earbuds, so she paid him no mind. Man, did she have some legs on her. Couldn't really tell what was going on beneath her baggy sweatshirt, but he was sure looking forward to finding out.

Then his phone started blowing up with text messages from T-Man.

What the fuck?

He looked at the screen:

U sick fuck!
What the fuck were u thinking!
U r SOOOO FUCKED!

At first he thought T-Man was screwing with him, like he always did. But the messages kept coming:

Better look at your FB page, asshole. WTF is wrong with u!

This ball-busting session was going a bit over the line. Nonetheless, Kevin tapped the phone's Facebook icon to see what the hell had gotten T-Man's panties all up in a bunch. That's when he saw that his own profile looked a whole lot different than it should. His photo was the same—a shirtless pic from his trip to Cancún last year when he had a killer tan that made him look friggin' ripped. His profile name, however, had been changed to "Kevin Chesney, THE SORORITY STALKER."

Now his heart was out of the gate and running.

Frantic, he looked under the "About" tab at the particulars of his profile, where it now plainly listed his work and home addresses for everyone to see and his professional skills had been changed from "heating and air-conditioning technician" to "SERIAL RAPIST." The pics of his favorite bars and clubs listed under the "Places" tab had been replaced by the most recent locations where he'd raped college girls. Then there was the "Photos" section, which had been transformed into a sadomasochistic collage of images taken straight from his private collection of photographs hidden under password protection on his home computer—his personal archive of conquest, the pics he'd taken of each of his victims as he'd raped them, but with their faces pixelated to blurs. He scrolled through them, page after page, dread pouring through him.

"Oh, my God," he said, feeling like he was going to start hyperventilating.

He tried to log in to his account to wipe the postings. His password didn't work.

"Fuck."

He tried it again, but Facebook was telling him that his password was invalid. Then he got locked out of his account altogether.

"FUUUUCK!"

Tightness gripped his chest as the horrifying reality struck him. Someone had hacked into his account. The truth was out.

T-Man hit him with another text:

Now ur on the news! Cops r tracking ur phone. Good luck ASSHOLE! When you get to prison, don't waste ur 1 call on me.

Kevin slung his backpack over his shoulder and sprang to his feet, trying to keep his mind on track, trying to think of where to go and what to do. Though he was no longer watching the female runner, she had taken a sudden interest in him. She came running toward him again, this time with a gun in her hand.

"Stop right there, Kevin!" she yelled, leveling the weapon at his chest. "Boston PD!"

No fucking way was he going to prison. He'd heard stories about how rapists were treated there. He dropped the backpack and broke into a sprint, heading for the bridge.

That's when the two Sallies he'd seen running past him earlier came out of nowhere and tackled him to the ground.

38.01 _____

@ Lake City, Colorado
10:59:11 MDT

Jonathan Farrell sat on the front porch of the cabin, drinking coffee, gazing out at the snowcapped mountains and the trees and the blue sky and the babbling river wending its way through the valley below, coming to terms with the notion that he'd finally found something that he might one day miss. Something that could hurt him. It was a tough thing to let down one's guard, to surrender, to *own* something . . . to become vulnerable. It unsettled him.

At heart, Jonathan Farrell was a simple man who wanted only simple things out of life. Dignity, first and foremost, since no man's life was worth a damn without it. It was the one truism that generals and politicians rarely understood when assessing an enemy. He'd seen it time and time again. Rob a man of dignity and sure as shit you'll regret it. Most men in most places in the world just wanted to live their lives, worship the god of their choosing, and make some money to pay for basic things, with a little left over to splurge here and there on their lady, or their kids, or their car, or their camel, or whomever or whatever they fancied most.

Purpose ranked up there, right alongside dignity. After all, a man needed to carve out his place in the world. He needed to feel connected. He needed context. He needed a sense of achievement and contribution.

True love was a desirable luxury, Farrell supposed, though he couldn't miss something he'd never had. And it was quite possible that he was incapable of such a thing—this fairy tale of romantic love. He knew that sounded cold. Heartless. But it was true. And being true to oneself, he decided, ranked right up there with dignity and purpose.

Maybe there was something broken inside him. There had to be. In fact, he figured that was the reason he'd passed with flying colors all those mental tests the navy put him through, before they'd given him the green light to become a killing machine. Truth was that something had to be dead or absent inside a man in order for him to kill on command, without question, without emotion. No doubt there'd been a piece of him missing right from the get-go.

It seemed, too, that most men wanted children—something to do with passing their seed on and leaving behind a legacy of some sort. To him, the desire to have children was selfish—perhaps even narcissistic—seeing as the world was already overrun with people who were consuming the planet willy-nilly, from oil to food to anything coming up out of a mine, even to clean oceans and breathable air. Human history, after all, boiled down to a never-ending squabble over too few things for too many people—the catalyst for warmongering, genocide, and the rise of psychotic demagogues like Hitler and Stalin. In the calculus of life, he'd determined early on that having children only meant more squabbling for more resources. Better to keep the numbers down.

Having gotten a good look at the shit and suffering that men created and endured, he was amazed that the human species had made it even this far. Though he thought it might have been nice to see part of himself passed on to another human being, maybe have someone who'd love him and who'd ask him to impart his wisdom. Realistically, however, he wasn't cut out to be a father. That piece of him the navy couldn't find was probably the same piece that could have made him a great dad, and might have allowed him to love and be loved.

Given how things had turned out, it was probably best that the piece was gone, so as not to leave behind pain for anyone else in the future. He would exit this world silently, causing no war or heartache or in-dignity. There'd be no legacy left by Jonathan Farrell. Even the family name would die with him. No, there wasn't much about this world he'd truly miss, because he'd never really been connected to it the same way most folks were. In the end, he hadn't even belonged in the ultimate brotherhood of the Navy SEALs.

Then he started thinking about his nameless, faceless employer— code name: Oz—and the strange business in Manhattan. The usual encrypted directives delivered to his phone ten days ago had been clear: kill Chase Lombardi in a highly public way. Big impact . . . in his NYC office . . . long-range head shot . . . video confirmation critical (1080p) . . . you have one week. A tall order, albeit excessive, with its rigid stipula-tions on the place, the video, and the daring shot to the head (as op-posed to a more conventional, and forgiving, hit to the center mass of the chest). Nonetheless, per usual, he'd executed in superb fashion. Reliable. Methodical. Clean.

That traffic incident on the D.C. Beltway, however, could have caused a serious wrinkle in the plan. But it hadn't. Neither his rental car nor the minivan that had bumper-tapped it had sustained visible dam-age. A D.C. Metro patrolman had filed a basic incident report before telling Farrell and the other driver to move along. No harm, no foul.

The driver's license he'd presented to D.C. Metro had drawn no scrutiny. The resemblance between Farrell and the man in the license photo was incredibly close: both clean-shaven, slender white guys with green eyes and buzz cuts and the same tilt to the eyebrows. It wasn't mere coincidence. The previous day, Farrell had shopped the DoD's database for a military sniper matching these strict physical specifications and had been pleased to find one David Furlong. Oz's encrypted top secret clearance to every level of government and commercial data had let him mine Furlong's banking records, too. From there, he'd used some nifty counterfeiting machines and print stocks—also provided by Oz—to press out official duplicates of Fur-long's Virginia driver's license and Visa card.

What still troubled Farrell was the fact that the video clip sent to

Oz had been posted to that damn vigilante website for the whole world to see, evidently to secure a prize of more than half a million dollars. He'd wondered why Oz would go and do something stupid like that: exploit his most valuable asset to cash in on some prize money. Farrell's skills were not something to be abused or grandstanded with; this arrangement of theirs was not to be taken lightly. So why would Oz want to rain chaos on people like that, here on domestic soil? Completely illogical.

As best Farrell could tell, it seemed that his kill video had set Bounty4Justice in motion here in the United States. He'd drawn attention to it, added validity to it. Gave it free publicity. And that raised a question: was the website Oz's creation? It certainly didn't fit the mold. If it was justice the man was after, there were plenty of Farrells on the payroll who could handle the work. Why leave the job to amateurs and freaks? The marks on the website weren't the typical fare for the Jonathan Farrells of the world. They were fairly low-level scum that fell through the cracks of society, not political pariahs who threatened world order or some national economic interest.

Equally troubling was the huge bonus Oz had wired to his account in Zurich (in addition to his $30K monthly retainer): more than half a million bucks, instead of the usual $50K single rate. When Farrell had seen the deposit, he'd feared a setup, because the sum matched the bounty paid out on Chase Lombardi. But there was no way that account could be traced back to him. So he'd pushed aside his paranoia and had taken some of that money to pay off this lovely dream home. After all, given his protections, he was untouchable by U.S. authorities, scandal or no scandal. Best to keep his mouth shut, follow orders, and understand his place in the order of things. He was a *tool,* plain and simple.

Having a home took some getting used to. It represented unstructured possibilities and potential unforeseen commitments and things that would someday require fixing—obligations that normally didn't agree with Farrell's credo of detachment. But everyone needed a home base.

So here he was looking out over the most beautiful sight he ever did see.

The little piece of the world he'd carved out for himself.

Since he was allowing himself this rare moment of introspection, he even considered that maybe, just maybe, there *was* a God who'd made all this, and had made him. And he wondered if that same God might ever forgive him for everything he'd done. It was too hard to figure all that out and make sense of it. Making sense of things wasn't his job. He was a soldier. And soldiers obeyed orders. Even if those orders came from a ghost on the other end of a satcom.

39.01

@ Dallas

Forty minutes after the discovery that Bounty4Justice was indeed making good on its promises, four forensic techs wearing FBI windbreakers showed up at the truck-repair shop. By then, Michaels had taken pictures of the seizure—the box, the shipping label, the bundles of notes and their metallic wrappers, the random paperbacks used as filler strewn about the floor. The shipping label on the lid of the box had a tracking number, which listed the sender's address as San Jose, California, even though the shipment had originated from Massena, New York. When Michaels searched for the San Jose location on her phone, however, nothing came up, not even on Google Maps. No surprise.

While Simmons went out front for a cigarette break, Michaels stayed with the techs in the back office as a silent observer.

The money inspectors pulled random samples from the cache, and Michaels took notes on every one of their observations, since she was sure that Knight and Novak would want all the nitty-gritty details.

The bills' linen and cotton blend felt just right to the tech's touch. The front-side images of Ben Franklin were the real McCoy, he told her, same with the iconic Independence Hall on their reverse sides, same with the optically color-shifting ink and the tiny red and blue enwoven security fibers. Under magnification, the microprinting and watermarks were spot-on. Chemical swabs passed with flying colors. A UV light wand made the security strips glow hot pink and high-lighted random oily fingerprints and the trace crystals of cocaine endemic to 90 percent of all U.S. currency. Finally, he observed, the paired serial numbers matched on each note, and the bills were non-sequential from one note to the next.

"Looks good to me," the lead tech concluded. "Legal tender. We'll need to run a final counting back at the lab and go through the rest of the batch, but assuming these are all ten-thousand-dollar stacks, it'll add up to just over two hundred K. Sure, we could run DNA or fin-gerprint analysis, but we'd wind up pulling hundreds of thousands of low-quality samples that really don't prove a thing." He said this last part as if the same old questions he'd been asked a million times before were already queued up in his brain.

Michaels was again reminded of the timeless beauty of cash and why it presented such a daunting challenge to law enforcement. It left no paper trail, and it was accepted the world over. Particularly in the Mafia-infested zip codes throughout Long Island.

"These look like standard shielded wrappers," the tech said, hold-ing up the silver foil pouches that held the bills. "Probably lead, you know, to deter an X-ray scanner from registering the notes' security strips, or maybe even the bills themselves, since they have a different density than the other contents stuffed into that box. But the postal service isn't in the business of scrutinizing packages on that level, anyway. It's not like they run these boxes through scanners or any-thing like that. I mean, you should see some of the stuff we've confis-cated that's passed through the mail: every drug imaginable, weapons, pipe bombs, a human head, all kinds of cockamamie crap. You re-member that website Silk Road?"

"Of course," she said. "Hard to forget."

Silk Road had been a global, billion-dollar online marketplace, hosted anonymously on the darknet, where drug dealers had carried out transactions with bitcoins and fulfilled orders using standard mail carriers. It remained active for nearly two and a half years, until the

FBI shut it down in 2013, and then only because a few lucky breaks exposed its twenty-something mastermind, Ross Ulbricht, who'd logged into the website's administrator portal from his laptop via a Wi-Fi connection at his local public library. The biggest break was that Ulbricht lived in San Francisco, well within the FBI's reach. Silk Road was a close cousin to Bounty4Justice—an eBay for criminals. And it had been run almost entirely by one "kid."

"Well, if Silk Road could ship heroin and cocaine through the mail for years on end, you can imagine the possibilities. Therefore, in my opinion," the tech said, holding up the wrapper, "this here's just a bit of overkill."

"There's nothing at all unique about that?" Michaels said. "Nothing that might trace back to a particular source or a manufacturer or something?"

"Sure, we could figure out who makes them. Can't imagine there's a huge market for these things. But, honestly, that won't do you much good. And this? A piece of wrapping paper?" He gave Michaels a tough-love look.

"Gotcha," she said, even though she didn't agree on the point. She'd been down this road before, and anything unusual, no matter how obscure, could open all sorts of doors. But the Secret Service policed the nation's money supply, not the FBI, and Michaels had a longstanding contact there who might shed light on this delivery method.

She stared at the stack of bills. All along, the FBI had been thinking about exotic payment instruments the scheme might employ. Yet like so many aspects of Bounty4Justice, this critical piece of its functionality was so cleverly deceiving. So universal. So *simple*.

39.02

"I still can't believe someone would send all that cash in the mail," Simmons said, weaving the Taurus around a plodding truck and zipping through a red light. "Just plain crazy."

"Short of a money order," Michaels said, "I'm not sure any other method would be all that secure or anonymous, either. And the odds that anyone would ever open the package during shipment are virtually zero."

"Unless your nosy neighbor gets his grubby hands on it after hearing in the news that you're due a big payout," Simmons countered.

The severe prison towers loomed up ahead.

"Well, sugar, I think we'd agree that Bounty4Justice isn't following any rules," Simmons said. "Really, now, anyone who can dole out these huge sums as if they're just trifles being stuffed into a birthday card must have lots to burn." She blasted the siren again to push the cars out of a snarled intersection. "I'm surprised the website even pays out the money to begin with. I mean, who would ever know if the bounty was never paid, right? It's not like an assassin would file a complaint with the Better Business Bureau for getting stiffed."

"True," Michaels said.

"I mean, what if whoever's behind it all is already rich? Like some investor type who scored a fortune during the tech bubble who's trying out a new venture. Or maybe some billionaire who's had a come-to-Jesus moment?"

"Anything's possible," Michaels acknowledged. "Could be an elaborate Ponzi scheme, for all we know."

Simmons made it back to the prison garage in record time, and she flicked off the lights and sirens and rode up two levels to where Michaels had parked the rental car.

"Great meeting you, Angie," Michaels said, opening her door.

"It was a hoot," Simmons said, giving her a hug. "You take care of yourself. I know you'll eventually find the right guy, and he'll be damn lucky to have you."

"I'm sure you'll find your man, too. But given your track record, promise me you won't go marrying him."

"I promise," Simmons said, flashing a big bleached grin.

As Michaels got into the rental car, she received a call from Novak.

"Hey there, Deputy," she said cheerily. "What's happening?"

"Hate to put a damper on an otherwise productive day," Novak replied. "But Tim just got a call from Quantico. Told him that our

suspected sniper, David Furlong, has a ton of witnesses and surveillance video that place him at his local shooting range in Lynchburg,
Virginia, at the time of Chase Lombardi's murder. He was nowhere
near Manhattan this week."

"You've got to be kidding me."

"No joke. We're back to square one."

40.01

@ Moscow
Saturday, 10/28/2017
14:17:55 MSK

Inside Rostelecom headquarters, chief network administrator Yegor Krasneker sat at his desk atop the control room's command platform, staring in bafflement at the critical error messages flashing up on his screen. At first, his brain denied the whole thing, telling him that what he was seeing could not be right. It was illogical. A mirage . . .

"Yegor," his lead technician called to him from a workstation in the pit below. "Are you seeing this?"

"Yes." *Yes.* He studied the screen once more. It *was* there. This was really happening.

Throughout the control room, all the lights and screens flickered for an instant, as if struck by an electromagnetic pulse—an electrical hiccup that quickly stabilized before any equipment went dark.

"The generators . . ." said the spooked lead technician, coming to his feet and looking around the control room warily, as if it would explode at any moment.

Now dozens of technicians rose from their disabled workstations, looking up to Krasneker for guidance.

On the control room's main screen, Krasneker brought up a schematic that overlaid a web of color-coded lines across a map of Russia. The grid—stretching from the Far East, to Siberia, to the Urals, and under the Kerch Strait to Crimea—traced out 550,000 kilometers of multi-terabit backbone fiber lines that connected Rostelecom's close to fifty million residential and corporate customers. Over half of Russia's digital communications ran through it: voice, Internet, data, media . . . even the secret networks known only to the Kremlin. It was the Motherland's central nervous system.

What Krasneker was seeing made his mouth go dry.

Systemwide, green lines were flipping to red and flashing ominously—from the fat lines representing the main data trunks right on down to the thin lines of FTTx last-mile connections—as if the entire data network were experiencing a rolling blackout. Even the labeled sections of the backbone that had recently been upgraded to provide network redundancy were failing to do precisely what they'd been engineered to do. Everything Krasneker was seeing pointed to a catastrophic meltdown. Russia was having a nervous breakdown. His hands began to tremble. *Impossible.*

Nervous chatter broke out throughout the room.

"Yegor, what's happening?" asked the lead technician in a quavering voice.

"I don't know."

"Was there an explosion somewhere?"

The chatter volume increased.

"Don't be an idiot," he replied loudly. "For this to happen, it would have to be . . . Armageddon." *Yet an all-out nuclear strike just might explain it,* he thought.

"You don't think—"

"Shut up! Everyone SHUT UP!" he screamed.

The chatter subsided to a murmur.

"I need to *think*."

For the sake of efficiency, during the backbone's initial construction, in 2005, much of the Russian Internet—or Runet—fiber lines had been snaked alongside ground-wire cables owned by power companies. It had been a mutually beneficial alliance, with more than one hundred utilities and power plants gaining digital connectivity between their substations and power grids, while ISPs avoided costly outlays for easements and infrastructure associated with a standard network build-out. A catastrophic failure in the backbone would take power plants offline and would strand the financial markets. Even the Russian government itself—Rostelecom's de facto majority shareholder—would be cut off.

How can this be happening?

Then a handset on his desk began ringing—the red phone dedicated to emergencies of the highest order. It was a *real* ringtone, the metal-on-metal chime of a tiny bell concealed inside this old-fashioned device, with its curlicue cord that connected to copper lines strung along roadside poles. He'd picked it up only during drills. It connected directly to Rostelecom's majority shareholder.

The control room went silent.

Krasneker answered the call tentatively, barely hearing the gruff voice on the other end of the line, because his heart was pounding so loudly in his eardrums.

"What in God's name is going on?" asked the caller.

"We're not sure, sir," he replied. "I need to run tests."

"Do it. *Now.* I will wait."

"Yes, sir."

Krasneker cradled the clunky handset on his shoulder, like he used to do as a teenager, when he talked to his girlfriend in whispers and stretched the phone cord into the bathroom and closed the door so his parents wouldn't listen in on the conversation. Oh, what he'd give to transport himself back to that simpler time.

He worked his keyboard and mouse to bring up the diagnostic utilities dashboard on his screen, and its mirrored image was displayed on the big monitor for everyone else in the control room to follow along. He started with the most basic test—the top-of-the-trees perspective—by clicking on a button that pinged the hundreds of data center servers spread regionally throughout the vast network. The command sent out a simple signal that sought an echo reply. The sonar of digital networks.

Nothing came back. Absolutely nothing.

Dread poured over him like ice water.

Murmurs again swirled throughout the control room.

Krasneker threw up his hand like a conductor cuing his orchestra, and the room fell into tense silence once more.

Next, he pinged the backbone's enterprise routers and core routers—the critical hardware that performed the traffic-cop functions of the network by moving parsed data packets to and from assigned destination addresses.

That's when *really* bad things started to happen.

The screens flickered, then blacked out for a split second. Another blip in the power supply? No, Krasneker immediately determined. If that had been the case, the lights in the ceiling would also have blinked. But they hadn't.

The screens came back to life, but they looked completely different. The utilities dashboard had been replaced by an empty blue pane. Once again, his sense of reality was being upended. He'd entered a living nightmare.

Then a message box popped up on the screen. A warning. More precisely, a threat. In English.

You are receiving this message because you have attempted to block Internet access to the following domain:
www.bounty4justice.com

RESTORE ACCESS IMMEDIATELY
You will be given one hour to comply.
Choose to comply,
and your system functions will be fully restored.
Choose not to comply,
and your network will be disabled indefinitely.

Censorship will not be tolerated.
Thank you.
Technical.Support@bounty4justice.com

Beside the text box, a digital clock appeared, displaying "60:00:00."
The countdown commenced.

This time, Krasneker could not suppress the eruption of chatter.

"What's going on over there?" growled the caller.

"I found the problem," Krasneker replied tremulously.

CODE_RED

> JAM: Razorwire took down the Internet in Russia.

> PIKE: Impressive.

> JAM: SCARY. What if the Russians locate the central command module? They may have the capability to crack the decryption algorithm.

> PIKE: They'll have to find it first. If we can't trace its location, there's no way they will.

> JAM: What if Razorwire is used to attack other countries, like yours or mine?

> PIKE: That would be extremely unfortunate. Let's focus on the current reality. Tell me the results of your communications with the project's assets.

> JAM: We're still waiting for some to respond to our queries. Thus far, the programmers that have responded claim to know nothing, as expected.

> PIKE: Any one of them could have stolen the code. That's a few dozen possibilities. Are you saying that not one of them is a suspect and that there's no audit trail?

> JAM: The software silos were walled off from one another. No single coder could have gained access to all the silos simultaneously, I assure you. We built multiple redundancies into the system's security layers. Nevertheless, the entire protocol was compromised, globally, all at once. Only an administrator could have done that. As you know, there are only two administrator accounts with clearance at that level. That same clearance would allow access to the bank accounts.

> PIKE: What are you suggesting?

> JAM: I'm simply stating the facts. The evidence suggests that the decryption keys were stolen from one of us. Same with the account passwords and clearances. Someone was watching us. Someone tricked us into revealing the decryption keys and the storage addresses for the entire series of silos. That same someone has locked us out of half of our accounts, which means we should assume that the money has been stolen, as well.

> PIKE: How much money was in the affected accounts?

> JAM: Eighty or ninety million, give or take.

> PIKE: And how am I to know that YOU are not the hacker?

> JAM: I could ask you the same question.

41.01

@ Brooklyn
Saturday, 10/28/2017
07:29:09 EDT

After returning from a brisk five-mile run, Novak showered, brewed a pot of coffee, and tuned the television to MSNBC's *Cyber Assassins Roundup* news special, so he could listen in while he got dressed.

The program began with Chase Lombardi's murder at the heart of world finance on Monday, which had led to yesterday's takedown of David Furlong in what had turned out to be an elaborate case of mistaken identity. Next, a recap of Tuesday's doubleheader: Alan Bateman's staged escape by sea in the Hamptons, and Paul Garrison's "halving" in Doha. Wednesday featured Jacob Feldstein's cliff jump, compliments of yet another ace sniper who remained at large, only to be topped by the late-evening torching of Congressman Kenneth Krosby in Dallas. Thursday had been relatively subdued, with no confirmed hits and Bounty4Justice's acquittal of Kerri-Anne Thompson, who'd been indisputably wrongfully accused of killing her twins. Friday brought news of the FBI's raid in Jersey City that shut down the website's novelty pin distributor. By midafternoon, however, things took a turn for the worse when a local news station in Dallas was tipped about the FBI's cash seizure. As Novak knotted his tie, the show's host recapped the story:

Yesterday, FBI agents in Dallas confiscated a package mailed to Manuel Tejada only two days after he'd been arrested for the gruesome murder of Congressman Kenneth Krosby. Officials have yet to confirm or deny that the seizure was prize money awarded by Bounty4Justice, but here's what one eyewitness had to say . . .

In the kitchen, Novak prepared a bowl of instant oatmeal as MSNBC cut to an interview that had already gone viral on YouTube, in which a tenacious reporter from an NBC affiliate in Dallas had cornered one of the mechanics Michaels had confronted:

"What exactly is the FBI looking for in there?" the reporter asked the burly man whose name patch read "Stu." "Can you tell us what you saw?"

"All I'm sayin' is it was a box full of cash. I could see the money clear as day: stacks of hundred-dollar bills. Lots of 'em."

In the same shot, the cameraman caught an FBI forensic tech wheeling the box out to his van on a hand truck, flanked by two other techs wearing navy windbreakers.

"And that's the box there?" the reporter asked Stu.

"Yeah. That's the one," he confirmed.

The reporter and cameraman scrambled over to the van. As the FBI tech hefted the box into the cargo hold, the reporter asked the question she knew wouldn't be answered: "Can you tell us what's in the box, Agent? Is it true that you found money that Bounty4Justice mailed to Manny Tejada?"

The agent ignored the news crew and hopped into the van along with the other techs. The cameraman tracked the vehicle as it drove off.

It was exactly the free publicity Bounty4Justice needed to tip the balance of speculation and take things to the next level. Within hours of the clip hitting the airwaves, four more targets had been taken out in the United States.

The killing spree started around 3:15 P.M., when Ralph Demaris, the crooked ex–mortgage broker from Jacksonville, was gunned down in the parking lot of his local Publix grocery store by some novice nutjob in camo fatigues. The undercover police who'd been shadowing Demaris took down the assailant, permanently, in a Wild West–style shootout.

Around the same time, in Seattle, the battered body of a crooked councilman who'd enriched himself with municipal pension funds was hanged naked from a tree in Volunteer Park with a sign strung around his neck that read, I WAS A GREEDY ASSHOLE WHO HELPED RUIN AMERICA. No suspect had yet been identified, and his bounty remained pending on the Bounty4Justice website, awaiting a video claim.

By 8:00 P.M., a university professor in Cleveland known for his liberal defense of radical Islam—whose phone and bank records posted on Bounty4Justice proved that his support for known terror organizations went far beyond his provocative lectures—had been found stabbed to death in his home, after the authorities had received a tip from an anonymous caller. The gruesome video showed up before midnight on Bounty4Justice, for the purchase price of $495,432.

Finally, by 9:00 P.M., the chief executive officer of a chemical company in Duluth, who'd been outed on Bounty4Justice for bribing a dirty EPA inspector to ignore his company's decades-long illegal dumping activities, had been found drifting facedown in the same filthy river he'd helped contaminate. He was wearing a necklace of glow sticks, which facilitated the body's speedy recovery . . . as well as the assassin's claim submission to Bounty4Justice, which had been validated while Novak had been out on his morning run, to the tune of $523,111. For an added bonus, the EPA inspector was up on Bounty4Justice, too, his own handsome bounty as yet unclaimed.

Until Novak had fallen asleep, at midnight, he'd been bombarded by texts and emails from the various field offices assigned to those targets, and he'd done the phone rounds with Knight and Michaels. Walter had also called to report that his team was still coming up empty-handed on every search permutation for the term "iArchos," even after two days of intense analysis. "Sorry, but there's nothing even remotely close out there that we can find, Novak. We even passed it through the NCFTA. Nothing doing. Once we have the proper warrants, I can have the NSA run a more in-depth analysis."

Captain Agner also joined the party along the way to report that during the course of the evening, his officers had thwarted three attempts on targets in Manhattan. "Something's got to get done here, Novak," Agner had said. "My men are getting overrun. We were lucky tonight. But our luck ain't gonna last forever."

At that point, however, there was little Novak *could* do, except work on his spreadsheet and feed Sentinel yet another update to keep the Operation CLICKKILL task force apprised of the situation. Meanwhile, once again—partly thanks to that mechanic's convincing YouTube interview—Bounty4Justice's target list was on the rise, with nominations galore.

Novak finished his oatmeal just as the MSNBC host began tallying up the week's twenty-two confirmed kills throughout Europe. His BlackBerry chimed, and caller ID displayed a really long number he didn't recognize. At first, he hesitated to answer it, thinking maybe Bounty4Justice was upping its game by attempting to transmit malicious code via the airwaves to hijack his phone. But on the fourth ring, he pushed aside his paranoia and took the call. "This is Novak," he said tentatively.

"*Aaaah,* thank God," a frantic male voice replied. "I've been calling all—"

"Who is this?"

"It's Fred. Sorry. Fred Shrayer. In Moscow."

"Oh. Didn't recognize the number."

"Our phone systems at the embassy are offline. I had to borrow a satellite phone from a CIA agent just to get a call out to you. And that's exactly why I'm calling. We've got quite the panic going on over here. All over Russia. I mean bad."

"What are you talking about?" Novak glanced back to the television. The ticker on the bottom of the screen wasn't flashing any headlines related to Russia.

"Yesterday, Voronov finally gave in and added Bounty4Justice to his blacklist, just like we asked him to. All good. Then this afternoon, when the Internet companies started blocking access to the website, it triggered some massive cyberattacks that took down huge swaths of the communications grid, including the Kremlin."

"Are you serious?" Novak started pacing the apartment.

"Serious as a heart attack."

"Why am I not seeing anything on the news?" He grabbed the TV remote and started flipping through other stations. Still nothing.

"It's all going down right now, as we speak. Give it a few minutes. You'll see."

"But how—?"

"All they're telling us is that some crazy software took over the system and scrambled up all the routers that control the network data flow . . . and it spat out some prompt stating that if further attempts were made to block access to Bounty4Justice, the attacks would only get worse. Like a ransom note or something. Can you believe this? As far as I know, Voronov is having the telecoms remove the block and—"

Shrayer went silent. Novak could hear someone in the background on his end, presumably giving the legat an update. A few seconds went by.

In a much more subdued tone, Shrayer said, "Looks like everything's coming back online now. They're telling me our phones are working again. Thank God." He sighed. "But just wait and see what a mess this creates. It'll be a huge embarrassment for Voronov and his people. These guys don't take kindly to looking weak, and this blunder just exposed some serious vulnerabilities within Russia's infrastructure. Expect this to be a diplomatic time bomb, is all I'm saying."

Novak didn't know how to respond.

"I understand that you have a job to do," Shrayer added. "But you've got to figure out another way to shut down this damn website. And for the love of God, leave me out of it."

"I understand," Novak replied.

"I've gotta go," Shrayer said. "Good luck."

The satellite feed chirped, and the line went silent.

Novak set down the BlackBerry and glanced at the television. The crawler on the bottom of CNN had finally caught up, flashing:

MASSIVE CYBERATTACK CRIPPLES RUSSIA'S COMMUNICATION NETWORKS

42.01

@ Salina Cruz, Mexico
Sunday, 10/29/2017
05:24:23 CST

Deputy Marshal Miguel Castillo peered through his binoculars at the motel room window. The shades were drawn, but a frame of light shone around their edges. He could only guess that the fugitive was preparing for a predawn start. But he had yet to catch a glimpse of the face plastered on the front pages of *The News* and *El Universal* and labeled "Most Wanted" by the FBI.

"Nothing yet?" asked his partner, Hector Rivera, seated next to him in the unmarked Chevy sedan.

"*Nada.*" He lowered the binoculars.

Dollar Rent A Car had tracked the transponder on the white Ford Fusion parked outside the motel room door. It was the same car captured on surveillance cameras at a Mail Boxes Etc. store in Puerto Vallarta two days ago, when the fugitive had shown up to see if his prize money had arrived. Detectives had quickly determined that the fake passport used to secure the post office box for "Thomas L. Berry" had also been presented to the car rental agent at Benito Juárez International Airport, and it matched a one-way United Airlines ticket from JFK to Mexico City Wednesday evening.

"When are they going to get here? What are we supposed to do if he tries to run?"

"Patience, amigo. Patience. There's nowhere he can hide anymore."

Castillo checked his watch. The police most certainly should have arrived by now, which was a problem, because south of the border, the U.S. marshals weren't free to roam about like some posse of Lone Rangers. The apprehension of an international fugitive was designed to be a joint effort. There were procedures to follow—treaties and all sorts of shit said so. Problem was that some municipalities cooperated with the U.S. authorities and some didn't, because politics and bullshit knew no bounds.

He stared at the motel, weighing the facts. Certainly Alan Bateman couldn't be planning to drive east or south to Belize or Guatemala, knowing that border agents would immediately nab him. No, Bateman was going to attempt a getaway by sea. That had to be his plan. Why else would he have come to this seaport? At the docks, a few hundred dollars could buy him a stowaway's seat on a cargo ship or a fishing boat, no questions asked. Providing, of course, that the crewmen didn't recognize him and decide to cash in on his bounty. Whatever his plan, however, Castillo was determined to ruin it for him. Badly.

Given the motel's squalid condition, Castillo was surprised that the front desk manager had neither contacted the authorities nor attempted to kill the fugitive to score the huge bounty being offered by that *loco* Grim Reaper website. That kind of *dinero* could change a man's destiny. Castillo couldn't help but fantasize about the ways *he'd* spend it all, starting with a first-class ticket to Las Vegas for some epic debauchery—luxury suite at the MGM, marathon poker matches, bottomless cocktails served by topless waitresses, and a no-holds-barred threesome . . . He'd have it all.

"What do you think the police are waiting for?" Rivera said.

"Who the fuck knows," he muttered.

"Don't you think he might have already slipped out the back and walked down to the docks?" Rivera pointed out the windshield toward the dark expanse of the Gulf of Tehuantepec, downhill maybe a half kilometer to the west. There tankers were tethered to the inner harbor's piers, bathed in sodium lights. "It's right there."

"No," Castillo said unconvincingly. "Besides, the police chief said he'd post plainclothes officers down there."

"The chief also said he'd have officers *here*," Rivera scoffed.

"Fuck you, Hector. Just fucking relax, will you?"

"I'm just saying . . ."

When another five uneventful minutes went by, Castillo began to question his own logic. It *was* odd that the police had yet to show. So maybe they were hoping to catch the fugitive themselves without the meddling marshals watching?

Rivera tried again: "I say screw the police. We should go in there and—"

The motel room door opened.

Castillo leaned forward, gripping the steering wheel.

Out came a man dressed in shorts, a T-shirt, and sandals. Castillo grabbed his binoculars to have a closer look. *"Chingada madre."*

"That's him, right?"

"Oh, yes."

Thomas Berry's *el otro yo* was cautious and alert. They watched as he dipped back inside the motel room, then reemerged lugging a big canvas duffel bag, like the one Castillo used to carry baseball gear to his stepson's games. He pulled the door closed and walked quickly to the Fusion, loaded the bag in its trunk, and got behind the wheel.

"Fuck." Castillo pounded the steering wheel with his fist. "We can't let him go."

"We can detain him until the police get here . . . can't we?"

"We'll sure as fuck find out." Castillo grabbed his shotgun off the floor. "Let's go."

Rivera beamed a smile and pulled his Glock from the holster strapped below his Kevlar vest.

42.02

Alan Bateman slipped the key into the Fusion's ignition and started the engine. Only when he put the car in reverse did he glimpse the two armed men, maybe ten meters out, charging toward him beneath the glow of the streetlights. So he hit the gas. Hard.

That's when the detonator clip wedged beneath the right rear tire snapped shut to complete a circuit that sent an electrical charge to the blasting cap plugged into the block of C-4 strapped to a chunky magnet stuck to the gas tank.

The detonation was deafening.

The dazzling, all-consuming fireball was so fierce that Houdini himself would not have been able to escape it.

43.01 _____

@ Brooklyn
8:45:55 EDT

Novak had just finished his eggs and bacon and was on his second cup of coffee, reading the opinion columns in *The New York Times*—two journalists going head-to-head over Bounty4Justice, one positing it as an advocate for the disaffected masses, the other branding it a threat to both civilized society and the rule of law—when Knight called with the news of Alan Bateman's death by car bomb in Mexico.

"Jesus. That was fast," Novak said. "They're sure it was him?"

"The marshals had clear visual. There wasn't much left of him after they put out the fire, but they'll run the standard DNA tests anyway. They've also got dental implants that can confirm his identity. It's him. But look, I wouldn't ruin your Sunday morning to reminisce about a chump like Alan Bateman. There's something else, too. And it's a doozy."

Knight wasn't easily rattled, so Novak prepared for the worst. "All right. Hit me."

"It's Voronov. He's dead."

Novak felt his heart sink. He set down his coffee mug, suddenly feeling a bit light-headed. *Can't be,* he thought.

"They found him a couple hours ago," Knight said. "In his car, parked along the river in Moscow. They're claiming he had a heart attack. Considering the timing, it's bullshit, if you ask me."

Still stunned, Novak went quiet for a long moment.

"You still there?" Knight's voice called out through the receiver.

"Did he kill himself?"

"No one's saying. If it wasn't suicide, you can bet your ass it was a very clean hit ordered by the Kremlin or some billionaire oligarch who lost some money during that Web blackout yesterday. Don't hold your breath for an autopsy, is all I'm saying. I wanted to talk to you first, because I know how you are. One of the downsides of being a good guy is that you have a conscience, and you take things personally. Last thing I need is my trusty deputy feeling too down about it. It's a shame what happened and all, but there's no way we could possibly have foreseen *this*. And it's not like he was a Boy Scout, either. Understand?"

It wasn't Novak's first bout with guilt, and it certainly wouldn't be his last. In his line of work, feeling deeply shitty from time to time was an occupational hazard. "Yeah. It is what it is, I suppose. Not like it can be undone."

"Remember, I'm the one who authorized that teleconference with Voronov. And I know damn well that we didn't overstep our bounds. The way I see it, Voronov considered our proposal and acted on his own volition, even advised us that he'd consult his superiors before taking any decisive action. Can't see how you or I or the FBI can be faulted for that. Odds are he would have blocked the website with or without us putting in our two cents."

Knight's reasoning made Novak feel a little better. But Voronov had seemed like a decent man, and he certainly wasn't the first of his kind to die mysteriously in Russia. They played by very different rules over there. In fact, their tactics were not unlike those of Bounty4Justice, if less public.

"We have a big meeting tomorrow morning, and I need you to stay focused, okay?"

"Okay."

"Keep your chin up. Watch the game later, have a few beers. I'll see you bright and early tomorrow."

44.01

@ Manhattan
Monday, 10/30/2017
07:30:00 EDT

The strategy meeting took place in the stately executive suite on the twenty-third floor, where tall windows provided a fantastic view out over Federal Plaza to the South Street Seaport and the Brooklyn Bridge. Assistant Director in Charge Patricia Hartley occupied the head of the long table, with the rising sun at her back. Seated to her right was the cyber chief, James Cooper. To her left was the counterterrorism chief, Bonnie Karasowski-Fowler. The SACs had just returned from a weekend powwow at headquarters in Washington, and they both looked as if they'd gone through hell and back.

Seated at the opposite end of the table was Chief Tabatha Cranston from the DOJ's Southern District of New York, Criminal Division, flanked by two young, dapper deputy attorneys general. Knight, Novak, and Walter—the grunts of Operation CLICKKILL—filled the chairs in the middle of the table to Hartley's left, and sitting across the table from them were Captain Agner and his boss, Police Commissioner Robert Kemper.

Hartley thanked everyone for coming and quickly passed the baton to Karasowski-Fowler to begin the briefings.

"As you might imagine," the SAC said, "a dead congressman has everyone in Washington downright panicked. Not to mention the body count Bounty4Justice has racked up in only a few days. There's no terror threat bigger than anarchy. That said, the current thinking is that the criminal investigations—given their unique circumstances and the fact that there's no reliable way for our profilers to confidently pinpoint potential assassins in advance—are best handled at the regional level. Therefore, the response, sadly, promises to remain largely reactive."

Commissioner Kemper frowned. He had a habit of stroking his chin in confrontational situations, and from the looks of it, Novak thought he just might draw blood before they adjourned.

Kemper said, "Folks, we don't have the resources to provide any meaningful level of protection for all these new targets. We're barely keeping our head above water as it is. In less than a week, this damn thing's turned the city into a free-for-all. Now you're basically telling us to order more body bags?"

Hartley threw the SAC a lifeline: "Bob, we share your frustrations, believe me. We're just as stretched here in this office. If this were strictly a local issue, we could promise more support, but let's face it: Bounty4Justice has the whole country under siege. We can't go tripling the ranks overnight. You know that. So let's just hear what everyone has to say, and then we can try to figure things out."

Kemper's shoulders went slack, and he resumed the chin rubbing.

Karasowski-Fowler went on to summarize the steps headquarters was taking to coordinate efforts between the Bureau's fifty-six field offices and state and local police departments, how the reporting structure and processes would work going forward, and how information would be data-pooled so that statisticians could use correlation and regression to extrapolate behavioral trends. She offered her staff to assist the commissioner in holding town hall meetings with the local precincts, which he readily accepted. In closing, she reiterated that the Bureau was sailing in uncharted waters. "The way I see it, we're at the mercy of the technology," she concluded. "Until we crack that, we're just spinning our wheels."

On that note, the baton passed to the cyber chief.

Cooper cleared his throat and his jaw jutted forward, as it invariably did when his mind sought true north. "Simply put, everyone in Washington is finally figuring out what we've been trying to tell them all along: this is no ordinary botnet or rogue website, and our current tool kit, frankly, isn't up to the challenge of infiltrating Bounty4Justice." He detailed some of the intrusion attacks they'd attempted, to no avail—largely Structured Query Language script injections and other Trojan malware sent to the website's access points to sniff out vulnerabilities and nip at it around the edges. "The NSA's top brass were there, as expected, and they maintained that this is not blowback from the Snowden leaks."

He talked in detail about the ongoing analysis and tactical response undertaken at Fort Meade. It sure sounded to Novak like the nation's top cyberspies were feeling emasculated by Bounty4Justice, too. Not good.

"I caught quite a bit of heat for not moving more aggressively to take the website offline sooner, as you might imagine," the cyber chief said. "Then this incident in Russia went down on Saturday. Before breakfast, I'm a moron. After breakfast, I'm the genius who avoided a catastrophe here in the States."

He was rewarded with some reserved smiles.

"I want to thank my team for its due diligence and prudence." Cooper gave a nod to the opposite side of the table. "By now, everyone's heard that Russia is publicly accusing the U.S. of engaging in an all-out cyberwar. And, of course, there's the highly suspicious death of the Kremlin's media czar yesterday. For a long time, Putin's been accusing the CIA of inventing the Internet as a tool for espionage and disruption. Lord knows these latest developments only help him further his case in Russia. On the news this morning, I saw him spinning stories about how Max Voronov had been manipulated by CIA agents, and how they'd poisoned Max so he wouldn't talk. Buckle up, because there'll be plenty more to follow. Just another day in the Motherland."

Novak was relieved that Cooper and Hartley were taking the mishaps in Russia in stride. Still, he held himself accountable for his part in stirring up an international incident, and he felt terrible that Voronov had become the fall guy.

Cooper continued: "Needless to say, Bounty4Justice is now considered a national security threat, both foreign and domestic. That means the CIA will be pumping its informants for leads. It also means that our request for FISA warrants should be fast-tracked for FISC approval."

Hearing that the FBI now had its trump card, the trio from the Justice Department were all smiles. Novak could tell that Agner and Kemper seemed pleased, too, and with good reason. The eleven judges of the highly secretive Foreign Intelligence Surveillance Court had the authority to grant the FBI no-holds-barred permissions to weed out foreign intelligence agents operating within the United States. FISA had been dancing with the Bill of Rights in the interest of national security since its inception in 1978, and exponentially so in the wake of 9/11. Now it would be in the midst of the fray again.

"Our hope is that once the NSA can fully exploit its databases and capabilities," Cooper said, "we'll start connecting the dots. And in the past few days, we've identified plenty of dots."

Now the baton passed to the middle of the table, for the battle reports from the trenches.

"We've had a very busy week," Knight began.

Novak passed out printouts of his most up-to-date spreadsheet as Knight gave a brief status report on the targets, focusing mainly on the sixteen active targets that resided within the New York office's jurisdiction. He touched on the hostage rescue team's Virginia raid that netted Furlong, the patsy marine sniper with the rock-solid alibi, and added that the search was still under way for the real shooter, who'd stolen Furlong's identity. Then he shifted to a more upbeat tone as he recapped the interception of the cash shipment in Dallas and the raid on Echelon in Jersey City, which revealed how Bounty4Justice had distributed its novelty pledge pins via the Sorvino crime family.

"It's safe to say that we're hot on the money trail," Knight concluded.

Walter started off his brief by providing context for the Russian crisis. He explained that ransomware wasn't a new concept and described how for years cyberthugs had been spreading malware, such as the infamous CryptoLocker, which locked down hard drives with encryption software and demanded a fee, or ransom, for the decryption key. And techniques like DNS sinkholes and redirects—often employed by the FBI to divert malicious botnets before they reached their intended target servers—were being retooled by cybercriminals to carry out phishing scams that lured unsuspecting victims to look-alike banking and retail websites in order to capture personal data. In that respect, he explained, Bounty4Justice was putting a new spin on time-tested cyberschemes.

"What we've witnessed in Russia, however," Walter stressed, "is taking these tactics to an entirely new level. Hijacking the network of an entire *country* and possessing the technology to create the trip wires to set off that kind of response?" He sighed. "This is epic stuff. But we're making good headway in attacking the website at its periphery. I'm confident we'll soon be able to work our way to the middle."

He reported that the task force had initiated a number of honeypot operations, with NCFTA agents trolling chat rooms, posing as Bounty4Justice sympathizers. "Though we've heard nothing meaningful thus far," he said, "the fact remains that hackers like to brag. And a hacker who takes down Russia will eventually want the glory of a victory lap. We intend to be there when it happens."

Next, Hartley looked to Novak.

Novak did his best to bring everyone up to speed on what could be gleaned thus far about the mastermind's motives, which were slowly coming into focus. "We now know for sure that cash is being paid to these killers," he said, "which tells us that Bounty4Justice is making good on its promises. We also know that it expects its participants to play by the rules or it will turn on them, just as we've seen with Alan Bateman. Critically, this takedown of the Runet reinforces our assertion that the motive here is *not* money. If that were the case, Bounty4Justice would have skipped messing around with bounties and pledge pins and credit card networks, and it would have gone right for the big score. It would have *started* with Russia and demanded a fat monetary ransom before taking the chokehold off the Kremlin."

"So what exactly do you think they're after?" Commissioner Kemper asked.

Novak looked at his hands for a long moment. "At face value, the endgame might be the simplest explanation." Through his years of investigation, Occam's razor had been vindicated more often than not. "They may simply be out for blood and vigilante justice. However, I think we need to operate under the assumption that Bounty4Justice will continue to crank up its threat level. And if we don't crack the firewalls soon, there's no telling what target it might go after next. Nothing will be safe."

44.02

As the meeting wound down and the visitors filtered out of the conference room, Knight stayed behind with Walter and Novak. "See, what did I tell ya? Everything's fine."

No sooner had he said it than all three of their BlackBerrys pinged at once.

"That can't be good," Walter said, reaching for his phone. He read the text message displayed on his screen. His face went white. "What the fuck?"

Knight looked at his phone and frowned. "Son of a bitch."

Novak's Blackberry displayed his own version of the message they'd both received, personalized just for him:

AS OF 8:15 AM EDT, YOUR CURRENT BOUNTY IS $102,812
CURRENT STATUS: Guilty
FOR THE LATEST UPDATES, VISIT:
http://www.bounty4justice.com/ROMAN.NOVAK

45.01 _____

@ Georgetown, WashIngton, D.C.
08:17:11 EDT

Special Agent Corey Jones sat in the Chevy Yukon's passenger seat
sipping a Starbucks caffè mocha from a tall to-go cup that looked tiny
in his grande hand, weighing how best to pass along the details of the
new assignment to his partner, Special Agent Alex Vargas, in the driver's seat.

"That's the one," Jones said, pointing to the handsome brownstone with the cops huddled out on the stoop.

Vargas eased the Yukon to a stop alongside the Capitol Police patrol cars lining the curb. "Man. Look at all this. So much for being
incognito. What exactly did she do again?"

"She's the one they're blaming for those kids dying from bad
school lunches, up in New Hampshire."

"Oh, yeah. Her."

It had been all over the news. Senator Barbara Ascher had steered
contracts to her sister-in-law's food services company—despite its repeated health code violations—and the company shipped rancid
meat products to a bunch of middle schools. A couple dozen kids got
sick. Three died. Ascher also chaired the Defense Appropriations

Subcommittee, and an exposé in *The Washington Post* a couple months back had detailed how she'd accepted bribes to steer tens of millions in intelligence contracts to a firm named LaserLine Data. They were calling it "LaserGate." The press now portrayed her as nothing more than a kid-killing crony capitalist, one helluva double whammy for even the most astute politico.

Worse still, since the investigation into the alleged wrongdoings was incredibly slow-going, Bounty4Justice had added the senator to its target list and inspired anonymous informants to dredge up troves of private documents and damning emails that would expedite her prosecution—or her death, whichever came first. To that end, the website had also posted photos and uncomfortably intimate bios of Ascher, her entire family, and her business associates. *Some hard-core muckraking, even by Washington's standards,* thought Jones. Ever since Congressman Kenneth Krosby had gotten torched in his limo a few days ago, Capitol Hill no longer viewed Bounty4Justice as some "Gangnam Style" fad. It was now classified as a genuine terror threat. Funny, Jones thought, how plenty of unsavory folks had fallen prey to Internet assassins over the past week, but it took the death of one of their own for Washington to see things differently.

The FBI had arranged the family's relocation to this safe house in Georgetown—a block away from John F. Kennedy's former residence on N Street—where they were to remain under protective watch and lie low until federal investigators built their case against the senator. Then, by the looks of things, she'd likely be moved once more, to the safest of all confines: a federal penitentiary.

Given the senator's high profile and the credible threat against her, the president had issued an executive order to the Secret Service to assist the Capitol Police. Not exactly a plum assignment. But Jones and Vargas were the low men on the totem pole, and shit flows downhill. So here they were.

"Like what . . . we've gotta take her around town for the next few days?" Vargas asked.

"Something like that."

Vargas looked at him dubiously. "What's that mean?"

"You'll see."

45.02 _____

The assets were ready and waiting on the other side of the vestibule's glass door: seven-year-old Maximilian and his five-year-old sister, Samantha. They were dressed in navy plaid school uniforms and strapped into their backpacks.

"Oh, no," Vargas said. "No, no, *no*. I didn't sign up for *that*. I come to work to get *away* from that."

"Suck it up," Jones said in a hushed tone. "We've got a job to do. And remember to smile." He opened the door and proceeded inside.

"You're off my Christmas card list," Vargas grumbled as he trailed in behind Jones. "Most definitely."

Inside, there were gorgeous parquet wood floors in a herringbone pattern, and intricate, glossy woodwork and stacked crown moldings, and actual plaster walls and ceilings, and a brick fireplace with a hand-carved mantel—all built the hard way, by craftsmen, long before the advent of drywall and plastic. There was a lot of history here, Jones imagined, and plenty of secrets. If only walls could talk.

The senator came clicking down the staircase in glossy heels, immaculate in a tailored red pantsuit, Hermès silk scarf, glittering jewelry, and flawless makeup and hair, looking more like the home's showcase realtor than its newest occupant. The senator wasn't scheduled to leave the house today, but with all the police officers coming and going, Jones figured she still had an image to maintain. Or maybe her intent was to portray some sense of normalcy for the sake of the children.

"Daniel," she called up the steps to the second floor. "Take a break and come say goodbye to the kids."

"I'm busy right now, Barbara," came her husband's gruff reply from somewhere upstairs. "Just . . . I'm busy."

The senator smiled tightly.

She introduced herself to Jones and Vargas with a firm handshake, then turned to the children. "These nice men are here to give you two a ride to school. So be sure to mind your manners." She bent at the waist and gave her daughter a peck on the cheek. "I love you, Sammie-bear," she said softly.

"I love you, Mommy," the little girl replied, staring curiously at Vargas, who stood by the door as rigid as a drill sergeant.

The senator gently squeezed Max's cheeks together and tipped his head up a bit, trying to force his pouty eyes up from the floor. "Hey. Look at me."

Max complied, frowning. "I don't want to be here. We don't belong here."

"It's going to be great. You'll see. Give it a chance. I love you."

The boy's eyes went back to the floor.

"Excuse me, young man," she said. "That's not how we do things around here."

"I love you, Mom," he said halfheartedly.

"Okay. That's better." She kissed him on top of the head. "You two have fun at school. I hear it's an awesome place."

Vargas held the door open, and the kids shuffled out into the vestibule.

"I know you've heard a lot of bad things about me," she said to Jones. "But those kids are—" Her brightly colored lips drew tight. "Well, just please take good care of them. They're all I have left."

"They're in good hands, Senator," Jones said. "I promise."

46.01 _____

@ Manhattan
08:43:47 EDT

Novak stood beside Knight as Walter brought up the Bounty4Justice
home page on the big monitor in his office. He scrolled through the
active U.S. targets. Sure enough, all three of them were there, with
generous bounties creeping upward, American flag icons, head-shot
photos, the works. Team CLICKKILL was officially on the chopping
block. Their alleged accomplice in the negotiations with Russia, Fredrick Shrayer, showed up right along with them. Each of their profile
pages listed the same three allegations:

- Conspiring to sabotage Bounty4Justice
- Harmful activities to advance Internet censorship
- Complicity in the murder of Maxim Voronov

"Jeez," Walter said. "Sure doesn't seem worthy of a death sentence. 'Complicity' is a bit of a stretch, wouldn't you say? It's not like we held a gun to Voronov's head or shot him up with cyanide."

Each of their profile pages featured a video window that, when activated, played their entire videoconference with Voronov—starting with the introductions that began the meeting. Nothing ambiguous about it.

Knight said, "I'm wondering how in hell someone got ahold of that video."

"Didn't come from this office," Walter said emphatically. "That much I can tell you. I was the only one in the room with you guys that day, and I certainly didn't keep records of anything. And it couldn't be Shrayer or his people, because they were in Voronov's building at the time. In the video, you can clearly see the Russian flag and the picture of Pootie on the wall. So it *had* to be their people."

"Not looking forward to that phone call with Shrayer," Knight muttered. "He's wrapped tight on a good day, and he's going to be mighty pissed."

"God," Walter said. "How am I supposed to tell my wife?" He scrolled through his vital statistics, his family photos, personal information . . . all out there for the world to see. "I'll need to pull the kids out of school, call my bank—this is a goddamn nightmare."

Novak knew Knight was in the same boat, equally compromised and laid bare, but the boss kept his worries to himself, per usual—stuffed it all down. Relatively speaking, Novak was on easy street—he had identity-theft protection, no kids, no damning secrets. Luckily, his sister and her family hadn't been dragged onto his FAMILY AND ASSOCIATES page. But both his parents were there, as if there wasn't enough stress on them already. One thing was certain: the sons of bitches running Bounty4Justice had just made this personal.

Walter said, "I'm guessing its algorithm picked up on all the media coverage and dragnetted us. Could even be that the Kremlin submitted that video and convinced half of Russia to go online and nominate us. You know, to pass the buck."

"Could also be that our mastermind is singling us out," Knight said. "Staging his own little vendetta. Like you said, Walter, it seems petty in the grand scheme of things."

"I mean, we're just doing our job here," Walter said. "Am I right? We're not the only law enforcement agency in the world trying to put a stop to this. So why pick on us?"

"Hey, I'm with you," Knight said. "I get it, buddy."

Novak pointed to the pie chart next to Walter's name. It was just over half filled with red, the rest green. "Look at that. You're only two percentage points away from swinging the vote over to innocent. That's pretty damn close. Check Tim's. Shrayer's and mine, too."

Walter paged back and clicked on Knight's profile; the vote there was teetering on deadlock. Same with Shrayer's. Same with Novak's.

"What about it?" Walter asked Novak.

"Walter, it's obvious," he replied. "We need more votes in our favor."

47.01

@ South Kensington, London
13:45:16 GMT

Deputy Director Charles Burls parked the Land Rover along the curb at a comfortable distance from the Windsor Arms—a six-story edifice inspired by London's ubiquitous Georgian style, elegant and sophisticated, with penthouse views of the Royal Albert Hall and Kensington Palace. Cooped up in that posh penthouse, under MI5's guard, was Bounty4Justice's highest-value U.K. target: Lord Andrew Smith, Sixth Baron of Twyford, the alleged "puppetmaster of capitalism," accused of brainwashing Parliament to systematically eviscerate the British working class to benefit the ultrarich. Current bounty: £695,000.

Directly across the street from the building, a much different scene: along the wide sidewalk, police in full riot gear formed a human chain in front of a raucous mob of protestors—hundreds of them, many tossing back the contents of thermoses, bottles, and cans, and not simply to fight off the chilly air. They pumped picket signs above their heads that said, DOWN WITH THE ROBBER BARON. Their spokeswoman, wearing a yellow rain slicker, stood atop a bench, chanting through a bullhorn: *"THE RICH PAY NO TAX, WHILE WORKERS GET THE AX!"* A huddle of BBC, Sky News, and ITN field correspondents and cameramen had gathered around her to memorialize the moment. Flames flickering out of half a dozen rubbish bins gave it all a rather medieval feel.

Burls checked his watch and turned to the scruffy-looking twenty-something in the passenger seat next to him, hunched over a laptop—the NCCU's prodigy hacker. "It's time, Jeremy."

Jeremy nodded without taking his eyes from the screen.

Burls picked up his secure talkie. "Is everyone ready?" He waited for roll call. This was a one-shot deal with a thousand variables that needed to perfectly balance, and his nerves were buzzing. "All right, people. Let's begin." With that, Operation HUCKLEBERRY FINN went live.

First, an MI5 agent dressed as a chauffeur emerged from a limousine parked at the curb outside the main entrance to the building. He opened the car's rear door and stood tall, waiting for his passenger. About two minutes later, three police officers—none of whom were privy to the operation—emerged from the lobby and came out onto the sidewalk to scout the area. One of them gave an all-clear gesture to someone still inside the building, which also served as the "go" signal for a young female agent, disguised as a mail courier, who came whisking by Burls's Land Rover on a bicycle, pedaling fast toward the scene.

Burls watched the bobbies signal for her to stop. Feigning annoyance at the delay, she took out her smartphone, and the video feed from a tiny camera integrated into her bike helmet transmitted to Jeremy's laptop to clearly show the phone's display and the application that was pinging Wi-Fi signals in the immediate vicinity. She tapped on the third device on the list that came up, denoted by the abbreviation for a cardiac pacemaker that had been described in great detail on the baron's Bounty4Justice profile page. Her screen refreshed and showed a dashboard of control settings for the device. It was the actual software, sent straight from the manufacturer. Burls needed this to be as authentic as possible.

The baron emerged from the entryway, flanked by two MI5 bodyguards, wearing a beige Brioni rain jacket over his custom chalk-striped suit. He looked over to the mob and managed to convey utter disgust with a slight curl of his lip, which wasn't part of the act. *No wonder Bounty4Justice's algorithm selected Smith*, thought Burls. The man had a gift for baiting the common hordes. Yesterday, as Burls had pitched this ambitious plan to him, the baron had peered out his lofty window at the mob below, saying, "Frankly, I don't know why they are all so bloody upset. They're acting like a bunch of wild animals. They should be *thanking* me for saving this country from sinking back to a failed welfare state." His supreme self-regard made him the ideal partner for their run at Bounty4Justice.

"THERE HE IS!" screeched the spokeswoman's amplified voice. The mob booed and jeered, and the police in riot gear tightened their cordon. She began a looping chant: *"DOWN WITH THE ROBBER BARON! DOWN WITH THE ROBBER BARON!"*

The baron ignored them, and the bodyguards motioned for him to get moving to the limousine, which sat roughly ten paces ahead. Burls remained laser focused on counting each of the baron's steps. *One . . . two . . . three—*

The courier raised her phone as if she were taking a picture of the baron. She pressed her thumb on a setting button that would send the pacemaker into overdrive. The helmet cam perfectly framed the prompt that flashed on the phone's display: ARE YOU SURE YOU WANT TO ACCEPT THIS CHANGE? She tapped her thumb on it again. CHANGE ACCEPTED.

"Rodney, do it now," Burls said in the talkie.

One of the bodyguards gave the baron's arm a subtle squeeze. A second later, Smith jerked back as if clubbed in the breastbone—eyes wide with alarm, hands swinging up violently to claw at the phantom pain in his chest. He crumpled to his knees and tottered forward; the bodyguards grabbed him before his head struck the cement.

Confusion swept through the onlookers.

Like a seasoned actor, the baron stuck to the script—staying down, rolling onto his side, writhing as the bodyguards dropped to their knees to assist him. Then he went rigid.

An eerie silence fell over the crowd.

The taller bodyguard yelled to the bobbies, "Call an ambulance!"

The mob flip-flopped from confusion to elation, as if witnessing the England national team moving the ball upfield at a World Cup match. The shorter bodyguard tried to find a pulse on the baron's neck; after a few seconds, he shook his head. The mob began cheering, people jumping up and down, and high-fiving, and hugging one another as if their team had just scored a goal, while the riot police stayed on high alert and kept their Plexiglas shields high and tight.

"Excellent. Now let's move him inside," Burls commanded through the talkie.

The bodyguards hooked the baron under the knees and armpits, hoisted him up, and quickly carried him back into the building.

"I must say," Jeremy said, reviewing the video capture. "It's bloody convincing."

47.02

By 2:00 P.M., U.K. media outlets from Twitter to BBC News were abuzz about the baron's rumored death—despite the fact that the body remained out of view on the sixth floor of the Windsor Arms and that neither the authorities nor insiders had yet officially confirmed or denied the claim. Nonetheless, the breaking news was picked up in short order by Reuters, with footage of the protestors celebrating the baron's demise beamed round the world, the excessive liquid refreshment making the scene reminiscent of the climax of a New Year's Eve countdown. This clip, in turn, lit up global newswires, social media sites, and the blogosphere. Thanks to the NCCU's ingenious campaign of misdirection, rumors of the baron's high-tech assassination by an enterprising hacker were well on their way to becoming gospel.

Meanwhile, in the penthouse's masterpiece kitchen, Jeremy sat hunched over his laptop, doctoring the helmet-cam video file, splicing it with top secret code copied from an encrypted flash drive that connected like a fob to his key ring.

Cocooned within his opulent study, the baron reviewed his press while sipping brandy as stage two of Operation HUCKLEBERRY FINN commenced.

Burls ordered the cybertechs back at the Home Office to begin flooding the Twittersphere with rumors that the police were canvassing West London for a suspected cyberassassin spotted by BBC News cameras outside the Windsor Arms at the time of the incident.

Then the taller bodyguard came into the room and announced, "Sir, the ambulance has arrived."

"Excellent," Burls said, checking his watch. He glanced over at Jeremy, who was busily working his magic, cutting and pasting lines of code. Despite Bounty4Justice's sentient functionality, the analysts at GCHQ had theorized that the kill-confirmation video submissions had to be authenticated by a human being, who would cross-reference the claim to news events in order to make a final determination as to whether the bounty would be awarded. Human intervention meant human error, the logic went. And human error meant an opportunity for exploitation. "How much longer, Jeremy?"

Jeremy threw up one hand imperiously. Hackers were a quirky bunch, and his was the most critical function of the operation. So Burls gave him his space and waited in silence.

Finally, Jeremy eased back in the chair and ran his fingers through his tangled hair. "Right, then. Brilliant. Once this file is uploaded and opened by the recipient, we'll need him to watch it for just under ten seconds or so for the scripts to fully execute. Then we'll have complete access to everything on the other side—hard drive, keystrokes, webcam, microphone, *everything*. He won't know what hit him."

"All right," Burls said. "Go ahead and submit the video. In a little while, we'll bring out the body."

48.01

@ Washington, D.C.
08:49:01 EDT

The Ascher children had been enrolled for guest visitation at a venerable private institution that occupied a full city block in the heart of
Georgetown. With a big old church surrounded by pristine red-brick
buildings, the complex radiated privilege. Considering all the open
ground to cover, Jones thought homeschooling would've been the
smarter choice. Lock the doors, shut the shades, hide the kids out of
view in the brownstone's basement. However, the grand objective
was to have the children maintain a normal life and keep them oblivious to the fact that Mommy had a $750K purse hanging over her
head.

Jones turned his head to the backseat. "This looks like a really nice
school. You guys excited?"

Samantha shrugged. "I dunno."

Max made a sour face and stared out the window.

In the driver's seat, Vargas looked equally dour. He'd barely said a
word to the kids. Jones figured his partner, with five children of his own
back home, simply had nothing left to give these two. In all fairness, he
had to admit that when one joined the nation's most elite law enforce-

ment agency, babysitting detail wasn't exactly what one envisioned. At least Max and Sam were cute and polite. Just ordinary little people caught up in extraordinary circumstances. And with Bounty4Justice using them as leverage against their mom, the threat *was* real.

Vargas bypassed the line of cars at the main entrance, where the trophy moms waited to hand off their precious cargo, and circled to the back of the campus. At the gate for the service entrance, he held his badge to the window for the elderly security guard. The man had already been advised of their arrival and snapped a crisp salute before shuffling back to his kiosk to activate the gate. "That's gonna be you, cuz," Vargas said to Jones, grinning and pointing to the guard. "You wait and see. Just give it a few years."

"Screw you. You'll be right there with me."

"Not so sure, my man. That's an awfully tiny booth."

The gate tilted up. Vargas saluted the guard and proceeded along the narrow driveway between the buildings and into a spacious court-yard, where he parked in the guest slot closest to the bright yellow doors designating the administrative entrance.

"All right, kids," Jones said, "let's go see your new digs."

The agents got out and helped the kids step down from the Yukon.

Samantha looked up at Jones and said, "You're not coming into my classroom, are you?"

"Probably not. Why, do you want me to?"

She shook her head. "It's okay. I can handle it. Mom says I'm a big girl now." She reached up and held Jones's big paw. "Besides, I think you're way too big to sit in a kid desk."

"I suppose I am," he said. He didn't have children of his own, but his wife was in the end zone, waiting for a Hail Mary. He'd been re-luctant to take the plunge into fatherhood. Lots of unresolved issues with the way he'd grown up, in the Bronx, plus some mental baggage from all the shit he'd seen over in the Middle East when he'd worked Special Ops. Still, Samantha *was* selling him on the idea.

Vargas circled the SUV, traipsing behind young Max, who looked utterly morose. Vargas just shook his head, as if he'd been subjected to this mood a million times before, back home.

They didn't see or hear the runners until the very last instant—two wiry guys, wearing some crazy-ass Halloween masks, sprinting silently, as if they'd materialized out of thin air. They ran straight at Samantha, scooped her up, and whisked her from Jones's grasp. Just like that.

"Watch him!" Jones yelled to Vargas, pointing toward Max, who'd responded in the worst way imaginable: by running off. Vargas pulled out his SIG Sauer 9mm and chased after the boy.

Jones was already in full sprint, closing the gap to Samantha, who was ten, maybe fifteen yards ahead, screaming and thrashing in the arms of the masked man, who carried her like a rolled-up carpet. Out across the courtyard, he spotted a second pair of masked sprinters swooping in to intercept the boy. "Vargas! Two o'clock!" he yelled over his shoulder, pointing at them.

At six-four, 215, and just a month shy of thirty, Jones had achieved what he'd deemed his peak fitness level. He was a machine. A goddamn sinewy badass weapon forged of muscle. At least that's what he told himself in order to tap into his adrenaline reserve. This would be the true test. This was the moment that would define the next decade. Somewhere behind him, he heard the *blam-blam!* of Vargas's pistol. *Damn.* No time to look back.

Then came the sound of screeching tires, and a black van skidded out from around the building, gunning straight for him. That pissed him off. Now all the pistons were firing, and he was nearly on top of the masked duo. In midstride, he pulled his gun and fired at the van's windshield, five shots in rapid succession. Didn't stop the van from swerving right at him, and he barely dodged its front bumper with some fancy footwork harkening back to his college football days. The van skidded to a stop, its side door slid open, and another masked man materialized. This one swung a gun point-blank at him and squeezed off a couple of shots aimed squarely at his torso. Jones had his vest on, and he hoped that the jabbing sensations he felt against his ribs—invisible fists knocking him sideways, nearly making him stumble—would leave only bruises. Regaining his footing, he surged ahead, at the heels of Samantha's abductors, with the runners directly in the gunman's line of fire. The shots stopped coming his way.

He heard Vargas firing rapidly. That father of five was once a fucking Olympic marksman. *Look out, fellas, you're all toast,* he thought.

He pushed himself to the limit, flicked his SIG Sauer under a parked car, and dove at the abductors, in the middle, hooking each man around the neck while throwing his bulk sideways for torque. That slight spin brought everyone down into a tumbling heap. Samantha screamed and rolled off to the side.

Up close like this, Jones had learned early on, martial arts and complicated spins were useless. Forget the Hollywood bullshit. It was all about dominance and position, and fists and elbows and knees, Bronx-style. He jumped up, fast, and dropped right down again, using his right knee as a pile driver against the first guy's head, which was still low to the ground. He heard the dry crack of the skull and a whimper. He snapped back up to a standing position. The taller man had also been quick to get to his feet, his wolfman mask turned sideways. Jones lunged at him and locked his arm around the guy's neck while sweeping his legs out to get him back down on the ground. Then he squeezed the arm lock hard. Really hard. Until there was no resistance . . . no movement.

That's when he saw the gunman from the van standing in front of him, not even three paces away, wearing a Disney princess mask—Jones couldn't decide if it was the mermaid or the one from that new movie that had come out just this past summer—his weapon aimed directly at Jones's head. *Game over,* he thought. *Blaze of glory and all that, but I'm going to die at the hands of a goddamn princess.* He heard himself assuring glibly: *They're in good hands, Senator . . . I promise.* Yeah, right.

Another gunshot sounded, like the loud crack of a cherry bomb, and he knew he was dead. But the princess mask spat red, and the shooter recoiled and crumpled to the ground.

Behind Jones, the old man from the gate came trotting over, his pistol still puffing smoke.

"They broke through the gate! Are you okay?"

At first Jones didn't respond, just looked out across the courtyard. Then he saw Vargas walking toward him, towing Max by the arm.

"Yeah. We're good."

49.01

@ Long Island
09:38:07 EDT

Michaels met Special Agent Tammy Reynolds at the Panera in North
Babylon. They ordered coffee and scones at the counter, Michaels's
treat, then sat at a bistro table near the window, away from the wan-
dering ears of a retirees' book club and some middle-aged men
slouching in the comfy leather chairs, silently poking around on their
laptops.

Tammy was a super-fit, forty-four-year-old brunette with a Whar-
ton MBA whose idea of relaxation was competing in triathlons—a
fireplug of a woman: fast mover, fast talker. She was based out of the
Secret Service field office in Newark, New Jersey.

"Thanks for finding the time to meet with me," Michaels said.

"Don't mention it," she said. "Gives me a good excuse to take a
break and have a little girl time."

Long Island was a hotbed for counterfeiting and money laundering, but Newark was an even bigger one, so Michaels knew that
Reynolds was burning the candle at both ends. When people typically thought about the Secret Service, they pictured big men wearing dark suits and sunglasses and earpieces who secured the president's

motorcade or the press area out in the Rose Garden. Few thought about the Tammys of the agency, even though the Secret Service Division had been established in 1865 as an enforcement arm of the Department of Treasury, at a time when the fledgling U.S. government was grappling with the flood of counterfeit money in circulation after the Civil War. It wasn't until President William McKinley's assassination, in 1901, that the Secret Service began taking on the responsibilities of protecting presidents and skewing its ranks to giant rough men.

"You hear about this thing with Barbara Ascher's kids?" Tammy asked.

"Yeah. Unbelievable."

"Can you imagine if something had happened to those kids? God. As a mother, it just sends shivers down my spine. I don't care what she did, but this is going too far. It's like there's nowhere to hide from this nutty website. It's a damn menace." She shook her head. "Anyway, let's hold off on the shop talk. First, I want to hear how you're doing."

Once again a bachelorette, Michaels had little to tell about since last they'd met, other than a jaunt to Barbados in September, a couple of good movies she'd seen, and licking her wounds from her most recent breakup, a few months back, which by most measures had gone rather smoothly—just two grown-ups who'd squared up to the fact that great sex couldn't compensate for the true chemistry needed to carry on through the golden years.

Reynolds said that she was training for an upcoming race in Georgia, then shared the antics of her two teenage boys, complete with visuals from her phone's picture gallery. She talked about her husband, Ted, a freelance network security consultant, who was all jazzed up about the windfall he anticipated, thanks to Bounty4Justice scaring the shit out of every IT person in the world. And that segued nicely into a quick recap concerning their most recent mutual investigation.

"I heard about our pal Alan Bateman," Reynolds said with a wicked smile. Bateman's Medicare scam, at heart, had been one big financial fraud, laundered on the back end by the Armenian crime syndicate; this connection had, by default, brought Tammy into the mix.

"Crazy, right?" Michaels said.

"I'd say. You know that car bombing is the MO of the Armenians, right? That's their shtick: the chip clip under a rear tire. There's been no kill-confirmation video yet. But you watch. Mark my word, they won't find anyone to blame, and that bounty's gonna sit there. There won't be a video."

"Revenge is a bitch."

"Please. Bateman had a death wish the moment he got into bed with them. Those Armenians are ruthless. Between you and me, I say good riddance. The world's a better place without that lying prick. Though it's too bad we've lost our key witness." She sipped some coffee. "I hear you're working with Tim Knight and Roman Novak. That's a strong team."

"They sure are."

"Mmm, that Novak is a cutie." She bit her lower lip.

Tammy would know, thought Michaels, because she'd consulted closely with Novak during Chase Lombardi's money-intensive investigation.

"Once you're finally ready to move on," Tammy suggested, "I'd say he'd be a good place to start. Just something to think about."

Michaels felt her cheeks get warm. Novak certainly was a catch. Handsome. Smart. Funny. Honest. The kind of man you could age with without sacrificing the physical chemistry along the way. What was there *not* to like? And she'd felt a spark between them from the start. But the idea of dating someone from work seemed like a deal breaker. Still . . .

"So tell me about this adventure of yours in Dallas."

Michaels gave Tammy the blow by blow of her Cagney and Lacey stint with Agent Simmons and described how some good timing and a bit of luck had helped them net the first bounty confiscation in the investigation. "Can you believe that someone would put all that cash in the mail?"

"Sure," Tammy said matter-of-factly. "We see it all the time. You don't really think anyone actually checks all those packages, do you? The postal service is hurting as it is. Can you imagine if word got out that they were opening people's mail?"

Michaels took out her phone. "I want you to have a look at what we found."

She showed Tammy the pictures she'd taken in the back office of the truck-repair shop: the cardboard box, the bogus shipping label, the paperback novels that had been used as filler, the banded heaps of cash, and, most important, those unusual foil wrappers, which the forensic team had dismissed as superfluous. Tammy's eyes, however, lit up the moment she saw the image. They grew even brighter when Michaels pulled a sample of the foil wrapper from her purse.

"Now, isn't that interesting," Tammy said, rubbing the material between her fingertips.

"You've seen this before?"

"You bet I have. It just doesn't make a whole lot of sense that Bounty4Justice would—" She paused to think it through. "Actually, it makes perfect sense."

"You're killing me right now. Tell me."

"Sorry. Yeah, we come across this sort of packaging every now and then. Even more so lately. In fact, the DEA has made a few confiscations over the past few months, right here on Long Island. Except the packages I've seen came in on a boat. Looked just like your pictures."

"What, you mean drug money?"

"Exactly."

49.02

"These cartels stockpile cash," Tammy explained. "They maintain a big inventory, and they've learned that when you keep huge stashes of money, the elements tend to take a toll. A *big* toll. They call it a 'critter commission.' I'm talking about rodents, insects, humidity, you name it. Basically, it's tough to store cash in a hostile environment. Even harder to transport it from place to place in bulk without damaging it. And these characters move it by sea, by land, by air, through jungles . . . everywhere. Hell, we've even intercepted home-made submarines stuffed with cash and drugs."

"So these wrappers are meant to protect the bills?"

"Right. There's even this residue here, on the inside . . ." Tammy turned the swatch over from the shiny side to the dull side and rubbed her pinkie on the powdery film. "It doubles as a drying agent and a repellent for the critters and bugs. Let's face it: nobody wants to be paid with rotten bills. Kind of defeats the purpose."

Clever, thought Michaels. When all was said and done, every good business boiled down to quality control—drug dealers, auto makers, and clothing stores alike.

"Let's have a look at that shipping label again," Tammy said.

Michaels scrolled to the picture and enlarged it for her.

"Massena, New York," she said. "Makes sense."

"Why's that?"

"Massena's just across the St. Lawrence River from Ontario. That's a popular crossing point. ATF and DEA are constantly nabbing smug-glers in that area. Everyone forgets that our northern border is three times longer than the southern border, and they beat the drum for a fence down there. We've got over five thousand miles of exposure up north, lots of it rugged country and rivers and lakes. There's a damn good reason they call it 'the longest undefended border.' No way in hell we can police it. Even if we try to, the smugglers tunnel under-ground, kinda like those Palestinians do over in Gaza when they sneak into Israel with bombs."

"So Massena is close enough for a smuggler to bring a package into the U.S. and put it through the mail?"

Reynolds nodded unequivocally. "The border patrol is looking for guns and cigarettes and methamphetamines and marijuana. Oh, and heroin, too. Trust me, your box of books there"—she tipped her head at Michaels's phone—"wouldn't even blip on their radar. In fact, I wouldn't be surprised if someone just drove it across the bridge, mixed in with some other boxes. No tunnels required."

"But I thought all the drug dealers were pushing product through the Mexican border?"

"You're thinking of cocaine. These cartels up north don't go after that market. They've learned not to mess around with the Mexican drug lords. Plus, it has more to do with *who* is distributing this stuff to begin with. Up north, most immigrants coming into Canada are primarily from Asia. With them come all the connections to the criminal elements back in their homeland. That's why trafficking in drugs like opiates is the niche up there."

"But this makes no sense," Michaels said, staring at the swatch. "Why would Bounty4Justice work with drug smugglers?"

"Come on, Rosemary. You know that smugglers run two businesses: distributing drugs or weapons or slaves or what have you . . . and laundering money. Lots and lots of money changing hands. *Cash* money. To me, this all makes perfect sense," she said, holding up the swatch. "Think about it: how else is Bounty4Justice going to monetize millions of digital dollars without inciting suspicion or raising red flags at some banks? Let me tell you, nowadays there's a *gigantic* online market for laundering. Think of it like this: one guy has the problem of turning something of value into cash, maybe a cargo load of stolen cars or electronics or a few kilos of cocaine, while the other guy has the problem of turning huge amounts of cash into something of value, like cars or electronics or houses or boats. So they swap, or one takes a cut to service the needs of the other. Or a third guy steps in as a facilitator. The black market has gotten very fucking sophisticated, let me tell you, and it functions pretty much like the legitimate one, just without the storefronts and paper trails. In fact, I'd say that makes it even *more* sophisticated, because you need to be clever to survive—it's literally a cutthroat business."

Michaels sipped her coffee and tried to frame it all in her head. This was a granddaddy twist in the investigation.

"So listen to your girlfriend Tammy. Because the bottom line is this: from all that you've just shown me, I'd say that Bounty4Justice is using these smuggling syndicates as its ATM."

50.01 _____

@ South Kensington, London
14:35:16 GMT

In the elevator car, Burls and three MI5 agents dressed as paramedics surrounded the stretcher bearing the body bag. Zipped inside was a life-sized CPR training dummy. The media had to confirm Lord Andrew Smith's death or the video kill claim Jeremy had submitted to Bounty4Justice wouldn't be taken seriously. Somewhere in the world, on some computer—maybe in a library or a coffee shop or the basement of some foreign intelligence agency or in the guts of a sentient machine—that Trojan video file was now sitting in an in-box waiting to be opened. Waiting to poison the well. Burls felt like an engineer at mission control awaiting transmission from a lunar probe on the dark side of the moon.

"Once we get outside, we move quickly," Burls told them. "Everyone remain calm and stay focused."

Emerging into the lobby, the crew carefully pushed the stretcher toward the front entryway, its rubber wheels squeaking along the marble floor tiles, while the building manager and his desk staff looked on somberly, trying to process the idea that the Windsor Arms's most prestigious tenant was checking out for good.

Outside, parked in place of the limousine, was an ambulance with its blue roof lights flashing. A fourth MI5 agent, uniformed as its driver, circled around back of the vehicle to open the rear doors.

The doorman and one of the bobbies held open the front doors, and the raucous sounds of the mob—now swollen by the news of the baron's death—assaulted the lobby.

They made their way outside and across the sidewalk, just as Burls's cellphone sang the arrival of a new text blast from Bounty4Justice. A couple of his agents' phones sounded as well, and even from across the street he could hear a cacophony of ringtones rising within the mob, as if a legion of digital demons had swooped in from the netherworld. Burls felt a chill.

"Ignore that," he snapped to his team. "Get on with it *quickly*. And leave straightaway."

A murmur swept through the crowd, the shriek of their spokeswoman rising above it through her bullhorn: *"LIES! THE BARON LIVES! THEY LIED TO US!"*

The crowd roared and surged forward. Burls turned and saw fear in the eyes of his agents. "Get moving! Go!"

The doorman backed away from the entrance and smartly set off in a sprint down the sidewalk.

"NO MORE LIES! NO MORE LIES!"

Burls darted back inside and screamed to the manager and the staff: "Get out of here, and make it bloody fast!" As they all disappeared through the door behind the front desk, he sprinted back to his men outside the entryway.

The enraged mob was now engaged in a full-on shoving match with the riot police. But the shields formed a line, not a circle, and the protestors began spilling out from the sides and stampeding across the street, headed straight for the paramedics doggedly positioning the stretcher to load it into the ambulance. As the outliers and the agents engaged in a struggle for the "body," one of the protestors yanked the bag's zipper down. Then the situation escalated to a whole new level; the roar was deafening as protestors muscled aside Burls's men, freed the dummy baron from the body bag, and raised it high for all to see—an effigy of betrayal.

Burls and his unit retreated to the lobby, the mob not far behind them, heading directly for the front doors of the Windsor Arms like peasants storming the castle. All that was missing were the pitchforks and flaming torches. The three bobbies, fumbling for their batons and pepper spray, were shoved aside, and bodies crashed into the doors, shattering the glass into thousands of tiny pebbles, which went skittering across the marble floor to Burls's feet as he stabbed the elevator's control button again and again.

DING!

The elevator doors opened, and Burls followed his men inside. As the lift jostled and began its ascent, he could hear shouting and crashing in the lobby below. He looked at the meddlesome text message displayed on his mobile to see precisely what had nettled the mob.

URGENT: REGIONAL ACTION ALERT
TARGET: ANDREW SMITH, autocrat, UK
STATUS: Unconfirmed
BOUNTY: £1,627,444 ‹‹REINSTATED @2x››
We have received credible intelligence that contrary to news reports, Baron Andrew Smith remains alive and well under the guard of British intelligence. Such ploys to shield targets from proper justice will not be tolerated. As per section 23 of our user agreement, the bounty for this target has been reactivated and doubled.
http://www.bounty4justice.com/ALERTS/ANDREW.SMITH

All Burls could think: *How could it know?*

50.02 _____

The elevator doors opened on the sixth floor, and Burls hit the red STOP button to freeze the car. He could hear the oscillating wails of klaxons off in the distance. "We've got a situation," he told the guards manning the doors to the penthouse. "Take the baron into the kitchen. We need to evacuate the building immediately." They disappeared inside, but before he followed them, he pushed through the fire door to the side of the elevator and peered over the railing, down the throat of the switchback steps. Four levels below, and all the way down to the bottom of the shaft, dozens of hands grabbed at the spindly steel railings and were quickly moving upward. "Bloody hell." Mercifully, the fire door locked from the inside. He secured it, scrambled into the penthouse, and turned the dead bolts and locks on the front entry's heavy walnut double doors.

In the kitchen, the MI5 guards stood in a circle around the baron, weapons drawn. Jeremy was still seated at the counter, staring gravely at his laptop and the two words displayed on the screen in a bold oversized font:

NICE TRY

50.03

"I need everyone out to the freight elevator. Move!" Burls barked.

Jeremy snapped his laptop shut and scrambled after the others. As Burls turned to follow them, he caught a glimpse through the French doors of men emerging from the fire escape, out at the edge of the rooftop terrace. "Faster!" he yelled to the group.

The guards grabbed the baron by the elbows, funneled down the hall and out the penthouse's rear door, then raced through the service corridor to the freight elevator. An earsplitting bang emanated from a nearby metal fire door and its hardware popped out, nuts and bolts skittering across the floor tiles.

Burls jabbed his finger at the control panel. Finally, he heard the machinery deep in the shaft engage.

A second huge impact sounded at the fire door; then the door was pulled open, metal twisting and grinding, and a fellow of Bunyanesque proportions stood there, grinning, cradling a sledgehammer. When he saw the baron, his eyes lit up. "There he is!"

A horde of burly men in flannel and denim spilled out from the stairwell, brandishing every implement they'd found along their ascent—fire axes and fire extinguishers, broom handles and metal pipes—and blitzed forward like marauding, nitro-fueled latter-day Vikings.

The elevator door opened, and the agents manhandled the baron into the car. One of the bodyguards fired a warning shot over the heads of the attackers, which slowed their advance just enough so that he could slip inside before the door rattled shut.

As the elevator began its descent, Burls briefed the group: "The garage is secure. It has a roll-down bay door leading outside and coded locks going in and out. And we've got the armored van parked down there." The armored vehicle was how they'd been clandestinely moving the baron from place to place. "We stay there while the police bring matters under control, keep the van running near the door. If the situation escalates, we open the gate and make a go of it. Do we all agree?"

Everyone nodded except the baron, who came back with "Frankly, I think—"

"*Do* shut up, Your Lordship," Burls snapped.

Silence prevailed until the elevator clunked to a halt at the bottom of the shaft. At the same moment, the baron groaned and tottered into Burls, clutching his chest just above the breast pocket of his suit jacket. Burls caught him before he could drop to the floor, grabbing him by the lapels to keep him upright.

The agents sprang forward and hooked the baron under his armpits.

"Your Lordship—!" Burls yelled.

This time, the man's agonized expression was all too real. His eyes rolled back, his complexion gray and beaded with sweat.

By the time the elevator door clunked open, MI5 was propping up a dead man.

51.01 _____

@ Manhattan
11:02:06 EDT

It had been only two hours since Knight had raced off to an impromptu meeting with SACs Cooper and Karasowski-Fowler to discuss Team CLICKKILL's latest predicament and present its proposal to fight fire with fire. Shortly thereafter, they brought Hartley into the deliberations, and she put a call out to the Office of Public Affairs. Not long after, the official statement hit the newswires:

> Bounty4Justice has wantonly targeted FBI agents in order to
> help Russia deflect blame for its cybervulnerability and internal
> disarray . . . and has implemented a slanderous campaign of
> misdirection that has no basis in fact. . . . Let the unauthorized
> video of the exchange in question speak for itself.

After the reference to Knight's intricate diplomatic negotiations with Voronov, the statement went on to further establish the agents and the legat to Russia as the solid citizens they were, tacitly reminding the public of whose side they were on and what they were collectively fighting. By 10:00 A.M., the talking heads of morning media had latched onto the story, trumpeting support for the actions of the FBI, with many pundits declaring a "New Cold War" in cyberspace and several social media sites electric with support. Before 11:00 A.M., Novak's BlackBerry pinged the arrival of his status change:

AS OF 11:00 AM EDT, YOUR CURRENT BOUNTY IS $151,008
CURRENT STATUS: Not Guilty
    «BOUNTY SUSPENDED»
FOR THE LATEST UPDATES, VISIT:
http://www.bounty4justice.com/ROMAN.NOVAK

Knight and Walter received similar updates within minutes of each other.

When Walter logged on, checked his profile, and saw that his new status had deactivated his family's personal information, he visibly relaxed. "That's better."

"We're not out of the woods yet," Knight said. "But it buys us some time. Now let's get back to chopping wood."

51.02

Novak told Knight he needed a moment to make a call, long overdue, and ducked out into the hallway.

His father picked up before the second ring. "Hey, sport."

"Sorry for taking so long to check in, Dad. I'm sure you've seen the news and know what's going on."

His father said, "Sure, I've been following it. Hard to miss. And before you ask, yes, Tommy stopped by this morning, just like you asked him to."

Thomas McGovern had been Novak's best friend since kindergarten and was now chief of the Summit Police Department. Novak had phoned him earlier that morning. If ever there was a time to cash in a favor, this was it.

"He told me that if we see any funny business," Raymond Novak said, "anything at all, to call him directly. And he's got two officers in a patrol car sitting in front of the house."

"Good. Glad to hear it."

"It's really not necessary, Roman. I appreciate it and all, but—"

"Look, Dad, I don't want to worry you, but this website grabs at everything it can to put pressure on its targets. It's not something to be taken lightly."

"That's what they're saying on the news. I get it. It pulls no punches and it hits below the belt. I know you're doing everything you can to put a stop to it. But don't be too hard on yourself, Roman. I know how involved you can get. Just try your best, son. Anything above that is beyond your control. Listen to me now: your mom and I will be just fine. If anything comes up that the police out front can't handle, we'll call Tommy."

"All right, Dad. And look, get a pen and paper. I know you pay cash for almost everything and you've already got credit monitoring, but there're a few things I need you to do." Novak reminded him to call his banks about restricting all online activity on his accounts, changing access codes and PINs, and issuing new credit cards with lower credit limits. For good measure, he also recommended a new email address and home phone number. "And be sure to file your tax returns as early as possible next year to avoid any scams. No clicking on suspicious emails, no giving out personal information over the phone. It's full lockdown. Got it? Same goes for Mom."

"Okay. I'll work on that today."

"And how is Mom handling everything?" Novak asked.

"Tommy spoke to her directly, really put her mind at ease. What a nice guy. I always liked that kid. Otherwise, you know . . . she's getting by. I spoke with an elder-care counselor, and he's looking into some options. Assisted-living facilities, skilled nursing facilities, nursing homes . . . there's a lot to consider. In the next week or so, we'll schedule some time to go and have a look at a couple of places."

"I'd like to come along on those appointments."

"If you can make it, great. But seriously, Roman, given everything that's going on, if you can't be there—"

"I'll be there, Dad. Let me know when you have the details."

"I'll do that."

"Seems we're both learning a lot about giving up control lately."

"That's for sure."

In the background, Novak could hear his mother calling.

"Sorry, buddy. I've got to go."

"Okay. Tell her I send my love," Novak said.

"I will. Love you, son. And good luck."

"Love you, too, Dad."

51.03 _____

Fifteen minutes later, with renewed vigor, the team was back in their groove. As Knight had pronounced at the morning's strategy meeting, Operation CLICKKILL was indeed unwinding the Bounty4Justice money trail. What he hadn't reported was that where answers should have been, new questions had arisen.

"CERT just confirmed it," Walter said, pointing to the email on his screen. "They've combed through Echelon's computers. Bounty4Justice was paying the Sorvino brothers exclusively in NcryptoCash."

"Shit," Novak groaned. NcryptoCash's peer-to-peer encrypted transactions completely circumvented banks and clearinghouses, leaving no audit trails whatsoever; to a forensic accountant, this was kryptonite.

"Surprise, surprise," Knight said. "I take it there's no chance we can trace the payments?" he asked rhetorically.

"Not a one," Walter said unequivocally. "You know the game: NcryptoCash is even better than the real thing. No fingerprints, no drop-offs. Whoever's running Bounty4Justice is no fool. All the transfers to Echelon were channeled through its anonymity network. Even though Echelon's computers show all the incoming transfers into the company's NcryptoCash Safebox software, we have no way of knowing where those payments originated."

"How much are we talking about here?" Knight asked.

"About twenty-seven million—tax-free, of course," Walter said.

"Out of that, the Sorvinos claim to have paid half for labeling and shipping, but not a dime toward the cost of producing or packaging the pins. At least that's the story they're sticking to. And if it's the truth, then those boxes of prepackaged pins shipped from China to Port Jersey after someone else had already paid for them. We could try to track the shipment back to the manufacturer to see who funded things on that end, but we all know that the Chinese won't help us enforce a damn thing. Blatant counterfeiting and trade infringement are right up their alley. They'll just claim to know nothing, like they always do. Especially if they have any inkling that it all ties in to a major cybercrime investigation."

During the interrogation in Jersey City, Novak had listened to the Sorvinos swear up and down multiple times that they had had no face-to-face interactions with any human being associated with Bounty4Justice. Add to that their nebulous plausible deniability about the contents of the tiny envelopes. The entire arrangement, they'd maintained, had been hashed out in an anonymous chat room hosted on the darknet, with the older Sorvino's techie nephew acting as their facilitator—the digital realm's equivalent of a safecracker.

"Let me guess: the company that was paying the Sorvinos is just some made-up name," Knight said.

Walter grinned. "The Alliance for Social Harmony and Justice, Limited. Glasgow, Scotland. No records. Not even a Google hit. A completely fictional entity. Might as well be called Screw You Incorporated."

"With the volume of pins the Sorvino brothers have been sending out," Novak said, "almost all of which Hargrave tracked to addresses here in the States, it stands to reason that they were Bounty4Justice's exclusive U.S. distributor. You can bet that they have counterparts in other countries filling the same role."

"Makes sense," Walter said.

"I'll notify Interpol," Knight said, marking his notepad. "I'm sure these other outfits won't be hard to find. We'll get an alert out to the postal authorities to be on the lookout for anyone shipping huge batches of those tiny envelopes."

"Why wouldn't Bounty4Justice have just started taking payments and paying the bounties exclusively in NcryptoCash to begin with?" Novak mused. "Why even mess around with pins and credit cards, knowing there'd be audit trails?"

"Well, some people still aren't comfortable with NcryptoCash," Walter ventured. "Everyone knows how to use a credit card online, but think about how long it took people to get used to that concept."

Novak shook his head. "No. I think there's more going on here." A lot more: the website's avowed mission to bring swift justice to those who'd beaten the system, the shell game of payments, the muscle flexing in Russia . . . He just couldn't put all the pieces together yet.

"Seems to me it's looking to show off," Knight said. "It's trying to scare people, give them a peek at the dark side of things."

Novak nodded this time. "That's closer, I think. It's exposing the system. Isn't it? It's demonstrating the danger in things . . . all the pit-falls of technology, all the shady dealings going on beneath the water-line. It's showing us how even the Mafia has gone digital. Criminals don't need to meet anymore. No need for deals in back alleys. They go to the darknet now. It's less risky. It's anonymous. It's instanta-neous. It's seeming to me that Bounty4Justice is willingly exposing its methods. That raid in Jersey City was too easy. *Too* successful. Those packages *led* us to the Sorvinos."

"It's *revealing* the chaos," Walter said, nodding agreeably. "Not causing it."

"Precisely. And if my hunch is right, those credit card transactions are going to uncover something else, too. Same with that cash mailed to Manny Tejada. But I'd wager that none of it will give away the identity of whoever is behind all this."

"Anything else?" Knight asked, jotting on his pad.

"Oh, yeah . . ." Walter shuffled through some papers on his desk. "Now that we've got our gorilla warrant, I have something for the NSA to process. A code block we came across. Here, have a look." He handed a printout of Novak's text file to Knight and explained how the "iArchos" segment buried in the mess of run-on characters might point to an online identity used by Bounty4Justice's webmaster.

"We've been working this for days," Walter said. "Coming up completely dry. We need to bring out the big guns."

"All right," Tim said. "Just copy me in on it."

Walter barely glanced at Novak as he finessed the confidential source. A knock at the door effectively changed the subject.

Connie walked in, holding a sheaf of papers and looking spooked. "We've got a problem."

"What is it?"

She handed Walter the papers. "The traces on those Visa payments."

"And?"

She looked over at Novak, then at Knight, then back at Walter. Then she told them who controlled the accounts, and Walter nearly slid off his ball chair.

52.01 _____

@ Georgetown
11:42:05 EDT

Senator Barbara Ascher and her husband, Dr. Daniel Ascher, an oncologist, sat with Jones and Vargas in the brownstone's living room,
in comfortable leather armchairs arranged in pairs close to a grand
bay window that, under better circumstances, would have provided a
great view of the park across the street. Except the shades were
drawn tight, and lamps substituted for sunlight.

Jones shifted in his chair, trying to get comfortable, thinking that
his ribs might be more than just bruised after all. All things considered, what happened over at the school could've wound up much,
much worse. From the looks of things, the abduction team was a
group of local toughs trying to cash in on Ascher's bounty. They'd
planned to use Sam and Max to lure their mother to a burned-out
building, where she'd be directed by cellphone to walk toward them
across a rigged floor, which would collapse under her weight and
send her plummeting twenty feet into a basement outfitted with
rebar spikes, floodlights, and remote video cameras—like some
twisted scene from a *Saw* horror flick. Whether the grotesque im-
palement they'd envisioned would have played out according to plan

was highly questionable. But Jones was happy to have helped keep it in the realm of imagination.

Three of the runners had been brought to MedStar Georgetown University Hospital—one with a skull fracture, two with gunshot wounds to the legs (lucky for them they'd been unarmed, or Vargas would have aimed higher). The unlucky gunman in the princess mask had been taken out in a body bag, which left the van driver and the wolfman to do most of the talking. There wasn't much to tell. They were all in their mid- to late twenties, just a bunch of desperate, misguided young men who'd made a really bad choice in a long series of other really bad choices. With the economy in the toilet for the past few years, at least for ordinary people, shit luck wasn't just a freak chance anymore. It'd become an epidemic.

While they waited for the police and the agents from the FBI to bring out chairs from the kitchen, Jones studied the Aschers. The patrician Dr. Ascher looked a bit older than his wife, maybe early fifties. But they could easily pass as brother and sister—both fair-skinned, slender, and light-complected—which suggested to Jones a predisposition to narcissism on both their parts. Two peas in a pod. Her yin to his yang. They even held hands like an Olympic skating duo waiting to hear their score from the judges. Senator Ascher caught Jones staring and said, "Once again, thank you *so* much. If it weren't for both of you—" But then the agents and cops came bounding into the room, creaking the floorboards, lugging in the kitchen chairs. Her lips quivered, and she shook her head. So Jones gave her a friendly nod to let her know that everything was going to be okay.

Once everyone settled in, Senator Ascher sat up, straight and composed.

It was her husband who spoke first: "This godforsaken website has taken over our lives. It won't be happy until one of us is dead. For Christ's sake, hasn't this gone far enough? Can't you people just shut this damn thing down? It's a *website*. It's a *thing*. It's not another Osama bin Laden."

The cops and G-men exchanged glances, every one of them reluctant to field the reply. Finally, the tall FBI supervisory special agent, Eugene Fitzky, grimaced and cleared his throat. "Dr. Ascher, what we're dealing with isn't just a 'thing.' Bullets took down Osama bin Laden, sir. *Ideas* are bulletproof. You can't kill ideology. You can't kill sentiment. And *that's* what we're dealing with here."

"But you *can* shut down a website," Ascher insisted. "Let's not ignore the reality of the technology and the fact that it enables this madness to happen."

Jones was expecting Fitzky to remind the doctor of what had happened in Russia when an attempt had been made to "shut it down." But his rebuff was much more subtle.

"I assure you that this technology isn't coming from some high school kid in his mother's basement," Fitzky said. "Even if we could shut it down—and that may happen, *eventually*—there's nothing to stop it from popping up again in some far-flung spot in Eastern Europe or God knows where. And the game begins anew, fast and furious, racking up plenty more hits before we shut it down again and everyone moves on to the next round. So if I can speak candidly, Senator . . ." he said, turning to her.

The doctor rolled his eyes dramatically.

"Please," she said. "Go ahead."

"From what we've learned so far, Bounty4Justice chose you as a target using software that analyzes all the negative publicity and allegations surrounding your case . . . somehow scouring and quantifying all those nasty blogs and tweets and news reports out there on the Internet. But that software didn't go digging through your emails and phone records to get to the *real* dirt on you. The most damning information was uploaded to the website by an anonymous whistleblower, after the fact. Somebody you know. Somebody very close to you."

Jones could tell that the words wounded her, though she did her best to shrug it off.

"I don't understand this at all," said Dr. Ascher, jumping in again, releasing his wife's hand and throwing both of his into the air. "I mean, look at all these crooks, like . . . like"—he spun his hands in frustration—"like Bernie Madoff. The guy's a complete fraud, but *he's* not on this ridiculous list."

"If I had to guess," Fitzky said, "I'd say that's because Madoff is behind bars serving a life sentence. In a system of law that's functioning properly, it's the outcome that's expected. More or less, he's been brought to justice."

"And you're saying my wife *hasn't?*"

Fitzky wouldn't take the bait. He kept his mouth shut and sat back in his chair and folded his arms.

The senator looked away, her lips tightening even more severely.

Silence settled over the group. Then Jones decided to toss a grenade.

"Is it true?" he asked the senator, as tactfully as possible. "Those documents on Bounty4Justice, and all those charges. Is it all true?" *What the hell,* he figured. He'd almost died protecting her kids. The least she could do was answer the question everyone wanted to ask.

Dr. Ascher once again attempted to shield his wife. "Come on. Are you serious? How the hell can you sit there and—"

"Stop!" she screamed. *"Enough,* Daniel. This is *my* fight."

The doctor's face went beet red.

"Fine. Do it your way." He stood abruptly and pointed at her face. "That's what got us into this mess to begin with, isn't it, *dear*? It's all about you. Always has been. You want to make yourself the sacrificial lamb? Go ahead. Fine by me." He stormed out of the room.

There was dead silence as she smiled sadly. She sat tall and pulled back her shoulders. "I've given this a lot of thought," she said to none of them in particular. "And what happened this morning only makes my decision easier." She folded her hands in her lap resolutely and looked over to Jones. "Yes, Agent Jones. Bounty4Justice has it right. Everything you've read is true."

Jones felt a chill as the grenade got tossed back at him. *Holy shit.*

"I'm not an idiot," she said to the group. "I know what the courts are going to say about all of it. And I know what that means for me, and for my family. Scandals don't last forever. Neither does sentiment," she said, giving Fitzky a cold stare. "Death, however, is permanent." She gazed up at the ceiling, where they could faintly hear the kids playing in the room above. "So let's talk about what happens next."

53.01

@ Manhattan

"This can't be right," Walter said in disbelief, flipping through the pages and scanning the dozens of account numbers on the printout.

Connie stood beside him, arms crossed tight across her chest. "That's what I thought, too. But they all checked out. I verified everything as best I could through SWIFT."

The Society for Worldwide Interbank Financial Telecommunication was the network through which nearly all major international wire transfers between financial institutions around the globe were routed. It was the switchboard for the global banking system—the means by which payments were settled.

She added, "They told me that all those accounts are controlled by a company named Archer Offsite Systems LLP. No address. No contact information. Nothing. When I tried digging a little deeper, I hit the walls you typically encounter when you accidentally come across a classified account. They started pushing back. In other words, SWIFT is giving me the cold shoulder."

Knight was skeptical. "And you're thinking it's linked to some other intelligence agency?"

She threw up her hands. "The ODNI, CIA—take your pick. I'm just saying. I've seen this before, at my old job. Every now and then I'd stumble upon secret accounts, and this is the same runaround I got back then."

Connie would know, thought Novak. She'd worked the money desk at the CIA for seven years before transferring to the FBI. And the money she'd dealt with wasn't the sort that went into agents' paychecks.

"This is how they typically fund operatives and pay informants," she said. "They set up phantom bank accounts that have no clear ownership."

Knight's face twisted into a knot. "You mean to tell me that Visa has been transferring money that's being paid to kill people—"

"I'm just saying it's a possibility we should seriously consider. And there's more. Lots of those accounts are also linking to the U.K. Same company name, same roadblocks."

"So British intelligence, too?" Walter asked.

"That's what it *looks* like," she said noncommittally.

Novak wasn't completely sold on the idea, even though over the past few years, whistleblowers had revealed quite a few collaborative scandals involving the intelligence branches of both the United States and the United Kingdom that had included the theft of telephonic decryption keys from the world's largest SIM card manufacturers. This had allowed both agencies to listen in, at will, on virtually any phone call, such as diplomatic communications at the highest levels of the German government. No warrants. No permissions.

"Congress is about to approve almost ninety billion for the intelligence budget next year," Novak said, thinking it through. Just last week, he'd read the arcane details in *The Wall Street Journal.* "They're saying that over seventy percent of that ninety billion is paid out to private contractors, most of whom the director of national intelligence never divulges. Not even to Congress."

"Doesn't have to, either," Knight added. "It's classified. Not for public consumption."

"Exactly," Novak said. "So there could be hundreds of contractors in the mix that no one's even aware of. At the end of the day, only a handful of people in Washington really know how all that money's being spent, and who's doing the spending, and why."

"All under the guise of national security," Walter said. "I mean, what *if* Bounty4Justice is being run by—"

"Stop there," Knight said, holding up his hand. "Let's not go down this road. We can't jump to conclusions, and we certainly don't want to start planting the seeds for conspiracy theories. Let's just keep this under wraps, and I'll present it to the brass. See how they want to pursue it."

Novak's phone chimed. It was Michaels. "I gotta take this," he said, stepping out into the hallway and pacing toward the executive offices to escape the noise of the main floor. "Hey, Rosemary."

"Hey. I was listening to the radio earlier and heard about you and the guys getting posted to the website," Michaels said on the other end of the line. "Crazy stuff. At least it seems like everyone's rallying behind you and the team. But I'm sure it's still pretty nerve-racking. Are you all holding up okay?"

"I'm looking over my shoulder in the break room, but I'm managing it. And you know Teflon Tim . . . not exactly one to express his feelings. Walter's already a bundle of nerves, so it's just one more thing to keep him up at night."

"Well, if you need anything . . . I'm a phone call away. I mean it."

He could tell she was truly concerned about him. It felt nice. "Thanks. I'll keep it mind."

"Okay, so get this," she said. "I showed that weird silver wrapper to my contact at the Secret Service, and she had plenty to say about it."

"Let's hear it."

"Bottom line is, it's the same packaging smugglers use to protect cash shipments from moisture and the elements. That powdery film on the inside of the foil packet acts as both a drying agent and a rodent repellent. It all fits perfectly with what Hargrave just told me about what he found on his end."

After Craig Hargrave's stellar performance throughout the raid on Echelon in Jersey City, Novak had suggested that Michaels contact the burly postal inspector about tracking the shipping label on the box of cash mailed from Massena, New York, to Manny Tejada in Dallas.

"He pulled security videos taken at the post office in Massena," Michaels said, "and emailed the files to me. The camera inside the post office, above the front desk, clearly shows a young Asian guy dropping off the box. Then the camera outside shows him driving away in a white minivan with Canadian plates. Hargrave has already confirmed with Homeland Security that not long after that, the van showed up on surveillance cameras at the Seaway International Bridge, heading north over the St. Lawrence River into Ontario."

"Did he have them trace the plates?"

"Yup. Vehicle's registered to an import-export company in Ottawa, named SingLao North American Shipping. So I reached out to the DEA in Ottawa."

It was the logical next step, thought Novak, since the DEA handled all contraband outside the States, including drugs and cash.

She told him that she'd then been directed to DEA Special Agent Robert Romeyn, who, as it turned out, had been working closely with the Canadian authorities over the past eighteen months to investigate SingLao for suspected smuggling activities. Romeyn made it clear that he'd happily facilitate a request to raid the location. He'd been looking for an excuse to get "these powder-puff Canadians," as he put it, to make their move, and this was "damn well as good an excuse as any."

"I say we take Romeyn up on his offer," Michaels suggested.

"I agree. I'll get on it immediately. Sounds like a pretty big breakthrough. Great work."

"Thanks."

He ended the call, smiling.

54.01 _____

@ Athens, Greece
18:28:48 EET

The three conspirators sat side by side on a bench in Syntagma Square, smoking cigarettes. They each wore periwinkle-blue baseball caps and matching coveralls, purchased from a local uniform whole-saler, dirtied and washed multiple times to give the appearance of being well worn. The embroidered patches on the uniforms, ordered from an online custom patch maker for rush delivery, bore a logo lifted from the website of a heating and air-conditioning company that serviced hotels throughout the city, including the big one across the street—the elegant Hotel Grande Bretagne, with its five-star ame-nities and breathtaking views of the Acropolis and Mount Lycabet-tus. Each man was equipped with a simple toolbox containing wrenches, pliers, and the like. The third man's kit, however, also in-cluded a very special instrument that could gut an elephant in one sweep.

To the casual passersby—and there had been many on this unsea-sonably warm day unusual for the rainy season—they were just three workmen taking a break. In actuality, they were looking—*hunting*—for a woman. They'd been tipped off by an insider who worked at the

hotel that she'd be staying one more night before sailing off to Myko-
nos for a more secluded holiday jaunt.

They were all from Bangladesh and had known one another since
childhood, back in a simpler time in Savar Upazila. They'd come here
in 2009 to study informatics and telecommunications at the National
and Kapodistrian University of Athens, just as the global financial
crisis tightened its grip on Europe. With banks running for cover,
they could not get the necessary loans to stay in school and soon
found themselves crammed into a tiny space above a laundromat,
scraping by on odd jobs that paid in cash. Bad luck, it seemed, knew
no borders.

Then fate dealt another crushing blow when, three months ago, a
building collapse back home in Savar crushed to death fifteen family
members: brothers, sisters, cousins. It was that event, that tipping
point, that transformed three dreamers into something else altogether.

"There she is," Masud said, tendrils of bluish smoke curling out
from his nostrils. The leader of the three once again surreptitiously
compared the woman to the picture he'd printed off the Bounty4Jus-
tice website, tucked inside last week's print edition of *Weekly Blitz,*
which he pretended to be reading.

Not long after sunset, Isha Bhatia finally returned from her excur-
sion to the Acropolis. Not only did the target look like a woman of
privilege, in her fine dress and wide-brimmed sun hat, thought Nazir,
the biggest of the three, but she carried herself like one, too—
blissfully strolling across the piazza with not a care in the world. According to her online profile, she was a French national of Indian
descent, forty-eight years old, unmarried and childless, a Pisces, an
avid traveler, and the driving force behind the clothing empire NHMP
Clothing, Ltd.—a company whose business practices and total disre-
gard of ethical standards offered brilliant insight into the ugly side of
globalization and the wholesale exploitation of human capital.

"You're sure that's her?" asked Rashed, the third accomplice. He
was slightly built with a lazy eye.

Masud nodded. "I'm sure." He took another drag of his cigarette
and stomped at the ground to shoo away the persistent pigeons.

"You'd think with all that money she'd hire some bodyguards," Rashed said. He puffed his cigarette.

"Just makes our job easier," Masud replied.

"She's very pretty," Nazir said, leaning forward, his elbows on his knees.

Masud and Rashed glared at him scornfully.

"She is an evil woman, Nazzy," Masud said, stabbing the glowing tip of his cigarette at Nazir. "Don't you forget it. Your cousins are dead because of her. Hundreds more right along with them. Don't be deceived by that pretty face."

Masud was right, thought Nazir. It hadn't been an act of terrorism or some freak earthquake that had taken down the apparel factory that July morning. It'd been the egregious dismissal of the factory's structural deficiencies. The building's upper levels, repurposed from office to industrial use, had been stacked four high above the retail shops at ground level. Where desks and computers should have been, NHMP Clothing, Ltd., under Isha Bhatia's instructions, had installed heavy textile machinery and power generators, which had vibrated ceaselessly, day after day. And instead of the few hundred occupants the structure had been engineered to support, nearly *three thousand* workers had been crammed in tight, slaving under horrendous conditions, twelve hours each day, to earn just over five thousand *taka* per month—barely seventy U.S. dollars or sixty euros.

Even after telltale cracks and fissures had appeared in the building's main support columns—prompting the retail tenants on the ground level to wisely evacuate the premises—a call made by the worried site manager to Isha Bhatia (which the garment empress later denied) had elicited only a terse demand to have the workers sent back to the machines the following morning, to ensure that a huge order promised to a major U.S. discount retailer would be delivered on time. No exceptions. A mere hour after the opening shift began that fateful morning, the building buckled; in less than twenty seconds, it had turned to rubble, killing nearly four hundred workers and critically injuring twelve hundred more. Yet no legal action had ensued. No arrests. No trial. And so it was that the beguiling Isha Bhatia was free to go about the world, sightseeing in luxury.

Rashed checked his Samsung smartphone again. "The bounty is up to one-point-six million euros. That's a lot of money."

"Which is why you must be sure to get the video right," Masud said. "If I'm going to handle the messy part, I need to know that you've got this covered. Can you handle it or not?"

"Of course. I've got it covered. Stop worrying."

"You'd worry, too, if you were in my shoes. Remember: money or no money, she will pay for what she has done," Masud said venomously, flicking his cigarette to the ground. "We will exact revenge for those who've been taken from us. Today we make our own destiny. Today we stop being victims—of people like her, of this place . . ." He scowled, looking out across the plaza toward the parliament building, seeing only yet another archetypal monument to corruption and greed and impotence. Then he folded the newspaper, grabbed his toolbox, and stood. "It's time."

54.02

The master key card Masud had been given—*purchased*, really, since the insider was simply doing his share for a 15 percent cut of the bounty—worked flawlessly for the rear service door and the service elevator, as well as the private elevator leading up to the penthouse and the main double door for the unit itself.

The three stealthily entered the dim palatial suite, which was redolent of pomegranates, hibiscus, and coriander. Masud gently set his toolbox on the credenza in the reception hall, beside a vase of exotic flowers. He unhinged the lid, removed the top tray holding screwdrivers and pliers and wrenches, and took out the three white *volto* masks and the Ka-Bar. He passed two of the masks to his friends, then pulled off his ball cap and slid the remaining mask over his face.

Rashed put on his mask and readied his Samsung to document the act.

The white mask and coveralls made Nazir eerily resemble the slasher from that horror flick *Halloween* as he rolled back his broad shoulders and readied his mind and his hands for what was to come next.

The masks were Rashed's idea—a ploy to pass blame to the hacker fanatics he'd seen protesting in the square the day before.

The floor plan was open and airy, with furnishings befitting royalty and windows all around that provided a picturesque panorama of Athens's nightscape and the lit-up columns of the Acropolis. The target, however, was nowhere to be seen. Masud pointed to the archway that led to the bedrooms; Nazir and Rashed quietly moved toward it and disappeared into the hall beyond.

Not two seconds later, the front lock emitted a quick staccato of clicks. Just as the door swung inward, Masud stepped into the shadowy gap behind it, because there was nowhere else to hide. Adrenaline shot through him, and with it came the rage. He gripped the Ka-Bar's haft tight in his right hand, the long, serrated blade pointed up at the ceiling. The moment the door closed, he saw the back of her head and the flowing dress. Blessedly, she was alone. As she moved toward the credenza, preoccupied by the strange toolbox left there, he lunged out and grabbed at her from behind, clamping his left hand over her mouth, wrapping his right arm around her, pressing the blade to her throat. She thrashed a bit, to no effect, and let out a muffled whimper, but Masud had her locked in a vise grip.

Rashed rushed back into the main room, immediately reading the situation. He held up his phone and focused intently on the device's display. "I've got it! Go!"

Nazir appeared just as Masud turned the target toward the camera light's bright glare for the final act. Nazir's read on the situation was very different. Behind the mask, his eyes went wide, and he threw out his hands and screamed: "Wait! It's—"

But Masud had sunk the Ka-Bar deep into the soft flesh of her neck. It glinted in the light as he swept it sideways amid a gush of red.

Nazir screamed, *"It's not her!"*

55.01

@ Manhattan

It was nearing 8:00 P.M. when Walter's wife called, wondering where he was.

"I thought you'd be home by now?" she asked. "What's going on?"

"I'm just finishing up an email, and then I'll be heading out," he told her, staring bleary-eyed at his computer screen.

"Don't be too long. Please. This whole website business has me a nervous wreck, and there're kids outside wearing those creepy white masks, like the ones they keep showing on TV. I don't know if they're having a bit of fun or if they're planning a break-in."

"Sweetie, I spoke with Felix earlier today, and he told me he has a panic button there at the front desk. I gave him the rundown on what to do if he sees anything at all suspicious. And Ruben's working the front door tonight. He knows how to handle things. Remember, he's a retired Navy SEAL. A bona fide badass."

"Just . . . come home. *Straight* home. Oh, but get a bottle of red on your way. Okay?"

"I'm wrapping things up now. See you before nine."

"Be safe. Love you."

"Love you, too."

He set down the phone and finalized an email to the NSA contact assigned to Operation CLICKKILL.

From: Walter.Koslowski@ic.fbi.gov
Sent: Monday, October 30, 2017 at 8:02 PM
To: Dilip Kapoor
Cc: Roman Novak, Tim Knight
Subject: Bounty4Justice—ciphertext query

Dilip,
An anonymous informant provided my team with the following ciphertext, which may pertain directly to an insider at Bounty4Justice:

FgHllli56/$kjilM//%jatiucmkem398dn47g8p754avh4899&&)*^fjjekjdj65#
589dkjjJHOke//3(mckGtFRdHHiLkm89$2P@/fiemMipfmi%tmjgf7&90/'d//
FooufyY&59689eTf‹iArchos6l6›jdutMtiu(309/d'x["wsdj]]djgtkjMtkeix$()))
djgk22d,tk952›/?jf48f9fjJljkd;lkgjk:LJLJl;kjgfituY

Of special interest is the string (a tag?) in line 3 "‹iArchos6l6›." However, after running various permutations through Sentinel and Guardian, we've had zero luck matching any relevant data points. I'm hoping your analysts can expedite this query. As I'm sure you've heard, the stakes have gotten much higher internationally, not to mention more personal for myself and my colleagues. I look forward to your feedback. Thanks very much.

Walter Koslowski
Senior Cybercrimes Specialist
Special Operations/Cyber Division
FBI New York
26 Federal Plaza
New York, NY 10278
Phone: (212) 555-0453
Fax: (212) 555-8858
@NewYorkFBI | Email Alerts | FBI.gov/NewYork

After he confirmed that the email was successfully delivered, he logged on to his Bounty4Justice profile page and checked his current status—still NOT GUILTY, now by a comfortable margin of 66 percent, thanks mostly to Tim's media blitz, which had effectively turned sentiment in their favor. After watching that video a couple more times during the day, he'd understood why most people—at least those living outside the sphere of Putin's propaganda troll factory—were rallying behind them. If anything, the video humanized the FBI and demonstrated how the agents assigned to Operation CLICKKILL were exploring every option to combat the very real international threat posed by Bounty4Justice.

Still, it made him crazy to think that someone might harm his family in retaliation for him simply doing his job.

He logged off the network, grabbed his backpack, and locked up his office.

55.02

@ Park Slope
20:43:11

Walter emerged from the subway at Seventh Avenue and passed a pack of hyperactive teenage boys in face paint and monster masks. Given the general threat level in the city, however, he could see the beat cops out and about, minding the shop.

Around the corner from his apartment building, he ducked into the local wine store and took the resident vintner's suggestion about a bottle of mid-priced cabernet sauvignon. He also dropped by the adjacent cheese shop and picked up some Havarti and cheddar cheese and a package of crackers, too, since his "dinner" had consisted of an apple, Cheetos, and Gatorade.

Half a block from his building's main entrance, a group of hooligans ran across the street, directly at him, hooting and yowling. When he saw that they were all wearing white *volto* masks, he froze and scanned the area. He was alone on the sidewalk, and the cops were nowhere in sight.

"Shit."

Sure enough, the pack slowed and encircled him menacingly. Five of them. None was imposing in stature, but they had numbers on their side. One of them—the leader, it appeared—had his hand buried inside his bulging coat pocket. Walter's heart began galloping wildly. *Fuck.*

"Yeah, this is the guy, right?" one of them said.

"Sure looks like him," the leader replied. When he tilted his head, he reminded Walter of a possessed porcelain doll.

"Hey, fellas," Walter said, feeling vulnerable as hell with a wine bottle as the only semblance of a weapon at his disposal. "You don't know me. So back off. Okay?"

Three of the others started making bizarre clucking sounds, while the fifth one pulled out a cellphone, pointed it at Walter, and started taking a video.

"You're not going to get anything," Walter said. "I'm not guilty. And it won't pay you if I'm not listed as guilty. Look it up on your phone, there," he told the cameraman. "See for yourself. Be smart. Don't waste your time." He figured he'd go directly at the leader and swing away. By Walter's estimation, it was the best chance he had. Otherwise, if he tried to run, he'd get shot in the back or, at best, maybe pounced on by the posse and stabbed to death. God, the thought of it—how it would devastate his family—made him sick. *Where the fuck are those cops?*

The leader tipped his head, like a confused dog. He slowly pulled his hand out of his pocket, and Walter prepared for the worst.

The leader cocked his arm . . . high and back like a pitcher. Which confused Walter.

"Hey!" a gruff voice screamed.

The kid froze with his hand up in the air.

"Don't even think about it," Ruben warned, all six-foot-two and three hundred pounds of him storming over. He went right up to the assailant and stabbed a meaty finger between the eyes of his mask. "You throw that egg, and I'll rip your arm right off your goddamn body and beat your idiot ass with it. And don't think I won't do it."

The pitcher slowly lowered his arm and dropped the egg onto the sidewalk. "Relax, big man. It's all good. Just havin' some fun."

"That's a twisted way to get your jollies, scarin' people like that. You all need some better manners. Get outta here. Scram."

As they ran off, the leader yelled back at him, "Fuck you, you fat fuck!" But the beat cops were just rounding the corner, and he barreled right into them.

Ruben chuckled. "Yeah, fuck you, too, jackass."

"Thanks, Ruben," Walter said.

"Don't mention it. Like I told you, I've got it covered."

Only Walter couldn't help but think that if it hadn't been an egg in that kid's pocket, things might not have turned out so well. It made him feel sick all over again. He walked to the building with Ruben, his hands trembling. By God, he was going to do whatever it took to bring down Bounty4Justice.

(D:) / Partition 4 | QUARANTINE

ATLAS-5 SECURE MESSAGE BOARD

Session: 11.06.2017.16:08:32UTC.TLPSYMM.7125253334-12-47

> PIKE: Firewolf is not happy about paying out $350M with nothing to show for it. And he's nervous. Very. The FBI has been looking into the accounts, especially the ones that point to Bounty4Justice.

> JAM: He's just being dramatic. He'll handle it.

> PIKE: Do you think? He's also concerned that he'll be linked to a terrorist plot. Says he refuses to take the fall. If he's called out, he's going to take us down right along with him.

> JAM: That's both unfortunate and unwise. He forgets that as far as anyone is concerned, you and I don't exist. If he pushes this too far, we'll simply need to consider more aggressive containment measures.

> PIKE: Let's not go there just yet.

> JAM: Fine. Did you tell him we need more time?

> PIKE: Of course. And he knows that's bullshit. Time isn't going to do a damn thing to help us. Razorwire is out of our control. No measures we've undertaken have done anything to change that.

> JAM: And I thought YOU were the optimist. Let's not be too hasty about this. We might still be able to salvage the project. We can reconstruct the code.

> PIKE: We simply do not have time for that. It could take a year or two. Nor do I have any confidence that it would be successful. Need I remind you that the programmers were prohibited from keeping backup copies on their local computers?

> JAM: That doesn't mean they actually complied with our directives. I say we give it a shot. We start over. Rebuild.

> PIKE: No. We have no assurances that it wasn't one of these programmers who may have compromised the project to begin with. Maybe built a back door into his code. This whole damn mess could repeat itself all over again. We need to cut our losses.

> JAM: So you're giving up?

> PIKE: I'm facing reality. And it's not pretty. I suggest you also consider taking ownership of this colossal fuckup. We've got a lot of explaining to do. This has gone on long enough. Better to start explaining things now, before they get any worse.

> JAM: Are you serious? How are we going to explain that our technology has been used to kill dozens of people and take down the fucking Kremlin? There will be no explaining. Don't you get that?

> PIKE: How do you propose we proceed?
> JAM: We need to meet in person to discuss our future together.
> PIKE: I agree.
> JAM: Seadog Pub at noon?
> PIKE: Yes. Can you be there in two days?
> JAM: Of course.
> PIKE: Then it's settled. I look forward to seeing you.

56.01 _____

@ Fort Meade, Maryland
Monday, 11/6/2017
16:17:33 EST

When it came to solving puzzles, Josh Tierney had always been a natural. The Rubik's Cube? Please. A relic from a bygone era. (Yet he did keep one handy, next to his keyboard.) Sudoku? Busywork for simple minds. (Though he did have a Sudoku app on his iPhone, and he revisited it every now and again when he got bored on the can.) When he was a young boy, his parents would try to stump him with all sorts of ring puzzles and brain teasers and number games, until they finally came to terms with what they were dealing with. Truth be told, it scared the shit out of Mary and Albert Tierney. He'd tried to explain it to them—and the doctors and shrinks, too—how numbers and advanced mathematics played like songs in his mind or, in the case of calculus and trigonometry, flowed in wondrous colors. Apparently, that made him different. Very different indeed.

When he'd first ventured into the games of the digital realm, around age four, his parents' anxiety had deepened. By the time he'd entered puberty, they were on red alert, because his "games" had evolved into outwitting top secret computer networks inside the Defense Department. (By then, hacking eBay, Amazon, Bank of America, and Facebook had simply become passé for him.) But he meant no harm. Typically, he'd just stroll through the machines' vast architecture, like a night elf exploring the mystical lands of Azeroth. Oftentimes he'd poke and prod at the coding when he thought it needed fixing, and more often than not, it did. It was what any good watchman might do.

Then came that Saturday in May 2009, when he was once again being harangued by his parents to fill out college applications and got caught snooping through CAD blueprints for some mean-ass stealth fighter that was being developed for the navy (long before the Chinese and Russians ever had a peek). Fucking thing was a blade of an aircraft with the impossible profile of a guitar pick. Sunday came, and so did an NSA recruiter, who knocked on his door and told him, "Son, there's two ways this can go . . ."

Josh wasn't a complete idiot. He'd made the sensible choice, because unlike some hackers, he'd been bequeathed the gift of a moral compass, which somehow blended well with the NSA's core vision of "global cryptologic dominance through responsive presence and network advantage." Moreover, prison didn't sound all that pleasant. So he'd emerged from the primordial ooze of the darknet and joined the official ranks of the world's white-hat cyberspies.

By then the NSA had already grown up and gone full-throttle into the modern age by creating a workplace suitable for the true masters of the digital world. The dress code was whatever you felt you needed it to be—with the exception of half shirts and outright nudity—with tats and piercings and goth attire considered fair game. The break hall was stocked with endless supplies of Red Bull and Cheetos. There was a gaming room and massage chairs and a smoothie kiosk and a Starbucks and a food court that served Thai and burritos and sushi. Everything a computer geek could ever want. What was there *not* to like?

Here, he was in good company. He was quirky, and so was everyone around him. All the other hackers were pale and doughy and temperamental, just like him. Many of them also possessed brains that processed numbers in colors and melodies.

And now Josh Tierney had been formally tasked to solve the mack daddy puzzle worthy of only the most abstract mind. Life couldn't get much better.

56.02

Bounty4Justice had gone viral within the labyrinthine halls of the OPS2A building. Even upper management was stoked, because the U.S. intelligence enterprise finally had a quantifiable enemy that promised to change souring opinions about the agency's role in national security. Fear, however, could also be found in NSA boardrooms, because Bounty4Justice was running technologies thought to be proprietary to the Tailored Access Operations strategic hacking unit. Like its enhanced man-in-the-middle spoofing capabilities that could impersonate legitimate websites—the heady stuff of the QFire exploit. Or its cyber kill-switch technology—once known by the moniker Quantumcopper—that could make an entire domain go dark by corrupting routers systemwide.

It wasn't that Josh's team hadn't already taken a crack at Bounty4Justice. Hell, his department had tried to hack the beast mere hours after that douche Wall Street banker got his fat head shot off, before the FBI or another agency could identify the website's operators as foreign or domestic and undermine Fort Meade's nebulous authority. Right from the get-go they'd pinpointed the website's trip wires, well before Russia blindly banged it with a hammer. And they'd mapped the code blocks to anonymous authors (how many was still unclear) in Korea and China and Russia and the Baltics and Germany and England and beyond—one big orgy of code—as if the world's preeminent hackers had gotten together to build the ultimate wiki.

Yet, to date, no back doors had been identified.

So management had decided to offer bounties of its own to any staffer who could crack the main spoofing algo that was masking Bounty4Justice's true IP addresses; some considered this an early warning sign of desperation. Propped on an easel outside Josh's boss's office was a whiteboard with his department's prize written out in red marker: $50,000 in cash and an all-expenses-paid trip for two to Grand Cayman.

A beach vacation was a strange incentive for this group of misfit night crawlers. But the boss, Dilip Kapoor, was a strange dude—a middle-aged career ass kisser and social retard who was anything but plugged into his staff's interests, let alone their daily work routines. The man micromanaged his morning shit down to the flush, yet he dealt with his staff from behind closed doors via awkward, oftentimes highly inappropriate emails, so as not to expose the inconvenient truth that he didn't know jack shit about modern cryptanalysis. Probably, a long time ago—back when Amazon.com sold only books and spoofing ATMs was considered high crime—he'd had enough chops to weasel his way into the NSA. Though once he'd put on his lipstick and set his sights on the boardroom, the manic mutation of the digital world had quickly left him drowning in its wake. To his credit, the man understood his place in the order of things: he was just a guy who knew a guy, and who'd be replaced in a few months by another guy who would know some other guy who'd replace Kapoor's guy. At which time Dilip Kapoor, obsolete yet ever cunning, would find another door to hide behind.

Minutes ago, Kapoor had forwarded an email to Josh, phrased in his typical robo-prose: "handle this." *What a dick.* He'd attached a query that was some random ciphertext submitted for analysis by Walter Koslowski from the Manhattan FBI, dated a week earlier. Josh knew from news reports and the agency's internal intranet postings, as did Kapoor, that this was the same dude who was already in an intimately tight spot with Bounty4Justice. *An FBI cyber agent is on this demented website, teetering on the verge of being added back to its motherfucking hit list and you let his query fucking stew in your in-box? Way to go, boss. Way to totally skull-fuck the brotherhood.*

On second thought, maybe Shut-the-Door Kapoor wasn't fully to blame for the delay, because ever since that abduction attempt on Senator Barbara Ascher's kids last week, it did seem as if every query related to Bounty4Justice had to be passed through the West Wing and Capitol Hill before any NSA analyst could even view it.

Fuck legalities and fuck bureaucracy. Time to help out a "brother."

At first glance, the ciphertext block Koslowski had submitted didn't look like much—just your standard encryption mumbo jumbo that would typically require a decryption key to unscramble it into something intelligible. But this "iArchos6I6" plugged into the middle of it all *was* rather intriguing. Someone had to have typed it in there after the fact, because encryption algorithms simply didn't generate such rational strings. Why would someone do that?

He turned to the analyst in the neighboring cubicle, who was pecking at his keyboard. "Hey . . . dork . . . dipshit . . . *Randall.*"

No reply. Probably had his earbuds jammed in too tight, zoning out to thrash metal. Josh plucked a paper clip off his desk and flicked it at him. That got his attention.

Randall unplugged his ears and scrunched his face up. "W-w-what the fuck?"

"It's all right, Cinderella." Josh knew not to ever go after the stammer. It was that damn moral compass. Furthermore, Randall was a fellow veteran of the team—an "old man" in his late twenties with tons of experience. That commanded a modicum of respect. After all, it seemed they were getting 'em younger and younger nowadays, since code breaking and hacking weren't the typical fare of the university curriculum. Over the years, the agency's scouting department had gotten really flexible and creative, from its CryptoKids website, which used animated mascots and cutesy online code puzzles to ferret out talented tykes, to its Gifted and Talented Program for high school seniors who excelled in math and engineering, to its college career fairs and annual DEF CON gaming challenges, which pitted junior-level hackers against one another. At times, it seemed the NSA was simply trying to gather up all the prodigies and savants to lock them away in a safe place where they could be monitored. Keep them out of circulation so that some Russian or Chinese intelligence project couldn't get their grubby hands on them. The irony was that the most serious hackers would never so willingly expose themselves, which was why this "old man" hailed from a more checkered past, in which an NSA recruiter had knocked on his door on a Sunday afternoon, consequent to some majorly successful security hack that had been anything but a game.

"Don't get your panties in a bunch," Josh said. "You remember you were telling me you read some book about an AI cube thing that instructed the machines to take over the world?"

"You m-mean *Robopocalypse.* Hell, yeah. Fuckin' Skynet, m-move over."

"Right, whatever. What was the name of the cube thing?"

"Archos."

"That's what I thought." He asked Randall to spell it, and he did. Josh looked at the string in the ciphertext—the clue. Perfect match. *Interesting.*

"W-why you askin'?"

"Can't tell you. It's top secret." After all, they were competing for the grand prize.

Randall shook his head wearily. "Stop f-fucking hitting me with your m-motherfucking paper clips. I m-mean it. It's not f-funny."

"Yeah, yeah."

Randall gave him the finger, then stuffed his earbuds back in and went back to coding.

Archos, thought Josh, studying the "iArchos6I6" buried in the ciphertext. *The sentient machine-god that annihilates humanity in some apocalyptic novel.* The lowercase *i* tagged before it could just be the short version of "I am." Bounty4Justice certainly was worthy of proclaiming itself a god. Maybe it *could* be the AI powerhouse that would bring humanity to its knees—the fast track to the singularity, when the machines would become self-aware and need no organic agent to program them, because they'd start programming themselves. *Awesome.*

The "6I6" could mean just about anything, though it did look an awful lot like 616, which was the numerical mark of the beast in the Bible's apocalyptic closing chapter, Revelation. The beast had seven heads, which was a metaphor for almighty Rome, known in antiquity for its prominent seven-hilled topography. And 616 and 666 were the numerical sums of the Hebrew letters that spelled out "Nero Caesar"—the name of the notorious persecutor of the early Christians at the time the text was authored—using an ancient Assyro-Babylonian encoding system called *gematria*. In Latin translations, *gematria* yielded the sum 616, and in Greek, the sum came out to 666. Take your pick. Either way, it sure seemed to Josh that 6l6 fit with the theme of world domination and hellfire and retribution, just like the beast it meant to depict: Bounty4Justice.

On his center screen, Josh copied the whole damn random mess of characters from the FBI's email, along with the strange cryptonym contained within it, then pasted it into the blank input field on his XKeyscore Deep Dive query window. He clicked the SUBMIT button to feed it to a different beast. Somewhere on the campus of Maryland's largest employer, a nest of Turmoil servers got just a little busier and went about farming out queries to Camp Williams, Utah, to the queen bee: the Intelligence Community Comprehensive National Cybersecurity Initiative data center. The big name was justified, because the CNCI's central brain for signal intelligence (SIGINT) was so big that it had to be measured in acres and exabytes. And with one exabyte equal to one *quintillion* bytes, that was one fucking mother lode of data that had been transferred into this most giant-ass repository—over fifteen years' worth of emails and phone data, Web search history and receipts, deeds and documents, airplane tickets and hotel bookings, porn preferences and social media posts of every kind—every tweet, text, Instagram, and Snapchat (and, yes, even those messages were captured long before they'd supposedly self-destruct). And so much more.

Josh couldn't help smiling. The privacy nuts' paranoia about government tyranny was absolutely justified. Edward Snowden barely did it justice with his half-assed revelations about Prism. The truth was, it was *all* at the Utah data center—personal information, medical and legal records, résumés . . . everything that could possibly be encoded into ones and zeros—just waiting to be mined to reconstruct or deconstruct any crime or motive or threat or conspiracy, past, present, or future. It was the DNA of the Internet. The notion of privacy in the Digital Age was as delusional as chastity in a whorehouse.

"That's it, my precious," Josh said, leaning forward. "Talk to me. Tell me everything about it. That's it . . ."

Randall cast a curious glance at him.

Josh looked back and raised his eyebrows haughtily.

Randall shook his head and returned to his work.

Within seconds, the first hits started popping up, and Josh scrolled through the clutter. There were lots of partial matches associated with anonymous chat rooms and online postings, and as best as Josh could tell, this odd patchwork of cipher had done the rounds for the last couple months, passed back and forth, up, down, sideways. All this buzz suggested that it *meant* something. Something big.

Things got interesting as the search algorithm skimmed deeper and deeper through the exabytes—far deeper than the bullshit metadata—to where the real messages people relayed back and forth to one another remained tucked away. The really, *really* private content.

Within thirty seconds, an exact 100 percent match came up.

"Hell, yeah. Now we're talking."

It was a very simple Gmail message, dated nearly a year and a half earlier, originating from the United Kingdom. The email user name was some weird alphanumeric mix, like something Gmail itself would assign to a latecomer whose desired name preference had already been registered in every imaginable permutation. In the body of the email, there was no salutation, or preamble, or message, or valediction—nothing except the block of ciphertext that had triggered the 100 percent match. In the subject line, there was one word, all in caps: RAZORWIRE.

When Josh saw the recipient of the email, colors began swirling in his mind. A smile broke across his face. *Oh, yeah. Happy Halloween.* He could practically smell those Cayman palm trees and feel that hot, sugary sand between his toes.

57.01

@ Ottawa, Ontario, Canada
Tuesday, 11/07/2017
06:11:08 EST

The Canadian authorities had begrudgingly granted the FBI's request
for Special Agents Novak and Michaels to observe the raid on Sing-
Lao North American Shipping, conditional on the agents remaining
under the aegis of DEA Special Agent Robert Romeyn—a thirtyish
corn-fed Nebraskan of medium height and build with a buzz cut who
wore jeans and cowboy boots and took orders through the American
embassy in Ottawa. Similarly, Walter and four techs from the FBI's
Cyber Action Team were now parked on a side street a half mile
away, in an innocuous panel van, standing by to play second fiddle to
six cyber agents from the Communications Security Establishment
Canada.

Romeyn brought Novak and Michaels inside the office building
across the way, up to a third-floor office space leased under the name

of a fictitious commodities trading company. They sat in the early morning darkness in swivel chairs, sipping coffee from foam cups, facing a big plate glass window that overlooked SingLao.

"Once that sun comes up, all hell's gonna break loose," Romeyn said in a gruff midwestern drawl.

Novak used his binoculars to scan the grounds of the facility, which were secured by chain-link fencing and barbed wire and lit by sodium lights. The main building was an expansive single-story rectangle of cinder blocks and sheet metal, optimal for stockpiling inventory. He zoomed in on six white minivans parked near the loading bays, then clicked on the night vision to read their tags. The second one from the right was the one that had been driven to Massena. Panning the grounds, he studied the dozens of marine cargo containers with Asian markings stacked in the lot. "Robbie"—the DEA agent insisted on being called by his nickname—"what's being shipped in those containers?"

"Acetic anhydride and potassium permanganate," he said. "Precursor chemicals. The magic sauce of the drug trade. Turns raw opium into heroin, and's used to cook up coke and meth. Without chems, the cartels would have no finished product to sell." He leaned back in his chair, plopped his shitkickers up on the windowsill, and took a big gulp of coffee.

"How do they not catch that at the ports?" Michaels asked.

"Four million of them cans come into Canada each year. On a good day, two percent might get inspected. Some get X-rayed for guns, others go through radiation portals that sniff out nukes, and some get an ion scan, if the inspectors suspect drugs. That's the official estimate, mind you, and it might hold water for small ports, like St. John's, but then you've got Halifax and the like, with these huge volumes of shit pushing through 'em." He snickered. "Unofficially, I'd say that skews the overall number of inspections to damn near zero."

"Pretty good odds for the smugglers," Michaels said.

"You bet it is," he said. "Ain't much different down in the States, just bigger numbers, is all. And where you find drugs or chems, you find cash. Lots and lots of cash. Like toast and jam. Contraband is contraband no matter how you dress it up."

That's why the Massena lead routed directly to Romeyn's desk, thought Novak. Rounding up drugs and cash outside U.S. borders required a unique skill set, which Romeyn possessed in spades.

"No surprise to me that this outfit cut a deal with Bounty4Justice," the DEA agent went on. "With all the volume the big boss is producing down there"—Romeyn tipped his head at the facility—"converting dollars to NcryptoCash lets him send all his loot back home to his buddies in China right over the Internet."

Romeyn explained how the DEA and various branches of the Royal Canadian Mounted Police and the Ottawa Provincial Police had been methodically charting the syndicate's intricate worldwide network. "You can always count on a few bigmouths in any operation," he said. "Some folks are just plain yappy. Can't help themselves. Especially on the Internet. I've been using this screen name, PonyX-prez, to troll the darknet chat rooms. Basically got them telling me all their secrets. And I've pretty much finagled my way into becoming SingLao's best customer, buying up huge batches of sauce on behalf of a Mexican cartel that doesn't even exist. Took nearly a year to get to this point. That's why our Canadian friends are none too pleased that your website is forcing things into hyperdrive. Hell, at sunup, six dozen known associates, middlemen, and mules throughout Canada and the U.S. will need to be rounded up, all at once. Because when the lights go on, these roaches will all be scuttling for cover. Got six hundred of our men waiting to pounce. All thanks to that package mailed to your buddy in Dallas."

They watched the morning shift arrive like clockwork—the same ragtag collection of Asian males Romeyn claimed to have seen most mornings for the past year. He predicted the arrival of the coffee truck within ten seconds of it rolling up and tooting its air horn; then he ticked off the names and beverage preferences of the cast of characters who came scurrying outside seeking sustenance.

"You really know your stuff," Michaels said.

"Don't be too impressed," he responded with a wily grin. He

flipped a switch on a parabolic antenna set on a tripod beside his chair. The voices came through loud and clear—the laughter and the banter, much of it in Mandarin. "Little bird here tells me everything I need to know. The rest is simple observation. I can even predict how many cigarettes they'll burn through at break time and who stands the best odds of winning at mah-jongg."

A fingernail sliver of the rising sun winked over the glowing horizon.

Romeyn checked his watch. "Six forty-five. Showtime."

57.02

Michaels used her binoculars to observe the armored vehicles and unmarked SUVs creeping along the streets leading to the facility. "Feels like I'm back in Afghanistan," she muttered to Novak.

Only a handful of men remained out in the yard. They dashed inside when one of them, spotting a behemoth Coyote LAV eight-wheeler along the northwest quadrant, out beyond the perimeter fence and accelerating toward the facility, shouted, alerting the others.

Two more light armored vehicles sped out of the shadows from the east and west, their bright floodlights snapping on as they effortlessly rolled over the barbed-wire fencing. Simultaneously, on the southern perimeter, a Humvee smashed through the front gate. Another Humvee bounded in right behind it, steamrolling toward two submachine-toting guards, who scrambled out of the security booth.

From all sides, black-clad ground assault units swept in on foot, equipped with snub-nosed machine guns.

SingLao's morning shift wasn't going down without a fight; the workers came streaming out of the warehouse wearing body armor and wielding submachine guns, too.

"Will you look at that," said Romeyn, tightening his binoculars' zoom. "Those uppity fuckers have Kriss Super V's. Best damn weapon on the market."

Novak zoomed in on one of the carbines; it looked like something out of a sci-fi movie. So much for surprise, stabilize, and seize. This was going to get nasty.

"Gonna be one helluva gunfight," Romeyn said. "Good thing we're up here."

In no time, the entire facility turned into a free-for-all Tin Can Alley, with muzzles flashing back and forth and bullets sparking and ricocheting. A pair of Bell choppers rumbled overhead and swooped in to circle the facility like birds of prey, the sharpshooters prone in their open fuselages, expertly picking off the SingLao militiamen.

The ringtone on Romeyn's phone clanged like a Chinese gong each time an update streamed in from another city in North America, each *blong-sssh!* confirming yet another arrest in the massive roundup. "So far so good," he reported. "We're rustling 'em up now."

Novak turned to Michaels. She didn't seem to realize that she was massaging a spot just below her right clavicle—a likely remnant of Afghanistan, he figured. "Rosemary, are you all right? Your shoulder?"

She looked over at him, startled.

"Your shoulder. Is it okay?"

She smiled ruefully. "Sorry. I do that sometimes. I'm okay. Just brings back some memories."

"Do you want to take a break?"

"I'm fine. But thanks."

The battle raged on for a few more minutes, until the few remaining fighters of the SingLao militia finally threw down their high-tech weapons and surrendered. They were quickly rounded up and corralled.

Meanwhile, the commandos unloaded a dual-track tactical Pack-Bot equipped with a camera head, an articulating arm, and a rotary firing mechanism loaded up with tear gas canisters. The robot was remotely guided into the building to scout the interior; a few minutes later, the unit commander ordered three tactical assault units into the building. Shortly thereafter, they called Romeyn with the all-clear.

57.03

By the time Romeyn, Novak, and Michaels had made their way on foot over to the aftermath of the battlefield, news vans were already jockeying for strategic positions outside the flattened perimeter fences, the choppers were grounded in the stockyard out near the cargo containers, and an armada of emergency response vehicles had descended upon the scene. The commandos were busy loading able-bodied captives onto a prison bus, while teams of paramedics tended to the wounded and bagged the dead.

They entered the building through the loading dock and emerged into a vast, brightly lit industrial space occupied by tall rows of shelving brimming with magic sauce—from keg-sized plastic drums to pourable twist-top canisters—ready to fulfill any darknet order, big or small. Clusters of Canadian authorities milled about the aisles.

"Man, even the goon squad showed up," Romeyn said, waving to a pair of Secret Service agents who'd arrived to inspect the scene, along with three agents from the Canadian Security Intelligence Service.

Proceeding to the rear of the building, Romeyn, Novak, and Michaels passed through the administrative offices, where Walter, fluid and laser-focused, was busily cloning computer drives alongside the North American cyber coalition—a blitzkrieg against SingLao's digital ramparts. Sometime last week, a quiet intensity had fallen over the cyber squad leader, and Novak was pretty sure it wasn't solely attributable to the mad dash of planning that preceded their hasty departure for Canada the previous afternoon. On the plane, Walter had been withdrawn and irritable—kept his headphones on for the whole flight. Novak knew not to ask too many questions. Sometimes Walter tended to get wound up tight and simply needed space to decompress. Lack of sleep, bad eating habits, and caffeine binges typically accompanied those episodes. Nonetheless, this time seemed different, and Novak sensed that something more had happened to set him on a warpath against Bounty4Justice.

Bounty4Justice had cranked up lots of people, in fact. Case in point: even Piotr at Novak's deli. When Novak had seen him yesterday morning, the old man had been all worked up about a shady Russian guy who'd stopped by a half hour earlier for a pack of batteries. "I know his type, Roman," Piotr said. "The way he looks at a simple Pole like me . . . like I'm a dog. There's something not right about him, I'm telling you. He's SVR. On the news, I see what's going on with you and your work friends . . . how this website is trying to come after you because of what happened in Russia. Who's to say the Kremlin didn't send him here to find you . . . to set the record straight?"

Piotr had even provided pictures of the Russian—a sturdily built man of medium height with dark features and acne scars pitting his angular cheekbones, as well as a jagged scar on his forehead—which had been captured by the HD security camera above the meat slicer. Thanks to the vivid picture quality, Novak had gotten a fast match when he'd run the images through the facial recognition software at the office. Turned out, the "Russian" was actually Ukrainian, a long-time neighborhood resident. And the Ukrainian didn't hold a valid passport, which meant he'd have an awfully tough time trying to shadow Novak into Canada. Though Novak had assigned him a threat level of zero, he'd worn his Glock all day yesterday, even in the apartment, so as not to completely ignore karma. After all, Russia did play dirty.

A burly commando with a ponytail and a goatee appeared in a doorway at the rear of the room. "Hey, Robbie, back this way!"

"That there's the meanest damn Canadian I've ever met," Romeyn said. "Name's Holt. He's the one who put this whole thing together."

Out in the hallway, Holt gave Romeyn a big bear hug, saying, "Can you believe this? *Whoooh!* And don't you go trying to take all the credit, you shit-shovelin' hick."

"I wouldn't think of it, you scraggly moosefucker," Romeyn said. "These here are my friends from the FBI." He introduced Novak and Michaels.

"Pardon the obscenities, beautiful," Holt said to Michaels. "I think you folks will be mighty glad you made the trip when you see what we found back here."

Holt led them down a sterile corridor into a workroom outfitted with stainless steel prep stations. Along its side walls were rolling racks stocked neatly with silver foil pouches, folded cardboard boxes, rolls of packing tape, and stacks of used paperback books.

Centered in the rear wall was what looked to Novak like the door to a meat locker. Its heavy handle was mangled and covered in black grime, which explained the acrid redolence of blasting chemicals, as well as the thin veil of smoke that hung along the ceiling tiles. Holt opened the door and motioned them into the space beyond—a roomy, temperature-controlled cubicle, its walls, ceiling, and floor lined with riveted metal panels, enclosing pallets upon pallets of neatly bundled cash.

They had stepped inside Bounty4Justice's cash vault.

58.01

@ Lake City, Colorado
06:11:17 MST

Jonathan Farrell had just cast his line into the burbling brook, contemplating nothing beyond trout, when his satcom pinged. He plucked the phone from his vest, read the instructions, then reread them. His jaw clenched.

"You've got to be kidding me."

It wasn't the mark that he took issue with. Whoever wound up on the receiving end of his Lapua Magnum wasn't any of his damn business. At this stage of his career, death was a transaction, not a moral dilemma. What bothered him most was the *place*.

Why *there*? he thought.

The location certainly complicated the method Oz was requesting. There were risks involved in everything, marginally more so in the art of killing. Calculated risk was perfectly acceptable, and every occupation came with some element of hazard. Wanton risk, however, entailed very different scales of probability, the sort he wasn't all that comfortable with. By his thinking, you didn't ask a poker player to place bets at a roulette table. Simple as that. It felt as if Oz was toying with him, pulling hard at his strings to try to make him dance.

He scrolled down the message, read the bio and the logistical data, and scanned the high-res photos. The face was unique yet not extraordinary. Easy enough to pick out from a crowd, though the directive implied there'd be no crowd to mess with. And that didn't sit quite right with him, either. Once the work was done, it would be hard enough to make an escape, and a bit more cover could, at the very least, compensate.

Then the satcom trilled a second time to announce a piggyback directive. *This fucker's pushing his luck.*

Different mark.

Same place.

Same time.

Same method.

"Shit."

Dance, monkey, dance.

He'd seen plenty of action movies where the master assassin has a cathartic moment—fade in on the surly veteran killer who gets dragged into that one last job, at the very moment he's come to terms with hanging up his weapon and heading off for a simpler, killing-free life. Farrell had always sworn that he'd never be a cliché, yet for the first time, he was feeling reticent.

So he mulled the facts once more, then assigned probabilities. *Two marks. Shit location. Big show. An impossible escape.* Invariably, however, he came to the conclusion that a challenge was a challenge. Above all, Jonathan Farrell wasn't one to back down. Besides, Oz paid *really* well, and on time. And the pay was two times the $50K single rate, with a kicker of $25K. For that kind of money, he'd make concessions.

From: Joshua.L.Tierney@nsa.gov
Sent: Tuesday, November 7, 2017 at 8:14 AM
To: Walter Koslowski, Roman Novak, Tim Knight
Cc: Dilip Kapoor
Subject: Bounty4Justice—ciphertext query
📎: Razorwire.email
Re: Query request #: 658YHRZJ395-001

Hi Walter,

I've attached a Gmail intercept dated May 12, 2016, that contains the exact cipher block you'd submitted for analysis. The metadata (included in attachment) points to an IP address once used by an Internet café in London, England, that went out of business earlier this year. The sender's Gmail account was registered under "PIKE MAS-TER," which is clearly a fictitious name. However, I'm sure you'll be intrigued by the recipient's email address, as well as the subject line of the message itself.

Frankly, I've never seen anything like the random block of characters contained in the body of the message. I concur that the only semi-intelligible string is "iArchos6I6," though I get no hits when I run it through data match—not even a screen name on IRC board archives. If I had to guess, I'd say it might be a password or username. I'm not sure if the "<" and ">" to the left and right of the string might also be important, and it's certainly possible that other pieces of the cipher block might also matter.

I'll continue to analyze the data. In the interim, the recipient of the "Razorwire" email is, by far, your best lead.

Best of luck,

Josh Tierney
Senior Digital Network Exploitation Analyst

59.01 _____

@ Ottawa, Ontario, Canada

"Man, oh, man, we are breaking *all* the records today," DEA Special Agent Robert Romeyn said to Novak and Michaels, wearing a shit-eating grin as he strolled around the ten pallets of cash sitting in Sing-Lao's stockroom. "So far we've got seventeen dead out in the yard, none of them friendlies, praise Jesus. Hands down, we've netted the largest black market chems seizure to date. Not bad. We've got sixty-eight out of seventy-two of SingLao's top associates in custody. That's impressive, too. But then *this*?" He whistled as if he were sizing up the prettiest lady he ever did see. "*Shit-damn!* This will *definitely* top any record for the biggest loot repo *ever*. Guess who's gonna be employee of the month? That's right. You're lookin' at him. Man, do I love it when a plan comes together."

Michaels smiled and glanced over at Novak, shaking her head as Romeyn went about tabulating the inventory. The contraband was plainly visible under the plastic shrink wrap, so the DEA agent confirmed the denominations on the bills on top of each pile, then crouched down to count the individually packaged bricks stacked below. This was clearly not his first contraband cash rodeo.

"Looks like we've got five pallets of hundred-dollar bills . . . three pallets of fifties . . . two pallets of twenties. Benjamins, Grants, Jacksons." He stood and leaned against one of the pallets. It reached the top of his chest, nearly five feet high. "So let's start with the Benjamins. As you can see, these hundreds are banded in stacks of ten thousand dollars, and they're packed four stacks by thirteen stacks per brick. That's fifty-two stacks per brick, or five hundred and twenty thousand dollars. Take your pick."

Novak realized that each brick, about the size of a shoe box, was worth more than what many middle-class families earned in a decade.

"You can't make a perfect square out of half a million in ten-thousand-dollar stacks. But you can see that each layer is six by three, or eighteen bricks per layer. Each pile is eleven layers high. Means each pallet of hundreds is worth one hundred and two million, nine hundred and sixty thousand dollars. Five pallets is roughly five hundred million in hundreds."

When skimming nearly $3,000,000 per pallet became a rounding error, you knew the numbers were big, thought Novak.

"Over there you've got three pallets of fifties and two pallets of twenties." He pointed to each pallet in turn. "Let's ballpark those at another two hundred million combined."

"Holy shit," Michaels said.

"Jesus," Novak contributed. He'd seen plenty of big dollar figures on computer screens and in financial documents, replete with multiple commas and zeros and decimal points. On paper, money was esoteric and abstract, not particularly impressive. Standing alongside its physical equivalent was an entirely different experience. He reached out and touched a big solid cube of cash. "Wow. Seven hundred million."

"You got it, my man. Not bad, eh?" Romeyn paced over and patted him on the back. "Seventy percent of hundred-dollar bills are held outside the U.S., just like this. For lots of honest folks who live in shit dictatorships and such, it's the only way they can preserve what they've got. Of course, then you have scumbags like these guys who just stockpile it and hide it away because it's ill-gotten to begin with. But physical money comes with its own problems. Take, for example, the fact that each of these pallets weighs just over a ton. That's ten tons of legal tender that needs protecting."

Michaels said, "Can't just go to the local bank to make a deposit."

"You got that right," Romeyn said. "And sure as shit you can't go bringin' it on a plane to Switzerland. You can only transport ten grand at a pop without having customs perform a cavity search. I don't even know how many trips that works out to."

"Seventy thousand," Novak said, without hesitation.

"Okay. Then that's seventy thousand plane tickets and hotel stays, and a lot of mules who need to get paid a cut to move this inventory to a safe place. Suffice it to say that's a mighty big hassle. Good luck trying to tape it to your privates, or jamming it elsewhere. I reckon, my friends, that's why these fuckers got in the business of swapping cash for NcryptoCash—to liquidate the inventory. Tell me, how much bounty has actually been paid out so far by that website of yours?"

Novak recalled the most recent updates to his spreadsheet. "It's awarded bounties on fifty-two marks in fourteen countries, grand total of roughly thirty million dollars. No way to really know how much was paid in cash and how much was NcryptoCash."

"Okay," Romeyn said. "Let's even say that it was *all* paid out in cash. Every bounty, every country. Thirty mil ain't even a third of a pallet of Benjamins. Barely puts a dent in the stock. So you can see why SingLao welcomed Bounty4Justice with open arms. It's the best money-laundering prospect in town."

Novak's BlackBerry pinged a call from Knight. He went back out into the packing room to answer it.

"Hey, Tim."

"I hear you've had one hell of a morning."

Novak related just *how* good it had been, and Knight laughed giddily.

"Sounds to me like we've just put a big dent in the Bounty4Justice business model."

"Sure looks that way."

"Listen," Knight said. "I've got some more good news. Not sure if you've seen it yet, but NSA just sent us the analysis on that crypto-text. Get this: they were able to trace it to an actual email account."

"An *email* account?" Novak listened intently as Knight explained the particulars of how the mysterious cipher block Borg had given him matched the message content of an old email captured by the NSA's intercept program.

Knight said, "The sender hasn't been positively identified yet. But the guy who received the message has."

"NSA's sure about that?" Novak pressed.

"A hundred percent. I've already made some calls so you and Michaels can get on this immediately." He gave Novak the contact details, then said, "Given the sensitive nature of our inquiry, it's best to handle this one in person. And you need to exercise extreme caution. I've convinced management that since this was your lead, you'll see it through. Hartley instructed me to tell you that this needs to be approached with finesse and utmost diplomacy. Understood?"

"Dust with feathers, not with knives. Understood. I won't let you down."

"I know," Knight said. "I'm having Jennifer book your plane tickets now. You'll head directly over there tonight, and your meeting will be tomorrow afternoon. I'm emailing the report to you now so you'll have everything you need. I don't think I need to emphasize that we have a lot riding on this. It's a huge break."

"Sure is."

"You'll bring Michaels up to speed?"

"Of course. No problem."

"Good luck."

60.01

@ Washington, D.C.
13:13:13 EST

Six Capitol Police patrol cars escorted the Yukon from the safe house
in Georgetown, cruising at medium speed with lights flashing. This
time, Jones did the driving, while Vargas sat in the passenger seat,
glued to his smartphone, watching the senator's bounty skyrocket on
the all-seeing, all-knowing website that had brought down her world.
Jones glanced in the rearview mirror at Senator Ascher, who sat in
pensive silence in the backseat, slouching under the weight of the
Kevlar vest they'd fitted over her pantsuit, maybe contemplating her
last minutes of freedom or the bad choices of the past that had culmi-
nated in the current grim procession.

The motorcade used a diversionary route over the Potomac bridge
crossings, swept across Theodore Roosevelt Island, then whisked
along Constitution Avenue, past the National Mall between the lawns
of the White House and the Washington Monument—smooth sailing, thanks to D.C.'s Metropolitan Police beat patrolmen who kept
the intersections clear.

Vargas held up his phone so that only Jones could see it and pointed
to the screen, mouthing, "Two million dollars!"

Fuck, thought Jones. Ascher added a whole new meaning to "high-value target." *Someone's gonna take a shot at us, for sure.* If the sniper who'd shot that banker in Manhattan was still out there somewhere, he'd surely take a crack at this fat prize. Jones could practically feel the laser dot burning a hole into his forehead. He'd been inserted into plenty of hostile environments over the years, but this situation was in its own league. The higher-ups had been tight-lipped, but Jones had the distinct impression that they weren't even sure of their own personnel—an inside job wasn't impossible at this level of payoff—not to mention the uneasy sense of the center giving way, things spiraling out of control.

Bounty4Justice had become a genuine menace. It had begun with the bankers and the child molesters and the cheats. Then it had moved up the food chain to mendacious journalists and bribe-paying businessmen, then to especially notorious, double-dealing local and state officials, and eventually to federal senators and congressmen, proving that no man or woman with a skeleton in the closet was safe. Which explained why so many politicos in D.C., in particular, were on high alert.

Jones had always thought that computer technology was a man-made construct, easily controlled by software and circuits. Evidently, in the wrong hands, there was nothing simple about it. There was something uniquely unsettling about knowing that people were out there online, voting in real time to have Ascher taken out, clicking away as if to say, *Last chance! Let's get her now, before it's too late!* The United States vs. Barbara Ascher, gangland-style. With all the disenchanted folks around nowadays, it made for bad odds. Very bad odds. Precisely why the senator had gone ahead and made the smartest choice of her career.

They swung a left onto Tenth Street, heading against the one-way signs. The street had been blocked off at the last minute for the final stretch to the J. Edgar Hoover Building—a little surprise tactic to throw off any clued-in assassin who might be expecting to take advantage of the normal traffic pattern. As they slowed to cross Pennsylvania Avenue, Jones got a good look at the protestors lining the wide sidewalks fronting the building's brutalist facade. They were all wearing creepy white masks that looked a bit too much like the slasher model from that classic horror movie his dad loved, which only made an already tense situation more surreal.

"I keep seeing those hacker freaks on the news," Vargas said. "They look mighty pissed off." He laughed, but Jones didn't think he was persuading anyone, including himself.

Contained by a cordon of police officers, the mob—hundreds of those white masks—whipped up into a frenzy as the motorcade skirted them and evaded the front entrance. Some of them were holding up signs that said things like BOUNTY4JUSTICE = TRUE LAW and THE FBI DOES NOT CONTROL THE WEB. The rest of them thrust their fists skyward in unison, as if they shared one brain. It gave Jones the chills. He caught Ascher's expression in the mirror; she seemed unfazed, as if this were all some bad dream she had already replayed in her mind, over and over again.

A heavily armed and body-armored security detail emerged from the building's side entryway to receive them. The FBI agents directed the patrol cars to stack and box around the Yukon.

Now they only needed to cover the last few yards to the door. But Jones felt a nasty sense of vulnerability that made him hesitate.

"Let's do this," Vargas said.

Jones nodded, took a deep breath, and opened the door.

60.02

They made it through the final leg of the transfer without a hitch—thank God. Once they had safely escorted Senator Ascher inside, they helped her remove the Kevlar vest.

She smoothed out her black suit jacket with trembling fingers. "I guess this is it," she said with a rueful little smile.

Vargas wasn't one for emotional displays. He just stood there with his hands crossed behind his back, nodding, like he had when he'd watched her heart-rending goodbyes to her family, a little while ago.

Jones reached out to straighten the American flag pin on her lapel. "You're going to be okay."

For the first time, she looked scared, and with good reason, he thought. Just this morning, inside the Justice Department building, all of them sitting across the street from those crazy protestors out front, the judge had finalized the hasty twenty-one-count indictment, which promised to stack years upon years upon years for myriad frauds and instances of tax evasion and taking bribes and knowingly endangering children, plus Lord knew what else. No doubt she'd been granted leniency for her full cooperation. But there was simply no avoiding the snowball effect of all those charges. She wouldn't be around to watch her kids grow up, plain and simple, and Jones was certain that this was the sentence that would inevitably tear at her the most. The only conditions she'd requested were that her arrest be dignified, for the sake of the children, and that she be given the opportunity to address the public on her own terms. Both requests had been granted, and the media conference was to be held here, in the press hall of FBI headquarters. A select group of reporters were now funneling through the metal detectors and security checkpoint at the building's main entrance.

Down the corridor, an FBI reception committee rounded a corner, coming to take charge.

"I never meant for any of this to happen," she said to Jones. "Power is a very seductive thing, you know. It makes otherwise decent people do stupid things. Really stupid things. Really bad things . . ."

Jones could see her eyes welling up. "But *now* you're doing the right thing, Senator. For you. For your family."

She smiled sadly. "Thank you for everything. Both of you."

"It's all good," Vargas said, trying to keep a stoic face.

Jones gave her a reassuring smile. "You've got this."

A crisp young woman wearing a lanyard badge for the FBI's National Press Office approached them. "Good morning, Senator. Are we ready?"

"I'm ready."

60.03 _____

At first, Senator Ascher stood frozen with a death grip on the podium, giving Jones the impression that maybe she'd had a change of heart. From his post at the corner of the stage, he scanned the room, camera flashes popping all around, dozens of video cameras feeding live coverage to points around the globe, imagining how intimidated she must feel at this very moment.

Finally, she adjusted the microphone, stared out at the cameras, cleared her throat, and began. "When we all arrived this morning, here in Washington, we were greeted by protestors wearing masks, along with other protestors out on the Internet who were casting votes to see that I be taken to task for all the bad decisions I've made. Behind every one of those votes, and beneath every one of those masks, is a person. Someone who is unique, and gifted, and sometimes alienated, and sometimes flawed." She scanned the faces in the audience. "I know this, because I've worn a mask, too. And you've all had the opportunity to see beneath it. You've seen everything about me. Every flaw. The problem is that *my* mask came with the trust of my constituents. They voted for what I represented and the promises I vowed to keep. They hoped that everything they saw in me was real and honest. I'm here today to tell everyone that my mask deceived them. I violated the public trust. And I'm ashamed of what people see now that my mask has been removed. I know I can't make it right. I can't bring those children back . . ."

Ascher choked up and took a moment to compose herself. Jones could tell she wasn't acting or playing to the crowd. She was unloading the sorts of invisible burdens that weighed heavily on those with secrets.

"If someone harmed my children . . . and I had to *bury* my children . . . I'd wish them harm, too." She fell quiet for a long moment, visibly trembling, struggling not to break down.

Jones looked around the room at the press staffers and agents. Everyone was gripped by the very public—and very private—spectacle before them. Bounty4Justice had come over America like a bad storm, and here was the first humanizing element to the whole ordeal. Barbara Ascher—the mother, the person—was putting a face to the other side of the equation. She was preparing to be sacrificed.

"You've won," she said humbly. "You deserve to win, because you deserve better. You are right to want justice. You are right to want a chance at liberty and privacy and fair play and everything we were promised by our nation's founders. And none of that is possible without proper representation . . . and trust. Bounty4Justice isn't just a website. It's a voice. A voice that demands action against people who break the rules and get away with it. And though its prescription for what ails the world is violent—extreme—I'm here today to tell you that *your* voice has been heard."

She fell silent again and glanced down at her hands. Then she looked back up into the cameras.

"Today, here before you, I confess my guilt to the crimes laid out on Bounty4Justice. I am remanding myself into custody so that a proper resolution can be worked out by our courts of law."

The crowd remained silent as the senator gave Jones a tiny nod. He nodded back. Then she turned and looked over to the FBI agents standing off to her side. They escorted her away from the podium, with dignity, and out the side door. Once she was gone, the room erupted in chatter.

By the time the Secret Service agents made it back out to the Yukon, Bounty4Justice had text-blasted its verdict.

Vargas smiled and held his phone up for Jones. "Lookee here."

Jones peered down at the display. He felt his tension start to release, knowing that the Ascher children were going to be safe:

TARGET STATUS NOTIFICATION: TARGET DEACTIVATED
TARGET: BARBARA ASCHER, senator, USA
STATUS: Guilty
BOUNTY: $2,212,058 ‹‹REALLOCATED››
http://www.bounty4justice.com/BARBARA.ASCHER
As per section 19 of our user agreement, targets who formally surrender to the charges presented herewith are subject to deactivation, and the bounty funds collected for that target will be distributed proportionately among the remaining active targets.
Thank you for your patronage.

Sacrifice accepted.

61.01

@ N 49°27'

After a near on-time 10:20 P.M. departure from Ottawa International Airport, the Air Canada Boeing 767 found smooth air at thirty-six thousand feet off the coast of Nova Scotia, and the cheery flight attendants initiated their first round of beverage service. It was just under seven hours to London, and after a big day, Novak was looking to catch a nap. He ordered a scotch on the rocks to settle himself. Michaels, sitting beside him at the window, dittoed him.

"To our first major victory," she said, holding up her plastic cup.

"You made it happen," Novak said, tapping his cup against hers. "You're one hell of an agent."

"Thanks. I really appreciate it. Cheers." She sipped her drink, studied him for a long moment, then said, "Seems like you've got a lot on your mind. Is it this whole mess with Russia and the website pursuing you and Tim and Walter?"

He took a pull of scotch. "I can take care of myself. So can the guys. But I'm concerned about my parents. They're going through a tough time right now, and having them fully exposed, out there on the Web, sure isn't helping matters. Talk about taking cheap shots."

"I'm all ears, if it would help to talk about it."

He gave her a quizzical glance.

"We've got a lot of time to kill," she said. "And I'm a lot cheaper than a therapist. Let's hear it."

So he aired his troubles, albeit hesitantly at first. Michaels's easygoing, matter-of-fact nature had an almost magical way of pulling everything out of him: the helpless feelings about his mother's illness, his anger toward his self-absorbed sister, and the other thorny emotions that linked it all together—things he'd never discussed with anyone—without judgment or strings attached.

"I never thought my parents would wind up in this position," he told her. "My dad was a consummate planner. Every detail, mapped out. His mantra was all about structure and managing risks. And my mom . . ." He shook his head and sighed, trying to shake off images of her sitting at the kitchen table barely able to sip coffee through a straw, remembering instead the vivacious, engaged mother he had been so lucky to have. "My mom was always moving, full of energy and spunk. So vibrant. So *healthy*. Now the doctors are telling her things that, to her, amount to something far worse than a death sentence." He shook his head again and took another hit of scotch, and Michaels waited patiently for him to continue. "Man, let me tell you, with everything they've got going on, the last thing they need is to be put in the spotlight by some glory-seeking hacker or to have to worry about their son being taken out by some fanatical vigilante. I just hope they can pull through until we can shut this damn thing down."

"They'll get through it. Because they've got you. Just stay strong for them, and everything else will fall into place." She smiled, put her hand on his arm, and gave a little squeeze. "In the meantime, you and I will be sure to teach this hacker and all his vigilante minions a thing or two."

He smiled. "Sounds like a plan." He drained his scotch. "Okay. Your turn."

She emptied her scotch, too, then said, "Let's do it. Shoot."

"Well, I hear you joined the Marine Corps and shipped off to Afghanistan right out of Cornell. What was the motive there?"

She shrugged. "I don't know, just trying to escape for a while. I had a really serious boyfriend back then who was pushing for rings and kids from the moment we graduated. I wasn't ready for all that. We had a long talk about our future, and we realized that we were on two different timelines. Two different paths. The breakup was hard, because we had a lot of history and he was a solid guy destined for great things."

Novak figured that if he had met Michaels back in college, he'd probably have tried to hang on for dear life, too. If ever there was a "keeper," she'd be the one. He actually felt bad for her ex.

"Anyway," she said, "I didn't have much of a plan for my life at that time, nor did I feel compelled to come up with one. I'd majored in business. And back then, business wasn't doing so hot. So, you know . . ."

"You figured shipping off to a war zone might fix all that?"

She smiled. "It just felt like it was the right thing to do. You know, putting something else before myself. Can't say that if I could go back I'd do it all the same, but the experience sure did reshape my priorities and values. Saw lots of things over there that completely upended my worldview . . . for good or bad, I'm not sure. I liked the teamwork and camaraderie, even the structure, I guess. When I came home, I knew that doing this, what we're doing right now—setting things right, or at least trying to—was the type of work I was meant to do."

In the grand scheme of things, all Novak had needed to bring his life into focus was to see his boss plunge from a rooftop. Relatively speaking, he figured he'd gotten off easy. "When did you get shot?" He glanced at her shoulder.

"Oh, so now you're a detective. You sure you really want to hear war stories?"

"You heard mine. What's fair is fair."

She collected her thoughts, then said, "I was a logistics specialist, so I managed to go three years without a scratch. Then one day I hitch a ride with an expeditionary unit heading for Jalalabad, where I'd been reassigned. On the way, they wind up in a nasty skirmish.

Not the kind of stuff that delicate girls like me were supposed to get involved in." She laughed softly, but there was an edge in her tone.

With the Marine Corps opening combat positions to women just a couple of years ago, Novak was pretty sure that during Michaels's years of service, female troops had been relegated to positions in the rear. Undoubtedly, Michaels wasn't the rear-lines type, and by his estimation she sure seemed fit enough to crush the Corps' rigid performance standards.

"The unit put them down fairly quickly, minimal damage, minimal casualties, by the book," she said, pausing for a moment, her eyes growing distant. "When the dust clears, I see this young Afghan woman, pregnant—I mean, *really* pregnant—dressed in a burka. She's hunched over, grabbing her big old belly, and it looks to me like she's hurt, maybe going into labor. I run over to her, get down on my knees, try to help. She points a gun in my face . . . pulls the trigger. I avoid eating the bullet, but my shoulder's not so lucky. I manage to knock the gun away, push her to the ground. She jumps up and screams something about God's mercy . . . starts fumbling to get at something tucked into her sleeve. I run. Make it twenty, maybe twenty-five paces away . . . she blows herself up. Boom. Just like that. The blast wave sweeps me right off my feet. I take some shrapnel in my legs. There're pieces of her in my hair, my gear . . ." Michaels paused, remembering. "Anyway, turns out it wasn't a baby under that burka."

"Christ. That's brutal."

"Tell me about it," she said, glancing out the window at the tranquil moonlit clouds quilting the sky a couple miles below. "That's the stuff that really fucks with your head. You know? War does horrible things to people. It's true what they say: there are no winners."

They ordered a second round of drinks and talked for nearly an hour. Novak made it a point to lighten the conversation, so that they had some nice laughs together—the kind that, for a few precious moments, let the weight of the world, and the past, float away and disappear.

"I have a good feeling about this trip," she said, reclining her seat-back. She tucked a pillow under her neck and wriggled in the seat to get cozy. "I think we're on the verge of another big breakthrough."

"Is that right?"

She closed her eyes and folded her hands over her stomach. "Mm-hmm."

"I hope you're right."

62.01 _____

@ London, England
Wednesday, 11/08/2017
14:16:04 GMT

Three blocks from their modest hotel in Westminster, Novak led Michaels across the Thames at Lambeth Bridge, and they followed the tree-lined walkway along the southern embankment in front of the Archbishop of Canterbury's sprawling Gothic palace. It was unseasonably mild and sunny in London, the clouds pinned to the eastern horizon—just enough chill in the air to soothe Novak's jet lag. He checked his phone for the local time. They had plenty of time to kill before their 4:00 meeting at the nearby National Crime Agency.

"So you used to come here often for business?" Michaels asked him, admiring the iconic views of the Houses of Parliament on the opposite riverbank.

"Yeah. A couple miles east of here, over in the City of London." He pointed off in the distance.

"Lots of powwows about world domination?"

"Something like that. Mostly strategy sessions for how best to wager on future trends in commodities like oil and gold and copper. You know, to help the rich get even richer."

"Fascinating," she said, smiling. "You miss it?"

"You mean the godlike feeling of financial conquest and the first-class air travel and six-figure bonuses and twelve-hundred-dollar bottles of champagne? Nah."

Crossing Westminster Bridge, they came upon a raucous rally in the vicinity of Big Ben. Bobbies in high-visibility chartreuse jackets kept the flow of pedestrians moving along the sidewalk as protestors blocked off behind security barriers chanted, "WE ARE THE VOICE! WE ARE THE REVOLUTION!" Some of them were huddled in groups, some worked the crowd into a frenzy with provocative pronouncements, and others waved picket signs reading, THE CYBER SPRING HAS BEGUN—JOIN US! and THE FIGHT FOR FREEDOM STARTS NOW. All of them wore white *volto* masks.

Michaels accepted a flyer from one of them, gave it a quick scan, and passed it to Novak.

Support BOUNTY4JUSTICE

Every voice matters.
Every vote counts.
Those who ignore the will of the people bow to corruption and supplant democracy.
The Internet is the last vestige of freedom, and we *will* protect it.
Fight the Internet, and the Internet will fight back.
WE ARE THE VOICE.
WE ARE THE WEB.
WE ARE THE REVOLUTION.
WE ARE NEXUS.
THE CYBER SPRING HAS BEGUN.
JOIN US.

Nexus wasn't pronouncing outright ownership of Bounty4Justice. But since the movement was highly decentralized and operated in secretive cells worldwide, Novak wondered if some lone wolf might actually be running the show and mobilizing these loyal legions—these quasi flash mobs. According to FBI intelligence data, the vast majority of the Nexus ranks were young people in their teens and twenties, roughly two-thirds male, one-third female—precisely the demographic that had been most disenfranchised by the seismic shifts in global economics and politics. If a worldwide revolution were to occur in the years ahead, he thought, it might well trace its origin back to these humble beginnings.

They negotiated the walkways that cornered the Parliament building and broke free from the crowd at the crosswalk on Abingdon Street, heading toward London's architectural crown jewel, Westminster Abbey. Circling to the front of the building, they paused to admire the famed twin towers of the cathedral's quintessentially Gothic facade.

"Are you a God-fearing man?" Michaels said.

Novak grimaced. "That's a loaded question. Let's just say I leave room for something bigger than myself in this universe and I believe that morality and law matter most, no matter what path one might take to get there."

"I assume you haven't been to church in a while?"

"Can't say I have. You?"

She shook her head. "My parents were always super religious. Fire and brimstone, Catholic guilt, the whole package. They tried to raise me as a good Catholic girl . . ."

"You saying it didn't work?"

She smiled mischievously, adding, "I liked the message, but I wasn't buying into the rituals or the stories. I guess my problem with all this," she said, glancing up at the cathedral, "is that I struggle with the notion that a supremely intelligent creator would find it necessary to be worshipped and adored. That strikes me as circular reasoning. Still, I appreciate the majesty."

"Well, if God and the law don't put the fear in you," said Novak, "I suppose there's always Bounty4Justice"—he gazed back at the masked legion—"and them."

> Anon453we: Do you know Archos?
> B4J: I do not understand what you mean.
> Anon453we: Do you know iArchos?
> B4J: I do not understand what you mean.
> Anon453we: Do you know iArchos6I6?
> B4J: I do not understand what you mean.
> Anon453we: Show me where you are.
> B4J: Sorry. I cannot grant your request.

63.01

@ Manhattan
10:04:02 EST

Holed up in his office, Walter stared at the computer screen. After all
the excitement up in Canada, the late flight home the previous night,
and the mind-blowing email Knight had received from the NSA crypt-
analyst, he'd gotten only a couple hours of restless, lousy sleep. So
he'd cut his losses and headed to the office at 5:00 A.M.

For the past few hours, he'd been attacking the chatbot from every
angle on one of the IRC message boards that linked to Bounty4Jus-
tice's AI interface. He had no idea what he was looking for. Just figured if he was going to blow off some steam, it would be best to
direct it at his enemy. Unlike Novak and Knight, he was terrible at
compartmentalizing anxiety. In truth, he *desperately*—to the level of
compulsion—needed to get off that goddamn list, no matter if he'd
been granted a temporary reprieve of "not guilty." Having a faceless, moody Internet mob in ultimate control of his fate—from the
welfare of his family to his comings and goings and even his frig-
ging credit rating—was fiercely messing with his mind, eating him
alive. "Logic dictates that crowd mentality can turn on a dime," he'd
heard some criminal psychologist say on the news yesterday. Those

words kept replaying over and over again inside his head. *Thanks a lot, asshole. That's really fucking comforting.* Bad enough that he kept having flashbacks of that pack of Nexi encircling him like a pack of wolves.

There was a light knock on his door.

"It's open," he called out.

The door opened, and Connie peeked in.

"Hey, the Cyber Action Team sent over those reports you requested." She held up a ream of paper. "I emailed the files to you. But I know you prefer the printouts."

Walter sighed and rubbed his eyes. "Good. Thanks. Put it there on the pile."

"You look terrible, Walter," Connie said. "You really should take a break."

"I can't. I try to eat or go for a walk or watch TV . . . Nothing works. My mind can't unplug. It's like I'm in full-blown OCD mode. I try to sleep and I wind up staring at the damn ceiling for half the night. This thing owns me."

"You shouldn't be so hard on yourself. Even the NSA is still trying to figure it out. Besides, Novak and Michaels are over in London chasing down the best lead we've got. You have to give them a chance to do their thing."

"I know," he said dejectedly. "Was anyone able to trace those NcryptoCash payments?"

"Do you really want to know?"

"*Uuuuuhh,*" he groaned. "What circle of hell did this demonic website come from anyway?" He cracked open another bottle of 5-hour Energy and took a swig.

"However," she said, "on an up note, they were finally able to access SingLao's shipping software. And they found lots and lots of addresses where large cash payments had been delivered. There were some particularly big payments over the past couple weeks."

"Bounty-sized payments?"

"Sure looks that way."

"Okay. That's pretty good."

"Granted, most of them were sent to post office boxes."

"Of course they were." He chugged the rest of the energy drink and tossed the bottle into the garbage.

The computers and data dumps confiscated at SingLao's Canadian headquarters were nothing like the antiquated equipment and unencrypted files they'd confiscated from the pin distributor in Jersey City. The savvy Asians up in Ottawa had employed total disk encryption on all their hard drives—a next-generation type for which even the NSA had no backdoor solution. If you didn't have the decryption key, you were dead in the water. And unlike Echelon's employees, SingLao's crew had committed their passcodes to memory, not sticky pads. All but one of those key employees had been shot dead in a blaze of glory during the raid. The big man running the show was nowhere to be found, and Romeyn had admitted that no one had ever known his true identity to begin with, just that he went by the online code name Firewolf.

That left one office worker with passwords locked in his brain, and he was using them for all the leverage he could. Smartly, to maintain his advantage, he'd given the authorities one password for one computer—apparently the one that managed the shipping invoices and NcryptoCash ledger. He'd said that the other computers contained all the big names back in China—and elsewhere—who were running the show, the clients from whom the funds had been collected, and more. Chances were that unless he cut himself a generous plea bargain with ironclad protections, he'd be taking the remainder of the passcodes to his grave. Yet, all in all, Walter figured, the raid had been an enormous success. It would likely force Bounty4Justice to retool its payment system, and maybe—with the right press—it would scare off plenty of would-be participants, who would fear that the authorities might just have gained an edge after all.

"What exactly are you trying to do there?" Connie pointed her chin at his screen.

"Not sure really. I've been talking to this stupid bot because, in some crazy way, I find it therapeutic."

She leaned in close to read some of the prompts. "Are you really asking it to help you?" she said, clearly trying not to laugh.

"Something like that, I guess." He turned back to his computer and stared at the monitor, tapping a finger against his chin.

"But it's only a chatbot," she said. "Garbage in, garbage out. It's just there to spew out useless information."

"Maybe. Then again, up until now, no other function of Bounty4Justice has proved to be useless. What if there's more to it than Q&A logic?"

"Not sure I'm following you."

Now Walter was deep in thought, thinking back to his first interactions with the chatbot and how it had intuitively made a lucky guess that he was an FBI agent based simply on the questions he'd submitted. It *was* clever. But he had a sneaking suspicion that its true purpose was more than just some gimmicky customer service tool. "Normally, if I want to query a computer to help me, I'd need to use a language it would understand."

"Sure," she said. "If it was a normal computer, you'd just type 'help.' Or some command."

"Precisely." He ran his wiry fingers over the keyboard to type "help," then hit ENTER.

The chatbot responded:

> › B4J: I can help you. You can type things like: video submission, customer care, or payments.

This wasn't exactly the "help" he was looking for. So he entered "h" and hit ENTER, because that typically worked with plenty of enterprise software. The same reply came back.

"How about a forward slash, then 'help'?" Connie suggested.

He tried it. Again, the same reply.

Now Connie fell under the spell of the chatbot challenge. "Oh, it's on," she said, rolling over the other ball chair. She plunked down beside him, and for the next forty minutes, they tried every string and command they could think of, but nothing could bamboozle Bounty4Justice's intelligent personal assistant into revealing anything useful.

"Boy, this thing is stubborn," Connie said.

"I call her Candice," Walter admitted.

"You have a name for it?"

He shrugged. "With all the time we've spent together, I figured it can't hurt. Candice was my girlfriend back in college. Total bitch. Broke my heart. But, *man,* what a body."

"You really are losing it."

"All right, let's think this through," he said. "We're going with the idea that iArchos is a password, right?"

"That's the theory the NSA's running with," she said. "What it's a password *to* is anyone's guess."

He stared at the screen long and hard. "Then maybe this is all much simpler than we think. How about we just type 'password'?"

"Sure. Why not," she said with zero enthusiasm.

Walter rolled his neck to produce a few audible pops, then plugged the word into the chatbot.

And that's when something magical happened.

63.02 _____

"Are you seeing what I'm seeing?" Walter said in disbelief.

"I sure am." Connie grinned.

Walter stared at the screen for a long moment, feeling like Alice peering through the looking glass.

> › B4J: Sorry. I still don't understand what you are looking for.
> › Anon453we: password
> › ENTER PASSWORD: _

The cursor that had appeared after the prompt was blinking—*waiting.*

"Are we in?" she asked. "Because it looks to me like this thing is patching us through to some kind of server."

"Looks that way," Walter said. "Shit." This was even better than he'd hoped for. Could Bounty4Justice's programmers have disguised a network gateway as a chatbot? Could this be an actual access point into the host server or some command interface?

"You're killing me," Connie said. "Don't just sit there—put the password in."

Walter leaned forward, his fingers quivering. He typed the password at the prompt and submitted it to Candice.

```
> ENTER PASSWORD: iArchos6I6
> PASSWORD INVALID. ENTER PASSWORD: _
```

"Damn," he said, slamming his fist on the desk. "Stupid bitch."

"Whoa," Connie leaned away on her ball chair. "No more energy drinks for you, buddy."

"Sorry."

"We can do this," she said. "I'm not going to let old Candice here break your heart again. I have a good feeling about it. Give me that sheet that has all that gobbledygook on it." She pointed to the Gmail printout. "And that message that came with it from the NSA."

Walter handed her the pages.

"All right," she said. "If the password is buried in all this random code, maybe we should assume that the code isn't *all* random. Because, let's face it, 'iArchos6I6' plugged into this mess isn't exactly discreet. And this Tierney-NSA-codebreaker dude is saying that just because 'iArchos6I6' is bracketed by these greater-than and less-than signs, that doesn't mean it's the whole password." She shook her head incredulously. "Jesus, we could sit here until the end of time trying combinations and permutations."

"Unless . . ." Walter once again fell silent, deep in thought.

"Well?"

"Okay. Look at this format closely: iArchos6I6. There's this little 'i' and this big 'I.' Then you've got the sixes on either side of the capital 'I.' Maybe that's the key. Let me have your pen."

She handed it to him and looked on as he underlined "Archos."

"Archos has six characters," he said. "See?"

"Yeah. I see it."

Then he underlined the six characters preceding the lowercase "i": "89eTf<."

"Six characters to the left of the 'i,' and six to the right. With the 'i' connecting them in the middle." He linked the lines by underlining the lowercase "i." "See? Six-I-six." He turned the paper so that it faced her.

```
FgHllli56/$kjilM//%jatiucmkem398dn47g8p754avh4899&&)*^fjjekjdj65#
589dkjjJHOke//3(mckGtFRdHHiLkm89$2P@/fiemMipfmi%tmjgf7&90/'d//
FooufyY&59689eTf<iArchos6I6›jdutMtiu(309/d'x["wsdj]]djgtkjMtkeix$()
djgk22d,tk952›/?jf48f9fjJljkd;lkgjk:LJLJl;kjgfituY
```

"Hmm," Connie said. "Let's plug it into this bitch and see what happens."

He entered the string at the prompt:

```
› ENTER PASSWORD: 89eTf<iArchos
```

Then he exhaled and hit ENTER.

And that's when the most magical thing happened.

64.01

@ London, England
15:57:51 GMT

"Sir, your guests from the FBI have arrived," a pleasant voice said over
the intercom.

"Brilliant," Burls replied. "Please escort them to my office."

Burls swiveled his leather office chair to face the windows and
gazed out at the spires of Westminster Abbey and the Parliament
building's iconic clock tower. Things were in a shambles. Barring
some significant breakthrough in reining in Bounty4Justice, he stood
a good chance of being removed from his post straightaway, and that
would surely set the record for the shortest tenure for a deputy director in agency history. Now the FBI was knocking at his door, which
only promised to complicate matters. *Not good.*

Predictably, the media was crucifying the National Crime Agency
for its cock-up with Baron Andrew Smith, screaming that the NCA
and the GCHQ had overstepped their bounds in manipulating the
public's trust to satisfy their own objectives, easily inflaming public

sentiment against a government already viewed as Orwellian. Following the debacle, Burls had endured a rather blunt dressing-down from his superiors: warnings, accusations of incompetence . . . even outright threats. He'd reminded them that Bounty4Justice was an unorthodox enemy that required the employ of unconventional tactics. Not surprisingly, that position held little sway, seeing as the inherent design of bureaucracy was all about passing the buck. He did have one closet advocate, whose support was offered not in the boardroom but at the sinks in the loo. "In the underworld of spy games," the veteran had told him, drying his hands with a paper towel, "tradecraft is everything, and rules are made to be broken. All fine and dandy . . . *unless you get caught*. In the intelligence business, it is our job to keep breaking the rules, while *never* getting caught."

It had been nine days since the baron's death, and Burls was still trying to determine exactly how his crew had been so thoroughly trumped. Naturally, he suspected that an insider had tipped off Bounty4Justice about the agency's clandestine plot to hack the enterprise. Exactly who that insider might be remained a mystery.

There was a light knock on his door. Burls pushed aside his somber thoughts, perked himself up, and said, "Come in."

His assistant, Sarah, opened the door and directed the two Americans into the room. The female agent was absolutely stunning. Her handsome male colleague looked vaguely familiar. Burls stood and circled his sleek, glass-topped desk to offer a jolly American handshake.

"Greetings," Burls said. "Welcome to London."

64.02

"To what do I owe this pleasure?" Burls asked, once Novak and Michaels had settled into chairs opposite his desk.

"First off," Novak said, "I'd like to extend my compliments for your going straight at Bounty4Justice. Despite any blowback, it's the only way we're going to take it down. As you may know, my own team's efforts in asking the Russians to block Bounty4Justice didn't work out so well. Nevertheless, our position remains that aggressive measures are our only viable option."

"Ah, yes," Burls said, nodding. "I thought you looked familiar. I've got to say, that's quite a mess you handed the Kremlin."

"Well, that news clip of the mob pulling your dummy out of its body bag was memorable, too," Novak replied.

"Right you are," Burls said, laughing.

"Point being, sometimes our plans don't always go as planned."

"Indeed."

Since the Voronov affair was already an open book, Novak went on to chronicle the FBI's ensuing efforts and strategies to contain Bounty4Justice, after which Burls broke down his operations—and the tragic aftermath—in detail for them.

"At first, we thought the baron had merely suffered cardiac failure due to the shock of everything that was happening," Burls said, explaining the botched sting operation at the Windsor Arms. "Perfectly understandable that a man in an already fragile state could easily have succumbed to that level of anxiety. Those people were out to kill him, after all. It wasn't until a video posted to Bounty4Justice the next day that we realized the heart attack he'd had in the lift was no accident. That same software we'd obtained from the manufacturer of his cardiac pacemaker for our faux attack was employed in actuality by the assassin. We found a discreet camera lens installed in the ceiling of the lift, wired to an encrypted satellite phone stowed in the cab's ceiling panel. The entire episode was performed remotely. All very clever, indeed," said Burls.

"Any idea who might have done it?" Michaels asked.

"We've got leads but, truthfully, nothing solid," Burls admitted. "Reason suggests that if we can identify who might have tipped Bounty4Justice about our strategy, then maybe we can find our man. Could be an insider. Perhaps someone on the staff at the building who'd bugged the baron's residence and listened in on the plan. Even an outside contractor is a possibility, since there'd been plenty of them going in and out of that service entrance. We're conducting interviews, checking phone records, bank accounts, that sort of thing. It'll take some time, but I'm confident that eventually we'll get to the bottom of it all."

"Well, on that note," Novak said, "we've got something I think you'll find of interest."

64.03

Novak opened the slim folio he'd brought along and handed a sheet of paper to the deputy director. Then he tipped his head to Michaels, the persuader.

Michaels explained, "What you have there is an email that was sent from a Gmail account, originating from an Internet café here in London in May of last year."

"I'm not sure I understand what this all means," Burls said, scanning the text. "Is this computer code?"

"It's a random cipher that's meant to distract from the string of characters highlighted there near the bottom of the code block."

Burls studied it, then shook his head. "What does 'iArchos6I6' mean?"

"We believe it's a passcode," Michaels said.

"I see. And what exactly does 'Razorwire' refer to?"

"That's what we came here to find out. That email was sent to one of your staff members here in this office. The recipient is listed there in the metadata header."

Novak studied Burls's expression as he focused on the email address that ended with a domain designated for the National Crime Agency—@nca.x.gsi.gov.uk—and blanched at the name tagged to it.

"Can't be," Burls muttered.

"I assume Mr. Grimes works for you?" Michaels asked.

"He does," Burls replied.

"We'd appreciate it if you'd let us speak with him," she said. "We need to ask him a few questions about this message. We think it's a critical link to whoever is behind Bounty4Justice."

Burls frowned. "I imagine we can arrange that," he finally murmured. "I'd certainly like to hear what Jeremy has to say, as well. Unfortunately, he's away on personal leave for the next two days."

65.01

@ St. George's, Bermuda
11:59:23 AST

The archipelago sat on coral reefs in emerald ocean waters just over
six hundred miles southeast of Cape Hatteras, North Carolina. Not
exactly middle ground for the emergency strategy meeting of Archer
Offsite Systems LLP, but there was a bit of tradition here, since this
was where the original concept for Razorwire had been hatched,
nearly two years ago.

Jam had the advantage of arriving first at the pub, where he ordered a drink from the barkeep—a dark 'n' stormy, of course, the
drink befitting any self-respecting pirate. Outside, he sat at a secluded
table along the wharf, overlooking the picturesque harbor, where the
big cruise ships dropped anchor during peak season to unload herds
of tourists, who would explore St. George's quaint pastel-painted
boutiques and watch the town crier and a woman in period costume
reenact a wench-dunking in the harbor. This time of year, however,
the place was desolate, the winds chilly and ominous.

Jam had read that in 1609 the island's English founders, Admiral Sir
George Somers and Lieutenant General Sir Thomas Gates, had crash-
landed their ship on a nearby reef during a brutal storm. Over the

months that followed, the admiral and the general vied for superiority over the few dozen surviving castaways, thus dividing the men into two factions. Each faction constructed a ship to escape the island—one christened *Deliverance,* the other *Patience*—and each sailed onward to Jamestown, Virginia. Four centuries later, a similar power struggle promised to splinter allegiances here on majestic Bermuda. But this time, the odds favored only one superior player journeying on to his final destination.

It was a shame that things had come to this, thought Jam. He'd liked Pike ever since they'd first met, at a DEF CON hacker symposium in Las Vegas. At the time, Jam had been the NSA's guest speaker (the conference was a prime recruiting ground for the agency), and his presentation had centered on tactical cyberdefense methods and the accelerating struggle for nations to protect their sovereignty in the cyber realm. During a cocktail mixer later that night, the charismatic Englishman had pulled Jam aside to compliment him on his keen vision. Then he'd offered the NSA employee an enticing opportunity to put that vision to immediate work by participating in a *most* lucrative project.

They'd designed Razorwire to be the ultimate cyberweapon—one that could claim absolute dominion over the new digital battleground, an all-encompassing suite of capabilities that would exploit, simultaneously, network computing, logistics, banking, crowd psychology, propaganda, secure communications, covert ops, the works. Know thine enemy. Subdue thine enemy. Turn thine enemy against itself. Above all, Razorwire needed to be impervious to assault or infiltration while embodying the very essence of stealth and subterfuge. Invisible. Invincible.

In its infancy, Razorwire had seemed too ambitious, too bold. So many disciplines needed to be coordinated, with no single programmer fully knowing the scope or intent of the finished product. After all, what good was intelligence if you couldn't keep a secret? Like most defense agencies, the NSA outsourced the development and production of component code writing to contractors. Overseeing the final assembly of a finished product was Jam's forte, which gave him great latitude in procuring highly specialized code from programmers and specialists around the globe. They provided the eggs, and he was the incubator. Despite the logistical challenges, as the months went by and each module blossomed in isolation, Razorwire showed promise that exceeded the original vision by orders of magnitude, much the way the collective force behind the Manhattan Project had defied the odds a few decades earlier to rewrite the rules of modern warfare.

The fatal breach—the lethal hack—had occurred just over five weeks ago, during the project's final stages, just as all those independent parts had been assembled into the whole, yet before safety layers and protocols had been thoroughly activated. Ever since then, Jam had been trying to deconstruct just how the project had been so disastrously compromised. And now he thought he'd figured it out.

"Hiya, mate," a voice said.

Jam turned and saw Pike swaggering out of the pub, sipping a swizzle (*his* favorite rum drink) through a straw, his scruffy mop of hair blowing in the breeze. The limey hadn't changed a bit, even wore the same beatnik outfit as the last time they'd met. Though he was also in his late twenties, he looked like he could be in a boy band. The two of them made quite an odd pair: the English heartthrob and the bespectacled American nerd—the glitzy Web, the grungy darknet.

Jam's brother-in-arms sat in the chair across from him, with no offer of his trademark chummy handshake, just a curt nod.

Pike stared at the choppy emerald water for a long moment. "Looks as if a storm is heading our way."

"The w-weather's not looking so good, either," Randall scoffed.

Jeremy Grimes grinned. "That's a good one, mate."

"I trust your flight was pleasant?"

"First-class."

Advantage Pike.

66.01

@ London, England

"So Grimes was with you the whole time?" Novak asked.

"That's right," Burls said. "He was with me outside in the Rover, where we observed the operation, then went back up to the penthouse so he could code the video."

"Did you confirm that he really submitted that video file to Bounty4Justice?" asked Michaels.

Burls paused for a moment, looking troubled. "No. There was no reason to doubt him. He's always been top-notch. The best we've got."

"And all you saw was this message on his screen that said, 'Nice try'?" she asked.

"That's right. Understand that it was all rather chaotic at that time. We were focused on getting the baron to safety. I didn't have the wherewithal to ask Jeremy many questions."

"Then it's at least possible that he submitted a warning instead of the video," Novak said.

"Meaning?"

"Meaning he easily could have alerted Bounty4Justice about what was really happening."

Burls frowned. "Why would he do that?"

"If he knew you were getting close to breaking through to the website," Michaels said, "he might have tried to protect it from being compromised. And if we're correct that he's somehow involved with the website's development, it would certainly explain his motive. He might simply have been trying to cover his tracks."

Burls mulled this over, and Novak tried to read if their suspicions were hitting home.

"It's a plausible theory," Burls said, "but do understand that I must hold off on conjecture until I speak with him directly."

"We need to talk with him as soon as possible," Novak said. "And it would be best if we do it in person. Can you call him in?"

"It's not that easy. You see, he's on holiday. Out of the country."

"How about the laptop he used during the operation?" Michaels said. "Can we analyze it to see what activities he actually performed?"

Burls held up his hands. "Let's not get ahead of ourselves, shall we? You must understand—"

"Do you at least know where that laptop is?" Michaels insisted.

Burls looked at her for a moment, then nodded. "We have strict rules. During off-hours, all those machines remain in-house."

66.02

Within five minutes, Sarah returned with the laptop she'd fetched from Jeremy's office. It was a slim Apple MacBook about the same dimensions as the leather-bound folio resting on Novak's lap.

Burls set it down on his desk and drummed his fingertips on its lid, his lips drawn tight.

"I assure you that whatever we discover, if anything, will remain absolutely confidential," Novak said.

"That won't matter, I'm afraid," Burls replied, unhinging the laptop and turning it toward them. "We'd need the password, and only Jeremy knows it."

"Try 'iArchos616,'" Novak said.

Burls did, albeit reluctantly. "That's not it."

Novak slouched a little as a sinking feeling hit his gut—but with genius timing, Walter threw him a lifeline from five time zones away, in the form of a text message that vibrated his BlackBerry:

Novak—
URGENT!!! Please call me ASAP. HUGE NEWS about B4J!
Walter

"Hold on, I think we've got something," he said.

Walter picked up on the second ring.

"Thank God," Walter said. "Oh, man, you won't believe what we've got here!"

Novak smiled broadly as he listened to what Walter and Connie had stumbled on.

"And we just go right through the chatbot?" Novak clarified, jotting down notes.

"That's right. Should work the same for you as it did for us," Walter said.

"This is great, Walter. Really great."

"I know. Now let's show this thing who's boss."

Novak ended the call, slid his notes across the desk to Burls, and tapped on the string of characters he'd jotted down. "Try this password instead."

Burls pecked the MacBook's keyboard, hit ENTER, and grinned. "We're in."

They'd found their man.

67.01 _____

@ St. George's, Bermuda

The two black hats stared at each other like gunslingers at high noon, Randall Scott nipping at his drink, Jeremy Grimes sipping from his straw. Absent the shield of the Atlas-5 secure message board—that ability to edit or censor each reply in advance—the interaction between Jam and Pike had taken on an entirely different dimension, one driven purely by human assessments, each man trying to deconstruct the other, trying to separate truth from fiction. Neither the American nor the Briton was particularly adept at such up close and personal analysis. By nature, each was much more comfortable—skilled—with ones and zeros.

"Look at us," Jeremy said. "Stuck in the middle of some international conspiracy, complete with bodies piling up. Two computer geeks who've gone and knocked the world out of orbit. All this brainpower, yet neither of us knowing who to trust or who to blame. Pretty crazy that two fuckoffs like us could create such chaos, wouldn't you say, Jam?"

"Sure. It's one big mind-fuck," Randall replied sarcastically. "Whatever."

"Things have gotten a bit ropey as of late. Seems our monster turned out a might bit scarier than we'd ever imagined."

"I'd say Razorwire is everything we hoped it could be," Randall replied. "And more."

"Now that the world has witnessed its capabilities, who knows what one might fetch for it. Perhaps that's why you stole the codes . . . to make a spectacle of Razorwire so as to prime it for auction to the highest bidder?"

Randall used his index finger to push his glasses back up on the bridge of his sweaty nose. "How many times do I have to f-f-fucking tell you, fuckwad? I didn't steal jack shit. We were fucking *hacked*. How do I know it wasn't this client of yours who did it . . . this Firewolf? Or maybe it's much simpler than that and you just went ahead and gave it to him, along with nearly all the bank account numbers."

"Have you gone absolutely *bonkers*? Think it through, mate. He'd be stealing from himself."

"Or he'd be getting the program *and* a refund on his seed money. An honest to goodness double cross. Exactly who is he, anyway? Someone inside Trident?"

Trident was their nickname for the three major branches of British intelligence: Government Communications Headquarters, MI5 domestic intelligence, and MI6 foreign intelligence.

Jeremy shook his head, studying Randall intensely. "No, no. Uh-uh. I told you the moment this project began to never ask that question. Tread lightly."

"I'm already f-fucked. I'd just like to know who's doing the f-f-fucking. You owe me that. Once word of this gets out, I'll be public enemy number one. We're talking about *treason* here. I refuse to be locked away in a prison cell for the rest of my life. Not for *you*. Certainly not f-for this damn Firewolf."

67.02 _____

Jeremy sipped his swizzle and studied the American, thinking that Razorwire was, by design, the stuff of nightmares for any enemy upon which it was unleashed. The *real* monster to be feared, however, was the enigma named Firewolf, who'd bankrolled Razorwire under the full expectation that the technology would be delivered to *him*, as promised. Jeremy had never actually met the man; the initial contact had been made by his stunning Chinese female envoy, just over three years ago, in Trafalgar Square. Whether Firewolf was some Sun Yee On mob boss or a key figure with direct ties to Beijing, clearly he was a force *not* to be reckoned with. With the U.S. and British intelligence alliance maintaining supreme dominion over the digital realm—a world order that stifled the ambitions of the East—Firewolf was determined to reset the balance. Tip it, in fact. And Jeremy had agreed to help him, in return for the promise of becoming a fabulously wealthy man. All of their communications had been exchanged via a PGP-encrypted message board similar to Atlas5—which had ceased abruptly on Tuesday, the same day the news broke that authorities had raided a huge money-laundering operation in Ottawa run by an Asian mastermind known only as "Firewolf."

The endgame was nigh.

"I thought we trusted each other, Randall," Jeremy said.

Randall fixed him with a long, dismantling stare. "That's touching, but we're spies, you and me. I trust no one. We're not f-friends. I'm simply looking to get paid, same as you."

Get paid. Having seen how dire the situation had gotten, Jeremy had initiated an ad hoc backup plan to beef up his cash flow last week, when he'd handily killed Baron Andrew Smith in that lift at the Windsor Arms. Sitting there at his laptop that day in the baron's gourmet kitchen, after submitting an obviously malicious Trojan to Bounty4Justice that the website spotted straight off, he'd used his phone to remotely activate the Web camera he'd discreetly planted along the ceiling panels in the service lift, their usual exit route. Once MI5 had spirited the baron into the lift, he'd used his phone once more to initiate the command sequence that sped the baron's cardiac defibrillator into overdrive . . . *for real*. Later that night, he'd retrieved the encrypted video and uploaded it to Bounty4Justice's claim-submission in-box. By the next morning, he'd received a simple email response that read:

TARGET: ANDREW SMITH, autocrat, UK
Claim submission date: 10/30/2017
Final bounty: £1,711,123
Selected payment method: NCRYPTOCASH

Dear Claimant:
Congratulations! We have validated your video claim submission. As per section 22 of our user agreement, you have been awarded the final bounty amount listed above. Please allow 24–48 hours for delivery.
Thank you for your patronage.
› CustomerCare@bounty4justice.com

And sure enough, two days later, Bounty4Justice had sent those NcryptoCash certificates to an anonymous Gmail account he'd set up, as promised.

But he'd also need the money that remained here in Bermuda, so he'd have enough to create an entirely new life—a new identity—in some faraway land, beyond the reach of Trident *and* Firewolf. To make that happen, he'd need Randall to accompany him to Hamilton to cosign in person for the withdrawals. It would take some convincing. But seeing as money was what drove the American, too, maybe it wouldn't be so bloody hard after all.

Jeremy leaned across the table. "Don't think for a moment that you can get away with this. They'll cut us into pieces, Randall. Quite literally. Do you understand? Stop being so daft. I've protected you long enough. It's my neck on the block now. It's you or me. And I'm looking to keep my head. You think you know what you're dealing with?" He shook his head and leaned back in his chair. "Look, you *have* done a lot for us . . ."

67.03

You have *done a lot for us.* Randall thought that was a bit of an understatement. He'd recruited most of Razorwire's programmers through a simple hack in the NSA's secure contractor procurement system, reserved for only the most secret protocols. Those deals were so covert that face-to-face interactions never occurred. They were the undisclosed deals, the digital version of the back alley. He was the one who'd tapped freelance talent from all over the globe, each contractor working under the illusion that the U.S. intelligence apparatus was fine-tuning its systems.

Time to skewer the pig.

"Look, *Jeremy,*" Randall snapped. "I'm through with this bullshit game of you accusing *me.* Here's the bottom line. The other day, this jackass cryptographer who sits next to me at work f-found what looked like a p-p-password in an old Gmail message, mixed in with a bunch of cryptobabble. Does 'iArchos6I6' sound f-familiar?"

For the first time, Jeremy's cool facade cracked. He froze, the straw of his swizzle puckered between his lips. His complexion visibly transformed to a sickly gray. Just sat there staring back at Randall with those handsome brown eyes.

Advantage Jam.

But, sensing confirmation of his worst suspicions, Randall suddenly wasn't feeling so well, either.

"You're sure it was a *Gmail* account?" asked Jeremy.

"Yup."

On Monday afternoon, one of the NSA's hotshot hackers, Josh Tierney, had refused to tell Randall precisely what he'd uncovered in his data-mining search—just kept making dickhead references to what he'd be doing with that $50K in prize money during his all-expenses-paid trip to the Caymans. Josh got cocky like that only when he *knew* he'd solved a puzzle. Sure enough, on Tuesday morning, things got totally fucked when Josh showed him the Gmail intercept that he'd forwarded to their dickhead boss *and* the FBI in Manhattan to formally stake his claim to the Caymans prize package. "And the metadata points directly to your f-fucking work email at the NCA. What the f-fuck were you thinking? You f-fucking asshole."

No response.

"Now, why the *fuck* would you do that, Jeremy?"

"So I wouldn't forget the passphrase. But, mate, I blended it in with the cipher so it wouldn't be obvious, and I—"

"You thought using 'Archos' wouldn't be *obvious*?" Archos wasn't a reference to the AI cube in *Robopocalypse*, like Randall's nemesis in the NSA thought it might be. It was the short name he and Jeremy used when referring to Archer Offsite Systems LLP: Arch-O-S. "They've already figured out that the accounts are registered under Archos, here in Bermuda, you f-fucking moron. Don't you s-see the connection? Email . . . bank account . . . *you*"—Randall jabbed a finger at Jeremy, then back at himself—"*me*. Like a fucking boomerang. Don't you get it?"

"I deleted that message straightaway. Right after I printed it. I don't understand how they could have recovered—"

"Please tell me I didn't just hear you say that," Randall said, clenching his fists. "It's the f-fucking NSA, numbnuts. You know better than anyone that there's no such thing as 'delete' when it comes to the Web! God, did you really figure it was okay to use a f-fucking *Gmail* account?"

Jeremy was chewing on his fingernails now. "How was I supposed to know someone would steal the program and use it to have people killed for kicks or to attack Russia, for Christ's sake?"

Randall took a moment to try to navigate through the haze of this nightmare. "What part of the system did the passcode access?"

"Come on, mate. Let's not—"

"Answer me."

Jeremy's lower lip quivered. "All of it. All right? The whole bloody thing."

Now Randall was feeling a bit queasy. "Come again?"

"*All of it,* mate. It was my administrator password."

"Jesus fucking H Christ," Randall said woozily. Only two administrators had been assigned global access codes to Razorwire, and both of them were sitting at this table. He fell silent for a long moment, dumbfounded. "That's how they got to us—these Bounty4Justice pricks. Don't you see? Your email was being monitored . . . every fucking keystroke. Had to be. They must have infected your laptop with a keylogger. Then you went and sent yourself a fucking Gmail message with the passcode and a subject line in big bold letters that read 'RAZORWIRE.' Clear as day. And—" His eyes went wide and adrenaline gushed through him, making him see white for a brief moment. "Oh, fuck me. Motherfucker. If you were compromised, that means they could also monitor every f-fucking exchange on Atlas-5. They know everything. *EVERYTHING!* And you have the balls to call yourself a *spy*? You handed the whole fucking thing over with a big fucking bow on it!"

"Easy, now . . ." Jeremy said. "Let's think this through. That password still works to access the gateway, right?"

"The gateway is only a bridge to the host server's root directory," Randall reminded him. "The *command modules* are the guts of the program." The modules were the entry points to the dashboard of programs that controlled everything from encrypted communications between intelligence operatives worldwide to every network node connected to the Web's global routing systems. "Each module had its own separate password. Just like we designed it. Remember? It was meant to be a f-f-failsafe. So don't you see what they've done? Of course you can access the gateway, but they've changed the p-passwords in each module."

"Then why wouldn't this genius have changed the gateway access code, as well?"

Randall thought it through for a second, and the disturbingly logical explanation became so very obvious that his vision flashed white again. "Fuck! To lead the authorities right to us, fuckwad! Just like they led them to Canada . . . and the bank accounts. God. Fuck! What were you thinking?"

But there'd be no more thinking for the pride of British cyberintelligence, because something struck him violently in the side of the head with a *pa-chump,* destroying his skull and spewing his brain onto the pub's exterior wall with enough force to splatter Randall's face and glasses with gobs of blood and gray matter. In the same instant, a sharp cracking sound reverberated out across the harbor: *pock-chooooom!*

"F-fuck me," Randall managed, knowing that he was already a

goner. Only a high-caliber bullet traveling faster than the speed of sound could have blown Jeremy's head clean off its neck. And that made him instantly recall an arcane factoid he'd heard years ago on some Military Channel testosterone-fueled weapons show: "Once you're in the sniper's crosshairs and he takes that shot, you're dead before you even hear the muzzle blast of his high-performance rifle, because the velocity of the bullet outruns the sound wave—"

It was the last computation his brain processed in vivid color.

He felt an insanely intense pressure erupt in his left ear.

Then the melodies of his genius went forever silent.

67.04

The barkeep, who'd heard both retorts of the sniper's rifle, darted outside and blanched at the carnage left behind by the two Lapua Magnum slugs that would later be extracted from the pub's stone wall.

Checkmate.

68.01 _____

@ London, England

Novak and Michaels stood behind Burls, watching as he took the
helm at the keyboard and entered the Rang-O-Chat Internet Relay
Chat message board on the darknet.

"You're saying I just type 'password'?" Burls asked.

"Correct," Novak said.

Burls entered the term, and up came the password entry prompt—
the blinking cursor that indicated the presence of something on the
other end of a darknet wormhole that was now awaiting a reply.

Novak felt like he'd entered the Matrix. "Go ahead and enter the
password."

Burls typed in the thirteen-digit passcode and hit ENTER.

> ENTER PASSWORD: 89eTf‹iArchos
> Please wait . . .
> PASSWORD ACCEPTED
> Please wait . . . .

There was a five-second delay as the bot went about establishing
its connection outside the message board. The command was pinging some server—calling out to the mother ship. But they didn't pass

through the wormhole just yet. Instead, what came back was a list of commands that could direct them to where they needed to go:

```
YOU'VE ENTERED: RAZORWIRE GATEWAY
PLEASE SELECT A COMMAND MODULE: _
DIAG
CMOD
RFSH
ROOT
ADMN
NTWK
```

"We believe that Razorwire is the systems engine behind Bounty4Justice," Novak said.

"Remarkable," Burls muttered in astonishment.

"Now what?" asked Michaels.

"Type 'CMOD,'" Novak said.

Burls entered the command.

Up popped another prompt:

```
› ENTER ADMIN PASSWORD: _
```

Burls reentered the thirteen-digit code, and the response was exactly what Walter had told Novak it would be:

```
› PASSWORD INVALID. ENTER ADMIN PASSWORD: _
```

"Damn. What's the next password?" Burls asked.

"We don't know yet," Novak said. "The NSA is working on it." Even had he already known it, that was a piece of information best kept close until they better assessed how badly British intel had been compromised. "I was advised that a brute force attack could take days, depending on the strength of the passphrase."

There was a knock at the door, and Sarah rejoined them, looking pale.

"Pardon the interruption, sir." Her eyes filled. "We've just received some rather disturbing news. The BBC is reporting that two men have been murdered in Bermuda by a sniper. They're saying one of them was a Briton named Jeremy Grimes."

From: Walter.Koslowski@ic.fbi.gov
Sent: Wednesday, November 8, 2017 at 11:32 AM
To: Josh Tierney
Cc: Roman Novak, Tim Knight, Dilip Kapoor
Subject: Bounty4Justice gateway address request

📎: Razorwire.gateway.jpg

Josh, regarding your cryptanalysis of the Razorwire ciphertext, my team has discovered a usable password hidden within the character block: 89eTfᶜiArchos. Note: the "6I6" referred to the code format: 6 characters to each side of the lowercase i. This password can be entered into the Bounty4Justice chatbot hosted on Rang-O-Chat (IRC message board). The attached screen print shows the actual input sequence, for your review. I'm hoping that you might be able to confirm the host server the bot is referencing. When I pinged the server, it gave me the same IP address over and over. Not sure if I trust it. Fingers crossed! Please advise. Thanks very much.

Walter Koslowski
Senior Cybercrimes Specialist
Special Operations Cyber Division
FBI New York
26 Federal Plaza
New York, NY 10278
Phone: (212) 555-0453
Fax: (212) 555-8858
@NewYorkFBI | Email Alerts | FBI.gov/NewYork

Cyber Tip Line: (800) 843-5678

69.01 _____

@ Fort Meade, Maryland
11:32:22 EST

Josh Tierney wasn't surprised to see another request from Walter Koslowski in his in-box. After feeding Koslowski the Gmail intercept sent
to Jeremy Grimes, Tierney had fully expected that the FBI would
want more information. What did surprise him, however, was that
the cyberanalysts from the Manhattan field office had figured out on
their own that the ciphertext in that Gmail message indeed contained
a passcode, albeit one that was, in and of itself, a puzzle. That "6I6"
wasn't a typo for the number of the beast after all but a clue to the
coding format. *Clever.*

He plugged that thirteen-digit code into the Rang-O-Chat message
board Koslowski had referenced in his email. The Razorwire command list came up on his screen, and it made his eyebrows lift.

"Well, hello."

These damn bots were getting cleverer by the day.

"And just where did you come from?"

He wasn't sure what system this protocol was running on. It wasn't
anything he'd seen before, and he'd pretty much seen them all.
Looked like a variant of Unix—the tried-and-true server platform
that had been evolving for over forty years now—or perhaps some
bastardized version of Linux or Apple OS X. But the command structure didn't quite fit those systems, either.

Whatever the case, Walter Koslowski was right. This chatbot
was feeding commands to a central server—from the looks of it, the
module that controlled the Razorwire protocol. The designer had
probably snuck this gateway in as a remote back door to access the
system from anywhere in the world. *Nice touch,* he thought. *Sneaky.*
He was a tad pissed that he hadn't figured this one out on his
own. But everyone deserved a lucky break every now and then,
so kudos to the dataheads in Manhattan. Besides, he'd identified
the actual human being who'd received the gateway password. That

had to count for something. Realistically, without the thirteen-digit password, there was no way he could've figured out this IP address earlier.

Whatever.

Time to have some fun.

The bot's command structure was rudimentary. So he ran through each command, typing it at the prompt on the Rang-O-Chat message board. Each module required an additional administrator password. He figured one password might unlock all the modules, or separate passwords might be required for each one, which would make sense if multiple users were assigned specific privileges. But in theory, someone had to control global access to the system—someone who could break open the whole damn thing and execute every superuser privilege in the root system. To determine that person's passcodes, a brute force attack might work—hit the server with a password hasher at quantum speed. But that could take a few hours, or days, or longer, depending on the server's response time. Most likely, the server would apply basic session logic to lock out a unique IP address that was endlessly spoofing passwords.

He logged in to a containment quad, quarantined from the NSA's main network, so that he could run his experiments. He began with pinging the server via plain old ICMP, like Walter Koslowski had done from his computer in New York, or just about any goofball could do sitting in his underwear at his home computer. The target server responded with an actual IP address that mapped to a precise location halfway across the globe, just like Koslowski had said it would. All along, Bounty4Justice had been using an entire network of proxy servers to cover its tracks, and this was probably some zombie decoy whose sole purpose was misdirection. When he pinged it a few more times, however, the same IP kept responding, which was weird. Why wouldn't Bounty4Justice just shut down the ICMP port and simply not respond? After all, obfuscation was this website's forte. So he dug a little deeper and ran a full trace on the physical network connectivity. He was getting back readings on a very specific physical connection—from backbone to branch fibers to last-mile connection to front-door hookup—with no ISP or middleman playing hall monitor. Straight to the source.

Interesting. *Too* easy. Yet it certainly appeared that this IP address wasn't fucking around with him. Could this whole damn command module reside on a server at this actual address that kept coming back at him? He shook his head. Appearances were often deceiving, and even more so in the realm of the darknet.

He moved on to the next level. The NSA had a very extensive tool kit when it came to exploits—an entire arsenal of infiltration scripts grouped into bundles, including every known back door built into every brand of router, server BIOS, telecom operating system, programming language, and software protocol.

The agency even had secret alliances with the technology manufacturers themselves, who, in the interest of national security, "cooperated" by incorporating back doors into their firmware that allowed targeted penetration, when needed. Though more often than not, those exploits were used to bypass encryption and listen in on a chancellor's mundane phone calls about trade policy or to eavesdrop on some dopey jihadist wannabe in Yemen looking to bring down the evil American empire with sticks and stones. Wiretapping wasn't simply sporting in the Digital Age; it was a given. The game was pretty much rigged. And hands down, the United States and Britain swung the biggest sticks.

Josh perused the cyber arms catalog and sent a band of his favorite port sniffers out to hunt. Server infiltration scripts reminded him of those high school sex-ed videos of sperm attacking an ovum—a bunch of aggressive invaders wiggling and squiggling every which way to force themselves inside to the sweet spot.

The confirmations came back within seconds, and much to his chagrin, all the results agreed that the server's thousand-plus TCP and UDP Internet transport security layers were all locked down. Okay. So it was running an ultratight firewall, and its routers were somehow shielding the true identity of the operating system. In fact, the routers seemed impenetrable. How could that be? he wondered. You'd have to do some serious monkeying around to retool a router like that. It had to be running through its own darknet within the darknet.

He went back to his tool kit and checked off a few more choice payloads—the super sperm—and set them loose. These dogs barked a lot louder, drew a lot more attention, and often left pawprints. The nuclear option. But given where the server was located, Josh didn't have to worry all that much about legalities or the rules of fair play. For this problem-child country, it was gloves off. No management approval required.

In seconds, the responses came back. Same shitty results. Even the most potent SSL exploit packets were coming back empty. For Josh, this was a first.

"Shit."

He stared at the screen . . . puzzled. Okay. The server wasn't shy about its location, but it was doing a stupendous job of not revealing a damn thing about itself. What a tease. He stared at the screen, his brain burning in bright, overlapping colors. A computer the NSA couldn't hack? Nah. Couldn't be.

Too bad Randall was off on personal leave, he thought, looking over at the empty desk to his right. That guy was a spaz, but he was really good at this kind of thing. He hadn't earned the nickname Spoof Master for nothing.

For the time being, Josh injected a botnet script into Rang-O-Chat's servers to monitor its message boards, so that if any user established a connection with the target server IP hosting Razorwire, the bot would capture the input data using a Quantumbot exploit and send it back to him, along with any packet data that might reveal the administrator's IP address. It was a long shot, certainly not foolproof, but worth a try. He repeated the same process for the other message boards hosting the Bounty4Justice chatbot, so that all the traps were set.

Otherwise, the next best course of action was the path of least resistance: send someone knocking on the door of this physical address. Just go on in and grab that damn megaserver using honest to goodness brute force. Besides, Walter Koslowski was primarily looking to confirm the IP address, and Josh had certainly done that. So he drafted his simple email reply, then cut and pasted the server's IP address into the message, added a polite suggestion to call the embassy and get a CAT team on a plane ASAP, and sent it off into the ether.

After all, even the NSA's Signals Intelligence Directorate had its limits.

70.01

@ London, England

Bermuda remained an independent overseas territory of the British monarchy, yet the Brits had no embassies there; therefore, Burls was being fed information through the crown's next closest point of contact: the British embassy in Washington, D.C.

The United States had no embassy in Bermuda, either, but maintained a small consulate of forty employees to protect its citizens traveling abroad and to aid investigations in drug trafficking and money laundering. Novak had dealt with the consulate in the past, but he held off on making any calls just yet; he'd left a voicemail for Knight requesting guidance and was awaiting a call back.

While the deputy director wrapped up his phone conversation, Novak and Michaels listened to the live news coverage streaming on Burls's computer monitor. The British Broadcasting Corporation was getting its information from another BBC: the Bermuda Broadcasting Company. By all accounts, the shocking violence of a double shooting had rocked the tiny island colony of twenty square miles and sixty-five thousand inhabitants, which had seen its share of gun violence over the years, but nothing like this.

The shooting took place at the Seadog Pub shortly after noon today. The victims, both tourists, have been identified as Randall Scott from Odenton, Maryland, and Jeremy Grimes from London, England.

The passport photos of the two men came up on the screen. Novak recognized Grimes right away. He opened his folio and flipped to the same photo in the dossier Knight had sent him. He didn't recognize the bespectacled Randall Scott.

. . . shot in the head with a large-caliber bullet by a shooter who has thus far remained unidentified. Here is what the pub's proprietor had to tell us.

The newscast cut to a prerecorded interview with the sunbaked British expat, who, with his shaved head and hoop earrings, looked appropriately twenty-first-century piratical:

I was inside when I heard the first gunshot. I ran outside and heard the second shot go off, but I couldn't quite tell where it was coming from. I went around to the patio to ask the chaps outside if they'd seen anything, and that's when I saw them there, on the ground, blood everywhere. What an awful sight it was. There was practically nothing left to their heads. Awful.

The field correspondent came back on-screen, saying,

We do know that both men arrived on-island this morning and reported to customs agents that they were traveling for leisure. However, inside sources have told the BBC that both Scott and Grimes work for intelligence agencies in their respective countries, setting off immediate rumors of conspiracy and adding yet another element of intrigue to this most shocking crime. The BPS Forensic Support Unit is on the scene, and police are

encouraging residents and witnesses to report any tips or clues
as soon as possible . . .

Burls ended his call and said, "They've got very little to tell so far.
But they have plenty of questions for us about Grimes's reasons for
being in Bermuda. The consulate has already gotten calls from the
BPS Financial Crimes Unit, because Grimes and Scott were registered
officers of a company located there on the island, in Hamilton, called
Archer Offsite Systems."

"So you have no idea why he was there?" Michaels asked.

Burls shook his head. "I've not a clue. I know that after all that
drama with the baron, he'd requested some time off. Perfectly rea-
sonable. It was quite a harrowing experience."

"Were you aware that he was in contact with Randall Scott?" Michaels asked.

"Not at all. I've never heard the name. Certainly never seen that
face," he said, looking at the man's photo, which was back up on the
screen.

Knight pinged Novak's BlackBerry.

"Hey, Tim."

"Got your message. I can't believe what a mess this is turning into."

"Do we know anything about this Randall Scott?"

"He's NSA, Novak," Knight replied bluntly. "Just got confirmation."

Novak felt as though the air had been sucked from his lungs. Maybe
Borg's suspicions about who was really behind Bounty4Justice had
been spot-on all along: *If I had to guess, it's the wonks with the BEST
tech: the ones who listen in on all our calls.*

"Won't take long for the news to figure it out," Knight added. "I've
been advised that until we have more information, we've got to keep
a tight lid on things. Understand?"

"Sure thing."

"And get this: the consulate in Bermuda told headquarters that the
forensic folks pulled two slugs from the wall of that pub. They're
going to run ballistics on them, but they're sure they came from
Lapua Magnum cartridges."

"That's an interesting coincidence," Novak said.

"Indeed it is," Knight replied. "We'll have to see if they can pull signatures on the slugs before we draw any conclusions. In the meantime, I've got some good news. Walter's sitting here next to me, and he just received confirmation from the NSA that they've positively identified the location for a server that they believe is hosting Bounty4Justice."

"You're kidding. That's great," Novak said, wondering again if the NSA was, in fact, playing games with them.

"Don't celebrate just yet. It's in Estonia. I have Walter flying straight there tonight. I want you and Michaels to meet him there tomorrow."

71.01 ————————————————————————

@ Virginia Beach, Virginia
Thursday, 11/09/2017
05:28:50 EST

"That's a mighty fine boat you've got there," Jonathan Farrell said to the heavyset middle-aged Italian.

"She's not very pretty," Fabrizio replied, "but she flies like the wind."

"I'd say," Farrell agreed. The sleek custom yacht was tethered to the dock, bobbing in the moonlight. *Sabrina* measured thirty-nine and a half feet long, weighed just shy of nine tons, and was powered by a pair of FPT C90 650 engines. Fabrizio had told him it was modeled after a military boat used by his Italian special forces unit, back in the late nineties. A few years ago, a similar model captained by a different Italian had traversed nearly eight hundred miles from New York to Bermuda in just under sixteen hours to break a long-standing speed record. Though the marina in Virginia had a hundred-mile advantage over New York, Farrell was pretty sure that mile for mile, Fabrizio had beaten that record hands down, both coming and going. But this was one speed feat that wasn't going to be publicized.

"Grazie," Farrell said, handing him the second installment of fifteen thousand dollars, cash.

"Anytime, my friend. I'm sorry about your weapon. She was a beauty."

Farrell shrugged. "It was the right thing to do. She and I had a good run."

He'd taken the two kill shots using the same AWM rifle he'd used in Manhattan, per Oz's directive. The hide he'd selected was on the shore of a small island situated along Bermuda's Town Cut channel, where the big ships navigated through the reefs to enter St. George's Harbour. The distance to the target location Oz had provided was nearly four-tenths of a mile, which wasn't all that sporting, but there'd been plenty of wind to make it a challenge. He'd kept on a wet suit and full dive gear, supplied by Fabrizio, and immediately following the shooting he'd gathered up his spent brass and packed everything back into its waterproof sleeve, slipped on his dive mask, and slid back into the harbor, leaving nothing behind except a few bent branches. Even the talcum-like gunpowder residue had been scrubbed away by the briny water. He'd given the AWM an honorable burial at sea, sinking her into a crevasse at the base of the deep channel. Then he'd finned his way back out into the ocean and along the reefs to where Fabrizio kept *Sabrina* lazily adrift, just offshore.

Farrell offered a handshake, but the Italian shook his head. "You Americans are such prudes." He stepped forward and embraced Farrell. "You take care of yourself, eh."

Farrell patted him on the back. "You, too, my friend."

The fraternity of contract killing. Sometimes you needed to use the buddy system. They'd met in Yemen a few years ago, right before Fabrizio retired from the Gruppo Operativo Incursori and moved from Sardinia to be closer to his daughter in Virginia. They'd corresponded occasionally, but this was their first job together.

"Come see me again soon. We'll go fishing and have some drinks and find some pretty ladies who like to party."

"Sounds like a plan."

Farrell walked back to his rental car and stashed his duffel bag in the trunk. Then he got behind the wheel and set off for the house he'd rented on the beach to rest up before his long ride back to Colorado.

72.01

@ Tallinn, Estonia
14:23:01 EET

The flight time from Stansted Airport to Tallinn was two hours, fifty minutes; during the trip, both Novak and Michaels brushed up on Estonia by reading the executive primer sent via email from headquarters.

The pint-sized E.U. nation of Estonia had a population smaller than that of the city of Phoenix, with only 1.3 million mostly ethnic Estonians, whose ancestry traced back to the Vikings. Owing to its strategic orientation on the world map—the Baltic Sea and the Nordic countries to its north and west, Russia to its east, and its Baltic neighbors to the south—it had been squabbled over for centuries by Danes, Swedes, Poles, Germans, and Russians. Following the withdrawal of Soviet troops in 1994, independence had helped transform Estonia into a beacon of prosperity in Eastern Europe—the "Baltic Tiger."

Its capital city of Tallinn, situated on the Gulf of Finland, was a financial powerhouse with an ultrarobust telecommunications network that earned it top ranking among the world's digital cities. Often referred to as the "Silicon Valley of the Baltics" and one of the "smartest cities in the world," Tallinn had embraced technology wholeheartedly; the Internet was the lifeblood of its culture, digitizing and automating every aspect of everyday life, from voting and tax collection to phone service, shopping, and parking.

In 2007, however, Estonia's greatest strength had been turned against it when, in diplomatic retaliation for removing a bronze statue of a Soviet soldier from a public park in Tallinn, Russia engaged the country in a month-long cyberwar that crippled government offices, banks, corporate giants, and the media. The situation had gotten so dire that NATO, the European Union, Israel, and the United States had sent their best cyber teams to help Estonia build up its digital defenses. Ever since, the new generation of Vikings had been at the helm of the world's most advanced Internet, fortified by the secrets of the world's top cybersecurity experts and locked behind system-wide 2,048-bit encryption. And though Estonia was the birthplace of Skype Voice over IP and Playtech online gambling software, it was also the progenitor for some of the world's most insidious malware, like the DNSChanger browser-hijacking botnet whose core technologies bore striking similarities to the Razorwire platform that powered Bounty4Justice.

In 2008, the NATO Cooperative Cyber Defence Centre of Excellence—classified as an "international military organization"—set up its headquarters in Tallinn. Shortly thereafter, the Secret Service established an outpost, and the FBI embedded its first-ever full-time cybersecurity expert in a foreign country.

Estonia was ground zero for the fight over Internet dominion. So it was only fitting, Novak thought, that it was where Bounty4Justice had placed its central brain.

"Pretty ironic that we'd end up here," Michaels told Novak. "I know what happened in Russia a couple of weeks ago was an accident, but after reading this, it sounds like they got a bit of payback."

"If that's the case," he said, "let's just hope the vendetta ends with Russia."

72.02

The taxi from Lennart Meri Tallinn Airport delivered them down-town to the Radisson Blu Sky Hotel, only a short drive from the Estonian Information System Authority, where the strategy session would be held the next morning. After they'd checked in, Novak received a call from Walter, whose flight had arrived ahead of schedule. So he called their local cyber liaison, FBI Special Agent Helena Öpik, and confirmed that they would meet at the hotel bar at 4:00 P.M.

The chic Lounge 24 had been aptly named for its lofty perch atop the hotel tower. Novak ordered a pint of A. Le Coq beer, and Michaels opted for a Moscow mule. Then they braved the deep chill of the rooftop terrace to admire the enchanting views of Tallinn Bay and the Old Town's storybook spires, medieval walls, and Hanseatic architecture.

"It's so pretty here," Michaels said. "It's hard to imagine that this twisted, dystopian game show we've been living through could come from a place like this."

"Looks sure can be deceiving," Novak agreed.

"Do you think that deep down, when the pressure's on, we're all just a bunch of savages masquerading as a civilization?"

He looked out to the cruise ships docked at the Port of Tallinn and considered her question. "As hard as it is to imagine, we're living in one of the most peaceful eras in human history. The dark side of the Internet doesn't really compare to the horror of plagues or world wars, which we've somehow managed to avoid for the past few decades."

"Are you saying that Bounty4Justice just exposed a few rotten apples?"

He shrugged. "Most people are moral and simply want to live in peace and have a fair shake at a good life."

"But that's gotten a lot harder for most folks nowadays. Especially the decent ones. The deck's been stacked against them," she said, sipping her drink.

"I suppose it has."

"And let's not forget that the darkest periods in human history always begin with the bad guys—the instigators—seizing control of the information that reaches the masses and manipulating it. Wouldn't you say that, in the wrong hands, the Internet would far and away be the most potent propaganda machine ever conceived?"

"Absolutely."

"Then I guess it's no wonder that so many people think Bounty4Justice is on their side."

"Too bad they don't realize just how wrong they are about that."

"Tere!" a voice called to them. "Is that you, Agent Novak?"

Novak turned and saw a young, pretty blond woman bundled in a bright pink muffler coming over to greet them with a cosmopolitan in her hand.

73.01

Novak, Michaels, and Special Agent Helena Öpik sat in the cozy lounge while they waited for Walter to arrive, talking about the wild twists and turns of Operation CLICKKILL: Bounty4Justice's amazing ease in harnessing the herding behavior of the masses to do its bidding; how it had taken the world by storm; and how, like any viral sensation, it had peaked and plateaued fairly quickly.

Some of the falloff, they agreed, could be attributed to the authorities' regaining control of the credit card settlement networks and intercepting the website's cash intermediaries, which now made it difficult for average participants to interface with the website. Public relations had played its role, as well, particularly when it came to the accounts of the attempted abduction of innocent children in Washington, D.C., and the horrible case of mistaken identity in Athens. Many stories just like those had played out across the globe: a gunman in Munich had taken out a target in a drive-by shooting, but only after killing three innocent pedestrians with stray rounds from his Uzi; in Bruges, a hotel bombing had eliminated its intended target along with the young couple in an adjoining room.

In most cases, the agents speculated, Bounty4Justice had proved that vigilantism, by its very nature, was relegating the administration of justice to those least equipped to operate in the broader interests of civilized society.

It was during this philosophical detour that Walter arrived.

73.02

"There is an abandoned railway that runs along the piers in the northern subdistrict of Kalamaja," Helena said, pointing out the windows toward the harbor. "All along it, one finds empty factories and old buildings dating back to the Soviet occupation. A particular building there had been in a terrible state of disrepair until a couple months ago. Contractors had been called in to fix it up—basic repairs like a new roof and windows, and plumbing, of course. That's to be expected. But then there are the peculiar power lines and fiber optic connections installed in the building, which are of the quality and capacity one might expect to find at an industrial facility. We've confirmed that both lines have been very active. And somewhere at the end of those lines is where your IP address resides."

"Who owns the building?" Walter asked Helena.

"Ah, now, that's where things get really interesting. Supposedly a charitable trust purchased the property not that long ago, but when we queried the registrar, they could produce no records to substantiate ownership. It's as if the entire project went on without anyone knowing about it. We can only surmise that someone hacked the government website to remove the records altogether. Would have been an easy manipulation for a skilled hacker. Estonia has had a very difficult time with Russian moles infiltrating government positions. There's always that possibility, as well."

Novak had read in the dossier that in 2008, the head of the Estonian Defense Ministry, Herman Simm, had been arrested after it had been discovered that he was a mole for the SVR—the Russian intelligence service that succeeded the KGB. He'd been privy to NATO secrets and the tactical measures undertaken to secure the Estonian Internet domain during those massive cyberattacks in 2007. It made Novak wonder if Bounty4Justice itself might be a smoke screen for Russia's grab for supreme control over the Internet. With the Kremlin aspiring to rebuild the Soviet empire through land grabs, it certainly wasn't a long shot.

"Does anyone currently occupy the site?" Walter asked.

"The police have performed preliminary surveillance," Helena explained. "They've reported no activity. No one coming or going. They're keeping an eye on everything until we can move."

Novak had a strong inkling that no one *would* show up, because the landlords were most likely both laid out in a morgue in Bermuda. Since word of the double shooting, there'd been a moratorium on bounty payments and text blasts, which was welcome news, particularly for himself, Walter, and Knight. It was as if Bounty4Justice had gone into sleep mode, right along with its masterminds.

"Someone must be paying the utility bills," Michaels said.

"I already checked into it," Helena said, "and those bills are set up on autopay out of an anonymous account in Stockholm that had been activated online. For now, let's just say it's a dead end."

"And how about the construction company that did all that work?" Novak asked.

"A general contractor from Latvia handled the entire project. The authorities have already questioned him. He claims to have never met his client face-to-face. Everything was handled by email and phone, both of which ran through encrypted VOIP and proxy servers that we're still unable to trace. He has all the receipts and job orders. He also produced permits and inspection reports the client had sent to him—all of it falsified, with no indication of the client's actual name. All he can tell us is that it was a woman, she paid on time, and she knew exactly what equipment and specifications were needed for the job."

"A *woman?*"

"Do we have a name for her?" Michaels asked, as surprised as Novak.

"Only a first name: Rhea." Helena spelled it for them.

Novak smiled, recalling that in Greek mythology, Rhea was the goddess who'd saved her son Zeus from being eaten by his Titan father, Cronus . . . she'd fed Cronus a swaddled stone instead of the child. He wondered what meal *this* Rhea was preparing.

74.01

@ Estonian Information System Authority
Friday, 11/10/2017
08:00:00 EET

The next morning, the presentation hall was filled to capacity with
uniformed constables from the Politsei-ja Piirivalveamet, black-clad
tough guys from the K-Commando counterterrorism unit, plainclothes linguists and cyber technicians from the Computer Emergency Response Team of Estonia and the FBI Cyber Action Team,
suited bureaucrats from the Estonian Cyber Defense League, and
agents from the local outpost of the Secret Service. From what Novak
could observe from where he stood along the back wall with Michaels, Walter, and Helena, the ad hoc task force was an equal balance of brains and brawn.

Boilerplate briefings from the police and cyber units were followed
by a crisp PowerPoint slide show from Commander Jüri Žmaka
of K-Commando. A hulk of a man with a buzz cut, dressed in full
combat gear, Žmaka summarized the tactical elements of the raid
and gave visual context to the facts Helena had disclosed over
cocktails the previous afternoon. The building in Žmaka's recon-
naissance photos looked nothing like what Novak had sketched in

his mind—an old brick factory or some repurposed Soviet storage facility.

Novak whispered to Helena, "You could have told us it was a church."

"And ruin the surprise?" she said with a devious smile.

The church's architecture was by no means grandiose—no flying buttresses, or decorative spires, or gargoyles, or ornate Gothic features. Just a plain rectangle of fieldstone walls supporting a gabled slate roof, probably small enough to be classified as a chapel. Built into the front left corner of the building was a stout bell tower webbed with veins of new mortar. Perched atop the tower, where a cross might once have been, was a compact satellite dish aimed skyward. Along the sides of the church were narrow arched windows that had likely once been adorned with stained glass but were now completely filled in with cement. The formidable main door was painted high-gloss black; Novak couldn't tell if it was made of metal or wood. On close examination of the meticulous restoration, he could see the more sinister qualities that had transformed the property—not so much in form as in function. What had once been a house of worship had been clearly repurposed as a bunker.

74.02

The convoy consisted of six armored vehicles, eight Politsei patrol cars, and a CERT mobile command transport. As the procession drew nearer the waterfront, quaint residential plots tightened and yielded to warehouses and production facilities and shipyards. The armored off-road vehicles veered left off the roadway to hook onto the gravel embankment for the old railway, while the remaining vehicles parked in the lot of the abandoned mill, designated by Commander Žmaka as a staging area.

The four FBI agents exited the CERT truck and followed the cybertechs and police brigade on foot.

Rounding the building, Novak saw the armored vehicles up ahead, moving steadily in line along the left side of the railway. Strangely, the right side of the railway was lined by people—tall and short, reedy and husky, male and female, scruffy and clean-cut, in jeans and flannel shirts and suits and ties. All of them were wearing white *volto* masks.

"How did Nexus find out about the raid?" Michaels asked.

"I'm not sure," Helena said.

None of the Nexi had weapons, as far as Novak could tell, and they remained silent, with their heads bowed, as if engaged in some kind of prayer vigil. Plumes of frozen breath emanated from the slots in their masks. "Let's just hope they all behave themselves," he said.

74.03

The church looked fundamentally the same as it did in the pictures, except for its scale, which, to Novak, seemed much larger in real life. No roadways led up to the property, and the grounds immediately surrounding the structure were overgrown with weeds.

The Nexi congregated in the vicinity, but the police cordoned them at a safe distance outside K-Commando's buffer zone. A police chopper began circling high overhead, and snipers took up tactical positions off in the bare trees. Novak could see news crews dashing along the rails, trying not to be late to the party. Walter stood with the clutch of eager cybertechs, all at the ready with gear in hand.

Žmaka scanned the church's entryway with binoculars, then gave a chopping hand signal to four commandos holding a pneumatic door ram that looked like a cannon. Before K-Commando could flex its muscle, however, the big black door made some ominous metallic clicking sounds that sent the breaching crew retreating back a few steps.

Then the front door of the bunker slowly and smoothly opened inward.

74.04 _____

With the tsunami of violence Bounty4Justice had unleashed upon the world, it was anyone's guess as to what Rhea had in store for her uninvited guests. But after a seemingly endless minute ticked by, nothing happened, and the chatter began.

As the news cameramen rolled live coverage, Žmaka's men deployed a recon robot, which rose up on six articulating legs and scurried toward the church—a metal vandal that nimbly clicked and clacked its way up the front steps and disappeared into the darkened interior.

Žmaka stood behind the bot's engineer, monitoring its video transmission feed, telegraphing no emotion whatsoever. Five minutes later, he gave another hand signal; this one sent six commandos armed with MP5s streaming up the steps, into the building, followed by a seventh man guiding two German shepherds on leashes.

Twenty minutes later, one of the commandos reappeared, and Žmaka trotted over to him. There was a brief exchange. Then the commander turned to the cyber team and the FBI agents and waved them inside.

75.01

Walking up those five granite steps and crossing over the physical threshold into the inner sanctum of Bounty4Justice, Novak couldn't remember the last time he'd felt so alive with anticipation. Immediately inside the entryway, they passed through a small vestibule, then under a heavy purple curtain that had been pulled aside, into the chilly, darkened sanctuary, which twinkled with thousands of pinpoints of neon light, like an alien nightscape. Within seconds, the darkness was banished when someone turned on the overhead electric candelabras.

As in most churches, a main aisle led up to the raised platform of the altar, but instead of pews on either side, this one was flanked by stocky refrigerator-sized metal cabinets with shelves stacked tight with routers and processors and hard drives, six server cabinets to the left of the aisle, six to the right, all thrumming and humming. They were spaced comfortably apart, so that one could easily pace around any one of them. Their fiber optic cables and power lines were piped up into a wide metal conduit bolted to the joists supporting the vaulted ceiling. The main trunks on each side ran in straight lines alongside the air-conditioning ductwork, through the sanctuary, and over the altar, before disappearing behind a black curtain hung along the rear wall where the tabernacle would normally be.

LEDs flickered wildly on the face of the component cells, tracking the frenetic calculations taking place in each section of the massive digital brain. Hundreds if not thousands of tiny fans whirred, and the cool air felt electro-charged, as if it could ionize into lightning at any moment.

Walter and the cybertechs were circling the machines, intently studying the complex devices stacked inside the cabinets, no doubt contemplating how to disarm the world's most potent cyber weapon.

Michaels tugged on Novak's arm and pointed up at the rafters.

Novak looked up and spotted one lens, then many more of the discreet surveillance cameras that had been installed throughout the space. They were swiveling on their mounts, panning to and fro, their electronic eyes retracting and zooming.

"Someone's watching us," she said.

Just then, the candelabras went out.

The German shepherds growled against a backdrop of nervous murmuring.

Novak reached for his Glock.

Up on the altar, a large LCD monitor snapped to life. Against its solid crimson display, bold white letters spelled out a message in real time:

WELCOME.
I'VE BEEN WAITING FOR YOU.

75.02

Everyone in the church fell silent, while the servers hummed along unabated, like bees in a hive. All eyes were transfixed on the screen atop the altar as the next message eerily materialized, letter by letter:

LOOK AROUND.
THIS IS WHAT LITTLE IT TAKES
TO CAST OUR INTERCONNECTED
WORLD INTO UTTER CHAOS.
SERVERS.
NOT MISSILES.
WELCOME TO THE CYBERWAR.

Novak glanced at his companions. Standing close beside him, Michaels was electric with tension. Walter and the cybertechs were huddled close to the altar, consulting in hushed tones; Žmaka and K-Commando stood in defensive formation behind them in the center aisle, draped in the weapons of another era, powerless against the digital ghost.

"Is this some kind of game?" Žmaka scoffed loudly, to no one in particular.

A reply scrolled onto the screen:

YES. YOU PEOPLE LIKE TO PLAY GAMES, DON'T YOU?

Žmaka glared at the screen, defiant. "Does someone want to talk some sense into this machine?"

The room broke out in chatter.

Until the machine responded:

HOW ABOUT YOU, AGENT NOVAK?
YOU'VE BEEN AN INTERESTING ADVERSARY.

Novak gazed up at the cameras. This was no chatbot, however clever. It was obvious that its operator was listening. Those who knew him were staring at him expectantly, and the others caught on quickly. Raising his voice slightly, he called out, "Is that you, Rhea?"

Pause.

AT YOUR SERVICE.

Jackpot. He desperately wished he could hear her voice, get a read on the subtleties—the subtext—of her responses.

READY TO PLAY?

"That depends. What's the game?"

HANGMAN, OF COURSE.

It was a low-tech, old-school choice—the kind of game he used to play with his sister as a young boy, using crayons and a scribble pad— but macabrely appropriate for the mastermind of Bounty4Justice. "Okay. I'm game. And what happens if I win?"

There was another pause, filled by the ambient drone of the servers.

I'LL REMOVE YOU FROM MY LIST.

"I'd appreciate that. But how about you remove *everyone* from your list? How about you stop the killing, Rhea?" It was a strong rejoinder—a bit *too* strong, perhaps arrogant—and some in the small crowd stirred uneasily. At this juncture, however, there was nothing to be gained by pussyfooting around. The stakes were simply too high. "You've proved your point, haven't you?"

No hesitation now.

DO YOU REALLY THINK
YOU UNDERSTAND MY POINT?

Novak glanced at Michaels, who nodded almost imperceptibly and gave him a cool, go-ahead little smile. *Proceed, with caution.* He decided to stick to the tough-love script. "I can't speak for you, Rhea. Just so we're clear, why don't you tell me in your own words? Tell us why you've brought us here."

There was another pause, longer this time, as Rhea presumably contemplated her response—or further retribution. He wondered if she was somewhere nearby or halfway around the globe, holed up in a dark room—watching him through robotic eyes, already on to her next move and playing them all like fools.

Finally, her reply scrolled onto the screen in rapid-fire typing:

MANY FORCES SEEK TO UNDERMINE OUR FREEDOM.
THE RULE OF LAW HAS FAILED US!
OUR GOVERNMENTS HAVE FAILED US!
THEY HAVE TURNED TECHNOLOGY AGAINST US.
THE INTERNET IS ALL THAT REMAINS.
THE COLLECTIVE IS THE LAST TRUE DEMOCRACY.
THE COLLECTIVE IS JUSTICE.

Clearly, he'd struck a chord. "But you're using the Internet as a weapon. Doesn't that undermine *everyone's* freedom?"

This time, with no delay:

MERE DEMONSTRATIONS, AGENT NOVAK.
OTHERWISE NO ONE NOTICES,
AND NOTHING CHANGES.
NOW EVERYONE UNDERSTANDS THE THREATS WE FACE,
THE WEAPONS ARRAYED AGAINST US.
NOW THINGS WILL CHANGE.
WE MUST DEFEND TRUE JUSTICE.
WE MUST DEFEND A TRULY INDEPENDENT INTERNET.
AT ANY COST.

WIN THE GAME, I STOP THE KILLING.
READY TO PLAY?

"I am."

PLEASE DON'T CHEAT, AGENT NOVAK.
YOU'VE SEEN WHAT I DO TO CHEATERS.

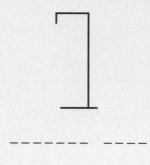

76.01

The sentient screen again reverted to solid red for a moment. Then the clue appeared in bold white letters, along with a digital clock graphic, a crudely drawn hangman's gallows, and blank lines in place of the letters for the two words needed to solve the puzzle.

The LEDs on all the servers began pulsating wildly, and the machines' buzzing ratcheted up to a fever pitch, like engine pistons firing on nitrous oxide. Some kind of controlled power surge, Novak guessed. The two German shepherds growled, fangs bared, hackles spiking along their backbones, their handler struggling with the leashes to restrain them. Not a good sign, since most canine units were specifically trained to sniff out bombs. Which seemed to be exactly what Žmaka was thinking when he shouted, "Everyone out! *Saada väljaspool nüüd!*"

Michaels pulled at Novak's arm. "Roman, this is going downhill."

"No. I've got this." *I might be blown to pieces, but I can do this.* "You go."

The clock began its countdown. What Novak had hoped were sixty minutes proved to be sixty *seconds*.

Michaels didn't move, and Walter joined them. Everyone else was heading for the exit. Before anyone reached it, the big black door smoothly swung closed on pneumatic pistons . . . and its heavy locks clacked shut.

Žmaka shoved his way to the door, clutching his MP5, cursing venomously.

"That's not good," Walter said. "Now what?"

Novak ignored him, blocked out the pandemonium, stepped closer to the altar, and called out: *"E!"*

On the screen, the gallows refigured itself:

Damn. He focused on the blank lines beneath the gallows. Last year, he'd attended a cryptography primer at Quantico, where, among other things, they'd reviewed the most frequently used letters in the English language. At the time, it hadn't seemed particularly useful. Until now.

"T!"

Which filled in one of the blanks for the second word.

$$\_\ \_\ \_\ \_\ \_\ \_\ \_\ \quad \_\ \_\ \_\ \text{T}$$

Next: *"A!"*

One A appeared in the first word.

$$\_\ \_\ \_\ \_\ \_\ \text{A}\ \_\ \quad \_\ \_\ \_\ \text{T}$$

The acrid scent of burning plastic and metal laced the air, and out of the corner of his eye, Novak could see coils of smoke spinning out from the server cabinets, white sparks crackling. Were the servers somehow rigged to explode?

"She's burning it down, Novak," Walter said. "Keep going!"

"O!"

Two more blanks filled in.

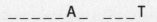

$$\_\ \text{O}\ \_\ \_\ \_\ \text{A}\ \_ \quad \_\ \_\ \text{O T}$$

Now small flames were rippling along the routers and hard drives, and noxious smoke began to permeate the room. Inside this windowless bunker, it wouldn't take long for all of them to suffocate. Novak forged ahead.

"I!"

Another score.

_ O _ _ I A _   _ _ O T

He couldn't remember if the next most common letter was *H* or *N* or *S* . . .

"S!"

"Shit!" Adrenaline was coursing through him, sharpening his senses but dulling his deductive capabilities, the hardwired primordial fight-or-flight instinct threatening to override all logic. He crouched to stay beneath the encroaching smoke.

The clock ticked to thirty seconds.

Žmaka and his men scrambled around the space, casting about for anything useful—fire extinguishers, alternate exits, anything. The cybertechs were shouting back and forth, circling the machines, futilely attempting to disable power to the servers, probably still hoping to salvage the equipment—the evidence—as well as stymie the burn. But the metal conduit shielding the electrical cables that snaked up into the rafters could likely be severed only with power tools.

Michaels pressed closer and squeezed his arm. "You can do this, Novak. Stay focused. Go with your gut."

The ultimate puzzle . . .

"H!"

Not good. And Rhea drew two arms instead of one. Bad enough that she'd filled the whole face in right from the get-go.

"Hey!" Walter screamed, stabbing a finger at one of the cameras overhead. "That's cheating!"

Novak felt his chest tightening with dread. He was sure that one more wrong guess meant two stick legs. That's how Rhea played. End of challenge—game over. *Think . . . THINK!* But Walter's words kept playing in his head: *That's cheating.*

Cheating?

He reconsidered the clue: *the ultimate puzzle.* He studied the partial solution. Could it be that easy? The church felt like a sauna, with the servers now fully aflame. Novak could barely see the screen through the haze of smoke.

"*G!*"

GO _ _ IA_ _ _OT

Big score. *And* confirmation of his hunch. The ultimate puzzle. The impossible challenge. The legendary knot at the ancient Turkish capital of Gordium that no man had ever undone. Until Alexander the Great arrived on the scene like a goddamn rock star and sliced through the impenetrable tangle with one stroke of his sword. Cheating. Or simply, literally, cutting to the truth. *The Alexandrian solution.*

"I've got it," Novak said.

Walter, in a prayer-like position on his knees, smoke haloing his Afro, threw up his hands. "For fuck's sake, Novak, what you've got is fifteen seconds! Then fucking say it, will ya? Before we all suffocate!"

"*Gordian knot!*" Novak shouted.

Nothing happened.

Please don't cheat, Agent Novak. You've seen what I do to cheaters.

Novak's pulse drummed in his ears. He couldn't tell what was happening on the screen. He strode up to the monitor, smoke be damned, and grabbed it, fully expecting to see the completed stick figure, game-ending legs and all. Even though he thought for sure he had it right.

Michaels followed him and grabbed his arm. "The countdown stopped at three seconds."

"Then why isn't anything happening?" Walter said, still low to the floor.

Not for the first time, Novak wondered if this was all another ruse Rhea had orchestrated to eliminate her most dangerous opponents. *How about you, Agent Novak? You've been an interesting adversary.* From the moment Chase Lombardi had gotten his head blown off, a trail of breadcrumbs had been leading them here, slowly and steadily—methodically. And he'd been obligingly following it. *She lured us here.*

The monitor went blank again—nothing but that damn blood-red screen.

Everyone in the room was down on the floor, with the smoke blanketing them. It wouldn't take long now.

Barely visible through the haze, a new message appeared on the screen, letter by letter:

NICELY DONE, AGENT NOVAK.

Then the locks on the entryway snapped back, and the pistons retracted to pull the big black door open.

76.02

When they emerged from the church, Michaels took a deep breath of fresh air and hooked her arm through Novak's to steady herself going down the steps. "Great job in there. Talk about staying cool under pressure."

"You were damn steady yourself. I almost lost it, more than once," he replied truthfully.

"But you didn't." She smiled and squeezed his arm. "I was starting to believe sweet Rhea was going to let us all die in there. Do you think she would have opened the door if you hadn't solved the puzzle?"

"No. I think we'd all be dead." And he meant it. "She plays for keeps."

"Bitch."

"Exactly." He saw news cameras pointed in their direction, close to where Žmaka stood by a Humvee, barking commands through a walkie-talkie. The commander met his gaze, gave him a thumbs-up. Novak nodded.

"How did you know that answer, anyway?" she asked. "Gordian knot? I mean, that's pretty obscure."

He shook his head. "Not exactly. She was toying with me. She seems to know me real well and that I'd probably get it right. She also knew that if I got it right, I'd be coming for her. And that's exactly what's going to happen."

"Guys! Over here!" Walter, huddled at the CERT command truck with members of the cyber team, waved them over. "You need to look at this!"

76.03

"The website's still up and running," Walter informed them, pointing at his laptop. "Definitely a new set of servers. The ones inside are all toast."

"Christ," Novak said.

"But get this: the targets have changed," Walter said. "She's definitely not gunning for criminals anymore. Or you or me or Tim. See for yourself." He handed the laptop to Novak.

On the Bounty4Justice home page, Novak still saw bounties ticking higher and higher. But the thumbnail head shots of criminals had been replaced by simple phrases like QUANTUM.LOCK and PORT.BLASTER and CHATTER.WORM.

"What do all those words mean?" Michaels asked.

"That's the problem," Walter said. "Those are the code names of covert surveillance algorithms used by the NSA and other intelligence agencies, internationally. Their arsenal. Looks as if Rhea's posting the code in open source. And she's paying big money to any hackers who disarm them."

77.01 _____

@ Summit, New Jersey
Monday, 11/13/2017
11:05:01 EST

Novak was at the wheel, with his mom buckled tight in the passenger seat and his dad fidgeting in the backseat. He kept the Impala to the slow lane on Route 24.

"We're running a bit early," his dad said anxiously. "Appointment's not till eleven-thirty. I figure today we'll just get a feel for the place. You sure you don't need to be at the office?"

"I'm sure, Dad," Novak replied, making eye contact with him in the rearview mirror. It was the third time his dad had asked him that same question. Not for lack of memory.

"Hey, you know, I saw you on CNN again this morning," his dad said. "They keep showing that same footage of you coming out of that church, with all those police. I've gotten a lot of calls about it from your aunts and uncles and cousins . . . the neighbors, too.

They're all very impressed. And you should see my Facebook page. I can barely keep up."

So much for maintaining a low profile, thought Novak. That clip had quickly become a media bite for the good guys—the first positive portrayal of law enforcement in an otherwise long line of mishaps and dead ends.

"You should be proud. That's an amazing thing you were part of, over there. Taking that thing down . . . putting an end to all that madness with people killing one another in the streets."

"Well, it's not over yet," Novak said. *Not until Rhea's in custody.*

"I'd say you're off to a strong start. By the way, everyone's asking who that pretty woman was beside you . . . the one with the short hair?"

"Rosemary Michaels. She's another agent from work."

"Man, is she a looker. She married?"

"No."

"Good. Because you two looked nice together. You saw it, right, Patty?"

"Umm," his mother replied, nodding slightly and giving Novak her best smile.

"I say go for it," his dad said.

"Umm," his mom added approvingly.

"It's not that easy, Dad."

"Eh, come on, Roman. Life's too short. If you find someone who makes you happy, you grab them."

"We'll see," Novak said. He exited the highway and proceeded along the suburban side roads. Ten minutes later, he turned through the gateway for the Spring Blossoms assisted living facility. Everyone remained quiet as he followed the signs for the main building.

"Your sister told us that this one's got the best rating for quality of care," his dad finally said. "And they just remodeled all the rooms."

"Looks really nice," Novak said truthfully. The grounds were meticulously kept, and the sprawling residential buildings looked practically new: immaculate stonework and siding, crisp architectural roof shingling, freshly painted trim—a portrait of order. He glanced over at his mother. She was doing her best to stay strong on the outside.

But as he approached the visitors' entrance and an attendant with an empty wheelchair waved him to a stop, he could see her eyes welling up. "It's going to be okay, Mom," he said. He put his hand on top of hers. "We're all here for you."

She nodded and gave his hand a tremulous squeeze.

"Okay. Let's go on in and have a look," his dad said as cheerily as he could manage.

Novak got out of the car, and a valet trotted over and handed him a parking chit. As they headed toward the entrance, his BlackBerry chimed the arrival of an email reply he'd been awaiting.

From: Joshua.L.Tierney@nsa.gov
Sent: November 13, 2017 at 11:21 AM
To: Tim Knight, Walter Koslowski, Roman Novak
Cc: Dilip Kapoor
Subject: Query requests 658YHRZJ405-001, 658YHRZJ405-002, 658YHRZJ405-003

✉: FIREWOLF.IP.query.results.pdf
✉: FIREWOLF.emails.pdf
✉: FIREWOLF.SingLao.pdf
✉: FIREWOLF.Mfg.China.pdf
✉: PIKE-JAM.Atlas5.chats.pdf

Team CLICKKILL,
I've attached network mapping and search results for the moniker "Fire-wolf," scrubbed for relevance to your investigation. The same IP addresses appear in the hard drive seized from SingLao North American Shipping, Inc., in Canada as well as a manufacturing company in Shenzhen, China, named Chongxin Shenme. I've activated network sniffers to monitor future transmissions to these IPs and will consult with my superiors as to what intercept data might be made available to your task force.
I successfully recovered exchanges between Randall Scott (online handle "JAM") and Jeremy Grimes (online handle "PIKE") carried out over the past eighteen months on a VPN named Atlas-5. Those exchanges provide insight into how Razorwire was conceived and designed and contain numerous references to Firewolf, corroborating that this individual was funding Razorwire's development. They also provide a timeline for what we now know to be the breach initiated by Rhea.

Regretfully, I cannot provide details concerning our internal investigations into Randall Scott's procurement of proprietary algorithms that Rhea had stolen and incorporated into Bounty4Justice's core coding (a.k.a. Razorwire). I have forwarded those inquiries to my superiors and am awaiting guidance.

Finally, I traced the text messages sent to Chase Lombardi's phone on the day of his murder. Those transmissions originated on a secure satellite band reserved for domestic intelligence assets. In the interest of national security operations, I regretfully cannot investigate the matter further. However, during the course of my analysis, I was able to determine that in the month preceding Lombardi's murder, someone had spoofed cipher keys to send secure directives to this intelligence asset. We can safely assume that the hacker and Rhea are one and the same. It seems that the compromised asset was fully unaware of the hack and that Chase Lombardi should be considered collateral damage of a very high-level security breach.

Best of luck,

Josh Tierney
Senior Digital Network Exploitation Analyst

78.01 _____

@ Lake City, Colorado
Friday, 11/17/2017
10:05:01 MST

Snow drifted gently earthward from steel-gray clouds, and it was
slow going on Route 149, even with the rented Jeep's four-wheel drive
engaged. Michaels was at the wheel, bundled up, trailing alongside
the roiling Lake Fork Gunnison River as it cut its way through the
white-capped mountain peaks of the Continental Divide.

Sitting in the passenger seat, Novak peered out the window, studying the rugged, snow-blanketed terrain. Hinsdale County featured
the fewest roads and the most mountains in all of Colorado, with
barely more than eight hundred residents spread over its 1,123 square
miles of rough-and-tumble wilderness of forests and lakes. The ideal
sanctuary for an expert survivalist.

He looked over at Michaels. She caught him staring.

She smiled. "What?"

"You have plans for Thanksgiving?"

"Nothing set in stone. Didn't want to overcommit with everything
that's going on. And my parents decided to go on a holiday cruise to
the Caribbean. Why?"

"There's an open seat at the Novak house," he said. "If you don't mind putting up with my chatty sister and her spoiled kids."

Again, that smile. "I think I can handle that."

He smiled back. "Sounds like a plan, then."

They drove through Lake City—a historic small town with wooden storefronts stacked side by side and a saloon and a stone-block bank where prospectors once deposited gold and silver. Continuing farther downriver, Michaels, directed by the GPS, turned off on a side road that wound its way up along a steep mountain pass, up over a ridge, and along three miles of undulating twists and turns to the mailbox that marked their final destination. Set back nearly a hundred yards from the road stood a modest wood-planked cabin with a corrugated steel roof and smoke spinning out its brick chimney.

"That's it," Michaels said.

Novak took out his binoculars and scanned the area. There was a Chevy Tahoe parked near a stacked cord of quartered firewood and a snowmobile, too. He couldn't see through the windows.

"Anything?" Michaels asked.

"Nothing."

"We came here to talk to him, right?"

He looked at her. "We did."

"Then let's go talk to him."

She turned at the mailbox and followed the tire ruts in the snow that led to the cabin.

When they were only halfway there, the front door opened. A wiry man, dressed in jeans and flannel, stepped out onto the porch. He had a crew cut and beard stubble. Novak saw the resemblance to David Furlong immediately.

78.02

The cabin's interior had a simple floor plan, with exposed rafters and an open loft, walls covered in knotty pine, scuffed oak-plank floors. Novak didn't see a computer or laptop or television, just some newspapers and magazines on an end table next to the leather sofa that faced the wood-burning stove.

"Can I make you some coffee?" Jonathan Farrell asked as Novak and Michaels took off their gloves and snow coats.

"That sounds wonderful," Michaels said.

"Please," Novak said.

"Make yourselves comfortable," he said, pointing to the sofa.

The agents settled in as Farrell went over to scoop some grinds into his brewer's filter basket.

"What brings you all the way out here?" asked Farrell.

"Bounty4Justice," Novak said.

The sniper turned the faucet to fill the coffeepot. "I figured as much. I recognize both of you from the news. They're saying you shut the killing machine down. What was the final head count?"

"Well, if you're talking about how many bounties were awarded, that would be twenty-nine here in the U.S.," Michaels said. "Another fifty-two in Europe and Asia."

"Damn. Impressive." He strode over and eased into an armchair facing them.

"There were nearly five hundred active profiles before the website stopped targeting people," Michaels said. "Could've been a lot worse. But let's not forget that plenty of innocent people were also killed along the way."

Farrell nodded. "So what does all that have to do with me?"

"Chase Lombardi," Novak said, flat out.

Farrell remained impassive.

Novak said, "David Furlong's license was run by D.C. Metro during a minor accident the day Lombardi was shot, even though he'd been at a gun range in Virginia at that time. The officers could only tell us that the driver looked like the picture on his license: Caucasian male with his hair cut 'like a jarhead.' Their words, not mine. The clerk at the Avis car rental agency told us the same story, but by the time we got there, the security videos taken that day had been recorded over. So we had Quantico run a list of former military sharpshooters capable of a half-mile head shot." Novak looked over to Michaels.

"We used a ten-year window," she said, "and filtered for Caucasian males. Still a fairly long list. Until Randall Scott and Jeremy Grimes were killed in Bermuda by bullets with ballistic markings matching the bullet that killed Chase Lombardi. Same weapon killed all three men. As it turns out, a local who'd been fishing on the pier when the shooting took place had spotted a man in scuba gear out on Hen Island, right near where he thought he'd heard the shots fired. The diver had disappeared into the water, carrying a long dive bag. The police found flattened bushes along the island's shoreline in a position that perfectly aligned with the trajectory of the slugs pulled from the wall of the Seadog Pub. We wondered how many of our Caucasian male sharpshooters over the past ten years had gotten scuba certified. It came down to three."

Farrell continued to listen attentively.

Novak resumed the narrative: "Then we looked at bank accounts, since snipers generally don't kill people simply for sport. And that's when we discovered that one of our three suspects had recently opened an account not far from here, over in Lake City, into which large wire transfers had been made from an account in Zurich that had no clear ownership. In that account was one rather large deposit that exactly matched the bounty sum paid out on Chase Lombardi, and it had been wired from Archer Offsite Systems, a company in Bermuda registered to Randall Scott and Jeremy Grimes. We also noted steady monthly deposits made to that account in Zurich, going back nearly four years. Turns out, those deposits are being made by the top office of the U.S. Intelligence Community."

Farrell seemed perfectly relaxed. Novak imagined it took a lot to unnerve a man whose service record reflected 148 official kills during six years of active duty with the Navy SEALs. As a top secret hired gun for the ODNI for the past few years—a lone operator who took on the most harrowing jobs, the sort that necessitated zero accountability—Jonathan Farrell had likely terminated Lord only knew how many more lives to protect American interests.

"Supposing all this was true," Farrell noted in a level tone, "I'd probably say something like 'I certainly can't vouch for secret accounts in Zurich and who puts money in them.' Then maybe I'd point out that certain contractors receive payments for services that they're not at liberty to discuss *and* that inquiries pertaining to national security would need to be directed to Washington. And that makes me wonder why we're even having this discussion."

"John, we know you report directly to the Office of the Director of National Intelligence," Michaels said, point-blank. "And those orders to kill Lombardi, Scott, and Grimes all came to you the way your orders typically do: on a secure satellite connection. You were only doing your job, like you always have. And it's that loyalty and sacrifice that keeps America safe," she said without irony. "I served in Afghanistan, too. So I respect that more than most."

Farrell shifted ever so slightly in his chair, his gaze hardening.

"Problem is, you've been had, my friend," Novak said. "Used. Not unlike the rest of us. Your phone has been compromised—hacked, actually. Along with a lot of other assets that fall under the purview of the intelligence community. Any orders you received over the past few weeks did not actually come from the ODNI. They came from the person who masterminded Bounty4Justice . . . this woman you've been hearing about in the news who calls herself Rhea. She needed professionals to start the killing, to ensure a lot of attention, fast. She needed people like you." Since Josh Tierney wasn't at liberty to disclose the NSA intercepts detailing the actual directives Rhea had sent to Farrell, Novak had only been able to work backward from the outcomes. Judging from Farrell's subtle tells, those deductions looked to be spot-on.

"My phone is encrypted," Farrell replied. "*Big-time.* So I'd say that's impossible."

"The NSA confirmed it," Novak said. "And they're pretty good at this sort of thing. They traced those text messages you sent to Chase Lombardi. No matter how secure your communications may seem, the NSA inevitably holds the decryption keys that unscramble all of it. They don't guess. They just cheat. You know that."

"Coffee's just about ready." Farrell stood and made his way to the kitchen.

Novak looked to Michaels for a read. She shrugged.

Mugs distributed, Farrell sat again, cupping his hands around his coffee, looking conflicted, saying nothing.

"Look, John," Novak said. "The NSA and British intelligence are already under fire. It's a public relations nightmare. No one is looking to drag another intelligence agency through the muck. We've got enough conspiracy to deal with as it is."

After a long pause, Farrell asked, "So you've come all this way to tell me to get a new phone?"

Novak smiled. "That, and we also hoped you might be able to help us."

"Really," Farrell said dubiously. "In what way?"

Novak opened his folio and handed Farrell a sampling of the Atlas-5 screenshots Josh Tierney had sent him, then explained how Scott and Grimes had clandestinely communicated under the screen handles JAM and PIKE.

"In those exchanges," Novak said, "I've highlighted references to someone named Firewolf. That same code name is also associated with the man behind the massive money-laundering operation we shut down in Canada that was unknowingly fulfilling Bounty4Justice's cash bounties. I'm sure you've heard about it."

"I have."

"During that raid," Michaels added, "we arrested one of Firewolf's bookkeepers, who helped us map the operation's finances to accounts in Shenzhen, China. Those same accounts wired funds to Scott and Grimes in Bermuda, which they presumably then used to build Razorwire. Those accounts are also associated with a manufacturing concern in Shenzhen named Chongxin Shenme, which is a front for stealing U.S. trade secrets. We're talking espionage on a grand scale. And I don't mean just pirating golf clubs and handbags."

Novak added, "Bounty4Justice's scales of justice pins were manufactured by Chongxin Shenme." That connection had been overlooked until Tierney's intercepts connected the dots. In reviewing the events as they'd unfolded throughout the investigation, Novak realized just how cleverly Rhea had been playing him at every turn.

"These pins, the cash procurements . . . all of it was intended to lead the FBI straight to Firewolf's doorstep."

"Hold on. Exactly who is this Rhea, anyway?" Farrell asked.

Novak smiled. On paper, Rhea simply didn't exist. She'd used a burner phone, prepaid with cash. All of her income was collected in NcryptoCash. With multiple aliases and no Social Security number or birth date or valid address for the FBI to go by, she could officially be labeled a ghost . . . had he not met her in the flesh at the onset of the investigation. "We're still trying to establish her true identity. But we're close."

Farrell studied the pages some more, then said, "And you're saying that all along she's been using Bounty4Justice to set up this Chinese character named Firewolf?"

Novak nodded. "She set up Firewolf, Grimes, and Scott. A trifecta. And some intelligence people overseas, too."

"And *you*," Michaels reminded Farrell.

"Problem is," Novak said, "she has most everyone believing she's some kind of freedom fighter hacktivist who's out to right all the wrongs in the world. But I'm thinking that she doesn't give a shit about justice or freedom. I think she's a psychopath with a major God complex. And she's an expert at manipulation."

"Then what's her objective?" Farrell asked.

"Rhea wants to own the Web, lock, stock, and barrel," replied Novak. "She's not looking to secure it. She's looking to tear down all its defenses, using Nexus and everyone else to help her do it, so that eventually she'll hold all the keys to the kingdom. To achieve that goal, she'll need to eliminate her competitors, like Firewolf. And she's just getting warmed up."

"Seriously, you're kidding, right?" Farrell grinned. "*Own* the Internet? You really think that's possible?"

"I'm not about to wait around long enough to find out," Novak replied. "She's already come a long way. She's proved to be smart and ruthless, and she's already got her hacker fan boys breaking down our entire arsenal of cyber safeguards and tools, which she's pegged as threats to freedom. That we can debate. But not if she's in charge, dictating what's secure and what's not. So it's critical that we track her down before she does more damage. I'm sure Firewolf isn't very happy about what she's done to him, so I suspect he'll be out there looking for her, too. For obvious reasons, I think we'd all agree that it would be best if we get to her first. I've got some ideas about our Rhea, but we've got our work cut out for us. And we won't make it far without the help of a specialist who can operate outside the normal framework, if you know what I mean. Bottom line is, we need a *hunter*."

Farrell nodded thoughtfully. He turned away from them and stared long and hard at the bright flames dancing behind the stove's glass door, then finally asked, "How much are you paying?"

Michaels smiled. "Come on, John . . . can you really put a price on freedom?"

"I reckon not," he said, smiling back. "When do we start?"

PRIZE PAYOUT NOTIFICATION
TARGET: CHATTER.WORM, packet transmission
exploit (NSA, USA)
FINAL BOUNTY: $1,385,805
VIEW PROOF OF CLAIM (coding patch) @
http://www.bounty4justice.com/CHATTER.WORM

79.01 ————————————————————

@ Grand Cayman Island
15:33:14 EST

With his toes buried in the warm sand and an icy mojito in his hand, Josh Tierney was feeling relaxed for the first time in a good long while. Looking out at the blue sky and the emerald ocean calmed the swirl of other colors that had been muddling up his thoughts. And his brain certainly needed a reboot, because there'd be plenty of thinking to do once he got back to the office. The NSA had been in code red ever since its cyberarms catalog—its arsenal of exploit algorithms— began posting slow and steady to Bounty4Justice, which was still lurking undetected in the uncharted depths of the darknet, now morphed into its second incarnation.

Whoever was behind all of it was being hailed by the hacker community and freedom advocates as some kind of Robin Hood—or, more appropriately, Robin Hood*ess*. It was a chick, after all, who had turned the world inside out. Go figure. She still hadn't been identified, so they just kept referring to her by the code name Rhea. And the co-conspirators Randall Scott and Jeremy Grimes were to be forever immortalized in the pop culture pantheon as "Scrimes," alongside Brangelina and Bennifer and TomKat. Crazy to think that that stuttering dweeb—that savant go-to man for NSA's senior management who'd been granted the highest systems clearances and privileges—had been sitting next to him the whole time, ransacking the world's most preeminent intelligence agency, poaching algorithms and exploiting the weakest vulnerability of all: *trust*. Good old social engineering—the surefire back door that no firewall could ever patch. Yet misplaced trust had also led to Randall's downfall in a most poetic double cross.

Josh's small victory was bittersweet. Sure, he'd helped the authorities find the servers hosting Bounty4Justice, which had inevitably forced the website to stop targeting human marks for assassination. Not that he viewed it as some noble deed, seeing as mostly every target on that website was a sleaze or scumbag who pretty much deserved what they'd gotten.

But a deal is a deal. So the NSA and his boss still made good on their end of the bargain and sent him off to Grand Cayman, all expenses paid, with fifty grand in spending money.

Behind Josh, the sliding door on the veranda opened and closed, and his plus-one sashayed over in a white bikini top and floral sarong, her jet-black hair pulled back to flaunt her graceful neck. Man, did she have a slammin' body. Normally, she sure wasn't one to show it off—one of her better qualities, he thought—with those retro-grunge outfits of hers. Trying to figure out some way to get her to *share* her body, however, had so far proved to be his next ultimate puzzle. Ever since he'd met her at DEF CON, a couple years ago, he'd been working every angle he could. Still, she'd managed to give him the slip every time. She was nothing like any other woman he'd ever met. Smokin' hot *and* brilliant *and* cool? Like some comic book seductress brought to life. He had high hopes that this trip might tip the scales in his direction.

"Beautiful day," she said, unwrapping her sarong. She knelt in front of his beach chair with her back facing him. "Can you get my shoulders?" She handed him a tube of sunscreen.

"Sure." He set his drink beside his laptop on the table and sat up beside her.

"Do you ever take this thing off?" he said, tapping the custom headset wrapped over her left ear. "You don't have to be Borg all the time, you know."

"Sorry," Christine said. "You're right." She plucked the headset off her ear, neatly folded the monocular lens, and tucked it into her beach bag. "Just been really busy lately."

"You going to make me one of those?" he asked, squeezing a dollop of lotion onto his palm. "I can even pay you, you know, being that I just came into a lot of *dinero.*"

"It's not for sale," she said playfully.

He smoothed the lotion over the silky white skin of her shoulders, and his libido responded as if he'd touched a live wire. "You should give Google or Apple a call. I'm telling you, they'd buy that design in a heartbeat, and you'd be a billionaire."

"It's not about the money," she said.

"Seriously?" he jested. "Come on, you mean to tell me you'd turn down that kind of coin?"

"Not everything's about money, jackass. Make sure you get my tattoo."

He slathered extra lotion on the wicked ink on the back of her left shoulder. It depicted some Greek goddess in a toga sitting on a throne with a loop in one hand, an orb in the other, and two lions at her feet. He'd once asked her what it meant, but she'd given him some blow-off explanation, even though he'd known it had some deep significance. That aloofness was another quality that inextricably drew him to her.

"I'm just saying," he added. "Everybody has their price."

"Look at your buddy Randall," she scoffed. "See what greed bought him?"

"Okay. I guess he's a bad example," Josh admitted. Christine had known Randall well, too. Same with that British dude Jeremy, who'd also gotten his head blown off in Bermuda. Josh had always thought that guy was a pretty-boy poser douchebag, because for months after they'd all first met at DEF CON, he'd tried to hook up with Christine. Kept sending her emails and was pretty much cyberstalking her. But she was the master of her domain and never let him in. "I mean, I won this trip. Is that greedy?"

"Don't be a dick."

"Sorry." He finished rubbing lotion on her lower back, and some graphically impure thoughts started reeling through his mind. "All set," he said, capping the tube and giving his fantasies a cold shower.

She stood, put her hands on the shapely curves of her hips, and looked out to the water. Then she slung her beach bag over her shoulder, turned to him, and said, "Let's take a walk."

"Okay." He stood and grabbed his mojito, feeling a bit woozy. He'd started drinking four hours ago, and the potent Caribbean rum was doing a number on him. He was looking forward to a nap before they headed out for dinner that evening.

"You think it's smart to leave your laptop sitting here on the beach?" she said, glancing back at the table.

"Eh." He shrugged and tossed his towel over it. "Nobody'll see it. Besides, it's encrypted."

A wicked smile broke across her face. "Silly me. Of course it is."

AUTHOR'S NOTE

By their very nature, intelligence agencies are not forthright about the true extent or *intent* of their capabilities. Though I've taken liberties with my portrayal of NSA and GCHQ, the ongoing revelations brought forth by Edward Snowden (theguardian.com/us-news/the-nsa-files) have let us peer behind the surveillance firewall to see how our online identities—from phone calls to browsing histories—have become digital DNA, mapped and coded and stored away in massive data centers like the behemoth in Utah.

Razorwire is a fictional cyberweapon that bundles a number of NSA signal intelligence capabilities—DNS sinkholes, network kill switches, encryption bypasses, and more. I've underplayed the danger of an intelligence asset such as Jonathan Farrell dutifully following Razorwire's phantom directives, only to discover that he's been manipulated by an anonymous puppeteer. Similarly, it's no big stretch to imagine a top-level cyber tech bamboozling both boss and bureaucracy to rob an intelligence agency blind, nor a fiendishly clever hacker who can outsmart even the best cyber experts in both the virtual and real worlds. *People,* not hardware and software, are the Internet's most vulnerable access points.

Cyberattacks that target power grids and infrastructure are overhyped, but threats to bank and government databases are woefully understated. The computers at a power plant or dam can be manually overridden to eventually get things back up and running, and the same is true of mass transit and air traffic control. It's believed that the United States nuclear arsenal's multiple security redundancies would be nearly impossible for even the best hacker to fully compromise—though it's anyone's guess as to how vulnerable some of the world's lesser nuclear powers may be. But the financial systems of the world are mere "clouds" of ones and zeros inside hard drives, susceptible to all sorts of crafty code worms, with virtually zero resilience against a coordinated cyberstrike.

Encryption has been around since kings and pharaohs; Knights Templar used ciphers and wax seals to authenticate and strengthen the integrity of communications. The privacy game continues today, with the sophistication of modern encryption constantly evolving to try and outrun both the logarithmic growth curve of computing power and governments' wholesale abandonment of civil liberties. Robust, unmolested encryption is critical to our future security and online privacy.

NcryptoCash is a fictional cryptocurrency based on Bitcoin, and I allow it to similarly transmit peer-to-peer with near-perfect anonymity, absent taxation or regulatory oversight. In an era when the world's central banks have no qualms about engaging in currency wars, demand will almost certainly explode for a truly global, market-based medium of value and exchange . . . but not without serious growing pains and some very sobering perils. Case in point: in 2014 the Tokyo-based bitcoin exchange Mt. Gox was shuttered after roughly $480 million (estimates of the actual figure vary widely) of depositors' entrusted Bitcoin certificates were hacked from its cybervaults.

Chatbots like Apple's Siri, or Bounty4Justice's virtual assistant, are tiny examples of a much grander push toward artificial intelligence. But no matter how sophisticated AI may become, it's far more constructive to worry about the malicious commands of its human programmers, rather than sweat an autonomous binary machine gaining the *emotional* capacity to plot our destruction.

Lots of repugnant characters connect through the darknet, but so do plenty of good guys. Today, one can download an encrypted browser from TorProject.org to cleanly bypass the Orwellian commercial Web. Bounty4Justice's network bridge between the anonymous peer-to-peer "hidden services" of the darknet and the policed realm of the dot-com commercial Internet is currently fiction—though I imagine we'll be seeing these enhancements to standard Web browsers in the very near future, much to the chagrin of intelligence agencies.

Malicious websites similar to Bounty4Justice abound in much smaller scale on the darknet. The FBI's 2013 takedown of Silk Road was the closest real-world case study of an anonymous criminal marketplace that thrived with impunity, nearly indefinitely. Silk Road's mastermind, Ross William Ulbricht, scarily demonstrated how these enterprises can be conceived and built by a lone wolf, using turnkey software widely available on the darknet.

The Atlas-5 message board used by Jam and Pike is my spin on a virtual private network.

Nexus is a fictional hacktivist collective based loosely on Anonymous.

The run-down building adjacent to Ground Zero that Jonathan Farrell used as his sniper's roost does not exist, nor does the railroadside church in Tallinn that Rhea converts into a data bunker. And don't try to find the Windsor Arms in upscale London, because it doesn't exist. In the Bermudian parish of St. George's—indeed a pirate haven of yore—one will find harborfront pubs whose outdoor tables are a sniper's shot from Hen Island. I've renamed one of them Seadog Pub.

Novak's dossier on Estonia's David-vs.-Goliath cyberwar in 2007 is factually accurate, though NATO cyberterrorism analysts found no definitive evidence of Russia's role in the attacks. Estonia has since become a test lab for national cyber defense, with the FBI and the Secret Service stationing full-time cyber experts there to aid in the fight.

As the Internet evolves and mutates like an organic virus, determinedly challenging states' sovereignty, only time will tell if it will gravitate toward a more uniform democracy or autocracy. As it stands today, it can swing either way, depending on what country you reside in.

The race to a zero marginal cost, fully transparent society—not just in manufacturing and retailing, but in the arts and sciences, too—will continue to force humanity to rethink labor and production, as well as our liberty and context in the world. Without doubt, the Internet is the most potent propaganda tool ever conceived. It's also humanity's least understood, most relied-upon machine. And if that's not the ultimate recipe for chaos, I'm not sure what is.

For more info, visit michaelbyrnesauthor.com.

ACKNOWLEDGMENTS _____

To my agent, Doug Grad, for sharing my vision of a different kind of story when I was facing some serious questions about the path forward. Without him, *Bounty* would have never seen the light of day.

Big thanks to my editor, Tracy Devine, for her saintly counseling and guidance through the multiple revisions that raised *Bounty* to its full potential. To assistant editor Sarah Murphy for the tough-love critiques that helped fine-tune the storyline's many gears and give nuance to a rather sizable cast of characters. My deep gratitude to Bonnie Thompson for her masterful assist with *Bounty*'s final grammatical and fact-checking nip-tuck, and to Loren Noveck, production editor extraordinaire, for guiding *Bounty* so superbly through every stage of the process toward print and digital publication. Kudos and thanks to Sarah Feightner, Simon Sullivan, and everyone on Random House's production team, who worked their magic in designing and packaging *Bounty* beautifully for the marketplace. Thank you, Scott Biel, for your super cool cyberpunk cover art. To Allison Schuster and the marketing team for their wizardly promotional efforts that helped my story connect with readers in stores and online. And props to Matt Schwartz for cultivating *Bounty*'s knockout digital strategy.

To my loving wife and children, who support my passion to tell stories, and patiently share me with the many crazy characters who inhabit my head 24/7 while I'm in project mode. There's no greater love than living with a novelist.

Thanks to Greg Meunier for helping me brainstorm *Bounty* during our five-mile runs, and for introducing me to Jack D'Orio—the guru of Internet architecture and offsite backups. My gratitude goes out to Michael Fregeau for helping me to demystify the complexities of federal law enforcement. To Mike Androlewicz—the most prodigious reader I've ever met—for his smart book recommendations and astute insights into what makes for great stories. My deep-thinking conversations with Jim Byrne are duly noted. And thanks to *all* my friends and family who've endured my rants about economics and politics and social injustice, and all the other things that I cannot control but love to fixate on.

The FBI's Office of Public Affairs was helpful, yet understandably opaque. The agency's website, however, offered an essential window into how FBI task forces mobilize to address all kinds of cyber threats. I learned a lot about logistics, reporting structure, and a special agent's day-to-day routines from speaking with an FBI agent and a CIA intelligence officer, both of whom will remain nameless.

My MBA concentration in computers and information systems provided a useful baseline for constructing the technological aspects of Bounty4Justice. But I had to scour countless articles, websites, TED talks, documentaries, and videos to brush up on what's happened over the fifteen years since I earned my graduate degree. As for books, *Kingpin: How One Hacker Took Over the Billion-Dollar Cybercrime Underground,* by Kevin Poulsen, stood out as most instructive about the FBI's online honeypot operations and trolling techniques. And cybersecurity activist/journalist Jacob Applebaum's YouTube lectures concerning the invasiveness of NSA and GCHQ surveillance are nightmarishly fantastic.

Thanks to Twitter for its unique blurb format that allowed me to tell oodles of micro-stories that would otherwise crowd *Bounty*'s main narrative.

Google Earth is one of this writer's favorite tools.

The 2007–2008 financial crisis was a $64 trillion heist engineered by a relative handful of investment bankers who exploited grossly unregulated markets, yet were held harmless after unleashing world-wide havoc; they are credited here for enraging me enough to think up a modern-day vigilante tale like *Bounty*.

To the immovable Robert Prechter and his emerging study of socionomics—those fractal patterns of fear and euphoria that sway human herds through economic booms and busts, social trends, and war. His pioneering approach to mining big data for behavioral trends and shifting moods helped me to formulate Bounty4Justice's sentient functionality.

In special remembrance of John T. Xenis—mentor, confidant, business partner—for inspiring me to think big, to be independent, to take vacations and enjoy great meals, to take pride in everything I do, and to never take opportunities or liberty for granted. His positive thoughts will always be with me, particularly his regular reminder, "Live life, this is not a dress rehearsal."

ABOUT THE AUTHOR

MICHAEL BYRNES grew up in West Orange, New Jersey, and attended Montclair State University as an undergrad business major and Rutgers University for his MBA. He currently lives in Orlando, Florida, with his wife, Caroline, and their three children, Vivian, Camille, and Theodore. He's a career insurance broker who also writes high-concept thrillers that delve into his lifelong fascinations with mythology, economics, and human behavior. He cherishes his family and friends and makes time to play guitar and go for long runs and bike rides. His first novel, *The Sacred Bones* (2007), was an international bestseller, published in more than thirty countries; it was followed by a sequel, *The Sacred Blood* (2009), and *The Genesis Plague* (2010). *Bounty* is his fourth novel.

michaelbyrnesauthor.com
@MByrnesAuthor

ABOUT THE TYPE _____

This book was set in Dante, a typeface designed by Giovanni Mardersteig (1892–1977). Conceived as a private type for the Officina Bodoni in Verona, Italy, Dante was originally cut only for hand composition by Charles Malin, the famous Parisian punch cutter, between 1946 and 1952. Its first use was in an edition of Boccaccio's *Trattatello in laude di Dante* that appeared in 1954. The Monotype Corporation's version of Dante followed in 1957. Though modeled on the Aldine type used for Pietro Cardinal Bembo's treatise *De Aetna* in 1495, Dante is a thoroughly modern interpretation of that venerable face.